WHEN THEY BECKON

KAY COSTALES

WHEN THEY BECKON

KAY COSTALES

CITY OWL
PRESS

This book is a work of fiction. Names, characters, places, and incidents either are products of the author's imagination or are used fictitiously. Any resemblance to actual events or locales or persons, living or dead, is entirely coincidental and not intended by the author.

WHEN THEY BECKON
The Witch Circus, Book 1

CITY OWL PRESS
www.cityowlpress.com

All Rights reserved. Except as permitted under the U.S. Copyright Act of 1976, no part of this publication may be reproduced, distributed, or transmitted in any form or by any means, or stored in a database or retrieval system, without the prior consent and permission of the publisher.

Copyright © 2023 by Kay Costales.

Cover Design by MiblArt. All stock photos licensed appropriately.

Edited by Tee Tate.

For information on subsidiary rights, please contact the publisher at info@cityowlpress.com.

Print Edition ISBN: 978-1-64898-371-9

Digital Edition ISBN: 978-1-64898-372-6

Printed in the United States of America

To those in the diaspora. We may be far from a home we've never known, but we may still yearn for it.

Chapter One

THE NAMES OF THE DEAD ARE TOOLS.

History is written by the victors, the ones who were ruthless and relentless. The soft-hearted won't find themselves anywhere but used by those with the courage to act in order to thrive—or at least survive.

Salome Visaya was alive, but her name was useless. The Alliance taught her those truths after finding her muddy-faced and barefoot, scrambling through a crumbling village with nothing but breadcrumbs around her dry mouth.

"I'm no one—I'm nothing!" she'd screamed when Gabriel, leader of the organization, grabbed her hand upon catching it in his coat pocket. She was only ten, small and skinny and desperate for food and coin. Back then, those fifteen years ago, she didn't know he would change her life, nor how true those words were.

"Do you want to be more?" he'd asked.

"Yes."

Always.

And then he and his partner Yvette noted her in their Book of Names. They took her under their wing and taught her to transform. How to change her voice and mannerisms so that while her face remained the same, her behavior belonged to other identities. They housed her, clothed her, and fed her, all the while reminding her that she would be free once she paid back all they'd provided. She was their servant, their puppet. She stopped being a little girl when her name was set on the page, when she signed her life over to the Alliance with little ability to read.

Away from her family, all she knew was the Alliance. They were her parents, her caregivers, and her mentors. They taught her how to transform and how to use that skill to their advantage.

Over the years, she'd become different people.

A servant, a fisherman's daughter, an orphan, a merchant's daughter, a witness to a murder... she could name them all in succession, every person she had become at Gabriel's command.

In the middle of a war, people died all the time. If no one knew of the death, if the news hadn't spread—it was easy to steal a life. The Alliance had no loyalty to a nation. Battlefields and fallen lands were an opportunity to borrow from a corpse or even a family, regardless of their status in Ilarya or its neighboring rival, Pavalla.

It was a war born of darkness and monsters and blame. Whoever won, whatever happened, it didn't matter. The Alliance's only concern was their latest mission.

Salome was to be a baron's daughter. The Ilaryan king's betrothed.

Rosalia d'Ilumias was dead, strangled and sunk to the bottom of the Viridian Sea. Now Salome wielded her name like a weapon, a tool to cut apart the path to the kingdom's riches.

For the better part of the last year, Salome trained to become the woman. Learning how she'd spoken, how she moved and existed. A poor hermit who didn't know how much power she could wield and failed to utilize it. The rest of the Alliance set on assembling the perfect team and all required materials. New gowns, false jewels, and portraits to replace the ones they'd burned and cast into the sea to destroy evidence of the real woman.

All this hard work for one last mission.

She participated in hundreds of cons over the years—big and small, some lasting weeks and others for days. In each one, she adjusted the sums and reported less than what there was, setting aside a little for herself. If she was caught, she'd be branded a traitor to the organization and tortured until they saw fit. It wouldn't end even if she told them where she hid everything that was meant for them, only when they decided she suffered enough. The last time that happened to someone, *enough* was when they were dead.

Finally, with this con, Salome imagined there was a chance to unravel herself from their schemes and live her own life.

The tip of a blade kissed the delicate skin of Salome's wrist, glinting in the dim lighting of the inn they were staying in. A downgrade from the dead baron's seaside estate, their temporary headquarters as they gathered everything required for this mission.

Jewels were forged, each member trained, the paths to take and the victims to target determined ahead of time. Every necessary detail and small portraits commissioned by starving artists employed by the Alliance filled a thick book that was burned to nothing right before they left the estate. It wasn't an easy task to rob the Ilaryan royal family. All decisions had to be plotted to precise perfection, all missions accomplished without flaw.

The blade didn't belong to an assailant. It was a member of the Alliance.

"When you head out, I'll be close," the man said. Abel, in his early forties, had black hair already streaked with silver. He claimed it came from having to keep an eye on Salome all these years.

Salome nodded. "Keep some distance between us and let me work. I'll signal to you if help is needed."

He glowered, but he trusted her. If he didn't, she would have been dead a long time ago. They used to bicker and he used to loathe being paired with her. But he was a watchdog, an enforcer for the organization. Sometimes he played her older brother. This time, he was the head of Rosalia's guards.

It was her place to survey the area in the night, not his.

With a wink, she tightened the opaque black mask over the lower portion of her face, and another dark, gauzy strip of fabric over her eyes. She blew a kiss before clambering through a window and down the side of the inn before darting through the city's streets.

"Make the most of the nights," Yvette told her before they left the baron's estate, her silver-blonde hair pulled in a tight chignon and her pale skin starting to wrinkle. "Waste no hour."

Once the sun set, something made Salome restless. The first night she stayed with Gabriel and Yvette, they found her wide awake, scrounging through their kitchen. The next night, they caught her sitting on a windowsill, admiring the stars. It amused no one. The organization had no use for children. And so, she grew up. Adapted. Transformed. Sharpened.

Maybe she was no one or nothing, but whatever she was, she was made for the night.

And so, it was often her sent out on tasks when it grew dark. Leaving notes under pillows in locked bedrooms, dropping poison into a late-night wineglass in an empty kitchen, switching real jewelry for forgeries, and whatever was needed to be done without notice. She didn't mind the little tasks between the larger cons. She saw opportunities to prove herself useful and seized them.

"I won't interfere," a woman said.

Perched the edge of a roof an hour into the surveillance work, Salome should have been alone. That wasn't always the case with team members who wanted to chance to show off and be rewarded. Amalia crouched beside her, her pale skin and vibrant red hair hidden behind a mask and a cap.

"There isn't much to see," Salome said. "Some additional guards, but not nearly enough to cause trouble for us."

Amalia nodded. "I saw Abel."

"I don't need both of you."

There were no accidents, no room for mistakes. She memorized names and titles, relationships and histories. She rehearsed what to say and practiced how to adapt if necessary. No one knew Rosalia, but she had to know all of them.

Years ago, another member of the Alliance, the one-eyed Euria, had her throat cut. She survived, only now she bore a scar for Salome's mistakes. Salome hadn't realized there were secret paths in a merchant's home or that she'd be caught with bags of stolen gold when he took an early morning walk as he did when he had nightmares.

She didn't know because she hadn't watched him long enough to learn he had nightmares after lightning storms. She hadn't paid close enough attention —and it nearly killed her accomplice. She vowed never to make that mistake again or give the Alliance any reason to think she couldn't accomplish their tasks.

It was lucky that Euria didn't loathe her, but Salome never truly decided if she was satisfied with having that incident dangled over her like an axe on a string. They were something like friends with secrets exchanged between them at least, with an agreement of *I won't tell if you don't* to keep themselves safe. Only Euria heard Salome speak of her resentment for the debt she owed to the leaders, though in the barest of whispers, and not a hint of her plans to escape.

"I'll check the other side of the city," Amalia said. "Elias will be with me."

Despite the spikes of jealousy that emerged between the two women every now and then, they agreed on one thing: they always wanted to win. When it came to the Alliance and their missions, Amalia and Salome learned that instead of fighting each other, they could work together and excel as a team. They still didn't like each other, but it was an improvement that they could at least trust each other to get the job done and do it better than anyone expected.

The Alliance encouraged rivalry and competition, believing that it could bring out the strongest skills, but Salome and Amalia discovered better results if they could get along. Still, they kept an eye on each other, waiting to see if the other might slip. If one faltered, there was one less person working for the Alliance, and the other would inherit more opportunities.

It was a war of their own, spies hidden amongst the armies. Not that the Alliance ever truly fought for anyone with a true crown. They had their men enlisted, but only to gather intel, never to die. If they got to that point, they were instructed to run.

Never lose your life for royals or nobles.

"See you before sunrise," Salome said, then flitted away. It was easy to lose whoever tailed her when there was no moonlight to touch her. In the shadows, she was lost to the world, safe and unseen.

Though she wasn't a child anymore, she still enjoyed keeping her team on their toes. If Abel had a hard time finding her in the dark, he stayed alert. Salome never imagined he'd falter, but that was what their team did. They made sure they were paying attention.

She liked to have fun and turn her tasks into a game. Most of all, she liked winning and the rewards that came with it. She was greedy for all things: having everything she wanted, knowing everything there was to know, being indispensable and therefore impossible to eliminate from the organization.

Abel was used to chasing after her. Before, he'd worry. Now he seemed to expect it and understood that when she moved quickly and stayed out of sight, she remained on task. There was no room for a pattern of excessive recklessness. The mission always came before life and safety. As long as the mission was a success and the Alliance wasn't outed, they did not mind when exact plans changed.

Everything was visible to her though, from the banners hanging from roof to roof, blue and gold waving in the breeze. The streets were cleaned, every brick on the ground polished, and large dark pots sat a metre apart on the paths to the side, overflowing with golden flowers and metal suns and stars posted in the soil.

Some balconies bore flags with the royal family's colors and sigil—midnight blue with a golden star surrounded by three suns. A few of them bore the sigil of the d'Ilumias family: a silver moon dipping into waves, set against black.

Welcome, the city said, *our future queen!*

It must have been a nice change, a deviation from the usual banners about enlisting in the army. The value of each life and the glory that could be bestowed upon a family. Though it wasn't yet mandatory to take up arms, that could change if the war dragged on.

A common person could die over politics and royal pride.

The new flags were a rug tossed over dirt and debris. They masked the mess with a pretty distraction. A promise of celebration, though it would go unfulfilled. They would never reach the coronation planned three months from now, and they weren't excited to meet Salome.

It was Rosalia d'Ilumias, daughter of Baron Oriol d'Ilumias, who commanded a significant portion of the royal navy in the ongoing war against the neighbouring kingdom of Pavalla. His victories were rewarded with the union between his family and the royals. Little did he know the prince she'd marry would become king after the deaths of his parents and siblings. That the royal family would crumble under the weight of drawn-out war and the advisors would hurry a marriage along with an ally. The family needed to be rebuilt. There needed to be heirs. The desperation was an opening that the Alliance could not ignore.

Rosalia herself was alive until a year ago when the Alliance decided they could make use of her identity better than she could. How unfortunate that her father went missing, and her mother and brother were long dead. How fortunate that she could be made to disappear like she was nothing but ancient dust in her family's tomb. A seaside estate might be beautiful, but it was far too difficult for one's screams to be heard over the crash of waves against cliffs and in the great distance from neighbors.

And so, when King Vincent d'Allorias met his betrothed, it would be Salome stepping out of the ornate, gilded carriage instead of the noblewoman he'd met once during their childhood. It had to be her, the only one in the Alliance similar to Rosalia's age and origins in the islands of Villasayas.

Salome climbed down from the roofs she was jumping across. The crevices in the bricks called to her fingertips and toes, finding them like a familiar path. When her soft-soled boots hit the ground, there was not even a whisper of movement.

She was like another shadow slipping between buildings.

Sometimes, she felt so embraced by the dark, she imagined it whispering to her, *This is where you belong.*

In this city, it felt like there could be something out there. A hand climbing up the back of her leg, soft as spider legs. A breath against her neck. A slight tug on a strand of hair. Someone was always watching, but it was likely the Alliance, not a monster in the dark.

Then again, there were rumors these days of such things. Rumors so intense they fuelled a war between long-time rivals, worsening the relationship between kingdoms. Ilarya and Pavalla knew only brief periods of peace. Every time an incident occurred, one side wanted to blame the other for the destruction. For the monsters someone allegedly unleashed.

A village overtaken by sticky, black substances. Houses that went up in smoke without a fire in sight. Creatures crawling out from places where candlelight couldn't touch. Children going missing in the dead of night.

Some warning signs were posted to shop doors and windows.

LOCK ALL DOORS!

COVER YOUR WINDOWS!

ALWAYS KEEP A LIT CANDLE CLOSE!

Superstition, maybe. Monsters didn't exist. Salome hadn't seen any. The only monsters *she* knew were the ones born from the Alliance. Their reputation was wicked, including public assassinations of their own members if they failed their tasks or risked uncovering details about the organization.

Yvette had killed her own son when she heard he'd said a little too much about his family to his lover. Out of love, she chose the cover of night to send an assassin to carve out his heart for having broken hers, sparing him such shame in daylight. Any loyalty was to money, to the organization, before blood.

The further into the interior of the kingdom, however, the more afraid people seemed to be. One would think the capital city of Ellasya would be busy, but there wasn't anyone. Maybe that should have scared her, but it didn't. It only made her more curious. Yet Salome still slid out one of the daggers from her sleeve. She was a liar most of the time, a fraud, but she could admit that a shiver ran up her spine when a cat shot across the street.

A harmless little cat.

Mist settled on the stony streets like a low veil. Salome imagined shadows curling around her ankles, or clawed hands ready to cut through her boots and delve into her flesh. She kept exploring though, peering through windows to find jewelry shops, or spaces tucked between buildings to use for discreet conversations.

The loudest part of the city was in the center of it. A bustling tavern with low music, dim lighting, the smell of sweat and alcohol, and a hint of laughter. A bookstore that promised history books the royal family would prefer to keep hidden. Even the offices of city security, candles lit but the guard at the window dozing off.

It was late at night, hours into her surveillance, before she decided to head back to the inn. The nights were warmer than they'd been in months and yet Salome shivered like a snowstorm blew through the city.

"Do you feel it?" a girlish voice whispered behind her. A voice with a breathy accent involving tongue-rolling, the kind that belonged to the people from Yoreal—a nation an ocean apart from this place.

Salome spun around. There shouldn't have been anyone around at all. She hadn't seen a single figure on the street in hours.

The woman was a tiny figure in the mist. Nearby trees seemed to bristle like they were eager to embrace her with their branches, like a mother's arms around their long-missing child. "The shadows are drawn to you, as you must be to them."

It had always been that way, but she couldn't recall when it began. It was why Salome adored running through the streets at night. Not only was it the perfect time for gathering intel and surveillance, it was like sitting in front of a blazing fire during the depths of winter, bringing life back to frozen bones.

"Soon, you'll know why," the figure said. Her hand curled around

Salome's wrist, her palm as rough as tree bark, except for her fingertips, which were soft as rose petals. "It's truly alive in you now. You'll feel it the moment I let go."

And then she did.

The world spun. When it steadied, Salome felt no different.

The night, however, felt alive.

Chapter Two

THERE ALWAYS SEEMED TO BE SOMETHING WATCHING, A SET OF eyes trailing after her. Even when Salome shared a cot with her parents, nestled in the middle of a straw mattress with a thin cotton sheet tangled around them and their clothes bundled as pillows, she felt the presence.

Something out there was waiting.

There were nights when she'd wake to the smell of burning herbs and the feeling of something hanging over her. Upon opening her eyes, however, nothing was there. Heart pounding, she'd clamber over her parents and search the tiny room that was home for signs of an intruder—under the bed, between the window and the curtains, on the empty chair.

Salome never found anything.

This time, as dawn spilled into the Alliance's suite at the inn, a whisper woke her. A hiss like a forked tongue darting between pointed teeth.

Finally.

Her eyes shot open, and she sprung upright in bed. Sweat dripped down the back of her neck as if the demon licked her and drooled.

She was accustomed to the sound of an army preparing for battle, of soldiers calling in the street for anyone willing to fight for their king. Even the little seaside town by the d'Ilumias estate endured such mornings, especially when there was an impending battle. If the demons were real, those were more frightening than being out on a field with some sorry excuse for sword and shield. At least war was predictable in its cruelty.

"Good morning," Amalia said. She sat by the window at a table covered in papers. "How late were you out? I didn't notice you when you returned."

Salome grinned. "Then I did a good job."

Their eyes met and they shared a look of understanding. They'd come a long way from days of petty insults and physical violence against each other. Amalia was like a sister, someone that Salome could trust with her life and any task they received, even if they didn't always like each other.

Salome stood and directed her gaze to the clothing on the bed. Months ago, Yvette commissioned an entire wardrobe with the finest silks and the most delicate gossamer fabrics. Everything had a purpose.

This first gown was golden and glittering, intended to draw all eyes when Salome was presented to the king as Rosalia. It hung off the shoulders, generously exposing plenty of skin. Diamonds and topaz would drip down her chest on a gold chain, with matching jewels in her curled hair. She was meant to be enchanting, to inspire love at first sight. He needed to wed and bed his wife before he too was lost on the battlefield. He needed to be encouraged to enjoy every moment they had.

And the gown was perfect for a thief with pockets for stashing jewels. Thin knives were also hidden at the hem, easily torn free should the occasion arise. Pins were also sewn into the bodice in case lock-picking was required.

From the corner of her eye, she caught Amalia staring. Though she'd never admit to it, the other woman was jealous that Salome would have such a spotlight. Being as pale and red-haired as she was, it meant she could not always participate in the jobs assigned by the leaders, not in this part of the world. Amalia learned her numbers and languages and all she could ever know to prove her use, but she could never blend in here in Ilarya where most people had brown skin tones and dark hair. Even Salome did not look fully Ilaryan.

She had brown skin, too, and hair like obsidian. What made her different was her flat nose and the angular shape of her eyes. Her features had her deemed exotic by merchants enchanted by the look of her, too invested in collecting her like a doll to realize she was collecting their coin in the handful of weeks she spent with them.

Men were weak. Men fell prey to a pretty face.

Men would give up the world for night in bed with a woman they never knew they could touch.

And Salome was perfect to play Rosalia, the king's betrothed, whose mother was from Villasayas, the group of thousands of islands west of his kingdom. That almost mythic place that Salome's own family was from.

She lacked the brute strength that Abel and Elias had, the two of them chosen to pose as her main guards. She wasn't like Gerard either, who could remember every detail perfectly. Salome could rival Amalia in her talent for languages and she, like Yvette, could recognize real jewels from false ones. Amalia and Salome would either be the stars of the charade or keep track of the potential number value of their hoard. Euria would confirm the price using her market knowledge, Leon would make a replica to return to the owner, while Elias sold the real ones on the black market.

Salome was the diversion, the clever smile and charming laugh. She knew how to move her body and flirtation rolled off her tongue like a native language. She was fun, she was mysterious, or whatever else she needed to be. She knew how to get close enough to use her daggers, the weapons she favored.

Somehow, as she finished applying makeup to emphasize the fullness of her lips and the dark of her eyes, Salome still felt this new presence that appeared after her encounter the night before. She thought it would disappear like remnants of a bad dream, but it hadn't.

"How true do you think the stories are?" Salome asked.

Amalia frowned. "Demons? We would have seen them."

"The city seems concerned, posters everywhere warning against danger. The other day, I heard a few children telling a story about a place outside the city where you can hear a dead witch's heartbeat." It stirred excitement in Salome, a flash of intrigue that made her want to go out and find it. To see if it was true—or purely nonsense.

She'd done that before when she was young, momentarily abandoning a job on a detour to follow a story that piqued her curiosity. It earned her a punishment from Gabriel which left thin, circular scars on the knobs of her spine. She still turned instinctively when she was out and caught threads of a conversation that made her mind wander. But Salome learned to catch herself before her body tried to follow where her thoughts drifted.

She wasn't a child. There were no excuses for her behavior. She never made such a mistake again, and her team knew that she wouldn't. It was a death sentence if she ever dared and she liked being alive.

Amalia looked at Salome. "Are you worried?"

Salome grinned. "Never." It was always more curiosity than concern.

When Amalia turned away, Salome glanced at the floor, at the shadows pooling beneath her gown. The sensation of claws around her ankles lifted the thin hairs on her limbs. It trailed shivers up her spine despite the rising warmth of a spring morning.

Salome hurried to another part of the suite.

On the carpet in the main room, Leon sat with oversized spectacles balanced on his wide nose, and his jewel-crafting tools scattered around him like he was piecing together a shattered skeleton.

At the door was Euria and Gerard, too focused on each other to care for the forgeries. One hand adjusted the black ribbon she draped over her left eye, the other traced the scar at her throat. Barely a few years older than Salome and already bald, the secretly self-conscious Gerard looked at her like he couldn't memorize enough, though kept his hands tucked behind his back.

Abel stood by a table covered in various weapons to be distributed among the group. Swords and daggers and vials of poisons of varying degrees of dangerousness. There were no accidents, no possibility for failure or defeat. No risks unmediated. He and Elias, Euria's twin who was broad with muscle yet had a boyish face, were the experts in weaponry.

It almost looked like the lot of them were strategizing for the battlefield, like this was a war meeting.

Euria looked up first and smiled at the sight of Salome, who twirled for her and curtsied.

Abel frowned. She waved him off, but something stirred beneath her. As if the ground shifted, or someone pulled the rug under her feet. It threw her off balance and she stumbled, despite not taking a step.

That caught Leon's attention and he lifted a hand to stop her from falling into his work.

A tingling feeling clung to her fingertips. She gripped the gauzy sleeves of her gown to rid of herself of them. Remnants remained, like grains of sand sticking to the skin no matter how many times they were brushed away. She wasn't unsteady; this wasn't like her. All these years, she proved that she was strong and confident and sure. Sometimes she strayed from plans, but she never failed. She always proved that any changes were necessary and ultimately what needed to be done.

"Something wrong?" Abel asked, approaching with an expression of concern, likely a mixture for her and the con.

Salome backed away, toward the bedroom, and collided with Amalia.

"The carriage is downstairs," Amalia said, then to Salome, "Are you ready?"

This was the biggest job she'd ever done, but not the first time she was at the forefront. She spent the early years with the Alliance accepting tiny assignments and promises that one day, she would get a chance. Eventually, they cast her as the lead, starting with small missions and building up and up as she proved she could not only handle them, but excel.

Because they trusted her, she had access to riches, and a chance to smuggle some for herself. It was all adding up to be enough to pay her debts in addition to the fees she already paid to the Alliance for their mentorship and protection. This con could be the last of what she needed to escape from their grasp.

So long as she didn't falter.

It was fine. There wasn't something sinister breathing down her back or something trying to twist around her wrist. Nothing but her own imagination. Though she couldn't shake the feeling that something had come alive and whatever she once thought was looking for her finally found her.

It was here, that thing that chased her all her life, always ten feet behind.

"Let's see this king then," Salome said.

Time to play the distraction while the Alliance set their players in the royal court.

She was sitting in the gilded carriage, her arms propped on the window to peer outside, when the rest of her entourage filtered onto the streets. The midnight-blue banners were brighter in the morning light, waving delicately, and the sun caught the gold threads of celestial shapes.

People gathered around the inn, many carrying armfuls of flowers and baskets full of sweets. Gifts, apparently, as they lifted them to the carriage until the hired guards shooed them back. The scene reminded Salome of what it was like in the early years of the war, when every victory was still celebrated in the streets. The little village where she'd lived with her parents were filled with jovial music and bright colors on those days when those in the army could return home for respite. Nowadays, only the largest battles that even the king fought in received a loud response when they returned home.

Amalia climbed into the carriage, making herself comfortable on the cushioned bench. She didn't seem to notice the spider-like figure under her hand, weaving in and out of the shadows formed by the movement of her adjusting her skirt.

Salome tried not to be transfixed by it.

Instead, she focused on the mantra she'd inherited from Gabriel. A reminder who and what she was: *she was nothing and no one.*

Most of the time, they didn't sting. There were moments, however, when such a motto felt like poison dripping down her throat, burning her inside out.

The crowd followed the carriage on its way to the castle, throwing flowers in its path. Salome waved gracefully and smiled, while Amalia was still and quiet. Their little parade was meant to be a celebration. Even a hermit could acknowledge the people who came to see her pass through.

They stopped at the gates, unable to enter and witness the momentous official meeting between king and future queen. Salome's heart pounded as they rolled to a stop in front of large stone gate engraved with the d'Allorias star and suns, the grooves filled with gold.

The doors swung open slowly, revealing a full courtyard.

Too many people to focus on a single face.

Abel offered a hand, expressionless as he helped Salome out once the carriage opened. He wore a black uniform with silver embroidery depicting a crescent moon above waves—the d'Ilumias sigil—over his heart. Despite a sheen of sweat on his forehead, he remained stoic and unaffected.

"Don't worry," she murmured for both their sakes.

In response, Abel nodded once. When they first met, reaching this point seemed impossible. He used to be so condescending, so distrusting and cruel. They used to disagree about the best course of action, fueled only by his insistence that his age made him wiser. It gave him the advantage of experience, but as time went on, as they worked on more jobs together, the gap shortened. They were professionals and needed to trust themselves and each other.

Besides, she always succeeded even when others thought she might fail.

She had the creativity and adaptability that a con artist ought to have. She proved she could handle everything she was given, including this mission.

There was never room for failure, and she always intended to win.

Maybe Abel didn't like her as a person, but he learned to respect that.

Taking a deep breath, Salome focused on remaining calm.

In the center of the courtyard, a man stared at her, stunned into silence. Broad-shouldered and dressed in a loose, midnight-blue shirt and fitted trousers, he could have been no more than a handsome soldier, if he weren't so differently dressed from the armed guards surrounding him.

Salome stared back at the man, unable to look away.

Kings shouldn't look like this. It was too tempting, this man-made magic.

People said he was beautiful, and yet she still wasn't prepared.

He easily towered over her, though she often stood eye-to-eye with men. Black hair curled over his shoulders as dark brown eyes peered at her in the morning sun. A thin beard enhanced his square jaw, and he ran his hand through the short hairs as he stared, mouth agape.

His handsomeness was a blade between the ribs. Sharp, deadly, and too close to the heart.

When she closed her eyes, she imagined the scrape of beard against her throat, the rough contrast to the heat of his mouth on her skin. The grip of his strong hands on her body. The thoughts sent heat rushing through her, flowing across her skin and within her veins. The feeling was like a threat, a warning that once she was closer to him, she might learn how it felt to ache.

She wouldn't mind stealing moments with him, taking advantage of their time together. It would be short-lived but savored. He looked impressed, but she needed more than that. She needed his hunger, and she would ensure to give him taste after taste until she was all he could think of, the one craving that only Salome could sate.

There was no time to be timid.

At first, each step she took was tentative, as part of her act. Amalia stayed a step behind, head bowed.

The king's uncle—General Bruno d'Allorias, medals and scars declaring his status and skill, white-haired with a scar down the length of his face and neck like someone attempted to cleave him in two—stood behind him, watching over the last of his older sister's children.

Salome stopped an arm's reach from the king and briefly glanced beyond him.

Smooth, black marble walls framed the castle. Imperfections were made mesmerizing by gold and bronze filling cracks and crevices. Towers loomed high as mountains with sharp peaks. Detailed arches surrounded every doorway and gleaming, stained-glass window. A wide staircase of polished black marble leading to the main doorway shined in the sun.

There was no chance she could scale the walls. She'd need to learn every passageway and every turn with more focus than she'd had during her studies prior to their arrival.

Salome offered the king a smile. His eyes never moved away. The way he looked at her was disarming, like she suddenly lost all her hidden weapons. Her shield was charm; she prepared to lift it in defense. Only the king could fall. Salome would not have such a luxury, though her mission was to ensure that he thought her as mesmerized as she needed him to be.

"Lady Rosalia," he murmured. His voice was a pleasant rasp, low and deep. It was warmth that somehow made her shiver. "It is a pleasure to finally meet you."

She bowed her head. "The pleasure is mine, Your Majesty."

Before she could rise, his hand gently came under her chin, igniting sparks where he touched her. He lifted it up, so their gazes met. His smile was charming, his eyes bright. She had no need to be attracted to him, no need to burn so hot under his gaze, but she did.

All she required were reminders of what she could appreciate. It made it easier to tolerate marks who weren't so pretty, to avoid recoiling in disgust.

But she didn't need to work to conjure attraction and longing.

The second their eyes met while they were so close, it felt like she was struck by lightning. Her heart stuttered once and it wasn't hard to imagine that he was feeling similarly affected, considering the slight shift in his expression. A suggestion of desire. Her mouth felt drier and she licked her lips to ease her sudden thirst.

He seemed to like what he saw, as did she.

His pleasure made her bold, loosening her tongue. "You don't look like other Ilaryans."

He had the same dark features and warm brown skin as most, though more deeply bronzed further by the sun. His features spoke stories, hints of other lands in his blood. The soft shape of his mouth, the sharp angle of his nose and his jaw, the cheekbones high and jutting like cliff edges. His look was a dangerous delight. It was easier to remain unmoved when the mark was ugly.

"The outcome of marriage for alliances. I like to think I'm a bit of everywhere in the world, even if I shall never visit those faraway places."

A sweet thought. Almost romantic. It encouraged her to smile genuinely.

"Your portraits, however, did not do *you* justice," he said.

Flattery did not coax a blush to her cheeks, but she needed that reaction. It was the thought of lewd acts that brought the heat. Her face warmed like a timid bride-to-be even before he kissed her knuckles.

Movement behind him caught her eye. Four hooded figures stood under the archway framing the main doors. For a moment, despite their stillness, Salome thought she saw their shadows move. She blinked, and the figures retreated inside.

The witch circus. Stories swirled across the world, whispers about a group of women capable of impossible things. Each one could bend an element to their will and bore an additional secret gift. They were here, though most seemed uncertain if they were friend or foe.

The king glanced behind him. "Is something bothering you?"

"No, Your Majesty." Scanning his face, she noted the dark circles under his eyes. "Are you well? Late night, perhaps?"

He hesitated. "You could say that."

"None of those demons in the stories keeping you awake, I hope," she teased.

"Of course not." He inclined his head. Then his smile dimmed.

The brief silence awakened doubt in her. Unacceptable. She opened her mouth to speak, but he swooped in first.

"Unfortunately, my lady, I am unable to spend the day with you."

"As the king, you must be terribly busy." Though she smiled, she wasn't the slightest bit pleased.

He nodded. "Nothing to concern you though. Not yet."

Something seemed to dawn in his eyes as he spoke, disappearing when he blinked. He bowed with his arms extended in a flourish. Any lower and he would have declared himself beneath her, as if she were queen and him, a mere peasant.

"Your presence shall be missed," she said.

"I hope, in the meantime, you will find a friend in Sylvia l'Essalia."

As he spoke, a pale young woman with white-gold hair came forward, moving unsteadily, with shaking hands clasped in front. Back bent, head bowed, she appeared small and fragile, at least a head shorter than Salome. The picture of deference—except for a fleeting moment when she lifted her eyes to trail the length of Salome's body with appreciation. Sylvia l'Essalia had a thief's quick gaze and a servant's quiet subservience.

"Sylvia is my family's ward and will act as your guide in my absence. She shall be truthful to you, and a friend, if you wish."

Her name was notable, her presence nearly an insult to nobility. Her father was a traitor executed for conspiring against the royal family. But she was valuable.

A guard in light armor trailed behind her, a tall man with brown skin and dark hair tied into a knot at the back of his neck. No crest, no colors, no decorations. No loyalty except to this small woman, evident by the intent way he watched her.

"My uncle, General Bruno, shall accompany you as well," the king added with a grin. "Our welcome would lack warmth if family was not involved."

The general stepped forward and bowed with a hand pressed to his heart. "It would be my honor, Lady Rosalia. Let us hope this face will not frighten you away." He gestured to the battle scars scattered across his cheek as if hundreds of blades had tried to tear it open.

Those words earned the king's laughter.

"I will see you tonight," the king promised.

Salome smiled despite her disappointment.

"At dinner. Perhaps before. There will be a special performance tonight in honor of your arrival." He took one of her hands and laid a slow, soft kiss on her palms.

If she were a more modest woman, she might have blushed at how sensual this first kiss was. But Salome wasn't inexperienced. When he looked her in the eye, she met his gaze without flinching.

"I shall think of you every moment until then," he murmured like a secret.

With that, he retreated to the castle, followed by the silent flock of guards.

"Rene and I are pleased to make your acquaintance, Lady Rosalia," the pale woman said, gesturing to herself and her guard. "Now, follow me, please."

Sylvia turned, taking Rene's arm. Her body trembled and her steps were slow, like her bones were too weak and brittle to bear her weight.

Salome glanced at her entourage, Abel supervising the Alliance members posing as her guards as they removed luggage from the carriage. Amalia came to her side, nodding toward their guide with narrowed eyes.

At her hesitation, General Bruno offered an arm with a grin. Salome slid her hand into the crook of his elbow and took the first step forward. As they ascended the stairs, Sylvia paused.

"You should know that some of the stories are true," she said. Her eyes shifted around. "There's true danger in the dark."

"How do you know?" Salome asked, earning a subtle pinch from Amalia. She wanted the stories of demons, of monsters stealing away those who ventured into the night and leaving destruction wherever they emerged. Things more fearsome than conscription and bloodshed from an endless, senseless war.

If the Alliance knew the truth, they weren't concerned. What mattered was getting their people within the castle, claiming riches and power where they could. One day, the Alliance might no longer work in secret. One day, they could rule.

All the jewels and coin they gathered along the way were mere embellishments to the grander plan. And monsters? The Alliance was among them anyway.

She didn't know how they might fare against the storied creatures of the dark though.

"Most who live here have seen the demons," Sylvia said quietly.

The general tensed. His grin vanished. Salome watched him, the way he walked in the glow of the sunrise, avoiding stretches of shadow. She wondered if he too could hear them like they were snakes, hissing and slithering and seething about being contained in the dark places.

The demons were real. Salome must have known some version of them all her life.

Such words should have rooted fear in Salome's heart. Instead, her curiosity bloomed.

Chapter Three

GENERAL BRUNO'S HAND RESTED ON THE HILT OF HIS SWORD, preparing for enemies who could leap out of the shadows. His presence suggested preparation for a fight at any time. He was the backup to the king's guards, the last stand to protect the final heir. The sight of him meant a family on the edge of being truly broken. It meant fear.

The kingdom seemed inches away from forcing anyone strong enough to stand and carry a sword and shield to fight. Thus far, all participants in battle were volunteers. There were only so many of those available.

And if the war continued as it had, it wouldn't only be the border towns at risk. Those who wanted to stay within their homes would find bloodshed on their doors if the enemy's armies pushed deeper into Ilaryan land. No victor had emerged in all these years. The worst felt inevitable.

It was only when they passed through the main doors of black wood engraved with the sigils of the noble houses that he took a deep, heaving breath, and the tension in the general's body seemed to dissipate. As opulent as the castle was, there must have been reinforcements hidden beneath the marble to ensure it stood against siege.

Salome swore there was a pleased grin on Sylvia's face that lasted no longer than a blink. The split-second of mischief made Salome like her immediately.

"Are there many distractions for the king?" Salome asked.

"His days are filled with private audiences with nobles and advisors, and now war meetings. We have never truly known peace with Pavalla, and now it seems any excuse is enough to call for battle," the general said.

There had been a small battle a fortnight ago, another town in disputed land near the border. It was so far from command that any story could be conjured to explain the fighting.

Sylvia mumbled under her breath about monsters. Without thinking, Salome glanced at the shadows creeping out through the crack beneath a closed door. Nothing sinister, however, as the extended figure shrank when its owner retreated further into the room.

"Have you visited the castle before, my lady?" General Bruno asked.

Salome looked up at the delicate white arches hanging above her with golden vines molded around them. The gilding glimmered in the morning light slipping through the tall windows stretching from the floor to ceiling.

"I could never forget a place like this." Her amazement required no acting. Though she'd been a daydreaming child, she never conjured up something so opulent.

General Bruno followed her gaze and smiled. "This has been the home of the d'Allorias family for hundreds of years, though it has been improved upon over time. You can still find the portraits of the queen who ordered this castle's construction."

"Her Majesty, Queen Xiana d'Allorias, who loved gold more than anything," Sylvia added in a monotone. "Some say there is more gold decorating this castle than there is in the rest of the world."

Ahead of them, Sylvia and Rene exchanged a few words in hushed voices like lovers. They turned to a hallway lined with marble busts. Salome immediately tried to count how many there were.

Before Salome finished, Amalia whispered, "Nearly two dozen."

She was always better with numbers anyway. That skill would be required of her for this con more than any acting. Much of what they'd take wouldn't have a history on the market. She would need to do her research and calculations to ensure they reported the most accurate details to the Alliance leaders.

"Queen Xiana's likeness will be at the end of the hall, with another in the main gallery. Not so beautiful by today's standards, but brilliant. That matters much more." He went on about how the first queen united families, bringing order to the land. Her domain was nowhere near as large as Ilarya came to be, only a smattering of estates.

He didn't touch upon the division of her land and how it led to battles within her own family and a history tainted with blood.

The politics of it all bored Salome enough to make her eyes droop. She kept herself awake by absorbing the details of the decor. One could make a fortune off the paint on the walls alone. They weren't here for that though. She peered around, searching for private quarters.

General Bruno tried to continue discussing Queen Xiana but before they could reach her bust, Sylvia turned into another hall. Less light reached this area, casting it half in shadow, lit only by thin lanterns posted between paintings in bronze frames. The paintings depicted innocent scenes of Ilarya: western sea-side views of sailing ships; the eastern Woods of Palvary with woodland creatures peeking through the trees; the northern mountains separating Ilarya from Laisia. Beautiful things unappreciated in the dark hall.

"The royal castle is a fortress, to be sure," Sylvia murmured as she led them through one hallway to another. Her footsteps were light, almost weightless, her slippers skimming across polished floors. "We have dungeons below and a nearly overwhelmed armory, though there's no need to show you that since the d'Allorias family would like to focus on pretty things."

The general coughed uncomfortably and tried to hurry them along. Sylvia always had commentary no matter where they went, hinting at something ominous in every dimly lit crevice.

It didn't help that, when Salome glanced to the corners the woman gestured to, she glimpsed a rotten-toothed smile and wide-eyes watching her in silence. When the eyes blinked, another appeared, then another. She imagined thousands of creatures clustered in the dark, focused on her.

Maybe these were the dead, the last remnants of those sacrificed to senseless war. Ghosts who condemned the royals and their army. She didn't know what she could believe more.

Salome sought Amalia's reaction, but it was as if no one else saw them.

General Bruno tried to show them the throne room, the doorways into it framed with white arches and lined with gemstones, some as large as Salome's fist. One polished gem would be enough to feed Salome for a year. Her stomach ached with wanting. The Alliance only provided meals to sustain their members, with the rare decadent treat to coax her into obedience. A decade and a half of this was torture. It was cruel, but it kept her in their debt. She could repay it all soon or have enough to escape their reach and disappear.

Her heart ached for that. She was desperate to get away from the danger and bloodshed, the family that could keep you safe or kill you depending on what needed to be done. Her real family was out there somewhere, and she needed to make sure they were okay and tell them that she didn't abandon them.

It could end in her death. That was always a risk.

But at least she'd have a choice.

The throne room sat in the center of the castle, surrounded by doorways in every direction leading to different hallways. It felt like they could wander for days and still not see all there was. It would be easy to lead a chase through these corridors and lose anyone trying to tail her.

Salome built a map in her mind. At night, she could not afford to see this place as a labyrinth. It was essential to know every path and exit. If she needed to run and hide, to avoid capture and execution, she had to know the route out of this place. It was required of her to assist with the mapping when she did the surveillance, to inform the rest of the team of how they could evade being held responsible for their crimes they were already committing against the crown.

"In here, all that remained of a servant girl who'd entered were bits of a charred dress," Sylvia explained as they passed a door covered in stained glass. No further explanation as she walked away.

Salome tried to peek through the keyhole. The general, however, tugged her onward.

"This room was once a private audience room for King Clement," Sylvia said of another room with a white door bearing a ruby handle. The man was grandfather to King Vincent and long since dead and buried in the royal tombs deep below the castle, further than the dungeons. "Though he only entertained his lovers here."

General Bruno choked at that. Salome stifled a laugh. It was certainly a room of interest. Gold and jewels were not the only things of value. Those linked to stories could fetch a good price. Sellers would over-exaggerate an object's historical significance to buyers. An object could triple in worth with the right story. The Alliance had a fondness for doing such that to raise the price, and Amalia would have to investigate how high they could go.

Despite the dark humor of Sylvia's tour, Salome learned that each doorway was an opportunity to display the royals' wealth. The family's long history was etched into the walls, carvings into marble made with skilled hands and sharp blades. Things to scrape off, to tuck into the secret pockets of her dresses.

Salome scratched her sharpened nails against her palm. Perfect for peeling off loose fragments.

As they made their way up a grand staircase of black marble steps streaked in gold, the king emerged from a meeting room. A pair of tall, brown-skinned, and dark-haired brothers followed him, the younger of the two sighing as he placed a hand on the king's shoulder. The older brother, heavily scarred as if someone slashed at him a thousand times, curled his lip in annoyance. They looked like they just escaped from an argument. The king's eyes squeezed shut as he roughly raked a hand through his hair.

"Nothing is simple in this war, is it?" the king grumbled.

Salome paused, her hand resting on the pale stone banister.

The younger brother suddenly looked in the direction of the tour group. His hand on the king's shoulder tightened then dropped to his side, before the brothers retreated into the room. But Salome saw the younger one grin.

King Vincent's gaze was heavy and serious despite his small, crooked smile. "Lady Rosalia, you look pleased."

"I wish I could say the same for His Majesty."

He laughed, though somewhat uneasily.

It was a small risk to speak so freely and one she was certain would work. A step toward more intimacy. She needed to make it happen sooner. There wasn't enough time to play patiently. When she glanced at Amalia, the other woman nodded almost imperceptibly. They had to do what was necessary to give the Alliance what they want and ensure the entire team benefitted from the con—and survived.

And there was a thrill in pushing boundaries. She craved danger like dragging her tongue along the sharp edge of a dagger. One wrong move and her head could be cut from her body. Some of the Alliance members—though none assigned to this mission—thought it was too blatant a crime to parade in front of royalty and nobles, to steal by slipping a hand into their pockets and waltzing into their private suites. It was a glorious opportunity that could only happen once in a lifetime. She volunteered herself even though it meant opting out of several other missions to have enough time to prepare.

She was a thief. She always took what she wanted. Gold, jewels, glory, and more.

This time, his attention was the treasure. She had no need of his love, only to keep his eyes on her so he would not notice what was being taken.

Their gazes locked like swords crossed in combat. She refused to budge. With a smirk, the king broke the moment and turned to the general.

"Unfortunately, Uncle, we require your wisdom. Shall I meet you in there? I wish to resolve this before the sun sets," Vincent admitted. "And to have enough time for a moment with Lady Rosalia before dinner."

General Bruno nodded and bowed, and the king returned to the room.

"This wasn't the life my nephew expected, but he does well," Bruno said. His eyes lingered on the door to the council room, his jaw tight, as if he knew what sort of battle he'd face on the other side. Salome was no expert on war, but she knew how tense strategy meetings could become when everyone had their own agenda.

"But some say the king is cursed to lose all he loves," Sylvia said suddenly. Her eyes dropped to the floor, her hands tangling in her skirts. Her guard placed a hand on her waist in a familiar touch. "Dead, dead, dead—all of them."

A long pause followed.

Amalia turned away, likely to hide her amusement. Salome was determined not to show her own interest. The king must have known Sylvia said such things, and yet she was here. How interesting. Was it kindness for another orphan?

The general was not keen on humoring Sylvia though.

"My sister and her husband passed nearly two years ago, as you likely know," General Bruno reminded them. The passing of the former queen and king placed the kingdom in mourning for several months. "And then my niece, Viviana, inherited the throne, but her reign was much shorter than anticipated."

Sylvia turned away, much like a child would when they held back some terrible thing they wished to say.

"May they rest in peace," the general added.

The red-haired handmaid looked down, back hunched like she held no importance.

Curious and willing to test the limits of the information the general and the ward might share, Salome asked, "What of his younger siblings?"

There was a younger brother and sister in the royal family, though their names hadn't been spoken in nearly a year. The king had no parents or siblings left. Everyone knew that. The details of their disappearance were hidden from the people. If anyone would share the secret, it would be this woman. If there was a chance, she had to take it. She always did.

There was a moment when Salome thought no one would say a word. The general was frozen, his gaze unfocused. Salome tried to look ashamed for even asking, but when she glanced at Sylvia, hope flared. Their eyes met.

"They are proof that the king should be more afraid of the shadows and what hides within them, not the eternal rivalry between Ilarya and Pavalla," Sylvia whispered, her voice strained.

Her guard kept her upright, a hand on her hip, fingers digging into it with more possessiveness than should be allowed of a guard. He had a purpose here like anyone else. Maybe he truly loved the woman he protected and maybe he was what kept her on her feet.

Salome knew monsters were real, though not even her parents believed her. All her life, she witnessed glimpses of evil living in the dark. Here, it seemed the royals and nobles were intimately acquainted with them.

If there was ever a story to chase, it was here.

Once the Alliance was satisfied with what she filched and their pawns were in place within the castle, Salome would meet the monsters face-to-face. For too long, she'd second-guessed the things she felt, saw, or heard. No more, not when they were here.

Being part of the Alliance and witnessing the way they exerted their power on those who failed them was terrifying. And yet she wasn't sure how it would compare to demons. Their reputation protected her from lowly criminals, deterring anyone from crossing those under Gabriel and Yvette's command, in fear of violent retaliation of the worst sort. Of torture before the release of death.

They weren't here to stop the ominous warnings come to life. They couldn't do anything to save her if she confronted those things, not when they did not have magic of their own.

When the meeting room's door opened, fragments of a loud argument spilled into the hall. The neighboring kingdom blamed Ilarya for demons spilling into their territory. They used that excuse to stake claim on the latter's land, as if it was payment for their troubles. It matched the whispers on the street and in the taverns, the talk in between alleyways.

The king was tired and frustrated. His side of the story was a bleeding wound, and he had no time to heal. She heard it in his voice, in the way it floated out of the room to her, like it was calling to her.

"I must go. Sylvia will take care of you." With a bow and one final look of warning to the king's ward, General Bruno rushed up the remaining stairs. The door slammed behind him.

The rest of the tour felt dull afterward.

Sylvia had less jabs at the royal family without one of them in her audience. She gestured with little interest to thick columns with cracks filled with molten silver, or windowed alcoves with lovely city views. She mumbled names when they passed portraits, swerving around sculptures depicting historic events.

Salome and Amalia focused on key details, like paths required to take in the night. The shadows would hide them as they did their work. While Amalia would hurry to the city to meet with messengers and spies, Salome searched the castle for things to sell or replace. She could take a tiara from the royal treasury and have Gerard remember and sketch, which Leon would then recreate. Elias and Amalia would sell the real ones in the night markets, and then the empty trunks they'd brought would be filled with the gold the Alliance sought from this mission.

There would be things she would keep for herself, as she had for years now, to sell when she had a moment alone. The Alliance didn't realize it, but every year, she was a step closer to paying off the debts she owed them. As a child, she didn't know what she'd agreed to do. Now she did, and it wasn't what she wanted, no matter how fun it was to play pretend.

If she succeeded in this mission and got what she needed, she could be free of the Alliance. They trusted her to do as they commanded, to obey and make them richer, to risk her life for their benefit. She'd bent to their will for fifteen years and picked up skills faster than they ever imagined anyone could. Every time she proved herself more than capable of accomplishing the tasks they assigned to her, her stash grew.

It might never be enough. They might not care what she offered them in exchange for freedom. There was even a possibility that they would kill her for daring to think she could leave the organization. But she had to try. If they wouldn't take it, she would still use it to fund her escape. She was a thief before she was a con artist, a beggar before she became an actress, and she always kept a little for herself.

The more she did, the more she earned, and the closer she came to freedom and finding her parents. If she did as she intended during this mission, she'd amass a fortune fit for the richest of heiresses, plus some for her family. The king was richer than should ever be allowed and this damned castle was proof of that. Her parents deserved just as much luxury, or more.

She'd give them the life they dreamed of. A seaside home, warm and cozy, with cupboards full of food and lush gardens outside. A home close to bustling markets where they could have anything they desired, with opportunities for adventure nearby. They were the ones to fill her head with stories, after all.

So she focused on memorizing all she could with the intent to retrace her steps that very night and learn the castle as if it truly would become her home, as it would have for the real Rosalia. Each hallway felt like another twist and turn to a labyrinth with no exit in sight.

Servants kept out of their way, though some glanced at Salome.

Let them focus on her while the Alliance planted ambitious new servants to act as their eyes and ears on the inside. She nodded to them and smiled, knowing they'd be gone soon.

But as they made their way through a hallway of busts—royal family members who never ruled—Salome swore their shadows twisted to watch her. *That* wasn't attention she enjoyed, especially when some seemed to smile.

At least they didn't speak—or call her name.

A few wicked grins were open-mouthed and smelled of rotten meat. Salome's stomach rolled with nausea. If the monsters were alive here, if the castle was rife with them, what would become of this place when the sun set?

"Could we continue our tour another time?" Salome requested, the words rushing out. Her heart fluttered like the wings of a frantic bird, desperate to escape. She couldn't tell if it was fear or excitement. "I would like to rest before greeting the court tonight."

Sylvia pursed her lips, frank with her disappointment, but nodded.

Salome's relief came too soon. Something touched her hand and when she glanced down, there was black smoke slithering up her arm like vines. Again, no one else noticed.

She'd wanted adventure and now she was likely in a dangerous one.

Chapter Four

Learning the path to her rooms was easy but pretending not to feel the shadows stirring in her presence was not. They were roused now, louder than they ever were.

There were teeth grazing against the vulnerable skin of her throat. Hands clawed under her skirt, snaking around her ankles, and climbing up her calves. They were cold and biting, like winter chill gnawing at her flesh.

"Slow *down*," Amalia hissed. "You'd think you were being chased by hounds."

When Salome's fingers twitched, it felt as though the shadows did too. They moved in time with each flutter of her hand. Behind her back, Salome flattened her palm to the wall and, suddenly, it was like the world went still.

A heartbeat later, the shadows were alive again.

She clenched a fist and gnashed her teeth together in a tight smile.

Eventually, after going in circles, Amalia went to fetch a servant to lead the way.

The second Salome was left on her own, she sagged against the wall. Wherever the servants were, they thankfully kept themselves out of sight. They must have secret passageways to avoid disturbing the nobles.

What was happening? It was never like this before.

She focused on a fleck of gold on the wall, the light dancing against it. The shadows quieted slightly. If they were merely waiting for some command, that was enough for her.

A few people passed her, soldiers or guards. They were armed but not dressed in the king's guard regalia. She smiled when they nodded at her. More fighters often filled the city in advance of another fight, groups gathering before making their way to the border.

By the time Amalia returned with a servant, Salome had removed some gold foiling to spread it across her nails like gloss. She had memorized the opulent chandelier and the smooth, delicate texture of the ivory curtains framing windows. She'd gained back some of her composure, too, standing straight with her hands clasped gracefully in front of her in the picture of a docile noblewoman.

Silently, the servant guided them to a wing of the castle filled with suites. Some were occupied, while others seemed untouched. Everything was shining and polished. Rosalia's chambers sat at the end of the wide corridor, labeled with two dark, wooden doors engraved with the night sky. The servant bowed to Salome, rushing away once excused.

"Hello, I am *home!*" she declared upon opening the doors.

One act for those in the castle. Another for her co-conspirators.

The only one who might know her truly was Euria. After what happened to her eye, Salome owed the other woman and offered vulnerability. It allowed Euria to hold something over her, a threat that if she was crossed again, it would not end well for Salome. There were plenty of things she could do. Informing Gabriel and Yvette that their little actress wasn't as loyal and invested in the organization as she pretended to be had the potential to be worse than being carved open and slowly emptied, bled out until there was nothing left in the body, not even a breath or beating heart.

It wasn't unusual to be resentful of the debt owed to the Alliance leaders. It was a problem if a professional thief couldn't be trusted by those who commanded her.

For her silence, Salome gave Euria a fraction of her own earnings, still managing to hide how much she truly hoarded for herself. And Salome never told Yvette of how Euria and Gerard sometimes spoke of settling down. The woman was worse than Gabriel, more vicious and vengeful, than the man who ruled beside her.

No one in the Alliance ever knew how long they'd remain in the leaders' good graces. When they had a chance of experiencing luxury, they had to enjoy it. Salome certainly did.

A small crystal and gold chandelier bore candles smelling of orange blossoms and promised to bathe the rooms in a warm glow in the evenings. During the day, crystal-clear windows framed in bronze brought sunlight inside, fracturing it into gleaming rays which made the metallic details of the rooms shine.

There was a small table of dark wood and marble for private dining and a section of loveseats and armchairs for entertaining guests, all adorned in midnight-blues and bronze fabrics.

And, to her relief, there was a lack of portraits in gaudy frames bearing down on her.

The Alliance had enough eyes and spies to make her paranoid.

Abel crossed his arms. "Did you learn anything valuable?"

Amalia busied herself with laying papers across the dining table. She tugged up her sleeves and started scribbling diagrams and listing names using charcoal.

"Places to go, people to rob, exactly what we needed to figure out." Salome plopped onto a couch and kicked off her shoes. "Amalia and I are off to a great start."

Amalia smirked and nodded. "There is plenty for us here. Salome has already been assigned a chaperone and a companion and will make use of those connections. We will have to work quickly to replace what we'll take from the fools."

Salome placed hand over her heart. "And I promise I will not spend this entire mission flirting with the *absurdly* handsome king. I will seduce him and gain his confidence before long. Then I'll learn all there is to know of the council's plans. We shall be out of here before an army arrives."

With the Alliance members, she tried to portray a greedy, fearless twenty-four-year-old woman—not the paranoid creature she'd suddenly become overnight. Her ability to blend with the shadows meant she was good at being unseen and listening. Her prettiness meant she could distract and keep eyes on her and away from the work being done.

The Alliance kept her for a reason. If they stopped seeing value in keeping her alive, she would have been dead before she could realize the shift. As she grew older, Gabriel became less interested in playing the doting father. Weekly visits became monthly, then yearly. In the first few years, she told Gabriel everything and he listened, especially after a mission. Now, someone else would interview her upon their return to headquarters, wherever it was next located since it never stayed long in one place.

The shadows, however, were a secret she never shared.

Euria snickered. Abel cast her a glare and silently ordered her to stand guard outside. She sobered instantly and obeyed. Gerard started following, until Abel held up a hand. She would do this on her own as punishment.

Once settled, they named some nobles to target for their wealth or influence. Amalia made notes, Abel made decisions, and Salome was expected to follow their lead.

She was the face of the operation and the one who would take the fall should it go awry.

They had three months to complete their mission.

They'd kept Salome alive this long, seeing something valuable in her when they found the muddy little girl, and she proved that all they invested in her was worthwhile. She made them rich and maintained the reputation they'd built long before she joined them. She tortured friends for them, stole from good people for them, earned their praise and the rewards gifted to her after a successful con.

But if she messed up once, if her littles detours led her down the wrong path, they wouldn't care about how well-behaved she'd been. They'd kill her and replace her before she was in the ground, if there was anything left of her at all.

Salome traced the arrowhead scar on her wrist that marked her as a member of the organization, often concealed beneath bracelets. She'd more likely lose her head than her hands if she failed.

As Abel examined the map, as Salome said, "The ward, Sylvia l'Essalia, owns nothing but valuable insight. I shall make good use of her acquaintance." An intriguing figure, with eyes like a storm and the demeanor of a woman who'd rather hide than seek approval from nobles.

Leon emerged from one of the smaller ones with his toolbox tucked under his arm. "Anything for me yet?"

Amalia tossed him a small chain with dangling gemstones. Leon caught the bracelet, then ducked back into his workroom and personal quarters shared with another member of their team, most likely Gerard. Rosalia's entire entourage would remain close.

"Elias will come with me to the city later," Amalia said. "Our contacts are settling in."

The Alliance had a few spies within the castle, but they needed more powerful allies to make bigger moves. While they were busy, perhaps she could see how active the shadows were here, if magic was becoming a more complex, living thing than before.

The witches were here. They could have answers.

But first, she had to do her job. Salome focused on memorizing the map's layout. The castle was the largest structure she'd ever encountered, but the drawing had gaps of information. Here, there were secrets—passageways and hidden rooms, or areas of the castle purposely kept out of her knowledge. Sometimes others in the Alliance doubted her, but she was clever and quick on her feet.

She could be a chameleon, and her talent for languages was a valued ability. Better to be seen as childish than scheming. But only a fool wouldn't think that any member of the organization didn't have their own agenda.

The tour hadn't included an entire wing, nor the lower levels where there were dungeons. This missing information would need to be uncovered. No mission was complete if there was anything left undiscovered. The organization was infamous for its hoard of secrets, including the ones about its operations. All their deals were done under the table and their puppetry went unseen.

For now.

Salome added the details she discovered, pointing out exit points and tricky corners. Routes to take to lose a tail. Rooms with multiple doors. Hallways that intersected. Places where there was more darkness than light, where one could hide and disappear. Her notes were added to the map and would be memorized. In a day or so, it would be destroyed to ensure no one outside of their team knew the strategies.

If the mission went well, the Alliance would have even pieces in play to assert their power than they already had, as well as a larger fortune to back up the work they intended to do. They could have their secrets, but they wouldn't need to hide behind them.

Certainly, if the king discovered who they were, the only reasonable response would be interrogation and execution. There was no other way to eliminate the Alliance. Death came to anyone who was caught with the mark of the arrowhead somewhere on their body, by authorities or by the Alliance.

The Alliance once burnt down a tavern to eliminate a member who was named a wanted criminal, certain he was hiding there with friends. All that remained was an arrowhead drawn in the ashes. Casualties meant nothing compared to the messages they wanted to send.

To be associated with the Alliance was to wield power like a weapon. No one would cross a member. Those in the organization were assumed to be the best at what they could do. To be within their ranks was like being royalty among criminals.

When Salome was little, a man once tried to take advantage of her. Before he could do any damage, Yvette personally cut off his balls one at a time and fed them to him. She ensured he chewed before he swallowed, that he wept before she released him, and that his blood left a trail in the dirt for anyone who wanted to find him.

A knock on the door made the entire suite go quiet. Salome slid her shoes back on. Amalia cleared off the table and made herself scarce before returning with a tea set.

Abel closed the door and turned to them. "The king is on his way."

"I'll handle it," Salome said.

Before anyone could speak further, there was another knock. Some laughter soon followed, low and masculine and vaguely familiar. Salome imagined the king standing with the two brothers from earlier, forming a handsome trio.

Abel maintained his seriousness as he opened the door. The king needed no permission to enter, yet he looked around with a bashful smile.

"Would you like some privacy, Your Majesty?" Salome asked, standing, then looking pointedly in Abel and Amalia's direction. To anyone else, it would look like a polite smile. A slight gleam in her eyes hinted at her delight to issue commands.

Her team wouldn't let any harm come to her or any asset they owned. The Alliance rewarded loyalty despite how wretched they could be. Only in the most extreme cases would a team member be left behind.

Once Abel and Amalia left them, the king crossed the room. Salome's arms dangled by her sides, her fingers toying with her gown and her head tilted in curiosity. There was a solemness to his eyes but gentleness in his smile. She momentarily fixated on the small, barely noticeable scar above his mouth. She could place her lips there, learn his taste and offer herself, if only she wasn't playing the part of a more innocent woman.

"It's good to see you, Your Majesty."

"Please, call me Vincent."

"Then you may call me Rosalia." The name rolled off her tongue with ease. Salome rarely spoke her own name aloud over the last fifteen years. To introduce herself with it seemed a far-fetched dream she refused to forfeit. All her hard work, all her successes and accomplishments, led her closer to what she wanted.

"A beautiful name to match a beautiful woman."

She laughed, a version that was sweet and charming and dainty, like she'd grown up with a more refined childhood.

"You do not agree?" Vincent asked. "Surely you know you are enchanting."

His gaze was dark and intense as it traveled the length of her body. It spoke of wanting, especially when his eyes lingered at the bare skin of her chest, above the dip of her dress. In response, she traced the lines of her collarbone slowly.

His eyes followed the back-and-forth sway of her hand. Her mind conjured the sensation of the scrape of his beard right where she touched, the heat of his mouth, his tongue. She sucked in a breath at the flash of desire in her, exhaling slowly until she was calmed.

"I think you are trying to win my favor by appealing to my vanity," she mused.

"Is it working?"

"I couldn't say." Truthfully, she did like being wooed.

"How about a gift then?" Vincent pulled a small package from his pocket wrapped in silver silk and a marigold yellow ribbon arranged to look like a flower. "I crafted it myself. I hope that does not offend you."

Salome raised her eyebrows in feigned surprise. She'd learned that the king used to spend his days drawing and painting as a young boy until more responsibilities were placed on his shoulders. A kingdom required ruling, and an heir to the throne needed to learn to defend themselves and their people, as well as develop an understanding their nation's history and politics. No matter how unlikely it was that they'd rule.

"That is very kind of you," Salome said carefully.

Vincent grew self-conscious, running a hand down his jaw and smoothing out his beard. His bashful smile was so sweet, her heart almost fluttered. But she knew charm and she'd met many handsome faces. She would not fall or feel anything except gratitude for what he had and what she could take from him.

"It is my hope that we can grow close and, perhaps one day, there will be love in our marriage," he said, as he placed the gift in her hands.

Ah, he was a romantic. Soft, sensitive. She wondered if there was more, if he was as lonely as she imagined, surrounded by death and unable to be attached. She could offer him intimacy, a bed to share to warm the nights and hold every secret thought he couldn't speak of.

Slowly, she began undoing the ribbons. "Should I open this while you're here?"

He nodded. So she continued, soon revealing the hand-painted deck of cards nestled inside. They wore thin, delicate brushstrokes of white and silver paint against solid black. It looked like the sky, each card unique, to be spread out to resemble the night itself.

On the other side, he'd painted the typical set of playing cards of hearts, spades, clubs, and diamonds. The first card she saw was the King of Hearts, faceless and dark-haired, dressed in ceremonial garb so detailed it belonged to portraits by a celebrated painter.

Such talent went to waste when he was king first.

She was a different kind of artist, but she could appreciate his work.

Suddenly, Vincent placed a hand over hers. "Do you like it?"

The contact warmed her skin. He drew back, though, clasping his hands behind his back.

If he was hesitant about their familiarity, then she ought to bring out his boldness. That would surely keep him distracted. She held the deck to her heart and closed the distance between them, placing her other hand on his cheek. The temptation to kiss him came over her like the sun shining in her eyes. She had to pause, blink, and try to see clearly again.

"Thank you. I adore them," she whispered.

He had a gentle heart. She could imagine how it would break from the starstruck way he stared at her now. Like she was glorious, and he was already halfway in love with her.

Salome pulled her hand away.

"How could I properly express my gratitude?" she asked. "Would you mind a kiss? I don't have anything else to offer at the moment."

When she looked up at him from under her lashes, his eyes were already on her lips. Eagerness bloomed in her, but she focused on bringing a blush to her cheeks, thinking of the two of them in the night. Comparing the size of him to herself, aligning their bodies, learning what he liked. Her body warmed and she breathed shakily.

Vincent cleared his throat, lowering his gaze to the cards.

"There is no need to thank me. It is a small thing. Besides, I am uncertain how the witch circus discovered my intention to share these with you, but they requested that you bring them to the dinner tonight," he explained. "For the performance."

She had to figure out how to keep his mind on her, but she didn't mind this diversion. It satisfied a curiosity she often had to stifle.

There were stories about what the witches could do, the magic they created. It was an honor to witness their performance, but that was not what intrigued Salome. She thought about the previous night, the woman in the city with vines on her limbs and a foreign accent. One of the witches, surely. They knew something about Salome. About the way the shadows responded to her, even now.

Salome took a sudden step away from the king. His brow furrowed.

It was as if he couldn't hear the hissing song that came from beneath them. Salome moved toward the window. It wasn't so sunny that afternoon, but still bright enough to quiet the shadows and ensure there was nothing to fear. And yet she was spooked like a child.

"I'm afraid I nearly forgot about tonight," Salome lied.

"If you are worried, there is no need."

She shook her head. "I ought to rest a bit before dinner so I may present my most charming self." There was a gorgeous canopy bed in the room calling for her to enjoy it while she could, though it was more likely to be a comfort won by battle—or simply being quick enough to get to it first. Amalia would surely try to claim it herself.

If there was any place Salome might find sleep, it would be that glorious bed with its mountain of pillows and soft, satin sheets. She and Amalia might share it, as they often agreed to do, otherwise they would revert to bickering and resentment. They had to keep such incidents in the past with their childhood.

"But Vincent, if we can be honest with each other, do not hide who you are from me," she began, speaking quietly. "We'll be husband and wife soon. I do not wish to be strangers."

If you want me, I'm yours, she attempted to convey in a way better suited to court.

Luckily, he laughed. He would make this too easy. How thrilling. This was a different kind of flirting. Bolder and sharper and a risk. She hoped he would take the bait and latch on. She hoped her expression conveyed the bone-deep wanting in her for a taste of this handsome man.

"We shall not be strangers. I promise that," he said, and smiled.

Something about him filled her with warmth. It felt like she basked in sunlight. It felt too good to be true, so long as the shadows stayed put. Too good, like dreaming of reuniting with her parents.

Fifteen years had passed since she left in the dead of night after dropping off medicine for her mother. It was one of the first major things she'd stolen. It was difficult enough for her parents to find work and feed themselves, let alone a little girl. By then, Salome knew how to be charming and how to go unseen. Leaving them behind so they would have a better chance without her seemed an easy choice. One less burden.

They could take care of themselves and build that life they'd dreamed of having when they sailed away from Villasayas.

Salome was born and raised in Ilarya. Most of her understanding of the world began here, as an Ilaryan. All she knew of the islands were her mother's wistful stories: trees so tall they must have touched the sky; enduring warmth more intense than Ilarya's summers; emerald forests housing magical creatures; some sleeping volcanoes and some awaiting eruption; jewel-toned oceans containing the most colorful fish and even water-dwelling people who could kiss you and allow you to breathe beneath the waves, or yank one down to drown and to be devoured.

When she was rich, she would go there. She would find the magic and see if the stories were true. There was something wrong there, though, that caused them to leave home behind.

The Alliance had brought her all over the world, guiding her in learning languages and cultures and to witness the breadth of their power. Villasayas was one place they dared not go. There was nothing to gain on those islands that they couldn't wrench away from merchants.

She had three months to figure out her next move to get closer to freedom. Away from the people who only saw her as a tool.

One day, when Salome was rich, she would be free. From the Alliance, from the lying, from the shadows that had followed her all her life.

Chapter Five

WHEN SALOME ENTERED THE THRONE ROOM, ALL EYES TURNED to her.

Tonight, she was dressed in another glittering, golden gown with long organza sleeves that touched the floor. Her hair framed her face and cosmetics enhanced her features, outlining her eyes in black and her lips painted a dark red.

The team had gone over the need-to-know details while Salome snacked on yellow mango halves sliced like a grid, like the ones she salivated over in markets worthy of strengthening her thief's touch. These ones, however, were ordered specifically for Rosalia and presented on a silver platter. A little treat from the king, who wanted to ensure she had everything she wanted, even the small things. He was courting her as much as she was courting him.

Not that it was personal. It was meant for who he thought she was.

Abel escorted her through the halls to squeeze in a lecture before her presentation to the crowd. She kept her mouth shut now, grinding her teeth to stay silent and listen.

Amalia also left Salome with a reminder: *you are nothing, you are no one. You can pretend all you like, but we know the truth.*

It struck her like a poisoned arrow to the heart. Even if she pulled it out, she'd still feel the effects and the only antidote was to prove them wrong.

For three months, she'd pretend to be Rosalia, but Salome was still the same hungry little girl who tried to steal from the leader of an infamous organization. They led her here, and they'd lead her to her grave if she didn't do what they wanted. She had to be more, and she had the tools she needed tonight: quick hands, light fingers, and a bright, distracting smile.

She wasn't a little girl anymore. She was grown and she was strong.

She had a chance here, in this glorious room, to prove yet again how brightly she shined.

White marble busts of former rulers lined the five walls, a pentagonal shape with doors at each angle. Several long tables and benches of onyx wood filled the room. Bronze chandeliers doused the room with light from floral-scented candles. Guests wore their finest clothing with gold and silver threads amidst family colors. A representative from each noble family was here to witness the future queen's arrival.

Vincent smiled broadly when he saw her. He sat in one of the two intricately carved bronze thrones, a table in front of him. His advisors were on either side of the thrones, nobles both young and old. They watched her—gaping, sneering, or uncertain.

She focused on the king's joy and steadied her breathing. Her eyes briefly sought out the exits and familiar faces. Abel and Elias were close behind her. Euria and Gerard were stationed at the different doors. Amalia took her place with the handmaids. Leon remained in their quarters, working on forgeries.

The team was ready.

Vincent came to her, propelled forward by long strides. Anyone in his way stepped aside.

She did not move, not until he was within reach, until Vincent bowed deeply.

Her heart thundered as she curtsied in response, rising only when he touched her hand.

"There are so many people," Salome whispered.

"All are eager to meet you."

And there would be more when the wedding came. She didn't care about their feelings or what they thought of her—she'd never survive as a con artist if that mattered. She only worried about the witnesses. If he called people to Ellasya before heading to the next battle, it could become even worse.

A woman approached, offered Salome a closed-lip smile, then immediately began speaking to Vincent about how dearly she missed her son, who was positioned near the Pavallan border and hoped he would be home soon.

Vincent consoled her quietly, then directed her attention to Salome.

The lady murmured pleasantries and curtsied, looked back and forth between them, then said her goodbyes. Salome watched as she rejoined a group of women, glancing back occasionally. This was not a job for the weak-hearted or thin-skinned. Salome looked to the king to stop her thoughts there. Only his attention truly mattered. His gaze must stay on her so the job could be done.

He took in the sight of her with greedy eyes, but when he reached for her, his touch was shy and tentative, grazing his fingertips on the soft skin of her wrist.

She needed to convince him to be bolder, to place his hands on her and tuck her close to him. Others came to speak about things from business to family matters, always greeting the king before acknowledging her. She made note of what she could pass to the rest of the team when they regrouped later.

A lord with a missing child. A lady discussing marriage between her daughter and a foreign noble. A merchant's heir offering their goods. As they spoke with the king, Salome moved closer to him. People noticed that more than her quick, busy hands.

She'd swiped a few things from those who brushed by. A bracelet that came loose at the touch, a jeweled button from a coat, a few coins peeking out of pockets. Few opportunities compared to city streets.

The entire team had a part to play.

Euria noted earlier of which guests held the most valuables. And Gerard would remember every detail of every minute, his perfect memory making up for everyone else's. Elias and Abel were on alert for any unusual signals or indications that their plans for tonight might go awry. If things were to turn violent, they could be trusted to protect her and the rest of the team, to get them to safety, wherever that might be.

Amalia stood in a corner, clustered with a group deep in conversation. Tonight, she was bound to gather plenty of worthwhile gossip. Both had an essential role in this game and would fill any gaps of knowledge or opportunity. The night would not be wasted. Information could be as important as a jewel, especially if it led to a bigger score.

Without warning, Salome slipped her hand into the crook of Vincent's arm during a lapse between conversations. He stilled, then placed a hand over hers. His touch was like sunlight, warm and sparkling in the sea.

"I hope you do not mind," she whispered. "All know that I am to be yours."

Heads turned in their direction at the sound of his laughter. It was wonderful: easy and slow. She decided to draw it from him whenever possible. The world would benefit from hearing it often, as if it could make the stars shine brighter. He leaned down to touch his head to hers, which had tilted in preparation for a kiss that never came.

Vincent was more serious and authoritative with others, except with the two brothers from earlier. He laughed openly, leaning forward with genuine interest while they conversed. Salome took a closer look at them. The elder brother was surly and heavily scarred. The younger appeared more open, though he bore a menacing scar stretching from his left eye to the corner of his mouth. Both were even taller than the king. She knew their names before they were spoken, recognizing faces from sketches included in her studies on the Ilaryan court.

"Introduce us properly to the lady, Vincent," the younger brother said. "No need for rudeness."

"Lady Rosalia d'Ilumias," she said, and bowed her head.

"As stunning as the sunset on the ocean," he stated with a bright, wide smile. "Pleasure to meet you, Lady Rosalia. I am Fabian l'Issalya, childhood friend of our woefully juvenile king—"

"And a nuisance," his brother interjected, perhaps noticing Vincent's glower.

Ignoring him, Fabian continued, "And a loyal soldier to the kingdom."

It was easy to be charmed, to laugh genuinely. Even Vincent chuckled.

"Pardon my brother, Oscar, for speaking so little. We can assume he falls mute at your beauty," Fabian nudged his brother with an elbow. Oscar merely glowered.

There was great kinship there, a fond brotherhood. It was different from the loyalty within the Alliance, the acceptance that they were safest and strongest within their ranks, if that made them anything close to family. That was all she knew—honesty to some degree, and trust and certainty that someone would kill for you if necessary. There was laughter and celebration, though perhaps not for the usual reasons. They didn't have to like each other and many of them didn't. There was a job to do and only success was the possible outcome. Everyone in the Alliance understood the importance of that above all.

She belonged among them no matter how often she dreamed of fitting elsewhere.

If she could belong somewhere else, Salome could only discover upon completing this con and escaping.

Vincent kept glancing at Salome, though, as if to let her know he hadn't forgotten her. Each time, he shared the light in his eyes with her, like taking a mirror to catch sunlight and direct it her way.

It was good to see that they could be in good spirits. From the look of them, they knew war. They knew death and pain and fighting, but they still had each other. Though his family was gone, he had these friends and that could dim the suffering.

Soon, someone came over to let Vincent know the food was ready. The guests then moved to their seats as the dinner was served. Salome sat beside him, overlooking the entirety of the room. There was lumpia and pancit and jasmine rice, and all kinds of stews—Villasayan dishes, prepared in honor of Rosalia's heritage—all finer quality than Salome had ever tasted, with the intended ingredients imported from the islands.

The man beside Vincent soon stole his attention, an older, brown-skinned baron with gray hair. She heard fragments of their conversation. A nearby village offered more young people for the army. A town at the Pavallan border wrote of their lingering militia. A few merchants complained of a beautiful girl who'd stolen their merchandise.

That last piece nearly made her choke, a laugh caught in her throat. They never would realize what happened. How terrifying it would be to discover how easily their world was infiltrated by criminals. Oh, how little they knew.

Ignored by the people flanking her, Salome absently picked at her food. She soon amused herself by swiping a bracelet from the lady beside her. The clasp came undone quietly, as Salome slid the jewelry into her pocket. A quick glimpse around assured her no one noticed. Not even the lady glanced at her unburdened wrist.

All her dresses had pockets, as was necessary for a thief. She'd had years to perfect her skills and recognized what tools and tricks were needed to pull off a mission. To learn how to hoard some for herself, separate from what she brought back to the Alliance.

A woman in a lilac gown stood out among the other advisors with pale white skin and light, vibrant eyes—a duchess, Salome recalled from her studies of the court. Likely the king's cousin, the infamous Irene d'Ellsaria, who knew all the court gossip and politics. She grinned and shrugged, as if to say *I wish I could help you, but we're sitting too far apart.*

Eyes wandering, Salome found Euria with Gerard, much closer than allowed. He brought her hands to his lips until she pushed him away, blushing and touching the silk over her missing eye. They soon resumed their positions, bashful and grinning. Later, they wouldn't play that game. They would find a quiet place and fill it with their noise.

At one point, Amalia called over a servant and whispered something to her. The girl nodded and hurried away. Likely an Alliance spy. If she could name all the spies scattered through the castle, she'd be satisfied. One could never know who to trust or who would report on her. The Alliance was planning something big. She'd need to unearth the details. They evidently weren't content working in the shadows anymore. Their power would likely soon grow.

While Salome indulged in her dessert of sweet, sticky purple ube halaya, servants began clearing plates until only drinks remained.

The performance was about to begin.

Candles were snuffed out and the shadows stirred like fog arriving ahead of a wicked storm. The hairs on her limbs rose as the sound of them awakening made her think of cold, distant laughter ricocheting off the walls of a deep cave.

They'd followed her all her life and now they were catching up to her. It must be the witches cursing her with this complication. She wanted to reunite with her family, rich enough to provide for them. She didn't want power or control. But there was something in the dark that called her name in a rasping, singsong voice.

No one else seemed to hear it or feel the icy touch on their neck like she did.

She was haunted by something alive.

Suddenly, drums began to sound. Slow, rhythmic, and deep.

Her heart pounded, however, faster than a hummingbird's fluttering wings.

A warm, heavy hand slid over her leg. Her eyes met Vincent's and he nodded. *It will be fine.* She laid her hand over his and squeezed. That touch there was intimate yet sweet and ignited her imagination. His hand between her legs, settled in the heat of her. Oh, the things that she could explore with him, the ways she could tease him and teach him how to find real pleasure. Such thoughts came to a sharp, sudden stop as the witches arrived.

Four women emerged from different doorways, dressed in all black with hoods and veils. Only their eyes were visible. They wove effortlessly between tables with drumbeats matching each surge forward until they were in front of Vincent and Salome.

The furthest on the left lifted her pale hands and flames appeared above her palms. At the opposite end, a witch lifted her dark brown hands with an ice crystal hovering above one and a large droplet of water over the other. The two in the middle lifted their hands at the same time, pale hands raising flowers and dark-skinned hands raising miniature tornadoes.

Each witch brought their hands together, palm to palm, extinguishing the illusions at the final drumbeat.

Applause echoed through the room.

"The witch circus has been waiting for you," Vincent whispered.

Her amusement drained away. A speck of fear flew into the vacant space.

"My parents requested their assistance for the kingdom," he said. "They provided the aid yet refused to perform until *your* arrival."

"Why?"

"They said it was *rude*." Powerlessness and resignation were loud in his voice.

What could anyone do when the other side had magic at their fingertips? Nothing.

He was human; they were much more.

Leaning forward, Salome peered at the flower-bearing witch, a pale and petite woman. Instinctively, Salome touched the base of her throat as if protecting it from attack.

The witches' eyes were heavy on her, like a trap clamped over her foot.

"Please, my lady, present the cards." The smallest witch's voice was high and girlish.

Any lingering doubt that Salome felt about this witch vanished. This witch was Salome's assailant from the night before. Warily, Salome removed the cards from her pocket, handling them like delicate jewels, and placed them on the table.

"Now, present them to your betrothed." The witch firmly grabbed Salome's hands and placed them over the cards.

Heart hammering and forcing herself to be steady, Salome lifted them. The witch released her. Vincent raised an eyebrow. She fanned them out for him, the intricate designs on the back mimicking a starry night.

"Choose, dearest king. *Please.*" The little witch's eyes lit up with amusement at the opportunity to command the king.

Unaffected, he reached into the deck and selected one, his fingertips skimming over Salome's hands.

"Turn it over, lay it down, and watch."

He did as instructed and revealed an image of a regal, brown-skinned, featureless woman with long, dark hair reminiscent of the portraits of his mother. A golden crown with pearls and diamonds perched on her head. Slowly, the portrait began to shift.

Salome exhaled sharply.

The new image matched her own features: loosely curled black hair, brown eyes, light caramel skin, full lips, soft round cheeks, dark brows, a mole on her left cheek. She grinned mischievously—alarmingly accurate, as if Vincent painted it himself.

"The Queen of Hearts, a faceless depiction transformed into Lady Rosalia d'Ilumias," he announced loudly, projecting for the guests.

No, Salome wanted to laugh. The card was a portrait of an imposter: Salome Visaya, a woman without title or truth. For a woman about to marry the king, to see herself was a blessing, a sign of hope. For Salome, this was a bad omen. Yet she forced out laughter and smiled so broadly for the audience, her cheeks ached.

"Take it as you will. Now, another card for the king, please!" The little witch clapped.

The other witches exchanged glances. Concerned but electing to not interfere.

Meanwhile, Vincent repeated the process. The new card was the King of

Spades, another featureless figure until the image shifted. She wondered how he felt, if it was entertaining or horrifying to see magic altering his art.

"The King of Spades." He exhaled. "My own image." He shifted his gaze to Salome.

She shook her head, unsure of what to say.

A faint whisper met her ears, fading before she could decipher it. It didn't come from the shadows. The cards, the magic—she almost touched it to coax it to speak again, as if that could work.

The nobles murmured excitedly, craning their necks for a better glimpse. The witch fell back into line with the other witches and bowed. As Salome organized the cards in a neat stack, hands trembling, sweat dripped down the back of her neck.

Vincent handed her the King of Spades. "Witches are a curious thing, are they not?"

"This is no more than illusion?" she guessed, returning the card to the deck. She was transfixed on it, running her fingertips over the details, textured with brushstrokes. As she lifted her fingers, the card returned to its original image, and she jerked her hand back in alarm.

"An illusion," Vincent confirmed, placing a hand over hers. "Nothing to fear. The witches have already taken their payment." His voice was light but tinged with bitterness.

Everyone knew this. The former king and queen offered their lives in exchange for the witch circus' aid, taking a risk in hopes of turning the war in their favor. They hadn't known if the witches would agree to the request for support, only that it could save lives in their kingdom. All they wanted was to protect their home and their people, and they died for it. Magic had a price, and swaying fate was no easy feat. Blood would be lost and so blood was demanded in exchange. They knew what would happen.

The king was haunted, darkness in his eyes, like peering into a grave. "We are grateful."

Salome wouldn't be as gracious.

Vincent turned away, keeping the witches out of view as they entertained guests. There were flashes of light and color, their performances small and personal. Bursts of laughter and applause scattered around the room in response to displays of light-hearted magic.

Vincent's expression became grave, and he lowered his voice. "My parents were strong when they went to battle. When they returned, they were so frail and sickly that they died in their sleep that first night back." Vincent clenched his jaw, hands curling into fists. He buried his resentment to allow his people to enjoy the witches' presence without the burden of his grief. This was his performance.

Quietly, Salome laid the cards on the table.

"Magic has a price, especially when bound in blood." Vincent sighed. "The destruction of an entire village, the death of livestock and crops, or the lives. We only know what is claimed once it's gone. They both knew the cost, whatever it may be, was worthwhile."

Salome placed her hand on his cheek. His skin was warm, his beard tickled her palm. "Thank you for telling me."

"I want you to know me," he murmured, trailing off as if there was more to say. He placed his hand over hers, then brought it to his lips for a kiss. Though it was soft, she felt his breath against her skin, the trembling and warmth of it.

The drums pounded once. Then again. And again.

Everyone rose from their seats. As servants cleared the tables and pushed them aside, the witches made their way to the center of the room. Their bare feet slid across the floor, chains with small gemstones around their ankles jingling as they moved. A breeze swirled around the witch stepping forward and separating herself from the others, ruffling her cloak. Silver eyes set against dark brown skin stared at Salome, odd and piercing, but not unkind.

"Let us give you all something to dream about," the bright-eyed witch declared.

The earth witch went first, bearing fistfuls of flowers, while the other three formed a barricade around her. She removed her cloak and veil, revealing a skin-tight suit covering her from neck to ankle.

Petals and leaves spun around her as the stones lifted her from the floor. She grabbed onto vines lowering from the ceiling like ropes, twisting them around her arms and legs, before letting go and falling headfirst to the ground. The vines around her legs pulled tight and kept her hanging upside down. Suspended, she pulled her body into distorted shapes, bending her limbs in impossible ways. When her performance ended, the vines retreated into the floor and the cracks mended. She was covered again by the time the next witch moved to the center.

The air witch ascended without strings or pedestals. She moved effortlessly once high up, twisting in an elaborate dance that had her gown and cloak fluttering like wings. Dust from around the room gathered and became a ghostly figure—a dance partner. Long braids of black hair slipped out from her hood as they twirled together. Finally, she returned to the floor, dust settling in an intricate web-like design around her feet.

The fire witch replaced her, surrounded by towers of flames. Sparks flew around her as all candlelight extinguished. The sparks looked like stars against the night sky. The flames in her hand became figurines, rising above to dance in the sky. At the end, the room became shrouded in darkness, before the chandeliers brightened the room once more.

Finally, the water witch moved to the center. She pushed up her sleeves and stood on her toes, revealing dark brown skin. Ice spread under her feet like a small rink. She spun on it, arms in the air, water spilling from her fingertips like ribbons. Long, black curls slipped out as she danced with slow transitions between positions of arched spines and stretched limbs. A wave of her fingers set the ice shards orbiting around her like delicate strings of jewels. Her performance ended with a deep bow, shards falling and shattering like a song.

Salome found herself longing for what they had. That magic, that beauty—it was astonishing, yet so different from hers. She couldn't take her eyes away. The audience was in awe, applauding, pleading for more. For power and proof of the impossible. Even Salome held her breath, leaning forward. Entranced despite the sorrow Vincent shared with her. He sat back, observing in silence.

With a dramatic swing of her arm, the tallest of the four gestured toward Vincent and Salome. "For the king and his…" the fire witch paused, "future queen." Her raspy voice was inflected with a Tyrean accent, stressing the final syllable of each word like a stab.

They all looked toward Salome. Eager, expectant. Terrifyingly so.

Her stomach twisted, chest tightened, mouth dried. She couldn't bear to look at Abel or Amalia. They would know something was wrong and she didn't want them to tell her it was all over already. Or had the Alliance known more than they shared?

It felt like something swirled around her feet like a fog. Her nose filled with the smell of burning herbs. Salome dared not move though, especially not while the witches were watching. The noise around her felt muted. All she could hear was a rattling like a snake's tail, mingling with hisses and snarls. Wild beasts waiting to pounce on prey.

Salome held her breath and waited. The monsters always went away. The shadows always retreated in the light. She just had to wait, swallow her screams, and smile.

Always a performance.

When Vincent applauded, she mimicked him, and the guests joined in.

The sound drowned out the shadows.

"For the king and his future queen," the witches chorused. They bowed, the drums silenced, and then, the witches drifted away. The rumors didn't do them justice. Omnipotent enough to claim the lives of the former king and queen yet benevolent enough to perform theatrics at a dinner party.

What was she to fear more?

The Alliance, the shadows, or the witches?

The shadows were unnerving but never harmed her. Maybe she could escape the witches, for they were interested but not threatening. When she caught Abel's eye, she knew it was them. The Alliance was more malevolent, holding onto debts like a noose and secrets like concealed weapons. Who knew of their true power and ambition?

She thought of Gabriel, fatherly until he was unhappy. Carving scars into her skin to claim her. Who else had done that? Who else could make her feel so trapped? She was fighting a war against her supposed allies, and it felt like she was bound to lose. Battles unlike the ones he knew, something secretive and unsure, more dangerous than an open field. She couldn't tell apart allies from enemies. They said they were a family, that she was one of them, but if she ever failed to do as they commanded, her life was forfeit. If she disappointed them, she wouldn't even have the chance to run before they destroyed her in the most vulgar, violent way.

Vincent stood, held out his hand toward Salome, and helped her rise to her feet.

"It is my hope that you all enjoyed the evening, that the food was delightful, and the entertainment was most fascinating." He laughed, fully and without restraint.

His dark eyes were wide with what looked like happiness and amusement, but something lingered. A flicker of grief, nearly unnoticeable. His hand warmed hers, his smile wide. She smiled too, amazed by his presentation of joy, how easily he wore this mask.

Being the deceiver that she was, she understood what it was like. And since she was eighteen, part of her performance involved getting in bed with a mark. She excelled at her job, even though she loathed it at times, the depths she'd sink to do it well. This time, she wouldn't mind adoring his body and how it might feel with hers. She'd seduce him eagerly and enjoy it. She'd take his mind away from politics and grief.

For once, she was thrilled by the opportunity. She didn't have to feign a blush.

"And it is my greatest hope that you are all as impressed with Lady Rosalia as I am."

Accordingly, she lowered her gaze and hid her smile with a hand as though she was a humble gentlewoman. Salome would laugh properly once safely in the privacy of her room. It always did amuse her to be reminded of how she'd fooled her mark.

"In three months, when we marry, she shall be our queen." Vincent caressed her knuckles with his thumb. The tender touch sent invisible sparks through her arm.

The nobles clapped, muttering amongst themselves. Regardless of what they said, she brought hope to the king and that meant hope for the kingdom. For now, she was pleased with the chance to pretend to be so important. With a bright smile, she bowed her head and touched her free hand to her heart.

"And finally, let us all hope for a happy ending to this war," the king declared, his voice more serious and pronounced. "I pray for the sunlight and for the darkness to fade."

All the guests applauded.

Chapter Six

"My lady, the night grows late, and you ought to return to your rooms," Amalia said.

Salome remained in the throne room with Vincent after all the guests left. True, there was a job to do. The rest of them had elsewhere to go and they did not need to stay. Salome could. If she could have more time with the king, it was all the better, wasn't it?

When she met Amalia's eyes, there was understanding. This semblance of responsibility was no more than an act. Later, they would go over what they collected throughout the event. Amalia would start on determining the sum of their score. The work would continue in Rosalia's private quarters as late into the night as necessary. No one on their team would worry about how much sleep she could get.

"I shall escort her myself," Vincent said, winking at Salome.

It warmed her like the first gulp of hard liquor, her chest filling with light.

Before Amalia could leave, Salome removed the stolen pieces from her pockets and discreetly slid them into Amalia's. "I promise I shall be safe with His Majesty."

She'd ensured that Amalia could complete her own task and confirmed that this was still the job. With a bow, Amalia departed, escorted by Abel and

Elias. Only Salome and Vincent remained, sitting on thrones in a room meant to hold an audience of dozens.

If one of them spoke, it would likely echo.

"Do you realize it has only been a single day?" he asked, voice quiet and contemplative. He slid his fingers over the back of her hand like it was a wondrous thing to behold.

This kind of touch made her feel like she was something holy and he was reverent.

"How unfortunate that it must end," he whispered.

"Does it have to?" Salome asked.

When he laughed, it felt like a match was lit and cast into a stack of wood. A bonfire grew between them. Then he leaned away, and the room felt colder. She only then realized his head bowed toward her. She exhaled slowly, watching him carefully. This was a duel of intimacy, and she was prepared to fight.

This was when she stood, moving to stand in front of him, edging between his legs. Her body urged her to climb into his lap, but it was too soon for that. Too bold. She stood there, draping her arms over his shoulders, bending forward to get closer. Slowly, carefully, she pressed her lips to his brow, then one of side of his head, then the other. She lingered before rising.

All the while, the king was silent, watching her. His breathing remained steady. Then he brought her hand to his mouth and pressed a kiss to her palm, lips dragging slowly across her skin like a promise of what the rest of her body might anticipate. Tender, gentle, and so sweet it could ignite heartache.

She shouldn't have felt a thing, but there was a flicker of longing and perhaps pity.

Except she wasn't sure who she pitied—the king or the pretender he kissed who wished for more than what was allowed.

"Being alone might not be the best idea," she murmured, closing her eyes.

He trailed his hands down the sides of her body, tracing the shape of it like learning a route on a map. As he pulled them up, the skirt of her dress caught on the callouses on his palms. Her breath hitched, but she remained still, behaving despite her instinct to steal intimacy she wasn't owed.

His expression was unchanged when she opened her eyes. "Why is that?"

"For our own good," she said. "Already, I am tempted." Bending, her mouth hovered over his. She breath shook as she exhaled, head tilted, ready to kiss him.

"How so?" His own voice was quiet, curious. His eyes were half-lidded and he inclined his own head. The instinctive movement nearly betrayed his best manners, if only he hadn't held back.

"Ah, we cannot speak of it this soon." She smiled shyly and stepped away.

Vincent raised an eyebrow, arms outstretched as if his hands wanted to follow where she went. His fingers twitched, hooking loosely to catch on her dress, but the fabric fell away.

"You're teasing me," he mused.

"Is it working?"

When he laughed, she smirked.

"Let us become better acquainted. Our affections ought to grow first," she said. "Court me. Woo me. Show me how romantic you are. Prove there is nothing to fear or regret."

He bowed his head. "If that is what you wish."

When he smiled at her, bright and warm, it felt like a summer's day. Standing on the shore of a white sand beach, the ocean's edge lapping at the land, the sky clear, the sun shining, and a light breeze drifting by. Birds soaring and swooping over the water to catch the tiny fish swimming beneath gentle waves. She was floating, absorbed in this feeling of safety with him despite the pounding of her heart and rush of heat flowing through her.

"Anything you wish, I shall grant it," he added.

"Then I shall go and, tomorrow, we can see each other again. We'll embark on a proper courtship."

As Salome smoothed out her dress, Vincent rose from his chair. Not once did his eyes leave her, as if she cast a spell on him. He was entranced, and she adored that look on his face.

"Well, perhaps not too proper," she suggested.

His soft smile curved into something wicked. *Oh, he must like the sound of that.* Good. With a light laugh, she pushed at his chest and backed away.

"Enough of that. You make me feel like a villain," she said. As she was. A thief in the night, ransacking his home when he imagined it to be a sanctuary. Perhaps he should have known better than to trust a stranger with a pretty face.

She moved to the nearest exit, but upon reaching the door, she looked back. Vincent laid a hand over his heart and bowed. She laughed again and hurried away, moving swiftly down the hallways. Smiling, she felt like she'd been basking in the sun.

"Goodnight," she whispered, though he couldn't hear.

Luckily, none of the Alliance was around to see her like this: lovestruck and silly. On previous missions, she'd felt the allure to a mark every now and then, chemistry capable of becoming overwhelming. This was a little different, a little more intense. She felt little pinpricks of aching and desire. A whisper to find a moment alone that night to reach between her legs and satisfy the growing desperation for touch. It wouldn't be enough all on her own, but it would keep her from losing herself to untrustworthy feelings.

She walked briskly down the halls, hardly noticing where she was until suddenly everything felt too quiet. A forest in the dead of night should have been filled with the orchestra of bugs and the rustling of leaves. A castle, too, should have noises of some sort. Distant footsteps, the howl of wind down a corridor, the faint suggestion of servants tidying up while the nobles rested.

There was nothing though. Not a single sound.

So, Salome stopped, held her breath, and listened.

A heartbeat passed, and then another. She focused her eyes on the lone flame of a three-candle sconce on the wall. It danced slowly, the gilding flashing as it caught the light.

Until it was snuffed out.

Now Salome stood in darkness in a castle as tall as a mountain with as many halls as there were streets in its capital city. In a kingdom where they said things could crawl from the places that light couldn't touch. Things that could kill and destroy, much more than any war.

She placed her right hand over her left arm, searching for the thin needle-like knives sewn into her sleeves. Always having weapons hidden across her body was a comfort, but she was still unsettled. She had no chance to rip a knife free when her wrists were seized by something unseen. Something cold and sticky.

Since childhood, she was trained not to scream when under attack. No matter the situation, to make such noise was to call attention to herself and that was never an option. *Death before discovery*, that was the rule. Die before anyone can find you in a compromising position. So she held her tongue.

Suddenly, four figures emerged in the dark. The witch circus.

"Hello, little one," the tiny one said.

"We wondered when we could finally meet," said another witch with a deep, coarse voice reminiscent of a wise old woman with smoke in her throat. A taller one, though Salome could not make out her face, until the witch's hands lit up with fire, illuminating the hall. As the light shone, the grip on her wrists slid away.

And Salome saw the witches properly.

Fair-skinned with amber eyes and brown hair, tall and broad-shouldered. The fire witch smirked, then gestured to the earth witch. Another pale face with honey-blonde hair and eyes of blue and green, too large for her round face.

The earth witch held onto one of Salome's arms with a grip like stone. On the other side of her, Salome met eyes as blue as winter waters, cold and sharp. The fire witch stood in front of them, beside a slightly shorter person who peered out from their hood with moonlight silver eyes.

They were much more than mere humans. It was terrifying and inspiring.

"You're lucky it was us who found you," the smallest witch said.

Salome was determined to seem unintimidated. "What do you want?"

"From you? Nothing," the silver-eyed witch said. "*For* you? Everything."

Salome yanked away in hopes of freeing her arms. The witches released her. She shook out her hands and glared at them, wondering what would happen if she brought out her blades. Would it do any harm? In the past, she'd used them well, drawing blood and opening bodies. Deadly skill was essential to thriving in the Alliance. If you were soft, you were weak, and anyone deemed such was discarded like trash.

"You wouldn't last more than a handful of seconds," the fire witch said.

There was a tranquility to her that rang with wisdom and knowing. Like she could peer into one's mind and examine every thought, wish, or dream. When she looked at Salome, it felt as though she could see everything she had done, all the crimes she committed. It made Salome shudder with unease.

The first time she killed a person, Salome was still a child. Only seventeen with her knife stuck in the hollow of a man's throat, pulled upward to split it, and dragged along the underside of his jaw. Yvette stood behind her the entire time, observing that test of strength. When Salome sliced his throat horizontally, she earned Yvette's disapproval.

It ought to have lasted longer.

"Maris—" the earth witch began, but the fire witch shook her head and continued.

"I see your thoughts and feel your intentions. There is no possibility of surprise."

Salome's jaw clenched. "Can the rest of you say the same?"

"I'd protect my sisters sooner than you could attack them," Maris, the fire witch, said.

"Enough, that is not why we're here tonight," the silver-eyed witch said. She waved her hand and wind pushed their bodies across the hall, putting distance between them.

"Yes, do explain," Salome said.

In a gentle voice, she said, "You needn't pretend with us, little one."

"There is no pretending here. I demand the truth." And she wasn't little. She wasn't a child, and she didn't have the innocence and hope afforded to one. All her experiences in life hadn't stripped her of dreams, but they had made her a cynic. The risks she took would always be more likely to kill her than free her.

"Be nice," the earth witch pleaded. "All of you."

"Della, this is not an easy thing to accept," Maris said. Affectionate, maybe, in a way that wasn't sisterly.

"Our purpose tonight is to inform you of a choice," the wind witch said. "The life you have chosen is not your only option."

Salome ripped her needle-knife from her sleeve.

Vines suddenly snapped around her wrist and held her still. They pushed the fabric aside and revealed a sliver of skin, a scar that was not so easily noticed, only slightly raised in the shape of an arrowhead. The sign of the Alliance, that this person belonged to them. She was trapped in their organization, a tool to wield. Didn't they know she must be afraid? To obey until she paid off a decade of debts to them, if she ever could.

The usual response was a mixture of fear and dread, wondering what sort of agony would befall them for crossing someone in the Alliance's command. How cruel was this person? How much violence did they wield?

None of the witches blinked, as if they expected to find such a thing.

"Do not dare to threaten my sister." Della's delicate voice now sounded deadly.

Salome held onto her knife. To her instinct to distrust.

They spoke as if they understood her choices, as if she had the freedom she aimed to reach. These witches spoke like it was easy to walk away from the people who raised her, who taught her everything she knew about the world—and herself.

She was nothing, and no one, and definitely not someone deserving of this attention. She was a nameless weapon to be kept until she lost her usefulness. A weapon that could not belong to anyone but those who trained her to become that dangerous tool. A creature that could slip away as quickly as she appeared.

"The only thing I want from you is an answer: what lives in the shadows?" Salome asked.

"Magic," said Maris, moving in front of Della. "Yours."

"I don't have magic."

"It was always there. A tiny ember that needed the right breath to set it aflame."

"Leave me alone," Salome said through gritted teeth. "Let me leave."

The wind witch was fearless, unconcerned of being harmed, as she stepped in Salome's way. Perhaps earlier, Salome might have tried to fight, but after all they said and the ease with which they used their magic against her made her hesitate about acting.

"Godiva—" Maris began, but the other witch raised her voice.

"This is not something you can run from. If you cannot control yourself—"

Godiva stopped speaking. Around her, the shadows stirred. Salome felt the movement as though she stood in the ocean and the water was the shadows, the waves rolling against her body. It came alive in response to her anxiety, the cold panic under her skin like splinters.

It ached and yet it filled her with relief to feel them. Alive, it was like she wasn't alone. She could wear different faces and clothes and adjust her accent for her character of the month, but the shadows were always there and now they spoke her name with more fervor and certainty.

Devoted and adoring and *eager*.

The eagerness terrified her.

It made her think of how Gabriel and Yvette would see her if they discovered this. The delight, the greed, the coveting. She would never escape them if they knew. They would never let her.

She couldn't tell if the witches could hear all that noise and chaos and the promise of wildness from the shadows. They slithered toward her like serpents on the polished stones. In the corners of the hall where the candles couldn't reach, eyes peered at the group. Watching the women, mere white diamonds in the dark without a pupil, unblinking. So inhuman.

And the smell—herbal smoke, reminiscent of a cleansing ritual.

Maris's hands became engulfed in fire, and she waved to the dark pooling around Salome's feet. It barely shifted, unafraid of the brightness. Maris gritted her teeth and glared. Della patted her arm comfortingly.

It was Godiva who offered some wisdom. "Some things in the shadows are beyond your control. They are not your magic, but creatures of the dark who long only to hurt, to kill. Note the difference and be careful, little one."

"How would I know?"

"Pay attention to their response to you."

The witches took a step back. The barrier they formed around Salome disappeared as they retreated further and further until she was alone in the hallway. Her chambers seemed a fortnight away. Especially in the dark, alone, and uncertain of what she'd experienced.

She walked slowly, one foot in front of the other, wondering if she might fall over and wake from the strangest dream of handsome kings and mysterious witches. If anyone witnessed her encounter with the witch circus, the con could have been ruined. Luckily, when she entered the rooms, there was no one to examine the expression she surely wore. Salome took a deep breath, standing in the middle of the main room as she collected herself.

Euria opened the door to the bathing chamber, her hair wet and empty eye socket visible. Her mouth turned downward in concern and she crossed her arms. Salome offered a smile as she shrugged and gestured to the back of her gown.

"What took you so long to return?" Euria made her way over to help with the buttons.

"The king wished to talk."

"And?"

Salome grinned. "Nothing happened." Between her and Vincent at least.

"That's unfortunate." Euria sighed. "I hoped for something interesting."

The last button popped free, and Salome exhaled with relief. As she stepped out of the gown and plucked out the hair pins, Salome looked at Euria with a raised eyebrow. "I've only just met him."

"When has that stopped you before?"

Salome answered by throwing the razor-sharp pins at her. While knives and daggers were her specialty, Euria was better at combat overall and dodged easily. The pins lodged straight into the wall behind her.

When Salome and Euria met each other's eyes, they laughed. Abel and Amalia could decide how they felt about the new décor when they noticed it. Their amusement almost made Salome forget what she was learning about the dark.

"Sleep with a candle lit," Salome advised once they quieted.

"Why? Are there monsters coming to get me? The guards here are so skittish. You'd think they've never been in battle." Euria laughed but took a candle with her to the other room anyway. Maybe part of her was slightly worried.

If Salome hadn't seen the wolfish mouth emerging from under the door to her bedroom, she would be laughing louder than Euria. Monsters weren't real. The ones who sang to her when she was a child, who scratched at her legs when she ran through the streets at night—those were different.

The witch circus warned her. But what was out there? What magic was in her?

She didn't have time to think of this.

And yet, tiptoeing to the bedroom, she kept her eyes trained on shadowed areas. That spot in the corner, the shade cast by her own figure, that bit of the wall that couldn't catch the light because of some furniture. She changed quickly into something soft and comfortable, trying not to blink.

Salome kept a dagger strapped to her thigh. Usually, she slept with a blade beneath her pillow and nothing more. For a moment, she stared at the door as she arranged the pillows around herself like a soft, feathery fortress.

There was danger everywhere now—the war, the Alliance, the shadows, the demons. And the only thing she could control was her performance and ensuring she always carried a blade on her. Was there anyone she could trust? Not the Alliance who would rid themselves of her at any moment, nor the witches, who had secrets they hadn't shared yet. And the king... as kind as he was, what she was doing was punishable by death.

Sleep felt unattainable, but she reached for it anyway. Amalia was already unconscious under the sheets, blissful as she rested.

Panic wrapped a hand around Salone's throat and squeezed. It whispered in her ear that Gabriel and Yvette would eventually learn if she had magic.

She couldn't wait to discover how they'd react, what commands they'd issue, what chains they'd force onto her, what they would do to keep her and ensure no one else could access the power of a witch, if that's what she truly was.

Salome laid in bed with one blade in hand, another on her leg, and a third under her pillow. Her eyes remained open so long, she didn't remember falling asleep.

Chapter Seven

"My lady will just be a moment, Your Majesty. She has been resting all day."

In her dreams, she conjured beasts with too many eyes and several rows of teeth with a lamprey's tunnel-like mouth. Horrors that left her feeling nauseous and unsettled. But she rushed out of bed now, cursing under her breath as she made herself presentable.

She plastered a smile on her face as she entered the main room.

The king bowed to her. "Lady Rosalia, I apologize for not visiting sooner. I wanted to see you and perhaps play a game." He scratched his jaw. "A card game?"

It took some restraint not to cackle at this man turning shy. How did a handsome, powerful man have such a gentle heart?

Most people she knew were cruel, thinking of only how they could use one another. People who hoarded their wealth and deserved to have it taken from them. People who took and took, thinking nothing of giving. Vincent did not fit in the world she knew, where his softness and generosity would be taken for granted. The Alliance would eat him alive. Even Salome wouldn't mind a little taste of him, though not of the same sort of violence.

"And I brought wine," he added, gesturing to a large glass bottle on the table. "As we are still getting acquainted, I was uncertain of your preference. I hope you will enjoy what I chose."

If Salome was younger and unused to handsome, charming men, she might have swooned on sight and fallen in love. But, as good as he might seem, she had long since learned to guard her heart.

No one could be how they portrayed themselves. There were always secrets. Her heart was broken once when she was still a girl and she vowed to never allow that to happen again, especially not by a king she could never have, a mark she'd come to distract. There was no room for sentiment in her line of work.

With a dramatic sigh, she asked, "Well, what did you bring me?"

"A personal favorite on the sweeter side."

"Ah, His Majesty has a preference for sweetness," she teased as she retrieved the cards from the fireplace mantle and placed them beside the wine. She sat first and gestured for him to take the chair across from her. "Then I shall be as sweet as possible."

Lust flashed on his face, and she licked her lips. The movement caught his eyes, and she relished the interest burning within them.

"Do not torment me, please," he murmured.

"Or what?"

"Anything you wish for, I would grant."

The sound plucked something in her chest, like harp strings. She had to swallow before she could speak. There was no possibility of trusting this man who had a way with words. To hear them meant she did her job well. That was all it had to be.

She shook her head. "You are generous."

"Merely captivated."

Perhaps he was. It seemed he couldn't see the shadows darting around him like tiny animals flitting around in a forest. Running, weaving between roots and under bushes. Though she could see flashes of action around them, she tried to ignore them. What would happen if she gave them attention? They could become braver, bolder—or perhaps dangerous. Though the shadows never harmed her before, they still could, one day. She didn't trust them, nor how she might influence them, especially since they'd changed.

She was used to holding the dark power that came from association with a deviant organization. The fear she could instill by flashing the mark on her wrist. The influence she could wield to bring a man to his knees if she uttered who owned her. She'd always only been property to protect.

"You do not yet know what kind of woman I am, Your Majesty," she said, leaning forward. There was a look in his eye that she didn't like, a spark of curiosity. She tapped the cards, drawing his attention to them. "What game shall we play?"

In his hands, they seemed small and fragile, as though they were made of glass, though he must have handled them countless times. Salome imagined him fussing and fretting and hoping she would appreciate this gift.

The Alliance favored weapons and jewels. Sometimes a velvet pouch full of coins, or a lesson from a master of some skill one longed to learn. Only for the most loyal and useful, of course. Something as small and sentimental as a handmade deck of cards—that never would have been an option. Long before she became the face of a con, she studied what the others delivered to the leaders. When her turn arrived, they marveled at her choices and praised her eye for finer things.

He smirked. "How about a scoundrel's game called the *Queen and Her Lovers*. Have you played that before?"

"Perhaps once or twice." A lie. It was her favorite.

When she was little, Gabriel used it to teach her how to read people. He even took her to taverns and inns to observe while he played a round or two with strangers.

Gabriel was almost father-like in those early days. It was how he planted the seed of loyalty: making recruits feel like they found a family. They then spent the rest of the time chasing the joy of making him proud. Even Salome was victim to that. If she began to stray, Gabriel was there again, reminding her why she came under his wing.

She would always link this game with her beginnings in the Alliance.

It wasn't something one would expect to play with a king called good-hearted and honest. This game required lying and deceit, where the goal was to collect the Queen of Hearts, another Queen, a King, and Jack. The latter three needed to be of the same suit. Whether it was easy or complicated depended on the players themselves. Many of the times Salome played, the card dealer would alter the rules as they wished.

As it was in life, the one with the power was the one who shaped the game.

Salome smiled. "It truly is a scoundrel's game. Should I be worried?"

"You have nothing to fear from me, dear Rosalia. If anything, I am the one to be frightened. You are beautiful and clever and I see that suggestion of mischief in your eye."

"As a child, I was a true terror," she admitted. "My father thought me a beast."

Both her true father and the figure she once saw in Gabriel.

Vincent laughed. "My siblings and I were seen similarly by the staff. Our parents thought to be our main caretakers and I wonder if they regretted that decision—or if the castle employees were the ones who wished they'd chosen otherwise."

When he spoke of his family, there was a brightness to him. She wondered if she looked that way when thinking about reuniting with her parents.

She began laying out the cards. They kept the rules simple, trading and discarding cards with an explanation. Give each their own story and try to distract the other from remembering what the card was.

Salome won the first round. Vincent pretended to be shocked, yet she had a strong suspicion he went easy on her.

"Would you tell me more about life here?" she asked as she dealt the next hand.

"Are you asking for scary stories or happy memories?"

She grinned. "Which ones are more interesting?"

"I shall tell you of the monsters, then. They will leave you with chills and you shall be tempted to spend your evenings with me." He watched her with a seriousness that made her wonder if she swallowed butterflies.

"To keep such monsters away?"

"Exactly. I could protect you."

Salome shook her head. "You do not know it yet, Your Majesty, but I am capable of much more than one might expect."

"I look forward to discovering what you mean."

Poor man. He ought to hope for the opposite. Though she did not gather any loot this evening, she could still extract information from him. Anything could be useful. A childhood tale of secret passageways or heirlooms they'd broken and hidden. Even a painting with a story to captivate a potential buyer. She'd have to convince the Alliance to bring their impressionist, but it could be worthwhile.

Waving her hand, she demanded stories, and he acquiesced. First, he claimed the dungeons were haunted by a girl who tried to save her father and ended up trapped in an unchecked cell, left to starve to death. That suggested an unguarded area in the dungeons.

Another story involved escaping to the forests on the side of the castle opposite of the city. The grounds were owned by the royal family, meant for hunting and leisure, safe from dangerous intruders. But there was a secret incident when they were children that they came across hooded figures burning herbs and burying something in the forest. Practicing magic, perhaps.

"Where are the monsters?" Salome grumbled as they finished their third game. Again, she had won, and she was becoming peevish about it. "And where is your sense of competition, Your Majesty? I thought I would have a true opponent."

"Call me Vincent," he said.

"Then play properly."

They stared at each other for a long moment. She narrowed her eyes.

"Let's make it more interesting. The winner gets a prize, whatever they want," he said. Something flashed in his eyes—mischief. "One never knows how much time they have in life, especially during war. We ought to enjoy what we can get."

The next time she won, Salome would demand a kiss, then more.

"I don't know much of the demons. They aren't much of a fright on the coast." She only saw those wretched flashes of images and strange things in her periphery.

Vincent nodded thoughtfully, running his fingertips over the side of the cards featuring silvery stars. She was entranced by his hands, knowing how calloused they were despite their delicate touch, until a clawed hand hovering over his shoulder snapped her from her reverie.

It disappeared quickly—there within one blink, gone the next. She wondered what that hand was attached to, if anything. Vincent, meanwhile, was telling her something. His eyes remained on his cards, his eyebrows drawn together in concentration.

"We have worked to contain them. Their presence is most often observed near the border to Pavalla, and the Woods of Palvary," he said. "I know the people call it the birthplace of magic in Ilarya. They might be right."

"Ah, so it is war and magic, entwined yet again."

These kingdoms had a long history of bloodshed. Of blame and battle. It would be a long time before they learned peace, especially when the princes were full of pride and the people were full of fear.

His voice was so solemn, Salome didn't like it. She reached out, grazing her fingertips over his knuckles. His gaze settled on her hand, even as she drew away.

"Would you take me to the Woods?" It was a dangerous request.

He didn't answer immediately, trading a few cards first. He offered weak stories, and poor excuses for giving them up.

Then finally, "That is not the sort of place you would take the woman you want to marry."

Salome swallowed a noise of frustration. She despised being treated like a fragile thing. How little he knew of her. It was better that way, and yet she craved his belief that they could fight fairly in war. Her eyes dashed to the swords displayed above the fireplace, wondering if she'd benefit from demanding a duel.

"There was a scout sent to the Woods," Vincent began. "They didn't return, nor did their horse. Another volunteered to find them, and returned with half a head within a helmet, covered in pitch. As though it had melted away."

She imagined a new graveyard near the Woods. Mutilated bodies ruined in all sorts of ways. What sort of damage did the demons do?

"Here, in Ellasya, we have not seen the worst of it." Vincent laid down his Queen and her lovers, achieving the set with more ease than earlier. At the shock on Salome's face, he grinned, but the light didn't reach his eyes.

She needed answers. She couldn't feel guilty for getting him to discuss this.

"What is the worst?"

"I shall tell you in a moment. First, I would like my reward," he said, and beckoned her to come over. She stood and did as commanded. Once she was within reach, he curled an arm around her and pulled her into his lap.

"Your Majesty—"

"Vincent," he corrected, smirking. "Could I keep you like this?"

She smoothed her hands over his chest. "You may, if this is the prize you sought."

"One of them."

"It will be difficult to play like this," she added.

They made it work somehow. His legs were thick with muscle, and she felt soft in contrast despite her own lean frame from training. She leaned away, easing into his steady arm, and held her cards close to her chest. Vincent held his own with one hand, tilted away from her. The other gripped her waist and stroked the side of her body. She tried not to shiver at his touch at first, then allowed herself to react when she met his eyes and saw fire. Smiling innocently, she wiggled in his lap as if trying to get comfortable, eliciting a groan from him.

It would be better if she could straddle him and give him a better understanding of what could be expected of intimacy.

Despite her teasing, they managed to continue their card game.

"There was a village by the border with no more than a dozen families." Vincent stacked the cards, then began to shuffle. The cards danced expertly from one hand to the other, then spun them between his fingers. He moved with the smoothness of smoke curling toward the sky.

Not to be outdone, Salome gathered up the cards when he set them down in her lap and shuffled them with even more extravagance. They flew faster and further, the crisp sound of the cards' movements filling the quiet space, weightless as they shot from hand to hand. She twisted them around, rearranging their position in the deck again and again until she was satisfied.

Surprise flit across his face before he chuckled, shaking his head.

"I promise I will be good if you finish the story," she said. "It is terrible that this kingdom has known such horrors. However, if I am to stand beside you, I need to be aware of all that has transpired, even the secrets and devastation."

She needed to know his plans. To be aware if the Alliance had to adjust their strategy. To ensure she always had time to escape.

They sat in silence for a full minute, the seconds ticking by slowly.

"You are correct," he finally said. "That village looked as though it was burned to the ground. The smoke smelled of rotting flesh. There were no bodies to be found, and the buildings—houses, churches, their market.... All of it was gone."

He took one of her hands and kissed the soft center of her palm. Her heart pounded in her ears as the heat of his mouth sent sparks traveling along her arm.

"I visited that village a month prior to deliver supplies and celebrate their freedom from Pavallan occupation," he whispered.

She cradled the side of his face in her hand. "I am sorry."

Death was a familiar figure in his life.

His parents lost in the bargain to bring the witch circus on their side. His older sister brought down on the battlefield when she led the charge after their parents' death. His younger brother, too arrogant and immature, slaughtered by Pavallans. The youngest, a girl barely in her mid-teen years, trying to play the peaceful messenger, only to be snatched by demons. There was nothing to bring back.

People whispered the news to one another, aching for their new king.

He cast his gaze down and busied himself by stroking her legs. Up and down her thighs lifting and twisting her dress. With a deep breath, he leaned forward and pressed his face against her neck. She felt his lips against her skin when he spoke.

"I am afraid of you."

Involuntarily, she shivered. Then, ever so slowly, he trailed his lips along her throat. As her head fell backward to allow him more access, movement caught her eye.

There was something in the window.

It pulled the heavy curtains, the shape of a hand appearing first, and then an imprint of a demon visage.

There was a large skull that could have been a big man hiding behind the fabric, if not for the lack of feet on the floor. What worried her, however, was the way the curtain seemed to be sucked inwards to a mouth with large canines spilling over the lips.

Her body tensed. Vincent lifted his head.

The shape vanished at the window, but it slid onto the wall, moving toward them. The silhouette inched closer and closer until it was an arm's length away.

And then, she heard a laugh.

And her real name, carried on a breeze as gentle as a breath on her neck.

Salome shuddered. "I may have slept too long. My eyes are playing tricks on me."

At that, Vincent turned to follow her gaze. She took his face between her hands and forced him to look into her eyes as she smiled.

"Please, trust me, there is nothing. My imagination wanders sometimes," she promised. Her touch seemed to leave a black handprint on his shirt, as though her palm had been coated in paint. When she lifted it, however, there was no mark.

He squeezed her waist. "Would you like me to stay?"

"Were you planning to leave?"

Smirking, he answered, "Not at all."

She moved over to one of the sofas, reclining with her legs tucked beneath her. Vincent didn't immediately follow, going to the door instead and calling for a servant. He spoke with them quickly, then joined her, pulling her legs across his lap. When he began to lift the edge of her dress to expose her calves, she let him. When he stroked the skin he found, she started to burn. Heat raced through her body, beginning between her legs before spreading though her limbs. Even her face felt too hot and she fanned herself slightly with her hands.

All the while, Vincent smirked and moved his fingertips over her legs, under her dress. They climbed to her knees and her breath hitched. Her body wanted to surge forward and climb atop of him.

She was a thief and her instinct was to take.

The prize she wanted now was his touch, and she coveted it.

Some time later, dinner arrived: a Villasayan dish. The scent alone was memorable. She would always recognize the fresh jasmine rice and chicken adobo with its brown sauce containing vinegar, soy sauce, and garlic.

The servants arranged a bit of a picnic for them on the floor. Salome watched in awe as Vincent assisted them in the set-up. Once they were gone, Salome sat down without a word and helped herself to a generous portion. They ate quietly, occasionally trading smiles, pretending that they had not been a moment away from devouring each other instead of food.

When they finished and he made his way to the door, she followed.

"Come visit more," she said. "And don't let me win. Earn your prizes and take them."

In response, he grabbed her by the waist and pulled her to him. She gasped like she was unaccustomed to the boldness, the sound stifled when he kissed her. Her body softened in his grasp though her hands squeezed his arms. When his tongue traced her lower lip, she opened her mouth to him, and moaned at the taste when his tongue met hers. He leaned back against the door and she leaned into him, still holding on.

It felt perfect. She might almost believe in fate for bringing her to this moment.

She had to be the one to retreat, though he chased her mouth. It made her laugh.

He stole one more kiss—softer, gentler—before he left.

Servants entered and cleaned up after he was gone. All the while, Salome sat on the couch, wondering what happened. He was too good to be a king, too sweet to be real.

And she would break his heart.

Chapter Eight

Before the sun came up every morning, Amalia and Salome discussed their progress. Whatever transpired in her meeting with her contacts in the city, Gabriel and Yvette weren't satisfied. It was essential to stay updated on what they managed to accomplish to ensure they made the most of the time they had, however long it may be. War could be unpredictable, and the Alliance did not want this team involved in a battle.

"You'll need to head out and find more than what we've filched during the day."

Salome groaned. "I thought so."

"Do you have a plan?" Amalia asked.

She didn't need to say a word to confirm. All Salome did was smirk. Long ago, Amalia wouldn't believe it was possible, but Salome proved again and again that, even if their plans fell through, she always found a way to win.

Because they were a team, though, she had to share. "The king needs a confidant. The nobles need amusement. If I keep them away from their rooms, that should be helpful, don't you think?"

Amalia shrugged. "Possibly. We might as well try."

Jobs worked when both had chances to prove their skills and talents. There was less jealousy, less sniping at each other. But like many of the cons that came before, these options were only possible if they agreed to it together.

Leon soon emerged from his room with circles under his eyes and dark fingerprint smudges on his forehead. He had worked tirelessly since their arrival, busy with stolen jewels and gifts from the king. Every morning, someone brought in jewelry. Gerard would memorize the details and draw them for Leon to recreate. At night, Amalia and Elias would sneak out to sell the real things.

Salome could only keep the cards. The Alliance's impressionist painter hadn't arrived in the city yet. Amalia claimed Gabriel was doubtful of their necessity, but Salome was convinced the king's art had value.

Amalia tossed a box wrapped in silk to Leon.

He caught it with fumbling hands and some cursing, then opened it. "A gold and diamond bracelet. Easy enough."

Salome liked that one, a gift the king sent the day before, which felt like satin against her skin. Something new arrived every day and, when she ran into Vincent, he always checked to see if she wore what he sent. If he couldn't stop and talk, at least he'd see it.

Sometimes the gifts came with a note. On occasion, there was mention of that kiss. His hands on her. Her body in his lap. A suggestion that he needed more and more and that maybe it would never be enough.

He wrote like whispers and ignited goosebumps across her skin.

Like the wealth she stashed away, she tucked in her bodice and hidden pockets for safekeeping.

Without another word, Leon returned to his workroom. He'd come out once finished and act as one of Rosalia's guards, if necessary. Their jobs never ended.

Abel pushed their plans forward. "There are plenty of rooms in the castle, ones left unattended. We will empty them of their furnishings, if necessary. Gold and jewels are not the only things of value within these walls."

The map they drew was rolled up and set in the bedroom, masquerading as a painting yet to be framed and hung. They discussed their tasks further—who would go where, what they would do, any contacts they must meet, and so on. Since Amalia would go into the city, Abel would stay close behind to ensure her safety. Salome would remain within the castle's walls and continue her surveillance of night activity. She tracked when guards patrolled, what their shift rotations were, how consistent the schedule might be.

All these years of one mission after another, she learned that the longer she watched, the more certain she could be. They didn't have the luxury of time, but they had enough of it. If she saw a gap, she took it, squeezing into unattended rooms and carefully avoiding any trace of entry. She picked up secrets from letters left on tables or personal items laying around in what should be sacred places. When you were accustomed to the work, it was easy to find meaning in the details.

And when one spent so much time wandering in the dark, one witnessed what was invisible during the day.

It was easier to say there was nothing wrong. Magic was rare. Who would believe she had it when even she was doubtful? Maybe Gabriel would, but she could never tell what he was thinking.

What frightened Salome most was the tingling in the palm of her hand, shadows clutching skin. When she turned her wrist toward the light, the feeling disappeared. Where there were shadows, there was a change of sensation.

This little test was a new habit, only a few days old. She wanted to know if it would happen again and again, if this change was permanent.

"Do I have time to rest?" Salome asked, not to request permission, but to confirm that she would not cause trouble.

Amalia looked out the window. "Minutes, maybe, before the ward arrives."

"I'll take it."

It felt like no time passed between closing her eyes and being shaken awake. Salome rose without complaint and readied herself as quickly as she could. Her gown was much simpler than others and required no assistance. Just a cap-sleeved dress in a creamy fabric, light and soft against her skin. The only opulence was the pearl-studded belt.

Amalia nodded in approval, then gestured to her bodice. With a grin, Salome pulled a thin knife from one of the pleats on her dress, then tucked it away. She would not go anywhere unarmed.

Abel would also be nearby to keep an eye on her and any indication of danger.

When Sylvia arrived, only her guard was with her.

"Sylvia!" Salome said with a smile. "How lovely you look this morning."

She bowed in return. "I thought we could go for a walk."

Salome didn't hesitate to take the lead, stepping into the hall, a stretch of sunlight beckoning ahead. There were already some nobles walking about. Curious glances followed her as she passed, trailed by Sylvia and her guard.

It was only when they reached the front doors that Salome paused. The king's ward moved to Salome's side, less than one step behind and in silence, they walked together with footsteps barely audible on the floor. Salome's slippers were soft and made for quiet. Sylvia, however, had shoes so worn-down, she might as well have walked on bare feet.

Neither spoke until they reached the garden. It was mosaic painted of emerald-green leaves and flowers from all over the world. A pathway curved through it all, wide enough for a pair to traverse side by side, and Sylvia led them onto it.

Magic was the only explanation for the presence of large flowers shaped like the sun and in all colors of the rainbow.

Salome glanced around.

The witch circus had to be there somewhere. If it wasn't the shadows or the Alliance keeping an eye on her, it was the witches.

The kingdom needed this brightness and color. A reprieve from death and darkness and destruction. No one knew when the world would end, or how that might come to be. The hopeless cycle would go on and on. Something to celebrate would make that easier to bear. That's why the king decided to marry and why it would happen so quickly.

"Did you enjoy the welcome dinner?" Salome asked.

Sylvia made a noncommittal noise.

"There were more guests than I expected," Salome continued. "All strangers to me."

"And you are strange to them."

For a second, she imagined Sylvia knew about her history with the shadows. But no one knew, except the witch circus. If Gabriel suspected, he never gave an indication of it. He had to know the witches were here and what might happen if Salome was within their reach. Once, she thought he knew everything, but not since she discovered she could keep some secrets from them.

"I do not know these people, but you do," Salome went on, even though Sylvia wouldn't meet her eyes. "I trust your judgment."

They eventually stopped at a marble bench beside a statue of a kneeling woman with wings. It reminded Salome of a bat-winged girl training to be one of the Seven, a sect of highly skilled assassins in the Alliance—who they might send if the con went awry.

No loose ends, no rewards for failure.

Salome looked away.

More people filled the garden now. They seemed curious about the future queen yet were unimpressed with the company she kept. As people passed them in the garden, the sentiment was clear: Sylvia wasn't wanted. They pursed their lips or turned away abruptly, like trying to avoid sneezing in another's face.

If someone strayed too close, the dangerous look in Rene's eye sent the eavesdropper scurrying away. The noble was close enough, however, Salome managed to free them of a pocket-watch now tucked away in the folds of her skirt.

"Do you know anything that might help me?" Salome asked.

Sylvia fidgeted with the long sleeves of her periwinkle dress.

"I know many things. I listen and I observe." Sylvia's gaze traced the patterns of the pathway's stone tiles and streaks of gold in the marble like rivers. "The king and I used to sneak around the castle like spies until we grew up... well, things changed."

Until her father betrayed the royal family. Until the l'Essalia family lost everything. Sylvia had been close to her father, and he'd supposedly valued all she ever had to say. They weren't just father and daughter, they were confidantes. Because she was only a child when he was convicted, the royal family claimed her, taking responsibility for turning her into an orphan. Years passed and she became a woman, though she remained within their walls and protection.

Salome linked their arms and touched her head to the top of Sylvia's.

"As friends, we can spy on everyone together, if you like," Salome offered, leaning back to display her grin. "I want to learn all that I can. Perhaps you can show me where you hid."

"Everyone has their secrets. All you have to do is watch and you'll see."

With a quick glance, Sylvia gestured to a couple sneaking off into a thicket of trees. They were laughing and trying to stay out of sight. A thief would know how to do that best and those two did it poorly.

Sylvia explained, "A servant and a marquis's daughter, meeting as they do every morning."

They stood, but stayed close, their arms linked as they walked. Sylvia's head remained down, her shoulders slumped. But she shifted her gaze sharply from one spot to another.

Though the sun was rising, filling the sky with a golden glow, some shadows of the statues spilled across the pathways. Trees arched over them, the gaps between leaves allowing in thin streaks of sunlight. Salome caught whispers of disjointed murmuring in dark patches. It could be ghosts of those who died too young in service for the crown, a warning to anyone who might join the fight. She couldn't decide which option was more ominous.

In those same places, Sylvia rushed for the sunlight like it was a shield. They followed the path, weaving between flower bushes and blooming trees.

An unfamiliar voice suddenly called out from behind. "Lady Rosalia!"

Salome set her lips in a polite smile. The duchess in the lilac dress from the dinner approached down the path. Today, she was dressed in a loose, mossy green gown with white sheer sleeves, her wide hips and softly rounded stomach visible against the silken skirt, unburdened by a tight bodice. She looked perfect and regal.

"That is Duchess Irene d'Ellsaria, cousin to the king. Her father was his father's brother," Sylvia murmured, turning away.

Irene d'Ellsaria, unfortunately, was very observant and well-versed in the social politics of the Ilaryan nobles. Getting too close to her was risky. She was a dangerous, powerful woman with a sunny disposition. The Alliance noted her as a potential useful connection but urged the utmost caution. Let the duchess make the first move, rather than seeking her out.

Salome maintained a friendly smile as she asked Sylvia, "What else do you know?"

"Nothing I could share now."

As the duchess neared, she bowed to Salome. Irene was a head shorter than Salome yet held herself tall and proud. She wasn't the prettiest girl, but her smile was lovely and the blush on her pale cheeks made her look flushed and lively.

"How unfortunate it was that we could not be introduced sooner," Irene began in a rush. Her eyes were bright blue and clear as tropical waters. Like her cousin, having such traits indicated a family built through politics, citizens of other countries matched with Ilaryans. Her amusement, however, flickered as she glanced at Sylvia. "Luckily, you were finally coaxed out so we may meet."

With the eagerness and boldness of royalty, she grasped Salome's hands. There was a flash of color, a myriad of them that momentarily stunned Salome as though the sun shined directly into her eyes. It was only when the duchess shifted her hands that Salome was able to see clearly again.

The moment she could, Salome pulled away, but not without removing a small, thin band of white gold with a pebble of an emerald from Irene's middle finger. It was so dainty, so easily misplaced.

"It's only been a few days," Salome said, then returned to Sylvia's side, taking her arm once again. "I couldn't resist the opportunity to spend time with my new friend, now that I am settled in."

"Ah yes, the more friends you have, the easier it shall be to grow accustomed to life here. I hope I can be a friend to you, as well. After all, we shall be family! My father was Duke Erasmo d'Ellsaria, brother to Vincent's father."

Salome already knew.

"Recently, I've become an advisor to my cousin on court affairs—gossip, really. Vincent cannot tolerate it in the slightest. However, someone must ensure the peace between the nobles." Irene waved her hand dismissively. Her movements were smooth and unrestrained, evidence of a young woman satisfied with her place in the world.

Maybe she wanted more. Those with power often did.

"I keep an eye on things for him, if I do not join him on the battlefield. Nothing quite compares to the loyalty of family," Irene continued. "I swear, you would have my utter devotion. My priority will always be this family and the well-being of our kingdom."

What she failed to say was something that Salome already knew: Irene d'Ellsaria was next in line for throne. This was the closest she ever was to wearing the crown since Vincent's siblings were all gone. If he fell, she would have her coronation.

Before Salome could speak, Irene barreled ahead. "Are you taking a walk about the castle? I should like to join you."

She spoke so quickly that the words seemed to tumble out as quick as raindrops during a sudden storm. Like someone who was raised without fear of her choice of words and the consequences of them. Someone with a stable position of power.

Sylvia tensed. Rene immediately stepped forward. Irene looked at him in alarm, her smile freezing. But Sylvia whispered his name and he moved backward, averting his gaze.

Salome shook her head. "Unfortunately, I think my mornings shall be set with Sylvia."

The king had requested their friendship. If only to respect his wishes, she sided with Sylvia. Perhaps the nobles wouldn't be so cruel to the ward if she was deemed important by the woman rising to power. Salome knew the worth of one who was unwanted by most, the secrets that one might know.

"Perhaps another time of the day instead," Salome suggested.

Irene beamed. "Wonderful! I shall coordinate our schedules and we will become the best of friends."

With a bow, Irene turned and departed.

Rene looked like he wanted to slap her for the suggestion of pushing Sylvia aside.

"The duchess may know as much as I do," Sylvia admitted once Rene relaxed, though his hand remained poised over his sword. "Perhaps more because of how connected she is—and well-liked, not only because of her position and direct relation to the king."

"She seems eager and lively," Salome said. "But I have enjoyed our morning together and I would like to do this every day, if you would allow it."

At that, Sylvia lifted her head, the smallest of smiles appearing on her lips.

A new friend, and new opportunities. Especially ones that provided opportunities to fill her pockets. They passed many familiar faces. By the end of their walk, Salome picked up enough rings to cover one hand, a couple of bracelets, a pair of diamond-crusted spectacles, and a few jeweled buttons that must have come loose and fallen into her pocket.

Chapter Nine

THE WITCHES WERE IN THE COURTYARD.

Salome watched them from the library, a cozy spot in a windowed alcove with a trove of tomes on the low table in front of the bench she reclined upon. She pressed her forehead and a hand against the windowpane, peering outside where a crowd of commoners gathered.

"Sylvia mentioned this earlier," Salome said. "She said the witches had informed the castle guards of a public performance."

As she spoke, the witches removed their hoods, having strangely donned such thick, dark things despite the warmth. And though the sun was setting, and the shadows would soon hide them, they wore thin lace masks over their eyes.

Smiles lit their faces. Warmer and more welcoming than they'd been with the nobles.

There was no need to frighten these people. The citizens were already hesitant, keeping several feet away from the stage of elevated stones and a canopy of blossom-infused vines.

The air witch brought in a cooling breeze that ruffled the flower petals and tree branches. Small columns of fire ensured there were no shadows around them. A few royal guards were stationed nearby—not that they would be much help when the witches had magic.

Salome caught only glimpses and fragments of the performance. The citizens gasped and applauded. Flashes of light caught on ice sculptures, on petals falling gently like snowflakes.

Standing near the alcove, Euria strained to see as well.

"Is your friend as honest as the king said?" Amalia wondered.

Salome answered in her Rosalia voice, "She seems true, and I enjoy her friendship. However, she did not elaborate on the purpose of this performance."

"Some children snuck out during the night. Their parents tried to follow them, but they were too far behind when the demons emerged. A near dozen children, gone," Euria explained, her voice low and hoarse. "A quarter of the city has been sectioned off for cleaning."

"Gone where?"

Euria grimaced. "To wherever people go when they die."

The threat grew more pronounced as one progressed deeper into the continent. On the d'Ilumias estate, there was only wide-eyed whispering to send the tales along. Snatches of these stories began passing from person to person nearly ten years ago.

The first appearance was in the east at the Pavallan border. A small town was evacuated. They'd said demons rose in the night and stole all light.

The rest of the kingdom called them superstitious fools.

Salome glanced at a lit lantern affixed to the wall, then the persistent patches of the dark between gaps in the shelves. Salome imagined clawed fingers tapping against a tilted book that created shadows. She imagined something viscous dripping from the hand, easing down the shelf but dissolving as it encountered light.

A whiff of rot reached her nose despite the rose-scented candles nearby.

"Be careful what you say to your lady," Amalia warned Euria.

What she meant was *watch what you say in case someone is listening*. Without knowledge of the Alliance's coded speech, anyone else would think a handmaid warned a guard from telling stories that might frighten away a docile noble girl. They could carry conversation without concern of who might hear.

"Did my father know of these monsters?" *Are Gabriel and Yvette aware of this threat?*

Amalia watched the growing crowd outside. "He knew of many things he couldn't share. Your father entrusted others to safeguard you."

Yes, they knew, but they didn't think it worthwhile to inform Salome. Abel and Amalia held onto information beyond than what Salome studied ahead of the con. The Alliance never forgot a misstep. They only shared with Salome what they deemed important above all. She was a little girl when she'd wandered off the path to follow a storyteller and yet that brief incident haunted her.

On one of her first cons, she'd heard a group of travelers from Veirelle talking over ale about a girl who'd risen from the dead and walked in the capital city. Salome got too entranced by the conflicting stories to remember to follow her target when they left the tavern. She caught up to him within minutes, but every second was a mark against her. An indication to the Alliance that she could be distracted.

Stay focused, that's all she needed to do. She'd never made that mistake again.

Outside, the witches jumped through hoops of fire and twisted in the air in ribbons of wind. The crowd's *oohs* and *ahhs* filled the air. This was the people's much needed reprieve from grieving.

Amalia cleared her throat. "Are you comfortable here, my lady?" *Are you doing as instructed?*

"It feels like home." Salome toyed with a strand of her hair. "Though much of it feels foreign, I could live happily here once I gather my bearings."

In other words, Salome was on target. Her friendship with Sylvia l'Essalia led to introduction to nobles and their secrets. It was promising.

"Any new friends?"

"Sylvia l'Essalia introduced me to the clever Duchess d'Aryllia and Lady Ofelia d'Amaya, who is sweet but clumsy." Salome pulled a pin from her hair, unraveling the curls, then stowing it in one of her hidden pockets while making it seem like she smoothed out her skirts.

With a smile, Salome continued, "I can hardly blame her though. It's easy to forget what is right in front of you when there are other things to see." *I stole some things that went unnoticed.* She slid a ring off her finger and dropped it down her sleeve to illustrate what happened. "It's a common problem." *There is more.*

"Let us hope you will continue to build friendships here," Amalia said.

Find others who are vulnerable and Euria will determine what we should take from them.

"I have my mornings with Sylvia, my afternoons to do as I choose, and my evenings with the king, aside from the weekly dinner with the court. Somewhere between all that, I shall find the time."

Three months. It had to be enough time.

There wasn't a set schedule, especially when the seamstress would come every now and then to prepare her wedding gown. It was one thing the Alliance was unable to create, thanks to the king.

Three months until the wedding. Three months to take advantage of the nobles before the king noticed something was off about her and her entourage.

It felt like there were eyes on her and ears straining to listen. It felt like the shadows peered through bookshelves, turned expectantly toward her.

Clawed fingers slid out between books, hands gripping the spines like a demon intended to shove them aside and emerge. The sight made Salome jump from the window seat. Amalia and Euria looked at her in alarm, the latter already removing a small blade from her sleeve. But the hands retreated.

"I am becoming restless." Salome laughed. "Let's return home."

She hoped it was only her imagination. Hallucinations born from all the stories rather than something more sinister in the library. Whatever the case, she was ready to leave.

Later, as the castle grew quiet, Salome donned her thief's uniform and explored the halls.

Night was a veil upon the castle. Though candles now lit the corridors, there were too few to illuminate every crevice. The light was weak—weary flames, eager to shut their eyes.

If there was one thing she could do, though, it was being unnoticeable when she wished it. She was more suited to melding into the dark than traipsing in the light. Preferred it, even.

All her life, she was drawn to the dark. Now it felt like it called to her.

She wanted to know what was out there, what beckoned her into the night. If she didn't find answers herself, then she would seek out the witches and demand their explanations. She also needed to grow comfortable with the routes through the castle in the dark. She had to be enough of an expert to know her way around without guidance or light. She needed to know the entirety of this place like it was home.

Her fingers tapped on her daggers' handles, using the rhythm to steady herself as she counted her steps and memorized the path.

Danger found her in the split-second she wasn't paying attention.

Hands yanked her into one of the darkest corners of the corridors. They smashed her against a sturdy marble statue, too heavy to do more than rattle it. Fingers dug into her skin, threatening to tear her clothes with blunt nails and a heavy grasp. She choked back groans of pain.

Tendrils of smoke, smelling strongly of burning flesh, curled around her. They crawled into her throat, choking her, as a viscous substance rolled slowly down her limbs.

She thrashed and struggled. They only held firmer, pulled harder, and yanked her with strength surpassing her own. Salome kicked out her legs and stretched her arms, swallowing the screams begging to be unleashed. No sound. Not even if she needed help or if she was dying. The risk of discovery was too high.

She needed this mission. She needed to succeed.

No giving up, no getting caught. No matter how exhausted she became.

The hands kept grabbing her—clawed, demonic things that appeared from nowhere. One snatched her braid, another blinded her with a band of black smoke, and another clamped over her mouth. Her arms flailed wildly, finding only empty air and a kaleidoscope of whispers whirling around her.

The dark had never been like this before.

She fought and fought and wondered if this was what it was like on the battlefield. What the boys who went to war endured. Or perhaps it was closer to the villagers' helplessness when the enemy arrived at their gates.

With every second, her eyes felt heavier. When a hand latched onto her neck and tugged, she choked on what breath she had left and closed her eyes.

Death before discovery.

Suddenly, something soft as velvet and scented of sage wrapped around her. It pulsed, throbbing like a heartbeat, and the pressure on Salome began to fade. She inhaled sharply and began to struggle again until she freed her arms.

The hands retreated. Salome's feet landed on the ground, but she stumbled, gasping.

The air felt thick with fog. A low murmur floated in the air like distant music, as the weight on her lungs vanished and quiet claimed the space. She didn't know if she liked what this was, but it halted the attack.

Salome leaned away from the walls, staring at the dark space she'd fallen into like a secret doorway. Her hands tightened on her daggers, twisting over the leather wrapped around the metal handles. She glanced around.

There was only darkness. No witnesses, let alone saviors. The emptiness made her shiver, but she straightened her clothes and her masks, then continued down the corridor.

She wove the daggers between her fingers as she walked, staying out of the light but away from the walls. The statues contorted in the dark, shadows turning them strange and grotesque.

A door slammed shut. Wind gusted through the halls.

As a little girl, her mother and father warned her from venturing into the night. In Villasayas, there were more creatures to fear. Monsters existed, like manananggals—creatures with bat-like wings and their body sliced in two at the torso—which would sweep through the starry sky in search of the vulnerable.

Girlish laughter spilled down the hallway as she reached an intersection. Her head jerked toward the sound, catching sight of a child with long black hair pooled at her feet.

Salome said, "Go back to your rooms."

But as she took a step toward the girl, the figure collapsed, melting like wax. From the black puddle, another creature rose in the form of a hound with fur dripping like molasses and teeth the length of her blades. White eyes snapped toward her. Curved, elongated claws scraped across the marble floor.

Each time she blinked, it inched closer.

When it lunged, she ducked, brandishing a dagger. But before the blade could meet its mark, light filled the corridor. The creature darted sideways, retreating to the remaining darkness. Its snarls faded to nothing, yet she still felt its presence.

Salome rose. A pair of pale-skinned women approached—one tall and brown-haired, the other small with golden ringlets.

The witches.

"Your candles aren't lasting long enough, Della," Maris said, fire swaying in her hand. Amber eyes met Salome's, a sharp nose turning upward and red-painted lips pursing.

"You ought to cast light another way then, *Maris*," the earth witch answered. She pressed her hand against the wall, fingers curling as the existing candles extended from the short nubs they'd become.

Maris focused on Salome. "Stay out of the shadows. We warned you."

"Not well enough then," Salome said.

Della smoothed her hands over Maris's arms, a tender and loving touch, more romantic than sisterly. Flower petals fluttered where her fingertips grazed, falling to Maris's feet. "We must all be more careful. Someone is extinguishing the light. Creatures roam. The halls aren't safe."

The two looked at each other.

"What we've done is not enough," Della said softly.

Salome frowned.

"No matter. Let us be friends. We must take care of each other to keep the balance, especially now." The solemn words were strange in Della's sweet voice. So strange that it brought back the creases on Maris's brow and etched concern on her face.

"What are they?"

Della glanced at Maris before she spoke. "They're either mimics, presenting as things familiar to us, or malforms, strange and unlike anything that exists naturally in our world… or a mix of both. The more malformed the demon, the more dangerous they are."

"Demons," Maris clarified. "Ones that now returned after centuries of their absence."

"They will keep coming back unless we can stop whoever or whatever is causing them to emerge. These creatures—they are not all the same. Some will want to hurt you. Others will want to claim you." It sounded ominous despite Della's whimsical voice.

Salome groaned. "Where are they coming from?"

"A long time ago, witches banished them. They have been freed again, called to action." Della's eyes drifted away as she wrung her hands.

Maris crossed her arms, the bell-sleeves of her maroon gown swaying. "You ought to heed warnings. Stay out in the dark."

"You have no idea what I should or shouldn't do," Salome snapped.

The fire witch raised an eyebrow. "I know your mind; I hear your thoughts. You cannot hide your secrets from me, but there is no need to worry. We could be friends, if you'd allow it."

Salome eyed her warily.

"Keep a candle with you always," Della said, unsticking a candle from its holder and handing it to Salome. "If you must hide in the shadows, hold the candle behind your back so the darkness won't be tempted to venture out."

Della performed the movements herself. She disappeared with the candle behind her, reappearing with a smile once it was in front of her. That smile faded at Salome's blank expression. Della sighed, reaching for Maris's hand, who grumbled, but obliged.

As a sign of friendship, the witch circus directed her somewhere she'd find valuables to bring the Alliance: the chambers belonging to the former king and queen. Their rooms were relatively untouched since their passing.

All their belongings, small objects and grand items. Her heart hammered at the possibilities. The kingdom was known for its wealth and prosperity. The war diminished funds, but support from people such as Baron d'Ilumias prevented any real damage to their wealth.

Royal treasures. Gifts, heirlooms, and more.

At night, the castle's corridors were almost labyrinthine, but Della had summoned vines slithering across the walls to show Salome the way.

"Be quick before someone follows," Della warned, waggling a finger.

Abel would argue against trusting them while Amalia would call her a fool for even speaking to them. But the witches gave her an option, a way to survive with knowledge of what hid in the dark. Perhaps there were more answers where they directed her.

The vines led to an area Salome hadn't seen before. Intricate designs covered the doors at the end of the hallway, swirls and vines that twisted and curled. She picked the lock with practiced grace and shoved the door open with her shoulder. It creaked so loudly, she winced.

Inside, it was dark. A thin layer of dust sat upon each surface—only framed paintings and mirrors on the walls bore evidence of someone recently wiping them clean.

Hesitantly, she ran her hands across the walls, illuminating the room with the candle. The thought of the shadows shifting into monstrous things made her shiver worsened by the night's cold draft.

It smelled of dust and a lingering perfume—sweet and floral, remnants of a woman who once lived here. This was a home. It wasn't hers to invade, to rifle through memories.

Rosalia belonged here; Salome didn't.

But she did what she had to do. The Alliance wanted their wealth. Salome had to keep them happy in order to stay alive. If she was deemed useless, then she was dead. She had three months here and she'd make the most of it, gathering as much as she could to pay off her debts for food, housing, and training.

Ten years led to thousands in gold coins she saved up, but she had a long way to go and hiding her repayment coins was not easy.

For several minutes, Salome searched frantically. Her feet slid when she rushed over a rug, silver and gold threads on furnishings shining when she held the candle over it.

Nothing she could steal. Only things to admire.

She did, however, spy a painting of a forest. Evidence of Vincent's childhood and one of the beautiful things he must have created. She imagined his rooms looked like this, cluttered with paint and tools for his art. A bachelor's unkempt rooms.

While this place belonged to his dead parents, a place where a family could find time together.

Her chest ached with longing.

But she soon sighed with delight every time she found a new jewel. Too many to count, too many for her coin purse and pockets. She'd have to return another night. There was a flicker of doubt, until she remembered that these things were unused. Nothing to be missed.

A small portrait of the former queen sat on the vanity table. A beautiful woman with dark hair and dark eyes, copper-brown skin, and lips painted a dark red. Salome imagined Vincent tracing the faces in the portraits and clearing them of dust and grime.

She exhaled and shook her head. Fondness didn't help her.

Once the clanging of her purse became barely audible, she turned to leave.

The sight of larger portraits of the royal family made her freeze. The former queen, dark-skinned and breath-taking, the king pale and handsome. They had the same kindness, the same forgiving eyes, and relaxed smiles as Vincent.

All four children were present as well. Vincent was a little boy in it, the second eldest. He was surrounded by two sisters and a brother, all of dark hair and darker eyes.

The beloved royal family.

She was nothing like them. She knew what she was, what she would always be unless she became free. A thief, a liar, a commoner.

With every con, it seemed less likely that she'd ever settle down and live a peaceful life. She was an adventure, not a happy ending. She had debts to the Alliance, and they might never let her go even if she managed to repay them. No one left the Alliance alive.

As clever and pretty as she was, how could she ever be the first?

The only thing special about her was her relationship with the dark.

Scowling, Salome tightened the ties of her masks and exited. The door screeched as it scraped against stone. Her breath stalled as she checked the corridors. Still empty.

Wax from the candle in her hand dripped onto her gloves.

She paused, waiting for the mocking laughter. There was only silence. With a sigh, she broke out into a sprint, keeping close to the walls in case someone came into view.

The shadows did not reach for her. No witches called her name. No humans caught sight.

Yet her heart was still pounding when she neared the corridor that led to her rooms. Abel stood outside the doors. He crossed his arms at the sight of her. Always so resentful.

"What? Everything is fine," she said. "The witch circus led me somewhere useful."

Abel scowled. "You can't trust them."

"Fine."

"Watch yourself around the king too," he warned. "He's asking too many questions about you. He's too interested and seeks to know more than what is offered. All that charm is not for nothing. He listens, observes, and *cares*. That can be dangerous for us all."

Chapter Ten

WHEN SALOME RETURNED TO HER ROOMS AFTER HER MORNING with Sylvia, Amalia had a satchel stuffed with letters, a pouch full of coins, a glass vial filled with poison, and short knives.

"I'm heading into the city," Amalia said.

They exchanged looks—Salome was intrigued; Amalia exasperated.

In silence, the two of them hid blades in sleeves and beneath skirts and in little pins tucked into their hair. They kept their pockets empty in case an opportunity arose to fill them.

Outside, a small, open carriage awaited them.

It wasn't nearly as extravagant as the gilded one that brought her to Ellasya but still subtly opulent. Onyx paint coated the structure with lines of gold and navy blue along the edges. Thick cushioned seats filled the interior, as soft as the mattress in Salome's bedroom.

Abel, Elias, and Gerard followed on horseback, armed and dressed in light armor with the d'Ilumias sigil.

Ellasya was a prosperous city. Pointed archways entwined with vines and carved with elaborate designs were at each entrance and exit. There were stone buildings of various ages packed tight together with dirt and stone roads winding through them. When they passed through other villages, Salome offered food to those who came to the carriage.

But here, she had no chance.

She never thought herself kind, but she remembered what it was like to be poor and hungry. She could never forget, nor live like that again. It was the only vow she'd ever made. The feeling of being on her knees on rough earth and the shame that came with begging would never fade. Some nights, she dreamt of it, and each time, she woke, sweating and panicked like it was the worst sort of nightmare.

Bruised, bleeding, begging—she despised it. She preferred being no one to that.

As they neared the city, the population grew dense. Clusters of citizens loitered by the main entrance into the city. Royal guards stood in the archway, casually surveying the streets.

People were scattered across the streets, crisscrossing from one side to another. They darted in and out of stores, eyes forward and feet shuffling quickly. Some bartered with vendors, comparing merchandise with sharp eyes and distrust. There were various languages being spoken, tongues she'd picked up over the years and understood to some degree, well enough to wear the right accents and converse with confidence to get out of a scrape.

Abel came around to help her out of the carriage. Albeit disgruntled and reluctant.

He'd only be so genteel for a role.

Even smiling graciously at him failed to inspire a hint of a smile as she stepped down. Elegance abandoned her momentarily as she stumbled, but she straightened out her lavender day dress, flicked one of her braids across her shoulder, and carried on. On the other side of the carriage, Amalia stepped out. Her head bowed in deference, while her gaze shifted almost imperceptibly.

Eyes followed Salome as she walked. They clung to the chiffon skirts of her gown, the rings on her fingers, and the gold pins in her hair. Some stared at the white velvet purse dangling from her wrist.

"I merely want to explore today," Salome murmured. *Who are we looking for?*

Amalia walked a step behind. "As you wish, my lady."

An evasion. Not even a coded answer.

She imagined one of the Seven was waiting there to get the signal from Amalia. Who would the Alliance kill today? Or tomorrow? It could have been her, as a backup plan if she failed her task. Salome forced a smile and turned into a jewelry store.

"Listen," Amalia whispered. "That's all you're required to do today."

Her talent for languages, her ability to untangle the tongues and translate conversations. That was what mattered here. The Alliance was certainly up to something. She tried to listen carefully, hoping to hear something to make sense of this trip.

She knew Gabriel and Yvette wanted more power.

How many of the people here were in their service? How many more did they want?

There were half a dozen customers in the store. Some leaned over glass counters, staring at cushioned pedestals bearing small gemstones. Couples clung to each other, grinning and laughing as they surveyed potential gifts. An elderly pair whispered to each other in Ilaryan. A younger set spoke quickly in Tyrean, an unusual language to accompany individuals with dark skin. It was a country of pale-skinned individuals, known for their resistance to outsiders searching for a home on their lands.

"Look for red hair," the woman said in Tyrean.

Salome tucked a lock of hair, flicking a finger toward the pair.

Together, she and Amalia approached a counter. As a shop girl opened her mouth, Amalia shook her head. "Only browsing."

They're lookouts.

The Tyrean-speakers slipped outside. After another couple of minutes of pretend-interest, Salome turned and exited the store. Audible disappointed sighs followed her, swept away when the door closed behind them.

A commotion outside made all other conversations quiet.

A pale face stood out among the citizens, bright as if she was part-sunshine.

Irene beamed at Salome. "Oh, you are here!"

Children swarmed around her legs. Since she wasn't very tall, some rose to her shoulders or higher. Dirt already clung to her pale-yellow skirts, handprints where children grabbed at her.

The l'Issalya brothers stood nearby, scanning the crowd for signs of concern. Both donned royal guard uniforms, playing guard for the duchess today. Fabian's eyes kept straying to her, like they were tethered together. Every step she took, he followed. Never more than an arm away.

"I thought I could join you," Salome shouted over the children's chattering, trying to weave through the small crowd toward Irene.

"Unfortunately, you missed much of the excitement," Irene said, crouching to look at a little boy. She brushed his hair out of his face then shooed him off to his mother.

A little girl wrapped a handful of Salome's skirts in a muddied fist. In her other hand, she held up a doll in a pink dress. "She bought presents!"

Irene shook the purse strapped at her waist. It was emptied of all coins, evidence by the silence, to the duchess' visible relief. That struck something in Salome, though she managed to prevent herself from visibly reacting. How privileged it was to find relief in empty purses.

The little girl attached to Salome's skirts wrapped her chubby arms around her legs.

It took a quick glance around to understand the necessity of this show. Adults and soldiers were clustered nearby, arguing amongst themselves at a recruitment table. Posters clung to posts encouraging citizens to join the army, to support the king and protect the realm. There didn't seem to be any enthusiasm. All those who wanted to be heroes would have enlisted long ago.

And then there was Irene, distracting the children so they did not focus on the fighting. On the possibility of losing their parents and guardians to a ceaseless war. Families were being torn apart. Gift-giving was a mere bandage to a wide, gaping wound.

"Is this what you do here?" Salome asked the duchess.

She blushed. "I have far too much money for myself. Sharing it is the least I could do."

Despite her nonchalance, there had to be more. People often longed for more power. If they could take it, they would.

Salome, however, didn't want to hold power. She wanted to be rich and free. That was her dream—to go anywhere, live her own life, without worrying about starving.

Around her, there were children brandishing coins of all sizes and worth. Some held bags of food, enough to feed a family of five for weeks. Others bore shining new toys: horses they held up and galloped across the sky; castles shaped like the black marble structure beyond the city; wooden swords painted silver. It was sweet to be so generous, but like starvation, a piece of candy wouldn't fill an empty stomach.

"Vincent and I used to do this when we were young," Irene said as she slipped out of the crowd, patting children's heads as she passed them. Their parents converged, keeping them at bay.

As Salome unraveled the little girl's fist from her dress, she noted, "You two are close then?"

"Yes, he and Sylvia were my closest companions. We all grew up together in the castle."

Salome lifted her eyebrows in interest. "And now?"

"Politics changed things," Irene explained. "Her father's decisions tore us apart."

Salome found herself slightly irritated on the ward's behalf. Averting her gaze, she searched for Amalia. A woman in a burgundy gown passed her, their arms brushing. Amalia curled something into her palms before the woman disappeared down an alleyway.

Whatever they'd come to do, it was accomplished in a single second. Quick and secretive. The Alliance was up to something more dangerous than usual. There was more to the mission than Salome knew.

Irene hooked her arm with Salome's. "How have we not had a day together yet? It is outrageous! I *demand* friendship."

Friendship with the duchess would be beneficial, despite the risks. Though Salome's purpose on this mission was to distract and steal, she could try to gather her own information. Maybe then she could be one step ahead of the Alliance and their plans.

Even if Irene wasn't one of their targets.

The duchess was too keen on social politics. If she spent too much time with Salome, she would figure out what was wrong.

"We *are* friends," Salome said. "Sylvia has my mornings; perhaps I can share my afternoons with you."

Irene pretended to consider before nodding. "That is acceptable."

They walked through the city together, flanked by their own guards. Crowds parted for them. Some children called for the duchess by name, waving frantically. She waved back and blew kisses like she was queen among these people.

It wouldn't have surprised Salome if she took the crown one day, if Vincent ever stepped down or died.

Died. It felt wretched to even think it. He was young and he couldn't be the last of his line. Fate couldn't be so cruel.

As Salome and Irene passed a row of stalls bearing fruits and vegetables, they encountered Sylvia and her guard. Sylvia carried a full basket and her wide gray eyes lowered to her feet as they neared.

Beside her, Rene stiffened, reaching for a hidden weapon.

"Sylvia!" Salome said. "You did not say you intended to come to the city today."

From the corner of her eye, she caught Irene's head twisting toward her. A sharp turn, almost like the snap of a neck. Vincent did not direct her to his cousin. Did he have doubts about her? Perhaps this visit enabled her to see Irene's ambition. She called for love from the common people. She made sure they knew who she was. It could have been troubling.

"Without servants to run my errands, I must do them myself." From the way her eyes dashed from Irene to Rene and how she inched back, Sylvia's discomfort was clear.

Irene patted Salome's arm. "Come, I'll show you where they announced your betrothal!"

Without giving Salome a chance to breathe, Irene whisked her off, deeper into the city. Salome glanced back at Sylvia, but she was already disappearing into the crowds. It wasn't until Salome lost sight of pale hair that she directed her full attention to the duchess.

Chapter Eleven

It was a gray morning with the threat of rain. A low mist hung over the gardens and many of the nosy nobles carried little umbrellas with them.

Somehow, Salome managed to filch a handful of things and slipped them into her velvet-lined pockets and wide sleeves—coins cut loose from a slit in someone's side pouch, rings from pinky fingers. A few murmurings followed hours later, servants questioned but no answers arising.

Thievery wasn't uncommon even among nobles.

That morning, most seemed reluctant to draw close. Excuses to approach were running low when she was introduced to lord so-and-so and lady whatever-it-was. Salome still smiled and waved them over for a quick hello, but they would spot Sylvia and eventually rush away.

At least no one could get intimate enough to discover the flaws in her façade.

Irene found her later in the day and, together, they spied on Vincent as he held an audience with the commoners.

Much of the complaints were of the war and the need for more soldiers in the army. Training was promised, limited as it was, and it did not guarantee if one lived or died. Many were displaced by the presence of soldiers and wanted to know when the conscription would begin.

It was not a matter of *if* it would happen. All seemed to expect it in the coming days.

The king would not eliminate the possibility, nor would he confirm it. There were promises of glory, of gold.

A few of the commoners complained of what the war had done to their villages, appealing to the king as a representative of the residents. The border towns were no longer the only ones affected. Soldiers of the enemy's army had begun to charge deeper into Ilaryan territory. Those on the battlefield weren't the only ones to face to suffering and violence. They were not the only ones who died.

The most demonic of men had come to reap whatever they wished. Blood tainted the earth and rivers, it splashed across floors and walls. Irene averted her eyes and seemed to fade away as these claims were spoken, but Salome listened and observed. At one point, Vincent caught her gaze and nodded.

As if they both understood the importance.

"Listen to the next speaker," Irene suggested, once she was able to stomach what she heard. "Her name is Yen. Only two of her children are present. She used to have three."

Salome leaned close to the railing on the balcony upon which they sat, laying her arms on the black-painted metal as she strained to hear. This time, it was not an army.

Yen lost her middle child, a little girl who followed her father into the worst of the attack. She witnessed demons drag her husband out of sight, and then her daughter. There was so much shrieking from countless others that her screams drowned in the sea of grief and terror.

Irene clenched her hands in her lap. "I tried to offer my help, but there's little I can do."

"Gifts won't heal wounds or bring back the dead," Salome murmured. "And they won't get rid of monsters, if they exist, or bring an end to the war."

"But it is better than pretending there is nothing wrong."

There was a shadow of mourning in her eyes and a hitch in Irene's voice. Perhaps she wasn't so kind to Sylvia, but she felt for the people. Salome had more to say but merely nodded and smiled, like she appreciated what Irene hoped to do.

There were many stories throughout the king's audience of monsters and wicked men. Vincent promised to send whatever he could, including guards and builders and whatever food could be spared. He even said he'd go himself.

"It's real?" Salome asked.

"It seems so," Irene said.

The witch circus was in attendance as well.

The wind witch—Godiva—spoke in her commanding voice. "This is why we are here. The root of the evil is magic being used to harm. We will use ours for healing."

No one applauded them. Though they performed like a circus, they were still witches. And if magic created demons, then magic was the enemy. It was one of the reasons Salome kept her relationship to the dark a secret. She never knew who would be disgusted by whatever it was, perhaps the dark taking a liking to her rather than an indication of her capabilities.

But then the witches had her join them on the platform.

She glanced at the king. He nodded, though she wasn't sure he truly had a say.

"My lady, perhaps you can offer some wisdom?" Della suggested.

"With the cards," Maris said with a knowing look.

Salome reached into her pocket. Vincent raised an eyebrow, and her face burned with embarrassment. There was no need to carry the gift with her, but it was the only one she got to keep.

As Salome shuffled the deck, she felt eyes on her, curious and judging.

"It may not say what we wish," Della whispered.

"At least we shall see what is to come," Godiva answered, her voice barely louder than a breath.

"Choose," the witches commanded the king, each holding up two fingers. "Two cards."

He chose the faceless Queen of Hearts and King of Spades again. While her image appeared with that same mischievous smile, the image of Vincent changed. On the card, half of his face began to melt. Like candle wax sliding off bone, flesh dripped and dripped until there was nothing but the ivory skull underneath.

Vincent was stunned into silence. Salome nearly dropped the cards, glancing at the witches in alarm. Della's eyes held no emotion. It made Salome shiver.

"Would you choose two more, Your Majesty?" Maris asked.

Vincent finally glanced up, fear in his eyes. Salome wanted to promise him everything would be okay. But whispers met her ears.

Death to the king.

A chill swept across her body, but he didn't react. Did he not hear them? Did anyone?

Her nose filled with the scent of rot. The urge to vomit clawed at her stomach.

With a heavy exhale, Vincent chose another card. The Seven of Spades, transforming into arrows with pearlescent fletching. A moment passed. He closed his eye briefly as he selected another card.

The Two of Hearts. The image bled, drops of blood sliding to the edge of the card.

"Magic is about attention, intention, and expectation," Della explained.

"Read the cards, my lady," Godiva urged. "What do they say?"

Salome recalled the words from last time: *take it as you will.* Panic seized her throat. Whispers brushed against her skin, like lips and tongues tasting her. She couldn't look Vincent in the eyes and reveal her emotions. No vulnerabilities. No truth.

The whispers rose again. *You understand. You know.*

The hairs on her arms lifted. She shuddered, hands now shaking. Vincent looked concerned, touching her wrist. Could the rest of them hear? Did they know?

She didn't have enough time to understand all this. She only had three months here and it had already been a week.

"What do the cards say, Lady Rosalia?" Godiva spoke softly, like coaxing a child.

For the king, for his queen, for life and death.

Hushed, desperate voice. Strange but familiar, like a forgotten friend.

Her lips formed the words, speaking them without sound. Then, exhaling, Salome closed her eyes. She heard arrows fly; flesh being pierced. Screaming and a frantic heart, pounding in her ears. When she opened her eyes, blood coated her hands and she wiped it on her dress, but no red stain emerged on the fabric.

Salome breathed unsteadily. A metallic taste clung to her tongue. The sounds spun around her, faint yet persistent.

"A King of Spades for a leader, the skull for battle and death. The Queen of Hearts for love. The Seven of Spades for an imminent attack, and the Two of Hearts, the suffering of lovers." The words came out like wine spilling from a shattering glass.

A hush filled the room. And all she wanted to do was run away.

The shadows had a life of their own and they chose to live it with her.

Later that night, the king visited her room with the intention of playing cards. He also brought a little post-dinner snack: lumpia. Crispy egg rolls filled with minced meat and chopped vegetables, with a sweet chili sauce for dipping. The crunch of each roll in Salome's mouth made her audibly moan, igniting lust in his eyes and laughter.

All she did was smile, wink, and continue their game. Still lying and cheating, except now the king didn't allow her to win easily. Now, he won more often than she did. It angered so intensely she threw the stack at him.

"You are terrible at losing," he said.

Crossing her arms, she said, "And you exceed at deceit. I am frightened."

"No, you are not."

"No, I am not," she agreed.

Their gazes met as they contemplated each other's posture and the interest in their eyes. His hands twitched on the table and his eyes kept returning to her mouth.

If he wanted to kiss her, she certainly wished he had the courage to do so. She pressed her feet into the floor to avoid launching across the table, taking that ridiculously handsome face into her hands, and claiming his mouth with hers. His lips looked soft. His rough hands on her skin would be a delight.

But when they finished their games, he only kissed her hands and left.

More had to be done if she was going to tempt him into acting on his lust. Her studies made no mention of lovers, if he had any. She'd figure it out once she released the coiled tension in her born from her own wanting for him.

Moments later, Salome darted out the door, dressed in dark clothing and daggers in hand. Water as frigid as a lake mid-winter splashed Salome in the face, sending her stumbling against the door. She wiped her masks and spat the fabric from her mouth.

"We haven't been introduced yet." The voice was dainty, as fragile as a crystal glass. "My name is Thema."

Salome lunged.

The other witches allowed her to get within an inch of the water witch's face, before hauling her backward with unnatural strength and ease.

"What was *that?*" Salome asked through gritted teeth.

"Please understand," said Della as they released her. "We needed to warn you before you took what shouldn't be touched."

"You sent me there before *and now you've changed your minds?*"

"We learned of an object in the royal rooms that shouldn't be there."

"Something important to our magic and what binds us to the kingdom was moved to those rooms recently and we had only just learned when we went to retrieve it ourselves," Maris explained. "You must leave it to us."

"The queen wore a crown when she enacted the blood ritual that bound us to the kingdom. If you try to claim it yourself, you put the balance of our magic at risk," Godiva said before Salome pushed them aside and carried on her way. She wanted gold and jewels. The more they earned, the sooner she could leave. The sooner they could leave this cursed place, the less time Salome would look at the king and be tempted.

Every night, she was closer to running out of time. She couldn't waste a moment.

She longed for a shield to hide from them, or something that could transport her directly to where she needed to go.

A doorway of a sort. That would be convenient.

The witches, luckily, kept their distance as Salome went to the abandoned royal chambers. But there was someone stepping out of them when Salome got to the hallway. She slid backward, hurrying into the shadows despite the witches' warning. Her instincts told her to trust them and so she tucked herself into the corner, cradled in the dark.

She inhaled deeply. It smelled of sage and burnt sugar.

"Did you know someone would be there tonight?" Salome asked the witches. She still needed to appease the Alliance. Returning empty-handed wasn't an option.

Della came closer. "Perhaps, but they weren't our concern."

"And I am?"

"Yes, because your life matters to us. *Your magic.*"

It was like she sang it into existence. The air shifted. The shadows stirred. Salome closed her eyes and counted her breaths, hoping for stillness and quiet, but the witches murmured to her.

Thema began a ramble about something she read a few years ago that would be of great interest to Salome if she decided to use her magic. Her own magic. What a strange thing to call it when it felt like a curse.

The figure at the chambers was coming close. The witches might have gotten away with being there, but Salome would be doomed. A fool returning to the scene of a crime when she shouldn't. It wasn't being a fool. It was desperation.

"You will have a choice to make very soon, little one. The people who you report to—you do not have to stay with them. There is another life waiting for you," Godiva said. Her voice was soft as a breeze, a gentle caress against skin. It meant to soothe.

And it ignited rage like a flint to fire. Salome felt a quick burst of heat within her chest that burned like flames. "You make it sound easy. *None* of this is."

Maybe it was an aching, a feeling of hopelessness that surged within Salome, so strong it felt like she was being blown backward in a storm.

In unison, the witches sighed. The ominous chorus brought chills over Salome's skin, and she continued retreating into the open. It wasn't the right time to discuss this. There was someone here and there, were things she needed to do and—

"Your life has been difficult, but you needn't endure it alone," Della said, eyes glassy with unshed tears

Godiva touched Della's arm. To Salome, she said, "One day, you could stand among us."

"Who's there?" a voice called.

The witch circus gathered, Maris standing at the front. She spread her arms wide. Without another word, the fire witch waved her arm over her head in a broad sweep. The witches vanished, erased from view with a bit of illusion. A mind trick, maybe.

They were gone, leaving Salome to contemplate her choices.

"I said, who's there?"

Salome was struck by the familiarity of the warm, rough rasp, though it lacked affection.

The king held himself tall and with authority despite being dressed like a commoner. Dark trousers, dark shirt, tall boots that blended with the dark. There was no silk or velvet, no gaudiness or opulence like his displays during the day. She liked him in the shadows, no longer pretending to be some bright, hopeful creature.

He had no armor, but he had weapons. A sword grasped in his hand, the hilt of a dagger peeking from the top of his boots, another at his belt.

Tonight, he came for a confrontation. He expected a fight.

Salome could easily give him one. "Your Majesty, the hour is late. Do you not rest?"

He walked slowly toward her with the swagger of well-trained soldier. Confident, unafraid. "Not when the likes of you intrude where you would never be allowed entry." There was danger in his voice, lower and threatening. Almost seductive.

Salome gasped. "How could you accuse *me*? What have I done?"

"You were here the other night."

"With perfectly good intentions." She touched the pouch at her waist. "Tonight, at least."

He wouldn't recognize her, not while they were half hidden in the dark and she still wore her masks. He might have, however, found the baubles familiar. She dangled the stolen jewelry in the light. Oh, rather, the forgeries of them.

Without warning, she threw them his way, and they clattered to the floor.

"You don't want them?" she asked. "Can I take them back?"

"They are not my concern; you are."

"Ah, so it will be a chase."

She was glad he could not meet her eyes properly. Not only would the intensity of his gaze terrify her, but she feared him peering into her soul and seeing the truth of her. They stood there, watching each other, waiting to see who would make the first move.

The hand over his sword twitched. Salome shifted her foot.

"Come on, my king, and chase me," she said, beckoning him into action with the curl of her index finger as she took a step back. The next one she took made him start to follow. There were still a couple of meters of space between them.

He lunged before she could leap, latching a heavy hand to her wrist. With a tug, he had her body slamming into the nearest wall, and he pinned her against it. Heat swept through her and her lips parted. A curse settled on her tongue, kept at bay by her teeth pressing onto it.

With his body on hers, she felt every hardened muscle of him. If she was forced to bear it, he ought to be tempted too. Salome moved slowly, rubbing her legs against his, pressing harder. He pushed a leg between hers to pin her in place, but that only summoned a flash of lust.

She had one hand free and used it to grab his head.

There wasn't much she needed to do. Already, he leaned in. He breathed deep. Their eyes never met, but their gazes were mirrored in their hyperfocus on lips. She didn't have to urge him, he came closer, ducked his head, and kissed her.

It was open-mounted, teeth clashing before lips touched. A hot, wet tongue that stroked and sought more to taste. She moaned quietly and drew a growl from him. Incensed him to push tighter, harder, pinning her to the wall in a delicious way that drove her through her body. Want was a fire between her legs and she needed relief.

He kept one hand on her wrist, pinned down at her waist now, and the other gripped her hip. He pulled and pressed their bodies together while his mouth moved over hers. It felt like being devoured, and she adored it. The sounds that came out of them were not at all courtly; they were almost feral.

It was only when one of them kicked the pouch of fake jewels, forgotten on the floor, that the sound of clinking stones brought them back to the moment.

Vincent drew back. His grasp loosened.

Salome yanked herself free and shoved him back. "Was this part of your plan?"

He wouldn't recognize her voice without the polished airs she wore for Rosalia. She shoved again and he stumbled back, giving her enough space to escape. As soon as she was free, she ran, and so did he. A new rush raced through her at the chase. It was a test, she imagined, a chance to prove she knew the hallways well enough to disappear.

Laughter spilled from her lips like sparkling wine from a bottle as she sprinted away, rushing from the chambers. The labyrinth of hallways made for a perfect route. Salome kept close to patches of moonlight when she careened down a hall of tall windows, all open and allowing the breeze inside. Her footsteps didn't make a sound, but Vincent's did. She heard him chasing her toward the dark.

No, she couldn't stop.

Into the dark she went, as did he. It was then that she came to a stop, sliding against the wall where he wouldn't be able to see her. A successful move that allowed her to see him run by her. She watched him as he started to slow. It was then that she came up behind him and stole the dagger from his boot. She ran her fingers across the details, the twisting vines around the jeweled cross-guards and golden handle.

Before she could make a clean getaway, he latched onto her wrist. Salome held tight to the dagger and yanked away. Vincent didn't loosen.

When he pulled, she fell against him.

The only correct way to respond was to slide out the knife tucked in her sleeve and plant it in the space between his ribs. More pressure was required to pierce the body, but it pressed tightly enough to his torso to feel it.

His other hand clamped over her wrist. "Is this a game to you?"

"Maybe. Did you like the taste?"

The wind suddenly disappeared. It seemed quiet before, but it was nothing like this. Her heart pounded in her ears. The shadows called her name and murmured a warning. She didn't know if Vincent heard them, but he noticed something.

"Stay still," he said.

He now looked to the dark, as if he could already see the creature that caught his attention. Part of her wanted to look. Another part of her wanted to run, and then there was a tiny voice that wondered if she could use magic.

A monster rose between them, tall and wiry with a torso like a trio of mangled trees twisted together and limbs like knotted roots. Whatever it was made of, it oozed. It moved like molasses, thick and heavy, with long drops dangling from its arms. It reeked like a corpse in the worst of its decay. So wretched that peering into its fathomless eyes might reveal maggots wriggling in the depths.

Salome inhaled sharply and stumbled backward.

The demon advanced on her, reaching with its dripping arm. When she ducked, it whirled on her and rippled once, then twice, vibrations pulsing in its body.

The shadows screeched with their own fury. She squeezed her empty hand into a fist to no avail. Nothing. She tried to copy the graceful movements she'd seen the witches perform. Still nothing.

"Run to the light," Vincent said.

"What happened to stay still?"

At the same time, the demon began splitting like there was a seam down the middle of its body. It convulsed violently. As the halves separated, new figures started forming.

No answer needed, Salome ran to the light, where the moon brought silver into the hall. Was it bright enough to be safe? Vincent followed, sword drawn, ready to play the hero.

The witches were in the hall when they got there.

"Run," they said in unison. "Forget one another and just run."

There was no time to think.

The hall filled with fire, acting as a wall between the king and the thief. As they'd sworn, they protected her. The demons were their duty to keep at bay. She had other concerns, a team back in her rooms that would demand information on the night. Did she do her duty? Were the forgeries returned? They couldn't know what truly conspired, unless they suspected something might occur.

Maybe they were waiting for something, like the shadows and the witches waited for her.

We're here, the shadows seemed to say. *But so are they.*

Chapter Twelve

HER EMPTY-HANDED RETURN TO HER ROOMS THAT NIGHT resulted in Abel using a knife to retrace the mark on her wrist that proclaimed her pawn and property of the Alliance. It was a scar painted in ink, carved into her skin again and again. Salome earned it the day she signed their Book of Names and received a new title.

Nothing. No one.

Except something for the Alliance to use.

Upon waking the next day, she already knew she needed to confront the witches, but had no opportunity in the morning. It was only when the afternoon came when Salome was meant to spend time with Irene that she had the chance to act.

After advising Irene of her intention to head into the city, Salome led the way to the courtyard where a small carriage awaited. All day, she'd had this feeling of rope wrapped around her middle, tugging her to the city.

The witch circus would be there, set to perform at sunset.

She climbed inside without a word and Irene followed, but with much more elegance.

During the night, Salome dreamed about waking to one of the assassins in the Seven forcing her mouth open to pour poison down her throat. In that nightmare, she felt every bit of her body reacting to the substance. The burning and roaring sensation of flames shooting through her insides while it felt as though someone peeled away her skin, starting at her fingertips.

She woke up screaming.

Then Amalia smothered her face with a pillow until she was silent.

On the short ride to the city, Irene laughed to herself and chattered about how a few of the ladies at court were in a war with one another about misplaced jewelry. Though Salome imagined them screaming at one another, slinging false accusations while she and Amalia cackled about their scavenging, the truth was much less aggressive.

Those with the same ring size blamed each other. Lost coin purses were found empty. Petty words were exchanged, side-glances and frowns filling any silences between suggestions of potential culprits.

The carriage brought them exactly to where the witch circus was. A crystal stage was erected for them with curtains of quilted vines drawn over where they would stand. People already gathered around the square though there were hours before the performance began.

The witches were not immediately visible. Salome scanned the area in search of them, twisting the gold ring around her finger all the while.

The duchess pressed a hand to Salome's arm. "Would you like privacy? I am terribly good at occupying myself in the markets."

Of course. Irene wore the most gorgeous dresses and jewelry. If the opportunity arose, Salome would eagerly snatch the emerald and pearl earrings dangling beside her round cheeks. It wouldn't have been a significant steal, but certainly a pretty one.

Once Irene went on her way, Salome climbed onto the stage.

No one stopped her, only whispered among themselves.

"Was that Lady Rosalia?"

"The king's betrothed is here?"

"What business does she have with witches?"

They could speculate all they wished. All that mattered to Salome was settling the panic bubbling in her belly. She stood there for a moment before the curtains rustled and figures emerged. Della appeared first, her face concealed by a mask and hood.

"Have you come to perform with us?"

Salome removed the cards from her pocket and pushed them toward Della. It was more violent than she intended, sending the little witch slightly off balance. An apology clung to the tip of her tongue, but she refused to let it out.

"What did you do to them?"

"Nothing!" Della said. "It was all you."

If that was supposed to soothe her, it failed. Fighting the urge to chuck at the cards at the ground, she clutched them to her chest. She gnashed her teeth together in frustration.

"Your magic is growing. We warned you," Godiva said.

"Clairvoyance can be a curse," Thema mused. She sat in a chair with her face tucked in the pages of a book. "Many witches with the gift covered their hands and avoided all triggers of foretelling. It is difficult to know what is to come, even with the vaguest of details."

Salome dropped to the edge of the stage and dropped her face into her hands.

"This situation shall only become more complicated," Salome said.

"We know," Godiva answered.

There were still people watching, wondering if anything would happen. Salome bit her tongue and considered her words. When she finally found her voice again, there was still only nonsensical thoughts, jumbled words, and uncertainty.

"And all my things, my rooms—"

Godiva sat down beside Salome and placed a hand on her shoulder. "Regardless of your choice, we will make sure that no harm comes to you."

Terrible things happened behind closed doors and if she remained where she lived, in close quarters with the Alliance, she was in danger. Hurting was not always physical. To hurt someone, all one had to do was find the weakness.

Salome was nothing. She was no one. The Alliance always ensured she felt that way.

With a wave of their hands, Thema and Godiva called upon a fog to form around the stage and a strong wind to conceal their words from others. It allowed them some privacy, a moment away from all the eyes and ears on them. Still, Salome remained unsettled.

"I'll need more answers. We cannot continue like this. It's too confusing and—"

"They will not own you forever," Godiva swore. "They can try to threaten and hurt you, and while they may succeed with humans, you have witches on your side. You have magic."

"They cannot stop us from freeing you from their grasp," Maris added.

Salome stiffened.

The Alliance offered death in response to betrayal. What if they found her parents the way they found another member's? What if they made a trail of body parts in their symbol, a reminder of what happens to those who failed them—or their loved ones? It kept their members in seclusion. Loyal, even if unwilling.

Absently, Salome rubbed the scar on her wrist that declared who she belonged to and who she had to repay somehow by gold or blood. A dark brown hand came over hers, warm to the touch despite the frost on the fingernails.

"You are one of us," Thema said. "And we take care of our family."

The word *family* was a hand around her throat. She felt strangled, lungs seizing with desperation. As Thema swept a hand over hers, a cooling sensation spread over Salome's skin, like splashing her face with fresh river water on a hot day. It soothed her feverish panic.

"I don't know what I ought to do," Salome whispered.

Thema pulled her into an embrace.

Salome couldn't remember the last time she was held this way. It had been years and years. Was it with her parents? Or had Yvette hugged her and kissed her forehead in moments when she pretended to be motherly? She couldn't fully recall, and it struck her as sad.

"Trust us. We cannot meddle with their every affair, but we can free you from their cage," Thema whispered.

"Quiet," Maris said suddenly. "Someone is listening and watching."

When Salome looked up, she swore she saw batwings at the edge of a nearby building. A girl in training to be one of the Seven. In a rush, she pushed Thema aside and straightened, dusting off her skirt and trying to regain her composure. There was still a fog, but it didn't entirely conceal them. From the right angle, anyone could see, and even if none could see them, there was a chance that someone could hear.

"I should not be consorting with you," Salome said as she backed away. Maybe they could defend themselves, but what if it sparked a new war?

Salome sometimes wondered if the Alliance had magic users, for all they had accomplished in such a short amount of time. Decades, no more, led by Gabriel and Yvette when they were barely more than teenagers. Their use of magic was never spoken or shown. They had people who were a little more than human, but if they had any gifts to manipulate the world around them, Salome wasn't sure.

Godiva sighed. "We know of the terrors inflicted by your people."

Della's hand curled into a fist and her face twisted with anger. A silly expression on her childlike face. "They are cruel and violent and possessive—"

Salome asked, "What about me?"

"Not everything must be about you."

Della shoved Maris for saying such things. It wasn't very nice, but then again, Salome did not deserve nice, nor was she used to it. She shook her head, still retreating. She'd deal with the consequences of this confrontation later, but she needed time, though she had very little. Had she only been here for a couple of weeks?

Choosing to be with the witch circus... Salome never dreamed of that.

"What was last night then?" Salome asked.

"A reminder for you of what you are capable of. It is not a thing you can ignore for much longer. Soon, you shall have to accept it," Godiva explained.

These weren't answers. They weren't enough. All they did was stir more frustration in Salome. She needed to find a better moment to get more information, to get clarity when it's been a blur. Where the hell did she stand in the world? What was her place expected to be?

"We'll always be close," Godiva promised. "That magic of yours—you will learn how to control it and there will be nothing to fear."

"Trust us," Maris said, hearing the doubt echoing in Salome's mind.

Salome left the stage area. She bumped into someone on the street, mumbling her apologies. When she looked up, she froze in fear.

Gabriel. He was here.

Leader of the Alliance. The one who recruited her to this life. He didn't often appear during a mission, instead choosing to stick to the shadows or observe from afar. His presence suggested there was more than what she was instructed to do. She stared at him in a long silence, dumbstruck and a little devastated, before she ducked her head.

Salome could have magic and the shadows and some affinity with the witch circus, but the Alliance still owned her life. Staring at him, she swallowed, and it felt as though all the fear she'd had as a child came flooding back.

Beside him were a pair of young people, a brother and sister from their similar appearance. Their arms were linked, and they held satchels filled with painting supplies. Gabriel brought the impressionists.

The job wasn't over. She wasn't dead yet.

"Pardon me, sir," Salome said.

"Watch yourself, my lady. You never know what sort of trouble might find you out here," Gabriel responded, his voice low.

It reminded her of being a child, scolded for failing in her studies. She had never been to school, too poor for tutors, with only her parents to teach her about the world. When the Alliance took her in, she could barely read. Gabriel was harder on her than anyone else to figure out how to read and write to perfection. Without his harsh nudging that often resulted in her tears, Salome wouldn't have developed her mind and tongue for languages. She had a natural talent, he insisted, and he wanted to make the most of it.

As a little girl, it meant the world that the leader of this terrifying group saw something special and valuable in her. She told herself that only someone who had love for her could encourage her so fiercely.

Was love supposed to be this painful though? So frightening? Not because of how strongly she felt, but because of the dangers she constantly faced.

Salome backed away from Gabriel and his new recruits to find Irene. The duchess wouldn't have much to offer other than a friendly face, but that was better than the near-paralyzing terror when Gabriel had his eye on her.

It couldn't be good to have his attention, especially not after what had just been spoken.

She once saw someone beheaded for simply uttering the Alliance's name to an outsider. This was so much worser than that.

In the chaos of the city center, Salome wandered in search of Irene. Citizens watched her go here and there, weaving in and out of shops as if she cared about the available wares. It felt like hours passed before they found each other.

"There you are!" Irene called from the middle of the street. "I hoped you had not imagined I abandoned you here. I had to do something kind when my little friend here appeared so eager to see me."

There was a child gripping Irene's hand, her knuckles white. A little girl with her black hair hanging down to her waist and skin as brown as Salome's stood beside the duchess. She wore a new, buttery yellow dress.

Salome smiled, but the girl's gaze focused on the ground, eyebrows drawn together in concern. There was a pool of shadows at her tiny feet, writhing dark figures knitted so tightly together that they could be a single cluster. As they gathered around her ankles, she scraped her foot across the floor.

They scattered like dust in the wind.

The little girl looked up at Salome with her face painted clearly with confusion. The only thing that Salome could think of saying was an apology. That, however, would draw Irene's attention to something she hadn't noticed. These weren't Salome's shadows if someone else saw them, unless there were others who had a trickle of magic that allowed them to see.

What if Gabriel was one of those people? And that was why he held onto her and made sure someone always had their eye on her. If they knew of her magic and wanted to use it, that was very, *very* bad.

"Was there more you intended to do? I have finished up here and would like to return home," Salome said, then bit her tongue. Home possibly didn't exist. All she knew now was that she no longer wished to be here in the city, where it felt like there were eyes everywhere and she couldn't escape judgment and scrutiny.

"I suppose I could head home as well." She patted the child on the shoulder. "Run to your mother and show her your pretty new gown."

To say the girl ran was an understatement. It was more of an escape. She didn't glance back once, disappearing into the city.

Be still, she begged the shadows. *Do not let them fear me.*

She needed more time, but there wasn't enough.

The shadows rippled like raindrops pelting the surface of a lake one last time before smoothing out. Again, and again, she begged and pleaded and urged them to listen. They took their time as if locked in debate before becoming quiet and unmoving. The pool became no more than her silhouette on the ground. Salome exhaled and hoped it would remain that way.

For the first time, Salome realized her potential villainy was not rooted in her upbringing, but her newfound magic.

Chapter Thirteen

THERE WAS NO HOPE IN HIDING FROM THE ALLIANCE. IN THE evening, though Salome tried to feign a deep sleep on the bed with the blankets wrapped around her and eyelids rattling with dreams, Amalia still woke her. The same violent shaking at first, and then later, fully shoving her body off the bed and onto the floor where Salome fell with a heavy thump and promise of bruising somewhere on the side of her body.

"Tell me what I heard today," Amalia said, crouching beside her.

Salome sighed. "I went into the city and confronted the witches." No point in lying. The punishment would be much, much worse than what would happen for honesty.

As leader of the Alliance, Gabriel never went anywhere alone. To enable him to blend with the crowd, his armed guards and countless spies remained out of sight. There were more people in the city than was originally advised. There were schemes beneath her nose that she hadn't noticed until the patriarch was in front of her, bearing a warning.

"And what was the point of that?"

"To confront them," Salome repeated. "About what happened last night, which I did not understand." No matter how many times she turned the words over in her head, nothing seemed right. She was gifted with learning languages, not being a poet.

"It's all a test. It always is. You should remember that," Amalia warned, standing up straight. "The witch circus's intentions are not always clear. There is a reason we do not consort with magic."

The more Salome felt her own magic stirring, the more she wondered what powers the Alliance truly had. Influence was one thing. A quick rise to controlling much of the markets and setting up a secret monarchy off the criminal underground while maintaining youthfulness and health—it was too lucky.

"But the Seven—" Salome began as she rose from the ground.

Amalia held up a hand. "They're an exception."

"I think you're scared. You've never seen magic so up close and personal before. Does it make you feel vulnerable? Do you doubt yourself when you see what the witches can do?"

When Amalia's palm connected with Salome's cheek, it forced her face to turn. Her skin burned red from the impact, yet she kept her arms to her side. As much as it hurt, she wouldn't react. Yvette hit harder than Amalia did.

It had been a long time since they'd resorted to petty fights. To kicking and screaming and slapping. They were far from children with knives they didn't know how to use. This hit was a statement. A belittling.

Silence filled the space between the two, tense as a chain pulled taut.

"Gabriel in here," Salome said.

"I know."

"What did he say to you?"

"I didn't see him." Her voice was stiff and final. It was always a touchy subject that Salome received more of the leaders' attention despite Amalia's capabilities and successes. It enflamed the odd rivalry between them. Amalia failed to see it as Salome did, that the Alliance wanted to keep an eye on only one of them, while the other had their full faith.

They kept Salome around because she was useful, not because she was loved.

Ungrateful, Yvette once called her. *Remember who loves you, who gives you food and clothing and a home to return to. It isn't your mother; it's me.*

Salome was loyal only out of necessity.

Amalia thought it was more meaningful than that, no matter how much Salome tried to convince her otherwise. There was no hope for that anymore. No point in trying to tell her there was nothing to envy.

After a moment, Salome said, "I have work to do,"

"Then go."

Soon after, Salome donned her black outfit and her masks. Amalia was with Leon, leaning over the latter's worktable, deep in discussion. He'd had an easy couple of days with Salome's failure to bring anything for him to recreate.

When he noticed her staring, he frowned, and it made her feel unwelcomed. She pretended to tighten her masks and turned away. The least she could do was act like she still obeyed the Alliance and keep busy.

"The painters are here," Leon called out. "If you're not going to bring me anything, at least get something for them."

She said nothing and left the suite.

The royal chambers called to her, promising more treasures that she could take, but when she peered into the hall, Vincent was there again.

There were other places to go. It didn't matter where she went, so long as it wasn't the dungeons.

Clouds rolled into the night sky, blocking out the moon and stars. The hallways were already brightly lit by sconces too. Her hiding places were nearly nonexistent, and the chances of being spotted were high.

It was tricky, but she'd adapted and overcome such an obstacle before. She'd proven herself time and time again that she had what it took to work for the Alliance. Perhaps, because of that, she'd never be free from the Alliance. Perhaps she had only these three months to figure out the exact escape route, or maybe she didn't. Perhaps Gabriel even already had someone watching her for evidence of magic and had safety nets in place to ensure she didn't become out of reach.

Regardless of what they discovered, she was only a tool to them—or a weapon.

The shadows began to hiss and seethe, and some of them crawled like low fog across the floor. Still, she didn't turn around. These ones wouldn't hurt her. She'd figure out how to handle the real monsters. If the witches could take care of them, then Salome could too, somehow.

With the shadows at her heels, she found herself in the portrait room.

There was a small frame fit for a locket tucked at the bottom corner of one of the four walls. Situating it there was asking for it to be snatched, easily removed from the hook keeping it elevated.

Holding the frame in her hands, it felt so much more than it seemed. It was a piece of art of an infant, important enough to be on display yet insignificant enough for a tiny portrait tucked close to the floor. Salome swiped her hand over the glass, then slowly began lowering her masks for a better look. But at the sound of the footsteps, she backed into the corner.

Vincent entered. At first, he didn't see her, so she set down the painting behind her feet, tucked into the shadows.

What was another bit of forgotten art to him? There had to have been hundreds of pieces scattered around the castle. Maybe some of the framed images in the halls were his creations. It warmed her heart to imagine his parents telling him not to spend too much time cooped away with his paints and brushes, yet eagerly displayed his finished works.

It took him a second of peering into the poorly lit room to spot her.

"What are you doing here?" he asked.

No, that tone of voice wasn't for his betrothed.

"I'm admiring the art," Salome answered.

He approached slowly and traced the shape of her with his eyes, as if searching for something. Salome braced herself and began reaching for her weapons, but the way he was looking at her made her feel strange.

She wasn't afraid. He wasn't angry. How confusing.

"What are you looking at?" She rested her hands on her hips once deciding there was no need to wield a weapon. There was a sword at his waist again, left untouched.

"I don't understand you," he said. "Coming in the night to look at portraits."

"Some people are very interesting to look at."

Each step Vincent took toward her felt like ages. His strides were slow, unhurried, and more terrifying than the possibility of a demon coming from the dark to destroy everything she knew of the world. It felt predatory and a thrill rushed through her at the thought of being his prey.

As he looked her up and down, Salome stilled, waiting to meet his gaze.

He caught her in some sort of trance. She felt locked in place, barely able to speak, let alone breathe.

"I've done nothing wrong," she murmured.

"Not tonight, it seems."

When he smiled, so did she. The remaining tension pulsed with something new and vibrant. It burrowed deep in her abdomen, but instead of terrorizing her body, it filled her with giddiness. This dangerous yet charming side of the king was something new and intriguing and exciting. Salome was almost tempted to remove the mask over her mouth and give him another taste.

He would be sweet. There wasn't anything else he could be. He was kind and caring and merciful. Another king would have tossed her in prison by now. Not him. Maybe he saw good in her.

That would lump him into a small group.

"Do you have something you want to ask?" she wondered. The look in his eye made her nervous. Maybe in a good way, like fingertips dancing down her back, traveling from her shoulders to her waist, igniting shivers.

"Many things. You would face an interrogation."

She grinned. "But not tonight."

Vincent frowned and crossed his arms. Even in the dim lighting, she saw the contours of his biceps, begging to be touched. Her fingers twitched, aching with that need. Giving into temptation had landed her in more beds than she'd admit, with all sorts of people. Kinds she shouldn't kiss and didn't deserve. Men who were cruel or women who were too soft-hearted.

But when Salome licked her lips, rustling her lower mask, something shifted in Vincent's expression. He loosened up and sighed, running a hand over his jaw.

"Looking is all I can allow," he said.

"It's not all I want though."

Before he could back away, she grabbed him by the shoulders and tugged him against her. He grew bold, pushing her backward so that she stumbled against the wall. He held her there, his mouth against hers, lips moving in a series of stolen kisses. Her breathing became uneasy, and it was all she could hear.

If she only had a little time with him, she'd be like a thief and steal these moments.

Frames that contained portraits of important people dug into her back. The sensation blurred when the king touched her leg, winding around her thigh like he was contemplating bringing it around his waist. She'd do that, imagining him lifting her up and holding her against the wall as he kissed her.

His mouth was warm. His lips were soft and full. He kissed her tenderly, but with enough pressure to reveal how much he wanted—much, much more than what they allowed themselves so far.

"This is terrible," he murmured.

His hand stroked along the length of her thigh, reaching around to touch her knee before sliding toward her hips. Heat pooled between her legs, and she couldn't help but tilt her pelvis toward him. He was hard, the solid length of him visible in his trousers, and she wanted to stroke it and see how he would react.

Her answer was to slide her tongue over his upper lip, urging him to open his mouth so she could steal a taste. He obeyed and she hummed with pleasure. The king would never kiss her like this. Not when she was acting as someone else.

Her head tilted back as his hand came around her throat. She tightened the leg around his hips, pulling him closer. He obeyed and leaned in, allowing her to feel his cock against her core. She rocked forward, desperate for more.

"You remind me of her," he whispered against her throat, breathing heavy and struggling to hold still. His body trembled slightly, and she hoped he was as delirious with lust as she was. "Of Rosalia. I shouldn't do this to her."

"This can be our little secret, Your Majesty. A one-time thing, if you wish it."

"But I'm hers, not yours. You're nothing." With that, he pushed away and stepped backward.

Salome's leg dropped to the floor with a heavy thud. Her body throbbed with aching lust and though the heat between her legs continued to burn, the rest of her suddenly felt cold.

Nothing and no one. As always. The shadows crooned her name and curled around her wrist like a bracelet made of velvet. Somehow, their touch was soothing and loving and strange. She instinctively opened her hand to them, and they crawled into her palm, shaped like a kitten.

Whatever she felt, it didn't matter. The king was nothing to her, as she was to him and the entirety of the world. Not for long, if her magic became known. What would she become? More than nothing, surely.

She couldn't have this. She couldn't even stay.

"Then goodnight, dear king. Go and dream of the girl you love."

Still, before she could leave, she kicked him between the legs hard enough to bring him crashing to the floor. That way, he couldn't follow her.

She couldn't be near him like this. She raced back to her rooms, taking a long route to get there rather than the direct path, thinking only about a private moment to relieve the aching.

Chapter Fourteen

Most of her team had their duties to occupy them. Leon guarded the rooms, nodding when she flashed the locket at him. She tossed it onto his worktable, then locked herself in the bathing chamber. Stripping her clothes, she gritted her teeth when she sat at the tub and realized she had no hot water. To get any at this hour, she would have to locate a maid, and there was no time for that. There was a basin of room temperature water and a clean cloth, and she used that to cleanse herself. It cooled her heated skin and she signed, leaning against the marble counter, looking into the mirror.

By the time she was dried and dressed in a robe, she stepped out.

Amalia entered the main sitting room a moment after, already dressed in her handmaid's dress. It certainly wouldn't have been what she wore to the city.

Before they could speak, there was a knock at the door.

"I have no scheduled guests at this hour," Salome whispered.

Amalia narrowed her eyes but went to investigate. She opened the door slowly and bowed her head upon seeing who was there.

"Your Grace," she said, her voice soft, as she stepped out of the way.

Salome pulled the robe tighter around herself and came closer. The king was in the same clothes as their earlier encounter. Perhaps, once she'd left him, he paced around before deciding to come here.

"I apologize for the late hour, Lady Rosalia, but I hoped to have a moment with you," Vincent said. He didn't spare Amalia a glance as he said, "Please leave us. It shall only be the lady and myself in these rooms."

Unsure of what to say, as Amalia did as commanded, Salome remained standing. She rested her hands on top of each other at her waist, waiting to see what he would do. There was still that lingering heat between her legs that she had wished to relieve, to tuck herself under blankets and find that sensitive pearl with her fingertips. She pressed her thighs together, hoping he couldn't notice.

She thought he might wish to speak, but when the door was firmly closed, he turned to her. Something unusual was in his eyes, something that didn't appear when he looked at her as Rosalia. It matched his expression earlier that night, the one that ignited her discomfort.

"I was thinking of you," Vincent said as he approached.

"What was on your mind?" She didn't move.

"How I've failed to do my duty as king, and as your future husband. I recall my mother speaking with my sister about how frightening the marital bed could be and how anxious she became. The wedding never came. But I thought about that and how a woman might feel ahead of marriage, how terrifying it might be as the night drew closer."

With every word he spoke, Vincent came closer to her. By the time he finished, they were face to face, their toes touching. He reached for her with slow, steady hands, and touched her cheek. Salome tilted her head, leaning into his touch.

"I'm not terrified," she said.

"Are you curious?" he asked.

"Perhaps you could clarify your intentions tonight, my king."

His eyes snapped up and their gazes locked. She almost regretted those words, smiling under his intense gaze. Then his hand dropped and settled on her waist, the other coming around the other side. He tugged her toward him, and she allowed herself to take a step closer until they were chest to chest.

The hands on her waist squeezed, then ventured lower to roam over her ass.

She bit her lip. "Your Grace?"

"Please, use my name."

The softness of his voice was like honey. His breath was hot as he leaned in to kiss her throat. She hummed in pleasure as he kissed her there, gentle at first, before his tongue darted out to taste her skin. A gasp slipped from her, and he took that as a moment to claim her lips. She sighed and sagged against him, her own hands finding purchase on his shoulders before she tangled one hand in his hair.

She parted her lips and he slid tongue inside to touch hers. It was heavy and hot and wet, stroking her tongue in a way that made her think only of his mouth between her legs. Wetness pooled at her core, and she longed to be touched there. Filled and satisfied.

"Rosalia—" he groaned, lips leaving hers to find her neck again.

She tilted her head back to expose it to him.

"Call me Sal," she pleaded.

"Not Rosa or Rose or—"

She huffed.

"Sal then," he said. She felt his smile against his skin. "Am I allowed to touch you?"

She certainly wouldn't mind, so long as he didn't see the mark on her wrist. She could keep it turned and out of sight; she'd done so countless time. All good thieves knew the importance of misdirection.

"Did you want a maiden on your wedding night?"

H groaned and took fistfuls of her robe, tugging as if he was desperate to remove it from her body. As if he hated this barrier to her skin. "It never mattered to me."

"Good," she said. "Because I am not a maiden, and if you want me, you could have me well before then."

She reached between them and undid the knot of her belt, the one thing keeping her robe closed. The silk slid apart.

A curse spilled from his mouth and his hands went into action. Calloused palms explored the light brown skin now exposed to him. First, he placed his hands under the robe to touch her shoulders and ease the fabric away. It fell slowly and quietly, pooling at her feet. His hands continued their exploration, traveling down her arms and once off her hands, moved to her waist and upward. He cupped her breasts and squeezed.

Salome groaned, arching into his touch.

"Your Grace—"

"Sal, use my name," he pleaded, then bent his head to take her nipple into his mouth.

"Vincent, please," she gasped, taking a fistful of his hair, and pushing her legs together.

Fuck, she was too warm, too wet. She felt an aching and emptiness, a desperation to be filled. Her hips swayed toward him, wanting more, as he suckled her nipple, flicking his tongue against it. She took a step back, hoping to edge toward the bedroom, but he held her firm.

If he wanted to fuck her on the floor, she would have let him, but wasn't she pretending to be a lady?

Vincent turned his attention to her other breast, licking at the brown areola before taking her nipple lightly between his teeth. The sensation made her moan. He massaged the breast he'd already lavished, squeezing and tweaking her nipple until he pulled away. She whined, about to grab his hand and bring it back, until he placed it between her legs.

This time, she swore. His fingers found her clit, brushing over it gently. It was already swollen, and she bucked her hips to chase his touch. But he dipped his finger between her folds, finding her slick, and groaning. She grinned, hoping he was pleasantly surprised by how much she wanted him, how desperate he made her. Vincent swirled his finger in her wetness, dragging her slick up to her clit and rubbing.

Her legs shook and she moaned. The sound had him lifting his head, taking her lips again as he rubbed circles between her legs.

"Do you like this?" he asked.

"I believe you know, Your Grace."

He growled and she laughed.

"Please, Vincent, don't stop," Salome said. "If you'd like, we can take this to the bed."

His answer was to lift her up, wrapping her legs around his waist, and carrying her to the bed chamber. She squealed with delight, gripping his shoulders. Before she knew it, they dropped onto the plush mattress. She was entirely naked while he was far too dressed. She made quick work with his shirt, undoing the buttons and pushing it from his shoulders and arms until his torso was bare.

Muscles greeted her and she honored their presence by pressing her lips to his chest and running her hands over his abdomen. There were ridges of hard muscle, evidence of a king who did more than sit on the throne. It was a soldier's body, one who knew hard work and battle. She imagined him toiling for hours in the early mornings, training in combat to the point of burning muscles and exhaustion, sweat dripping down his body. She kissed his skin, nibbling here and there, moaning at the salt on the surface.

Vincent pushed her back until she was laying on the bed, pushing her toward the pillows.

Salome was about to pull him up, but he settled between her legs, head bent.

"Let me worship you," he said. "My queen."

Then he flattened his tongue to trace her folds. She leaned back and cursed. He teased her with his tongue, gently trailing around her opening. It must have been evident how wet she was, and he seemed to appreciate it, licking up her juices like it was the most divine wine.

"Please," she whispered.

And he let his tongue find her clit and licked. He flicked it back and forth, teasing her, drawing on her nerves. She couldn't help the moans that escaped, the sighs and whimpers as she lifted her hips toward him. Vincent took one of her legs and hooked it over his shoulder as he focused on his attention at her core. He licked and sucked and then placed his fingers at her opening. She twitched at the fingertip that teased her.

"Would you—" he began.

"Yes."

One thick, long finger slid inside her. She arched her back and groaned, biting her lip. He worked it in and out, the wet sound of the movement turning her on even more. It felt like she was burning up, every muscle in her body tightening as the pleasure built up and up. He continued to lavish attention on his clit with his lips and tongue, all the while his finger filled her. Then he added another and began to move quicker. She chased his hand and mouth, grabbing his hair to hold him in place and squeezing her leg on his shoulder.

Laughter rumbled from him, adding vibration that made her moan louder. He pushed more, gliding those fingers in and out of her core, drenched in her slick while his tongue rubbed her clit.

Her climax built up, her breaths coming shorter, her sounds becoming higher pitched. His movements grew more fervent and intense, desperate to bring her to the edge—until she nearly screamed as the pleasure rolled off her. The waves were sharp and unrelenting, her hips bucking, his fingers continuing. Vincent had lifted his head though, watching as she chased her pleasure to the end, as she came on his hand.

She slowed, her breaths remained heavy, but he pulled his fingers from her.

Before she could speak, he stuck his fingers into his mouth and licked her juices from them. She bit her lip and reached for his trousers, pushing them down his hips and freeing his cock. It sprang free, long and wide, so hard that veins bulged along the length. Salome wanted to flip him over, to take him into her mouth and taste him, but he kept her down.

His weight on top of her was delicious. His gaze was intense.

"Rosalia," he murmured. "Sal. Do you want this?"

She laughed. "Sweet king, I believe you already did me a great kindness. It would be very generous if you offered more."

Vincent grinned and took himself in hand, positioning the tip of his cock at her entrance. He let it glide over her folds and around her opening. The contact of their skin was so wet, so loud. She bit her lip as he coated his cock in her slick, then began pushing into her. She gasped.

"Fuck," he groaned. "So tight. So wet."

"More," she pleaded.

He pulled back, then pushed in further. Back and forth, entering inch by inch. She gripped his hips, urging him to feed her more. He was so thick, he stretched her wonderfully. Every bit more than he filled her, she moaned, tilting her pelvis to take more until finally, he was fully seated in her to the tilt.

Both cursed at how it felt to be joined like this.

"I'd wed you now to have this forever."

"Fuck me, Vincent. Please," she said.

And he obeyed.

Slowly, at first. He thrusted into her steadily, stretching her more and more. She wrapped her legs around him and pulled him closer. Then he moved faster. Harder. Pushing into her so deep that she threw her head back and bit back a scream.

"Let it out, love. I want to hear everything," he whispered. "Show me what you like."

She moved her hips to meet his, urging him faster. The good king was kind. He did as she insisted, hitting that spot inside her so perfectly that she couldn't help the loud moans that grew and grew. As he sped up, she felt the scream coming as she soared higher. She was almost at the peak and Vincent seemed to know. He placed a hand between them, right above where they were joined, and massaged her clit with expert fingers.

Until she yelled and squeezed his cock with her insides. As she flexed around him, her muscles convulsing, he continued to thrust relentlessly, faster and faster until suddenly he stilled as he came too.

She was still in the throes of her pleasure as his seed filled her, the heat unlike anything she'd felt before. No man ever came in her. She forced them to pull out, even willing to suck the man's cock to keep his seed far from her womb, to take it into her mouth and swallow it for the certainty. But she allowed him this, not only because his betrothed shouldn't worry, but also because she wanted to know what it was like.

And it was heavenly.

She thought it was over when he pulled out, but he demanded to bring her to the peak once more as his fingers found her clit again and urged her to weep from the pleasure.

Chapter Fifteen

IN THE MORNING, THOUGH IT RAINED PROFUSELY, AND SHE AND Sylvia could not go out for their garden walk, Salome was in the most pleasant of moods.

Last night played in her mind again and again. Her lips tingled and sparked with the knowledge that she enjoyed a taste of the king who wasn't hers. She throbbed between her legs as well, as if she was just freshly and thoroughly pleasured. He was in expert in bed and kissed her until she was too sated and languid to move. Ever the gentleman, he didn't even leave her like that. He helped her into the nightgown that had been draped on a chair for her. Then he tucked her under the blankets and kissed her, groaning as he hardened again inside his trousers. He couldn't stay, though he expressed how much he wished he could.

Salome had fallen asleep before Amalia returned. Whatever was discovered, no one said a word, but when she'd woken, Amalia grinned at her.

"Well done," she'd said. And that was all was exchanged as they readied for the day.

Salome's chiffon dress was a blue so dark, it mimicked the midnight sky, with gold stars on the bodice. She even set a few gold pins in her hair to match the embroidery on her outfit. They always dressed her up in case the king saw her. If she could capture his attention entirely, it allowed the others a moment to take advantage of.

When Sylvia arrived, she led the way to the portrait room. It took incredible effort for Salome not to smirk as they entered, pretending to scan the images with nothing but casualness.

They paced around the room for some time before Sylvia seated herself on one of the two sofas situated back-to-back in the middle of the room. Despite the thick cushions and the pillows on it, she sat stiffly, her back straight and legs pressed together with her hands clasped in her lap.

Their guards remained at the doors. Rene looked grave and stood with a hand on the pommel of his sword. In contrast, Gerard seemed in good humor as if he'd enjoyed a pleasant night with Euria. With his superior memory, he could replay every second, perfectly.

Oh, she truly envied him in that moment. To recall the exact sensations would be an absolute delight, though highly distracting. Rene and Sylvia might not care, but she wouldn't want to draw Gerard's attention to it. Then he'd certainly have something to report. The team knew something had occurred. The details, however, were out of their reach.

"This is a beautiful room," Salome eventually said.

That earned her an unimpressed look from Sylvia. "Let us not engage in such small talk."

"Is it offensive?"

Sylvia said, "It's dull."

Shaking her head, Salome did another turn around the room. The gold frames gleamed in the bright light set off by the two gold and pearl chandeliers. Even this room was an ornate exaggeration of the kingdom's wealth.

Salome peered closely at the largest portrait. It was set in direct view of whoever sat upon the sofa facing it. Two frames surrounded the painting to emphasize the importance of the woman it displayed.

A beautiful young woman with olive skin and long black hair that fell to her feet. She was dressed in a silver gown with detailed sleeves cut so sharply, they resembled armor. Jeweled stars decorated her curled hair and silver dusted her eyelids. In one hand, she held a sword pointed to the earth. In the other, the sun hovered above her palm.

A bronze plaque below said *Queen Xiana, first Queen of Ilarya*.

She was only twenty-three when she united the provinces, younger than Salome was. Hundreds of years had passed since she died as an old woman of nearly a century, surviving much longer than anyone anticipated and leaving behind a dozen children with different fathers. She believed the best path to peace and ensure her family held the throne was to remain unmarried.

Though young Salome wanted to be like her, her father laughed and told her of all the responsibilities placed upon a monarch. That made Salome change her mind. Instead of being queen, she'd be content with only being rich and beautiful.

Someone else could bear the burdens.

"Is there something on your mind?"

That startled Salome from daydreaming, picturing herself in a similar gown in gold instead of silver, holding shadows instead of the sun. As she thought of them, she swore she heard them crooning with delight.

Smiling, Salome said, "Oh, no, not at all. Do I seem thoughtful?"

"Don't be suspicious," Sylvia said, eyes narrowed.

Salome laughed. This morning, everything made her feel light and giddy. It felt like she'd come across a treasure trove and longed to recreate that feeling.

"Did you know any of these people?"

In a deadpan, Sylvia answered, "No, I'm not old enough to have known the first queen."

That wasn't what Salome meant. She waved a hand dismissively. "Of course not, but there are plenty of people on these walls, not all of them long dead."

"My father foolishly used to want to be remembered here," Sylvia noted. "He was a lord, but a lowly one with nothing to offer. The idea of power... it always appealed to us. To his optimistic heart."

At the nostalgia entangled with bitterness, Salome laid a hand over hers, and for once, Sylvia didn't immediately jerk away. Instead, she turned to look at Salome.

Sparks filled Salome's vision, like a flurry of shooting stars racing across the sky. They were a series of colors like slashes in a thick curtain blocking out light, offering thin slivers to peek through to see the mosaic on the other side of a window. She swore she saw a battlefield, and then the figure of an enormous beast, and perhaps a graveyard.

This time, Salome yanked her hand free.

Sylvia turned away, kicking off her shoes to place her feet on the sofa. It was the first time Salome had ever seen the ward get comfortable in a public place. Making herself at home.

Quietly, Salome removed her own slippers, curled her legs underneath the skirt of her dress, and stretched her arms above her head. A yawn slipped out of her mouth, loud and unladylike. Sylvia relaxed, and even smiled. Now they matched.

"Let's stay here for a while," Salome decided.

"I hope you are not expecting to exchange gossip."

That made Salome grin. "Only if you had something to share."

The side-long glance that Sylvia made was suspicious. The corner of her mouth tilted upward. What happened when people treated you as if you were a ghost they couldn't see, even when you often passed them in the hallways? How many secrets would one have?

"Share," Salome said. "Please."

"Lady Irene's husband—you have yet to meet him—is a very kind man, to most. He tends to spend the warmest months at his estate in the north," Sylvia began.

People's living situations weren't the least bit interesting. Salome prodded Sylvia with an elbow. *More*, she demanded. *Offer something fun.*

Sylvia rolled her eyes. "If it wasn't for political alliances, he'd be with a certain man."

A little more intriguing, though not surprising. Many of the nobles were with their spouse for one reason or another, and many were not love matches. It was a common problem in the couples that led to miserable unions, though not all the time. The former queen and king were arranged to be married and still lived happily together.

And then there were pairings like Salome's parents, deeply in love but living in poverty. Better these days, she hoped, without so many years with the burden of a child.

Salome looked at a portrait of not only Vincent and his siblings, but his cousins as well. Irene was among the many children, all of them dark-haired with skin in different shades. Some as pale as the duchess, others as dark brown as the late queen. The mix of features and colorings revealed lineages spanning the continent and further, as a result of politics.

Humming thoughtfully, Salome said, "I imagined Irene loved her husband."

"Not romantically."

"How unfortunate."

"Do you believe it will exist in yours? *Love?*" Sylvia's gaze was so intense that it brought a blush to Salome's cheeks. Her stubbornness prevented her from looking away, though, no matter how much it felt like her soul was being pierced.

Sometimes, when Sylvia looked at her, Salome wondered if the ward was able to see all that she'd done. All the good and the bad, the people she pretended to be and the people who died because of the family she found. But that was impossible.

"How could the king not fall in love with me?" Salome flipped her hair over her shoulder.

It caught Gerard's attention, so she winked at him. Abel would have scowled. But her guard this morning only laughed and shook his head, then resumed his emotionless stance, ever the professional.

It took some more coercing and teasing and prodding, but eventually Sylvia gave in. Her insight confirmed details already known by the Alliance, including how an older noble family sold their heirlooms to newer nobles in order to keep their estate. She also shared where some paintings were done, and which portraits were recently commissioned. Unsurprisingly, there were some small busts done by Vincent, his signature in the bottom-right corner of those pieces.

"Any stories about magic?" Salome peered at a portrait of a girl at the Woods of Palvary.

"Once, there was a d'Allorias princess who joined the witch circus many decades ago."

"What do you know of her?"

"One of my ancestors was part of a blood magic ritual to erase her name from history," Sylvia said ominously. "None recall it."

It was so serious and spoken with such a dark look in her eyes that Salome couldn't stop herself from giggling. Perhaps part of her should be afraid and concerned for her fate. But if she had magic of shadows and the witches intended to protect her as they already had, perhaps what was destined for her wasn't so terrible.

"Does that mean there's magic in your family?"

Sylvia scoffed. "No, not at all. But there is in Irene's side of the family."

Sadly, she had nothing more to offer. They spent the remainder of their morning sitting in silence, until Amalia came to fetch Salome for lunch.

Before they left the gallery, Salome went to the corner where she forgot the little portrait the night before. She reached into the shadows but found nothing. Slowly, she straightened and turned to find Gerard watching her. He peered into the hallway, then back into the portrait room.

"Were you expecting to find something there?" he asked.

"Maybe."

When she settled in for a quick nap before seeing Irene in the afternoon, she found the tiny frame tucked in the shadows behind her pillow. Salome brought it over to Amalia, who promised to send it over to the impressionists. Let the Alliance remember her usefulness, though she wasn't sure if they should know how she managed to steal it.

Part of her worried they already suspected and were waiting for proof.

Then, during her nap, Salome dreamed about peering into the shadows like they were a doorway into another world. All she saw was black.

Chapter Sixteen

"Good morning!" the duchess sang, coming toward the doors to Salome's rooms as Sylvia moved aside. "Are you ready for a day together, dear Rosalia?"

Irene's light-brown hair was braided intricately with emeralds and pearls, spilling over her shoulder when she curtsied. Her gown today was soft green with floral gold embroidery. A young, teenage girl lingered beside her in a matching gown, as if the two of them were a set of dolls. Trailing behind them were the l'Issalya brothers, dressed in partial armor. The two men looked prepared to spring into battle at any moment.

Salome bowed her head. "Duchess d'Ellsaria, how pleased I am to see you again."

"It's Irene, remember? We'll be family soon. There's no need for formality." As always, Irene's way of speaking was all speed and energy, the words tumbling out like acrobats. Salome half-expected a flourish at the end of each sentence. "Oh, and this is Eulalia d'Aryllia, my husband Ezequiel's littlest sister."

Eulalia's round face was youthful and elfin, framed by curly black hair. She beamed and bounced on her toes with enthusiasm that rivaled Della's.

"You've been alone here for so long! When the king said I could meet you

—" Eulalia stopped, catching Irene's eye, and smiled sheepishly. "I mean, I am delighted to make your acquaintance, my lady."

Irene shrugged, still grinning. All forgiven. "Do not mind Eulalia. She's very eager. She is correct, however, that my cousin thought you'd like more company."

"Does he think me lonely?" Salome raised an eyebrow.

"Well, perhaps I convinced him that I *long* to spend more time with you." She didn't look the least bit ashamed to admit to that. "I did meet your father once, years ago. He had a small portrait of your mother, you know, and carried it everywhere—*so* romantic. I assume you look more like her."

"Oh, yes." Salome gathered some unshed tears in her eyes. The family was long gone, and no one would miss them, but someone needed to pretend to care.

"Forgive me, I've heard he is missing, and I have no intentions of upsetting you."

"There is no need for forgiveness," Salome assured her.

"I think we could be great friends. We shall have fun together, I promise!" Straight white teeth shone between her thin, pink-painted lips as Irene smiled.

But Salome couldn't mirror the pleasantry.

It should not be known that the baron was missing. That information would create further questions about the family and, eventually, the discovery of what the Alliance had done to them. Gabriel and Yvette were too careful to allow that.

Unless they wanted people to know, or to send some sort of message.

Whatever it was, it didn't bode well for Salome. The Alliance must have known of her waning loyalty.

"There was an incident last night. It's not pleasant to discuss," Irene said. Though she temporarily dimmed, she didn't slow. "More shadows, more demons. A messenger sent word this morning. I thought we could visit and offer our condolences and support."

Sylvia would not join them. Irene had no interest in spending time with her due to her history and poor reputation.

Lord l'Essalia destroyed his family's standing by wanting to dethrone the d'Allorias family. He was not alone in his many attempts, but the others were never identified. To keep them from trying again, Lord l'Essalia hanged, his body on display for days. Sylvia had sat in front of it and apologized profusely to his corpse until they took it away. She screamed, begging to bring him home and entomb him.

People said Sylvia wailed until her throat dried and the sun burned so intensely that spectators blistered in the heat.

Wherever she went, the story followed.

She loved her father and didn't care about the accusations against them and made certain all knew that she believed his punishment was unfair. To even suggest that was treasonous and that may have cost her all her friends.

As they left Salome's rooms, Abel whispered that he'd meet with someone in the city.

The nervousness twisted her organs and tied up her tongue.

How many people knew that Baron d'Ilumias was missing? What else had been discovered? Perhaps the news was why Vincent encouraged Irene to spend time with her.

He was dead, not missing. He was in an unmarked grave out on the sea. No one was supposed to be looking for him or realizing that perhaps they should.

Salome wasn't the worrying sort, but a flicker of fear sparked in her as they made their way to the stables.

The l'Issalya brothers trailed behind them, with Abel, Elias, and Euria close as well, forming an armed entourage that was much larger than necessary. The brothers cast an uncertain look at the Alliance, even allowing the latter to venture ahead and lead.

Irene spoke of politics and idle gossip, discussing who would fight in the next battle against Pavalla, who was the richest, who planned on marrying soon. Her expertise. Some familiar facts Salome recalled from when Yvette grilled her about the court. Others were bits of knowledge from Sylvia.

Once they reached the stables, it became clear their little trip was preplanned. Irene had gloves waiting in a saddle bag. Then, stripping off her skirt in a single, smooth motion, she revealed a pair of riding trousers.

"I'm always prepared. The castle gets dull." As Irene spoke, she effortlessly launched herself onto the saddle.

"Well, it is still new to me. I've needed to explore," Salome replied as she mounted another horse, though with much less elegance. Her horse was snow-white and gray-speckled with dark, long-lashed eyes. Its nostrils flared like it smelled something strange on her when she approached.

Did it notice the wisps of shadow weaving between strands of her hair and smelling of burning herbs? Perhaps the horse was sensitive to magic. Luckily, it waited patiently as Salome made herself comfortable.

And then, grabbing the reins and kicking her legs, Irene sped forward with wild laughter. Her hair came loose in the wind. Salome chased right after her, trailed by Eulalia and their entourage of guards.

Irene's face was flushed when Salome caught up to her on the path.

"You know, both you and my cousin are lucky," the duchess said, slowing.

Eulalia was now a few feet behind them with Fabian and Oscar.

"What do you mean?"

"A beautiful woman, an honorable family, and someone he enjoys spending time with. Before you came along, I was his dinner partner," Irene said. "We doubted he could find love again and now... perhaps he has."

"Love," Salome repeated quietly.

"Would you allow me to share something with you?" Irene whispered.

"Of course, anything."

"It's hardly a secret. My husband and I do not have the love you could have with Vincent. We care about each other, but he'll always prefer men. I grieve for him, truthfully, and how he is unable to be with who he truly loves." She gestured to Oscar, who scowled and quickly looked away, pretending to survey their surroundings.

"There is no shame in his feelings, but duty comes first. Our families wanted the alliance." She shrugged. "If you find love, hold onto it. That is what I wanted to say."

Salome never imagined truly marrying. Only for a con, as anyone but herself.

"Enough of that," Irene said, waving her hand dismissively. "Let's hurry."

As Salome spoke, the duchess had already urged her horse faster, whooping loudly. Was she fighting for optimism in a world plagued by demons? Perhaps this was how she coped.

The excitement, however, died down the second they entered the city.

A woman with black and white hair stood directly under the arch covered in vines at the city entrance. Her voice was hoarse, like she had been yelling for hours. Hope filled her eyes when Salome and Irene approached.

"My husband—he's gone! Taken! Killed! The shadows—the demons..." The woman released a piercing wail. "I want him back. I *need* him back!"

Salome cringed away.

Amidst the bright colors of the street vendors and the shop-signs waving above vibrantly painted doors, the bleak details stood out. A man demanded the witches be cast out. Fury and hatred filled his voice as he blamed them for the war.

Children begged for food, bearing empty bellies and ribs prominent against their skin. A woman held her bleeding baby. A skeletal man stood on shaking legs. This was all she could see, not the colorful roofs or the painted signs. Those were blurs in the background.

Many of the able-bodied were off with the army. Those who remained alive could have their wages sent to their families, but those who perished could offer nothing. Salome didn't know what happened to the families who lost that income. Surely the king would still compensate and send condolences for their loss. Perhaps it simply wasn't enough.

The king was powerful and rich, but they were the opposite. The castle was safe, yet not a sanctuary. Here was the evidence that a kingdom's riches couldn't eradicate war-born suffering worsened by demons.

Deeper into the city, smoke billowed from a charred building. Only one wall remained standing. A black, gooey substance oozed down the sides, seeping between the stones. A pile of bodies covered in soot-stained sheets lay where doors must have been, victims pulled out from the rubble. The lampposts around the building had collapsed, bent in half and the lantern and its candles lost within the debris.

People moved aside, staying close to the buildings. More hid in narrow alleyways.

The sky was clear, but the scent of unwashed bodies and dirt remained.

And the decay—already, the rancid scent of it filled the air. Death had touched the city last night when demons visited.

Irene dismounted quickly and headed straight to the children. When one reached for her hand, she provided it. Soon, weak laughter resonated as Irene took children into stores, buying them whatever they desired. She purchased loaves of bread and offered pieces to each child. Her kind face drew them toward her. Her smile inspired matching ones.

Grateful murmurs and sighs of relief soon replaced hungry wailing, grief, and resentment. Some people still looked disinterested, distrusting, though. Some turned up their noses and twisted away.

Salome understood how they must have felt. She remembered kneeling on the road, covered in mud and desperate for food or coin. A night of crawling through streets, picking up a grimy, half-eaten orange and devouring it to fill the void in her stomach.

After some time, Irene returned to Salome's side. "I cannot do nothing."

Her charity kept the people distracted from the night before, an interlude from sorrow. Children were the most trusting. They could forget more easily, at least for a little while.

"You'll hear no complaints from me," Salome said.

"We can only offer what they will accept. Most tend to keep their distance." Irene brought an entire purse of coin for charitable intentions. It seemed she intended to empty her pockets to supply food and clothing before returning home.

It wouldn't rebuild homes or bring back the dead, but it was something. A speck of hope before the war reeled them back to the bleak reality. The harsh, narrowed-eye gazes that followed Salome made certain she knew who they blamed for the war and presence of demons. The royals, the nobles, the people in power who couldn't establish and maintain peace with the neighboring kingdom.

A senseless war. An endless parade of battles.

And now otherworldly things to rip them apart.

Salome followed quietly, smiling when someone glanced her way. To offer anything more was to ask them to remember her. It was better to forget and be forgotten.

The l'Issalyas and the Alliance guards remained on their horses as well. Eulalia soon dismounted, racing to join her sister-in-law to play with the children. They danced, spun, and chased each other around, like they'd been friends for all their lives.

Abel urged his horse beside Salome's, fingers tapping against his saddle.

Then an arrow shot through the air. The wind of its trajectory scraped across Salome's cheek before it landed in a child's chest.

The peace shattered.

A woman shrieked. A man howled. Someone wailed in horror. The child fell to the ground, eyes open as blood spilled from their wound.

Bile climbed up Salome's own throat.

This couldn't have been happening and yet it was. Bodies pushed around as people tried to get closer or retreat from the scene. It was directionless chaos.

Her heart pounded in her ears, a dull throb of a headache like drums amidst war cries. This wasn't a battlefield though and she had no armor to protect herself, no proper weapons to fend off attackers. Her needle-knives wouldn't do much here.

A whisper brushed against her; the words unclear.

All she did was stare at the corpse.

Soon, all she heard was screaming around her, colors blurred and the world out of focus. She didn't know if she was standing or sitting or swaying. It felt like she was seasick in the middle of a hurricane.

The crowd was getting closer, surrounding them. Someone grabbed at her skirt. She struggled to move away, stumbling. Her instinct was to attack, but she kept her hands tight on the reins and urged her horse back.

Everywhere she looked, there were eyes. Bloodshot, blazing with rage and hurt.

She had never witnessed such hatred before.

Fabian was the first to move, parting the crowd to get to Irene and Eulalia. Irene grew stern, snatching Eulalia's hand and tugging her from the crowd. Both managed to mount their horses and move away, sticking close to Fabian, Oscar, and Salome.

Nearby adults lifted children away, pulling them from the scene. High-pitched screeching and crying trailed after them like ringing alarms signaling approaching danger. It was too late though.

The danger was here.

Assassins. The word hissed among the citizens like a curse. Salome looked around, still unable to focus, searching for the archer. Likely one of the Seven, the subsect of the Alliance rumored to be demons themselves, sent to kill those who failed to fulfil their debts to the Alliance. Salome was lucky to have never met them. Until now, perhaps.

They could have easily killed Salome if they wished. The Seven didn't make mistakes.

Here was another message. If she wasn't afraid before, Salome certainly was now. Cold terror that dripped down her spine like wax on a candlestick.

She clutched the reins tighter, her knuckles white as bone. They were here, watching her. They were going to take her away—

Or kill her.

Terror was a knife at her throat, already slicing.

"You did this!" a man shouted at Salome and Irene. "You're causing trouble."

"Flaunting your money," another woman said.

"Go back to your castle!"

"You'll get us all killed!"

She didn't know where to look or where the voices came from. It felt like she was surrounded, buried under the crush of filthy bodies. She couldn't *breathe*, releasing the reins to claw at her throat like she was suffocating.

They turned so quickly, their trust easily broken. Irene kept apologizing, despair plain on her face. Others chimed in, throwing harsh words in sharp contrast to the lightheartedness only moments ago. Hands grabbed at them, pulling at the saddle, the reins, their legs. More people came closer, yelling obscenities and threats. Rocks and stakes and anything they could grab became weapons.

They converged, separating Salome from all the guards.

Nails dug into her skin, ripping her sleeves, her skirts. They yanked her down, bringing her down without mercy. They dragged her from her high place and brought her where she belonged.

She hit the ground hard, getting lost in the mud and feet and the hands pushing her lower. Rocks and other debris cut through her dress and scratched her skin. Blood dripped from new cuts and soreness all over her body promised bruises. Every time she moved to rise, they forced her down again. Desperately, she tried to turn, rolling onto her stomach, and hoping to scramble away.

She was ambushed. She was trapped.

They had her hair in their fists. They screamed and spat at her. They smashed her body into the ground, violent and relentless. All the combat she ever faced was nothing compared to this angry mob.

She wanted to weep. She wanted to scream that she was one of them, that she was nothing and no one. But they would never believe her. They saw her clothes, who she was with. Wealth and nobility. A target for assassins, a scapegoat for a child's death.

Let us help, a voice whispered. Smoke brushed against her skin.

Yes, she decided. *Help me. Please.*

They didn't respond yet she knew what they wanted her to do.

Eyes squeezed shut, she threw her arm up in defense. Her body surged with the feeling of fullness and energy. The fingertips of her raised arm tingled. The pressure of the converging bodies disappeared. At the same time, she was filled with a feeling of rightness. It was peaceful and soothing, like someone brushing her hair and humming a lullaby.

There was a *boom*, a sudden gust of wind.

And then, everything quieted.

When she opened her eyes, Salome inhaled sharply.

A shield hung above her. Formed entirely of shadows, but solid unlike a normal shadow. Smoke-like, gray extensions shrunk into the shield as Salome curled her hand into a fist, slithering like snakes. Salome drew her arm close to her chest and stood up quickly. The shield faded instantly. Her body shook violently, limbs unable to straighten. She still couldn't focus, couldn't figure out where to look.

It had taken offensive action and launched them away from her. Several people laid sprawled across the streets, blown back by some explosive force. Some cradled their bodies, curled into themselves in agony. They looked at her with fear now, keeping their distance.

She found Abel corralling the crowd, keeping them away from her. Fabian and Euria rushed to her side, urging her to move. Oscar was looking around, searching for the threat. Elias charged through the streets after the archer.

Cursed, she had to be cursed. This was what the witches wanted to tell her.

"*Witch.*"

She thought it was in her head, until it was spoken again.

"Witch!"

Immediately, she turned toward the voice. It was the man from earlier, the one filled with animosity. Whatever progress the witches made in gaining their trust in magic faded now. Terror was a noose and the words that followed tightened the knot and strung her high. These words condemned her and promised she would never return to the life she knew, whether she wanted it or not.

If the Alliance were unsure about her magic, they weren't anymore.

But would they keep her or kill her for what she was? There was no escape. The truth was out now.

"She's a witch."

Chapter Seventeen

Witch. Witch. Witch.

The word was a curse, ringing in her head, as Fabian lifted her onto her horse.

"Lady Rosalia, listen to me. You're fine. You're *safe*," Fabian kept assuring her. His voice sounded like Vincent's, low and warm and soft. It was the kind of tone one longed to hear when they were trying to claw their way out of a dark place, a light at a tunnel's exit.

She ought to have felt better.

All she felt was the crowding darkness. Shadows curled around her hair like silk ribbons. Her fingers twitched with the urge to physically rip them away from her. This magic was a curse, pulling her away from the Alliance and toward the witches. It forced her onto a dangerous path where she had no choices if she wanted to live.

There were no more doubts about what she was.

Her body was numb and beyond her control now, the brothers urging her to move with gentle hands. They shielded her from view but couldn't block out the shouting—all hate and fear, noise and chaos behind them.

Where was Abel? Her own guards?

She wasn't sure her safety mattered. Perhaps they got what they needed and were onto the next steps of whatever was planned. She wondered if they wanted to be rid of her, if they'd decided that she wasn't worth any trouble. She didn't know what was real, only what she was told.

You are nothing, and no one.

The words echoed in her head. Now, though, they collided with a new title: witch.

What did that make her now?

Oscar took her reins. All she could do was hold onto the saddle and stay low. Wind whistled by her ears as they escaped, the force pulling strands of hair from her braids. They charged straight across the expanse of grass and dirt.

Witch, they said. It wasn't a secret anymore.

There was no more pretending about this. No more acting as though something hadn't shifted in her when they arrived. The Alliance would surely kill her when they discovered she had no intention of becoming a new sort of tool to them. To use her face and her body and her talent for tongues was one thing. Her blood and abilities were something else.

How would they try to restrain her? What chains would they use on her now?

She couldn't stay or let them wield her as they willed. If she did, she'd never be free.

Her limbs felt weightless and weak. Her heart matched the rhythmic forward movement of the horses' feet pounding against the earth. Her life wasn't meant to be this way. She was only ever a con artist, a criminal, nothing and no one.

Witch, her mind corrected. *Witch,* the lingering shadows declared.

The witches had warned her, but not well enough.

As they raced to the castle, the brothers kept glancing back. No one followed. They didn't want her, regardless of who she was. All they knew was what she could do.

Witch.

It wasn't a surprise, but acknowledging it felt like waking up to a knife at her throat.

Though the sun hung lower in the sky now, it glared down at her, bright and accusatory. Mud and grime covered her sore body. Her skirts were torn, her sleeves darkened by dirt. All the court would see how the people turned against her, the future queen. But perhaps this could free her from the betrothal that wasn't truly hers.

A weak flickering of hope. The world wasn't kind enough to allow that.

Witches were not regarded kindly in the past. There was a long history of magic-wielders abusing their powers, often at the expense of the commoners. Salome didn't know she would be the one to remind them of their suffering at witches' hands. They had enough dark magic tormenting them.

The l'Issalya brothers and the Alliance yelled at each other along the way back. Curses and frustrations passed between them without restraint.

Abel knew. This horrible charade of cluelessness made the nausea rolling through Salome even worse. It felt like she'd swallowed some creature that now clawed its way up from her belly to the back of her throat.

"Elias went after them. He'll find answers," Abel said.

A second after his eyes met Salome's, he averted his gaze. Fear was never something he expressed with her, but now he did.

Oscar groaned. "Who were they aiming for?"

Feeling a gaze heavy as bricks on her body, Salome looked up. The younger brother shook his head, but his eyes met Salome's.

She looked at Abel and Euria. The latter shook her head, no answers to offer. But Abel set his jaw. Elias was still in the city. Maybe he knew who they were. Maybe that was who Abel intended to meet. He could have sent the signal to the shooter.

She wasn't safe with them.

All four witches were in the courtyard when Salome and her company arrived. A wall of bodies in formation, barring them from bursting through the front doors. They looked like harbingers of death in matching black gowns and menacing, half-skull masks made of onyx.

It seemed Maris heard the panic swarming Salome's mind like a hornet's nest. Her gaze set on her in an instant.

The fire witch offered one almost imperceptible nod.

We take care of our own. No one spoke the words aloud, but Salome felt them settle over her like a cloak. Warm and velvet soft, she leaned into the feeling. All the while, she stared up at the castle and its black walls streaked with gold. Was it a cage or a sanctuary now?

Godiva's hand flexed around a blade as she stepped forward. "She should not have left the castle."

"*We* were there to guard her," Oscar growled.

Abel added, "There were plenty of us to keep an eye on her."

Godiva drew herself taller, blade rising.

Oscar turned from her as he dismounted his horse, throwing the reins to a waiting servant. Abel's feet hit the ground at the same time, and he went to Salome's side. She gripped the saddle tighter and looked away from him.

"That isn't enough!" Della hissed. Maris held her back as Oscar shot her a glare.

"She's safe now," Fabian said. His eyes darted anxiously between his brother and the witches as he handed his horse off and helped Eulalia dismount. He turned to Salome, but she waved him away, her legs shuddering as her feet found the ground.

She lifted her head, searching for Maris, and silently pleaded: *get me away from him.*

"What happened?" Irene asked as she dismounted. "I couldn't see."

"It was incredible!" Eulalia said.

Abel glowered. "We learned something of Lady Rosalia, though it may not be wise to share such news with everyone."

There was a spark in Abel's eyes though. The corner of his mouth twitched, fighting off a smile. This was a look of someone who was plotting.

Dread placed her at the bottom of a frigid lake topped by a layer of thick ice.

"Do not speak of it," Godiva warned, gentler toward Eulalia. "Now is not the time—"

"That is not up to you. She is under *my* protection," Abel said.

Warning flashed in Maris's eyes, as threatening as a wildfire. "As one of ours—"

"May I see the king?" Salome interjected. "And change?"

Her guardians exchanged glances. Almost queen, but still powerless.

"She will come with us," Godiva decided. "You are soldiers, not guards."

"We would not oppose going together," Oscar said.

Fabian turned to Salome with a hesitant smile. He reminded her of Euria —easy-going and friendly despite the battle scars.

Godiva gritted her teeth, glanced at her sisters and back, then nodded. The witches must have wanted to send everyone away, as Salome hoped. How unfortunate they all failed in that. Irene and Eulalia stood aside. The latter looked eager to speak, but Irene squeezed Eulalia's hand and shook her head.

For now, Salome needed to escape the openness, pushing ahead to climb the stairs to the main doors. The rest of them followed. As she ascended the steps, a trail of mud followed. Salome ran a hand through her hair, all knotted and tangled from the rush of their return.

When the castle doors opened, Vincent was already rushing down the white marble steps of the grand staircase. But upon seeing Salome, he softened, shoulders sagging with relief.

She wanted to be comforted too, but her mind kept returning to the scene, the shadows hanging above her, the whispers turning to laughter. Even now, with sunlight streaming through windows and filling the entryway, the shadows sang for her. Salome wrapped her arms around herself.

The witches instantly positioned themselves like a barricade.

Maybe it was the fact that her own magic was dark, but Salome saw the possibility of empires crumbling if they sought destruction instead of peace and protection.

"What happened?" Vincent demanded.

More guards followed close behind him, fully armored in the same leather and iron and steel as Fabian and Oscar. All wore the d'Allorias sigil on their chests, following like the king's own bloodhounds.

"In private, please," Salome said. Too many eyes, too many ears.

Servants pretended to busy themselves with various tasks though they were straining to hear. Even some nobles began crowding the foyer to see what the commotion was all about.

Vincent approached and offered his arm. "Please."

She took it, silent as he led her inside. Along the way, he spoke quietly to a passing servant who ran ahead. Their combined entourage of guards followed. Amalia joined them too, walking a step behind with her face painted in concern.

Rather than taking Salome to her own rooms, Vincent led her to his. His guards positioned themselves around the doors, but Vincent opened them for her. She glanced back at the witches and the guards.

"We'll be here," Fabian promised. Abel and Euria nodded in agreement.

She ducked inside, escaping all these eyes and expectations.

His rooms were disorganized, as if a storm swept through. Books were strewn across tables. Bottles of paint occupied the remaining space on tables. There were several canvases propped against walls and furniture. Splashes of paint clung to surfaces—emerald greens, gleaming golds, blues as bright as the ocean. A spilled bottle sat on the floor beneath an obsidian table, the bold red paint spreading like blood from an open wound.

The world existed in dull tones, but his home was alive and vibrant against gloom.

This was not a bachelor's suite. This was an artist's studio.

"Welcome home," Vincent said.

For the first time in what seemed like hours, Salome felt safe.

Chapter Eighteen

A BASIN OF HOT WATER AND A PORCELAIN CLAW-FOOT TUB SAT under an arched window with stained glass that depicted a sunny day waited inside in Vincent's bathing chamber. A tunic lay across a chair for her, a simple navy-blue design with a black belt, along with trousers. A tray of bite-sized pieces of bread and sliced fruit sat on the small table beside the chair.

Vincent remained in the sitting room, leaving her with only Amalia to keep her company.

Salome focused on the ceiling as she wrung her hands. An artist painted a more abstract aerial view of Ellasya, as though they stared down at the city from a cloud. A dreamier interpretation in metallic and pastel colors.

"What happened?" Amalia tugged at the dress and yanked at Salome's hair, focused on efficiency before care.

Reluctantly, Salome relayed the events.

The water quickly darkened with mud and blood. Salome stole bites of food between scrubbings. Amalia tried to help, but she was too rough, too impatient. As exhausted as she was, Salome took care of herself. Her arms shook with the effort.

"What you can do—it's *valuable*."

Despite Amalia's amazement, Salome felt sick. She didn't want to reinforce her worth this way. She didn't want them to latch their teeth on her throat or brandish her like a blade. Especially now, when she found an escape route, and discovered she was more powerful than anyone realized.

"But the attack—"

The gleam in Amalia's eyes darkened. "That was necessary to ensure you knew that they wouldn't hesitate to deal with potential liability or reason for lost trust."

In some ways, the Alliance was predictable.

This job was still an important one and it wasn't over yet. Trust was a thin, wooden shield that could easily break once beaten. They wanted to know how hard they could hit.

Once Salome was clean and dressed, she called for Vincent.

Amalia exited as he entered, but not without casting a warning glance at Salome. The king's gaze was set on Salome though, as if only she mattered. Not for the first time, the intensity of the way he looked at her was disarming.

Feeling like she was on the ground with a sword at her heart, Salome waited.

His hands flew to Salome's face, her neck, her arms, touch wandering down until he reached her hands. He touched her like she was delicate, made of glass and already cracking. It made her feel more vulnerable and exposed, and rivaled the terror brought by the shadows and the Alliance and near-death.

Their bodies were more familiar now. A new bond forged by pressing themselves into a moment that forced them into intimacy and trust. It sped up this feeling of closeness and maybe they weren't in a place where they loved each other without condition or loved each other truly at all—but there was something possible. A flower bud ready to bloom if they continued the journey they started.

Finally, Salome managed a small smile that existed because of the spark of hope he provided. It was small, almost significant, but Salome saw it and felt it. All because of a man who didn't seem to care about her magic or her money or what she could do for him.

She was a person to him. A woman he could love, if he wasn't already starting to.

It was so ridiculous to hold onto that, knowing she was lying to him. But he lied to her too, and that made him a little more real. She forgot for a moment that she wasn't the person he thought she was.

Except for this tiny revelation that she had magic, exposed to everyone now.

He kissed her before either of them spoke a word. He pulled her close until his body aligned with hers. He held her like he thought she might slip away, pressing his lips to hers before trailing down her throat, before his hands too began to explore, as if he could hardly believe she was here. As if he relied on touch to confirm that this was real.

A thick leg snaked between hers, urging to use it, as he pressed into her. He squeezed and massaged her body before reaching into the trousers.

"Let me soothe you," he murmured.

And so she allowed him to touch her until she had to bite her lip at the sensations. He intended to distract her and she didn't mind it. He used his fingers to work her well as he kissed her, encouraged her to lose herself to touch and forget about everything but how it felt. She climbed up and up, breath quickening and body tightening until release came.

She came down slowly, eyes closed as she regained her breath. Vincent continued to kiss her throat before finding her lips again. She let him think for a moment that he was in control, that he alone could quiet a storm—but it was short-lived. All games had to end.

Finally, she grabbed his hands. "I am not fragile," she said, lifting them away. It felt like his pulse searched for hers when her fingers found his wrist. His heart in her grasp. "I am not about to break."

"Tell me what happened," he pleaded.

It wasn't a king's command. It was a soft request, a door open. *Trust in me.*

If she had to build something with him for however long they had, she had to offer him some truth. Some evidence that yes, he was in her confidence.

And so, she paced around the room as she recounted the day, only intent on avoiding naming the Alliance.

Salome hesitated before admitting to the shield, the magic she hadn't intended to enact.

An unsettling sensation of uncertainty coiled around her stomach. She felt like she was reverting to the little girl who felt like nothing but trouble to parents she adored who struggled to survive.

"Does it change anything?" she asked. "This... magic."

"You always have me as an ally." His eyes were kind, his voice like a soft caress of fingertips across her cheek.

Salome nodded but didn't have an answer for him. Didn't know how to make sense of the maelstrom in her mind and what she was supposed to say. She'd always been no one, nothing, not this. Stronger, more powerful, stranger and more unusual—and perhaps a bigger part in the world than what she'd thought.

There were no rehearsed lines for this moment.

Vincent cleared his throat and averted his eyes. "The witches warned me of the possibility before you arrived. You already know that they were waiting for you. It was not my place to tell you why. Not yet."

As she stilled, he lifted his eyes to hers.

Her feet remained firm on the floor. She balled her hands into fists at her chest.

"They told me you would not immediately understand."

Anger emerged, bursting from her chest with an explosion. "You *knew*?"

"A warning of awakening magic, not a full explanation," Vincent clarified, reaching for her. "I'd only known days before you arrived."

"Your future queen has magic. That must be wonderful for you."

She wondered if he thought it was fate, that the woman he'd chosen to make wife—the one he thought her to be—was a more powerful ally than anticipated.

"I would not force you to use it for any reason," he swore.

"How could they know?" Her eyes met his, finding sympathy where she wanted answers.

"That knowledge is not mine to bear. I wish I could help you more—"

Sal shook her head and raised her hands, palms outward as she took a step back. Without all the glamour and flair in her façade, she was a woman raised by criminals. She was accustomed to being used and played like an instrument, strings plucked, until she produced the right melody. A thief with a pretty face and a talent for languages. A girl raised into a woman who took advantage of the gullible, accustoming to stealing and seduction.

"What else do you know?"

His encouraging smile faltered and there was a flash of knowing in his dark eyes. Regret, too, like the first streak of silver in someone's hair.

He took her hands in his, setting her fingertips in his palm. The instant she traced the center line in his hand, lights flashed before her eyes like a bolt in a storm. Golden, at first, then red and blue and green. Golden again, before clearing to a battlefield.

In the image, she saw herself on the ground through his eyes before she saw him. There was pain in his eyes, blood on his face, and new bruises bloomed over his body. The suit of armor around him was dented and dotted with rust-colored splatters.

Before she could rip her hands away, Vincent placed a kiss on her knuckles. She felt his breath on her skin, his trembling exhale. If she was foolish enough, she could pretend that such emotion was real and belonged to her.

"Will you forgive me for wanting to spare you pain?"

"It hurts to know you hide important things from me," she said quietly, then added, "Irene said my father is missing."

The king searched her face, gauging her emotions as they passed like the shadows of clouds over a ship's sails on a windy day. She stared back at him, demanding answers and offering nothing in return.

"I have sent people out in search of him on land and sea. I hoped to find answers before breaking your heart, to lessen your worries." He spoke so softly.

Her stomach twisted with annoyance. He had no right to treat her like a child. She knew worse things than he'd could ever imagine. Her childhood was marred. Innocence vanished long before she first bled between her legs.

"Do not hide things from me," she commanded. Her voice broke, as she wished for something she didn't deserve. She was made of secrets and weaving them into a performance and yet she begged him for truth. It wasn't fair.

A woman like Rosalia would be frightened to the core about her father's whereabouts and well-being. He was the last of her family. She imagined herself to be a frightened animal, caught between fight and flight, ready to lash out in order to survive.

The fear in Salome was spawned by something more dire, more certain. When the Alliance came to make her into a tool, she needed allies, and she hoped it would be some as caring as this king. "I would rather know."

"But—"

Before he could continue with his rebuttal, Salome yanked her hands away to snatch the knife from his belt. She held it low, right to his guts.

Vincent raised an eyebrow.

"I fear for my father, for what might have happened or may happen. If you know anything, I want to know as well, and if there is anything I can do, I want to do it," Salome said. "He's all I have left. Promise me that you will share all you know of him."

Though she spoke of Baron d'Ilumias, it wasn't him she thought of. Her real father was still alive, she hoped, and he was the one who taught her to be brave. Without how encouraging her father was when she was young, she wouldn't have the strength to run away and leave them less burdened. It hurt to go, but she felt she had to do it for them.

And then there was Gabriel, not kind or loving but wanted her strong and raised her to be dangerous. Not someone soft or breakable. He expected her to stand and fight.

That was necessary to survive in this brutal world.

Her real family was out there, somewhere. To find them, she had to survive. She had to figure out a way to navigate the changes that were coming and escape before lies caught up to her. She'd do anything to get an advantage, to get ahead and go far, far away.

She didn't deserve honesty from Vincent, but she sought things she didn't deserve all the time. Usually, it didn't hurt this much, and she wasn't so afraid.

"You cannot threaten the king," Vincent said.

"He must know how serious I am," she answered.

He nodded slowly.

Before he could speak, Salome continued, "I can handle the truth, whatever it is. I am stronger and braver and more fearsome than you could imagine. You want a queen? You shall have one."

They stood there in silence that hung between them like an executioner's axe. Her breaths came heavy, while his remained steady. Smirking, he placed a hand over her wrist. It reminded her of their encounters in the night, of playing cat and mouse. Her skin was the night sky and this feeling was made of shooting stars.

And then with one hand, he yanked her close, making her stumble while his other hand came around her neck. She tilted her head out of instinct and began to close her eyes. Vincent gave her what she wished, as though she whispered it aloud.

He kissed her.

His lips were softer than earlier, less urgent but still heavy with desire. She parted her lips with a sigh, almost defeated, though he took it as encouragement. With the knife between them, this kiss held more danger than anticipated. He released the offending wrist to snake an arm around her waist, the hand on her neck climbing up to cup the back of her head.

Her own free hand gripped the spot where his neck met his shoulder. His heartbeat slammed against her palm, and she dug in her fingers, urging him closer. He kissed harder, more desperate, and she released a low sound of delight. She grinned when his tongue traced her lips before darting between them.

He tasted both sweet and salty, with a dash of mint. Her breath grew ragged as an aching need built up inside of her, golden hot like the sun and just as agonizing. She leaned into him, the blade threatening to burrow between their chests, and their kisses slowed, turning more affectionate. Too personal, unlike the ones she preferred.

When he pulled away, Vincent said, "From now on, no secrets and no need to threaten me to swear it on my life. I will be truthful."

He said it with such conviction that she believed he meant it.

"Please." The knife fell with a quiet thud to the floor.

All the while, she would uphold her own lies.

He stepped closer once again and offered a hand. "Come with me?"

She allowed him to hold onto her fingers, guide her out of the chair, then into the corridors.

He motioned the l'Issalyas and the Alliance guards to keep close without a glance in their direction. Abel and Euria looked to Salome for answers, but she ignored them. Messengers would come in the night to deliver the orders for how to proceed.

If Salome wasn't a tool, she was a liability. The outcome for either was awful.

The witches were nowhere in sight. She hoped they were close and were figuring out what they needed to do to separate her from the Alliance. Then again, she was raised never to trust others with her life.

If she wanted freedom, she could only rely on herself to make that happen.

Wordlessly, Vincent led her through the castle. She kept her head up. Rosalia was noble from birth, raised to believe herself better because of her bloodline and history. A woman like that had to be proud, especially if she had a king at her side to encourage her strength. She ought to be emboldened by such an alliance with the king.

The king led her to a large, rectangular room filled with soldiers. Bronze racks of weaponry covered the walls—swords, spears, arrows, axes, and more. Soft leather covered the floor, dark as soil, with glass windows on the ceiling spilling sunlight across the room. Wax candles that smelled faintly of sandalwood and pine lined the walls in single sconces, and yet, the scent of sweat persisted.

Images of learning combat in various Alliance headquarters filled her mind. A dungeon in a forgotten fortress, a new manor taken from someone rich, a tunnel under the city. A makeshift sort of place to practice and enhance their skills, not like this. This was for elite royal forces, for people like Vincent and the l'Issalya brothers.

Vincent brought her to a training room.

He released her hand and moved to the rack. His attention was set on the swords. There was no reason for him to hide his skills, unlike Salome. She wouldn't make a point to stay away from the daggers, but she wouldn't reveal how well she could wield them.

As he moved to the wooden weapons meant solely for practice, the room's occupants moved to the side. A show was about to begin and, this time, the king would be the performer. Training always brought her a unique rush and a distraction from life. She missed the sweat and intensity. She liked the look of excitement in his eye too, so boyish and eager.

"Do you intend to teach me to fight?" she asked, hands on her hips.

"If we intend to fight side by side, I'd like to be certain of your capabilities," he said.

Daggers, dirty tricks, and luck—that was how she fought. But he couldn't and wouldn't know that, not while he knew her as Rosalia. What she liked were the weapons used in close encounters. It was easier to hide the violence in an embrace.

"You like to fight?" she continued.

"I like to be thrilled."

Oh, that was a beautiful thing to say. It gave her a shiver of pleasure.

He threw her a wooden sword. As she caught it mid-air, making a slight show of fumbling, he claimed another one for himself.

"Do you know how to use it?"

"The basics," she said.

Still, Vincent made a point to go over what he considered the foundations of sword-fighting. Simple things like how to hold the sword, for starters. Maybe he wanted to hold her and move his hands over hers. *There was no need to make excuses for that*, she whispered to him when he bowed his head while explaining something, hoping to make him blush.

He showed her movements and stances, teaching her with more pleasantry than her previous teachers. While this wasn't her expertise, Salome held more advanced knowledge than this. Still, she let him explain what she already knew.

Salome lifted the sword. "Hold nothing back, Your Majesty."

This wouldn't be like their early card games, when he allowed her to win.

The king lunged, intending to take the first strike. She blocked it and grinned.

Back and forth, they swung at each other. Fearless, unrelenting, competitive all the while. When Vincent paused to apologize after scratching her arm, Salome attacked. Her movements were clumsier than intended, unused to the sword. But her mind quieted as she found comfort in this method of unleashing emotion.

"How do you feel?" he asked when their swords crossed.

Laughing, Salome replied, "Better."

He shoved her back and their fight continued. Her face was red with exertion, sweat trickling down her temple. He paused to watch it slide down her neck.

"Do you want a taste, Your Majesty?"

Their audience laughed. Vincent cocked his head and waved her toward him. She flew at him, sword prepared to strike, but he knocked it aside with ease. She tried not to grit her teeth.

Servants filtered in and out of the room, offering refreshments to spectating soldiers. Vincent interacted quickly with servants, passing them and giving instructions without losing his breath. At times, their swords crossed, and they shoved at each other, ruthless but playful. He held back but wasn't gentle. Though she sometimes lost her footing, he remained steady.

"Again," he commanded after each pause.

She loved this relentless side of him. In battle and in bed.

She threw herself into it. He won often, graceful with his weapon poised to kill. But he would always demand a kiss, and she would feign displeasure.

His brown eyes gleamed, becoming golden. His smile glowed. He was sweating and laughing, pulling her around the waist toward him if she wasn't careful.

Her heart pounded. Her lungs were bursting, gasping for air.

It would be easy to love him, honestly. Too easy to fall in love.

As they laughed and sparred, a servant girl entered the room and waited by the weapon racks with a tray of goblets. She kept her head down and stayed out of the way.

Salome pinned him against a wall with her training sword at his neck.

"I let you win," he swore.

"I hope not."

Suddenly, with their gazes locked, an image filled Salome's mind of a dark hallway. A creature laying on its belly, a body almost human-like, but too long with over-extended limbs and a torso twisted like a pair of trees entwined around each other. Black foam spilled over its shark-like teeth, two forked tongues darting out.

It rushed toward her, and Salome loosened her grip on the sword.

Vincent noticed the shift in her and nudged his leg against hers. Shaking her head, she mumbled an apology. He leaned back against the wall, lifting a hand to push strands of hair that had fallen over her eyes.

"What happened?" he asked quietly.

Visions. She was having visions, like all this new magic was rising like a quiet sea brought to life to by a storm. "Let's not discuss that now."

"Magic must be difficult to deal with," Vincent said.

He smiled at her, and she was about to speak, when an arrow flew past them and pierced Vincent's hand. Salome whirled around, eyes wide and searching for the source. The servant girl stood there, face unhidden, as a bow dropped to her feet. It was the same one who had spoken with Amalia on a few occasions.

An Alliance spy.

Unconscious guards slouched against the walls or sprawled across the floor, goblets around them. There was no audience anymore.

Salome only saw the servant girl and her two blades.

The daggers flew toward Vincent and Salome, fast as falcons flying for their prey.

Chapter Nineteen

SALOME'S ARMS SHOT UP IN A POOR ATTEMPT TO SHIELD HERSELF. Simultaneously, shadows gathered in front of her and formed a wall. Hands wrapped in tendrils of smoke emerged from the wall, catching the daggers, before sending them back at their assailant.

She felt their glee when the blades pierced the servant girl. One through the chest, the other through the stomach. A hundred voices chorused, filling her head with delight and disgust over the gore. She was safe.

But she just killed someone in full view of others.

She felt cocooned in the cacophony, suffocating. The world blurred, bordered by the fog-like barrier protecting her and the king. She couldn't find her voice, as if she'd swallowed it. She felt sick.

As if they understood, the voices became quieter, but remained unwilling to fade.

Blood poured out of the wound caused by the arrow in his palm as he removed it, grimacing. He tested the usefulness of his injured hand, or rather, the lack thereof. That bothered him more than the blood and the displeasure turned to disbelief.

All the while, Salome looked back and forth between the discarded arrow and his wound. Salome felt that pain once, two years earlier. An arrow had pierced her lower back, caught by a lookout before she could escape. A small, puckered scar remained.

Blood spread around the servant girl, the daggers still embedded in her body. A different assassin from the one in the village. She was clever enough to go unnoticed until the end.

Where was Abel? Or Amalia? Or any of the Alliance? Were they still here or did they leave her here to deal with this on her own? Had they known it would happen?

There was one attack earlier. Now, two in a single day.

Collapsing to her knees, Salome's hands shook uncontrollably. When she tried to breathe evenly, she gagged. The smell of death hadn't yet registered, but she was already imagining it—the excrements, the decomposing, the foul stench. She gagged again. It wasn't her first kill, but it was death wrought in a new way. Death wrung without her conscious control.

Her mind returned to the cards, the diamonds turning to bleeding arrowheads.

One arrow, two daggers thrown. Four more to fly.

She wanted to weep and scream.

The four witches entered, followed by Abel and Euria. Salome immediately lifted herself from the floor, dusting off her clothes with trembling hands.

Abel and Euria exchanged a glance. The Alliance warned her of the witches. Now, they watched Salome find reassurance in them. For a second, there might have been fear in Abel's eyes, as if she truly was beyond control now.

If that was the only good thing to come of this magic, it might be enough.

"We felt the magic," Della explained. She crouched in front of Salome, leaning forward with wide, worried eyes. "How are you feeling? That was pure, instinctive magic."

Half-numb, Salome mumbled, "I killed her, didn't I?"

I killed her, I killed her, I killed her. This horrible song played in her head. She'd murdered before, as was required for jobs, but with daggers and poisons and rope. What she'd done this time was like any other time before.

Della said, "It was an accident."

Lowering her voice, Salome said, "I know who sent them."

Maris glanced their way suddenly, and shook her head, then tilted it toward Vincent. This wasn't the place to speak of it yet. It had to be done in private. Salone knew enough of discreet gestures to understand what Maris conveyed.

Still, Della said, "We can talk about it later."

"My instinct is violent." And her magic was dark. Perhaps the witches wondered if it was necessary to fear her more than protect her.

"It was an accident," Della said again.

Maris and Thema were checking the king's wounds before anyone else. He came first, of course. Their blood magic bound them.

"Thema can draw out poison," Godiva said, standing behind Della. "She'll take care of everyone affected." Her normally stiff voice was sweetened with understanding. As if she knew how Salome felt, shuddering with sorrow and rage.

Maris and Thema pressed their hands over Vincent's, murmuring. Their gemstone necklaces slid forward, brushing against his body. As sunlight caught on them, the stones gleamed.

All the while, the shadows offered hushed, honeyed crooning. She wasn't strong enough to silence them. They were tendrils of smoke, slithering like serpents on the floor and around her.

"Can you hear them?" Salome asked quietly.

Della shook her head. "But I know how it is. The earth sings to me."

If anything, it was sinister, an ominous chorus.

Della's hands left Salome's hair, a tight fist held in front of her. When she opened it, a yellow rose sat on the palm. Touching it felt like it would tarnish the sweet gesture of friendship.

"Do not fear," Godiva promised. "As one of us, you will not endure this alone."

One of us. It sounded like both an accusation and a reassurance. This was what she wanted, right? To join them and leave the Alliance? To let them teach her everything they could offer?

Gentle wind whirled around Salome, drowning out the shadows. The shaking of Salome's hands slowed, but she didn't want to rely on others. "Tell me how to take care of *myself*."

"We will teach you to manage it, but it will take time," Godiva said.

This wasn't a skill she could pick up like learning a song in a new language. The king soon came over.

"Apologies, Your Grace. This magic is all but instinct. She shall need to learn how to control it."

"I will," Salome said. "I must."

"I trust you shall," Vincent answered, regarding her calmly. "But allow me to swear this to you, I will never be afraid of you or what you can do. You may not believe me, but that is the truth. Whatever you do, it will not change how I feel."

Their eyes met. It was too early for love and too much was feigned for it to be true.

"I told you before that I am haunted by what I have lost. I will not lose you too," he added.

Salome nodded and Vincent looked to the others. His smile faded, even as Thema helped them. They woke soon after she lifted a fallen goblet to their mouths. A glimmer of light shone in the drugged liquid inside, summoned from their bodies.

They still looked pale and green, eyes slightly glazed. A few looked at the witches with blame. But others murmured their gratitude.

As the unconscious awoke, Vincent redirected his attention to the dead girl. Salome hoped her Alliance mark was well-hidden, or removed, as was done to assassins in high risks situations. She felt the urge to touch her own branding, to scrape it away.

"Could she be associated with the archer in the city?" Vincent asked.

If there was a mark, no one would know Salome had one herself. The dead can't talk. Salome should be relieved, but she was horrified and ashamed. She killed her.

"Lucky girl," Fabian muttered. "Won't have to face the dungeons."

Those words earned him a harsh, silencing look from Vincent.

"I could have read her mind if she wasn't dead," Maris said.

"That helps no one," Della chided her.

Godiva sighed. "We will not find answers like this."

"Stay with Rosalia," Vincent commanded the witches and the l'Issalya brothers. Then, to the guards and servants, "Remove the body and clean the mess. Let's keep this contained."

When his attention returned to Salome, his eyes roamed her face. She tried to be impassive, to hide her terror. "Two attempts in one day, Rosalia, and we do not know why." With a soft smile, he assured her, "But you'll be taken care of, I promise."

Vincent tucked her head to his chest and stroked her hair. Her arms dangled awkwardly at her sides until she wrapped them around him. The warmth ignited a flickering memory of a long-lost mother's touch and a low lullaby.

"Thank you," she whispered.

"I hate to leave you, but I must. Please forgive me," he murmured. And then, with one last lingering look at Salome, he vacated the room with a swarm of guards.

Fabian and Oscar were among the unconscious. Abel and Euria were present now. There was a knowing spark in Abel's eyes, an awareness. How convenient that they weren't present. The dead girl was taken away, blood seeping through the cloth they'd wrapped her in and leaking onto the floor. A trail of blood formed on the path they took. A servant remained close to mop up after them.

"Come now, please," Della said softly, tugging on Salome's arm.

Salome covered her ears as they walked, trying to drown out the shadows' incessant whimpering. Suddenly, a low-pitched hum like mountain-top winds filled her ears, silencing all else. Godiva met Salome's eye and nodded.

Salome inhaled deeply. It was like walking through a garden, the scent of blooming flowers all around her from the candles Maris lit along the way. They wanted her to focus on sensations and meditate on that. She knew teachings were not always spoken. She let herself to be taught, to focus on what she heard and smelled and saw, rather than what was in her head.

When they reached her rooms, Abel opened the doors. Fabian and Oscar remained outside with the two of the Alliance guards. As Salome passed Gerard, he raised an eyebrow at her. She shook her head, nothing to say to him.

The witches entered first. Della stuck her tongue out at Fabian as she walked by, drawing a laugh from him. Maris cursed under her breath and pushed her forward. Thema kept her head down, while Godiva held her head high and shoulders squared, pausing to look each man in the eye before entering.

Oscar turned to Salome. "We'll be here if you need us."

"I'd rather not fight witches just to lose," Fabian muttered.

His brother jabbed him in the side with an elbow.

Abel had nothing to say.

By the time the door closed behind Salome, Della was filling an empty bowl on the table with yellow flowers. Della then bounded over to Maris, already stationed by the corner window.

"Leave us, please," Godiva said to Amalia.

Not even Leon was working in his room. Salome couldn't hear the clicking of his tools. And so, like the rest of the Alliance, Amalia was banished. Only the clench of her fists at her sides hinted at the displeasure beneath her placid exterior. Her silence, however, suggested fear. She wouldn't disobey when she knew she was powerless against them.

Salome kicked off her shoes and settled onto an armchair, her legs tucked beneath her.

Godiva and Thema took a seat on the couch across from her. Thema stretched her legs and raised her arms above her head, yawning dramatically, while her sister massaged her temples and closed her eyes. Around others, even Vincent, the witches were conservative with what they revealed. Not with Salome though.

"It's about time we did this," Maris grumbled.

With a sigh, Salome undid her braid. "I suppose we can't keep dancing around it all."

"Your magic calls to you," Godiva began.

"I think she got that much."

Della swatted Maris's arm and shushed her with a smile.

"You are a witch, and you are lucky, for you won't have to go through any of this on your own." Though Della generally seemed youthful and naïve, the wisdom in her eyes belonged to an old woman.

They weren't human. And, if Salome was one of them, neither was she.

Thema cleared her throat and nodded. "There is *so much* to learn, so many amazing and wondrous things. We shall guide you the entire way."

"My sister has spent some time gathering books for you," Godiva said.

"I'll bring them to you tonight," Thema said.

Salome, for once, truly didn't know what to say. Every rehearsal was useless. All her training and experience never led to this moment.

"We shall need to work quickly. There are demons unleashed in our world," Godiva said. "Ones born of darkness, awakened by magic with only the instinct to kill and destroy. There have been countless casualties in the last few years—too many, and more in Pavalla than Ilarya."

Della continued, "Only those who have light magic or dark magic can allow them to pass into our world."

Godiva and Della met each other's gaze like an unspoken conversation. There was a bond between them, different from the romantic one between Della and Maris, and between all four.

"It wasn't me," Salome swore.

Maris snorted. "Obviously not."

Della ignored them. "Someone awoke the light witch's magic and conceals her from us—from me. I can sense when an element witch is ready, when the buds of magic burst open and bloom. But for this one... I felt *nothing*."

Maris pressed a kiss to the top of Della's head. They leaned into each other.

Godiva continued, "The king knows you could not have caused any of this, especially since your magic lay dormant until your arrival."

"Not entirely," Salome admitted.

Della frowned. "You experienced your own magic before we found you?"

"A little bit."

Maris and Godiva exchanged a surprised look. Thema leaned forward with interest. A proud, vain part of Salome imagined this meant she was more powerful than anyone anticipated.

"Then I suppose you could say it's my fault more is happening to you now." Della smiled sadly. "It was only days after we made a deal with the former queen that I knew you were coming. Once we met, your magic awoke."

How whimsical she made it sound, like fate was wrapped in pretty ribbons.

"Is there a way to make it go away?"

Then perhaps Salome could disappear. The Alliance wouldn't chase her all over the world, especially if they thought her dead.

"I have the ability to cause... a hibernation of sorts for another witch's power. It is a last resort, though... a punishment," Godiva said. "I shall not do that to you."

Was it meant to be kind? Salome sighed.

Godiva placed a gentle hand on Salome's knee. "Manage your emotions for now, let us teach you, and help us find the light witch. We all have our own elements and our counterparts. The light witch is meant to balance your shadow magic."

"But someone has either taught her how to shield herself, or done it through blood magic," Maris said.

Closing her eyes, Salome asked, "But why *me*?"

"Why are we who we are?" Thema wove her hand through the air.

Godiva smiled. "Despite the long history of magic, we have yet to determine the meaning of it, or how one is chosen to have magic. Those like us with elemental magic tend to identify as women and there are never more than five at one time. Another takes our place once we die, and one with awakening magic like Della can sense us. Other types of magic are more complex and difficult to track."

"What we must focus on now is finding the light witch and turning her away from this destructive path," Thema said.

Godiva removed her hand from Salome's knee, leaving her feeling cold. She couldn't remember the last time she felt comfortable enough to seek out reassurance. It was always train harder, fight harder, focus harder.

"We cannot use magic to find her, though we have tried," Godiva explained.

"We help Ilarya and keep searching for her." Thema sounded so hopeful.

Salome paused. "And Pavalla?"

"It's a cycle," Godiva said. "A demon attack in Pavalla they blame on Ilarya, a battle, then a truce. Eventually, it starts again. Thus far, we know it all started in Ilarya, hence our deal with the king's parents."

Like the flow of ocean waves, the battles were inevitable.

"This war—it started during the time of the First Witch, and when a human queen divided her land between her two children," Thema said. "Royal pride keeps us here."

"We must focus on the present." Godiva cast a stern look at her sister.

Not long ago, Salome assumed demons weren't her problem. If she didn't think of it, it wouldn't matter. Now she had a part to play and a wedding to pretend to anticipate.

Her time was running out. She was here for almost a month now.

"What happens when the demons attack again?" Salome asked.

Godiva smiled sadly. "Then we go to battle."

Chapter Twenty

That night, a stack of books was left at Salome's beside table. Amalia tried to inspect them, but when she pried open the covers and flipped through the pages, all she saw were blurs.

Uncertainty flickered in Amalia's eyes. A flash of annoyance appeared too.

It seemed they didn't know each other anymore.

Their dynamic shifted like the earth had moved overnight, mountains trembling and waters rushing over the shore. She said nothing, jaw clenched. It felt like they had stepped backward in time to when they were two little girls fighting for attention from their leaders. Like they hadn't worked together, side by side, on countless occasions over the years.

It was a dangerous thing to become unknown. It was lost trust.

The only reason she wasn't already dead was her potential value to the organization.

"I can't stay there," Salome said once alone in the library with the witches. She sat on the cushioned bench by the stained-glass windows with Della beside her.

"Once you understand your capabilities, they will be afraid of you," Thema explained, already perusing the closest bookshelves.

The Alliance's fear meant they'd assert more control to keep her within their power.

"I still have a part to play, don't I?" Salome asked quietly.

A future queen, not a con artist. She rearranged herself, smoothing out of her dress—an elegant ivory piece with gold accents and sheer cape sleeves.

"For now," Maris said. "Until we can decide on what to do about...them."

The Alliance, Salome thought, and Maris heard. She nodded.

"What is our purpose here today?" Salome asked aloud.

"Sylvia l'Essalia has been informed of your whereabouts and will join you shortly," Godiva pulled a chair toward the bench and seated herself across from Salome. "We have some time before she arrives."

Thema leaned against Godiva's chair. "Time for a lesson."

Before anything else, they focused on breathing. Losing control of this natural function meant losing control. Regaining it enabled one to assert power over themselves and their magic again.

All magic was dangerous without proper control, especially that of the dark or light.

"I know how to *breathe,*" Salome argued.

"And yet we can all forget. Have you ever had such an attack on your body? When your lungs seize, and you can't seem to catch your breath? You panic and it feels like you're dying so you panic more."

"It feels like your heart is going to burst the longer it goes on and, eventually, that inability to breathe properly will lead to losing sensation in your fingers and toes, before spreading through your body."

"If that doesn't scare you, then you don't understand," Thema said. "And as witches, we cannot allow ourselves to lose control like that."

Godiva paced around them, like a guard on patrol duty. "Do you know what happens if I panic? If I infect the air around us? Or if Maris becomes a living beacon of fire? What if Della is so overcome she causes the earth to tremble and split open? And Thema—though the cleverest of us, even she can become overwhelmed. What if her uncontained magic sucks all moisture from the earth or from human bodies?"

They could perform shows and little tricks to impress their audience, but it was nothing compared to what damage they could do.

"Your magic is young," Della said. "You don't know what you're capable of."

"No one wants to discover what evil you could conjure," Maris added. No sweetness to coat the truth of the danger. Salome didn't need them to be nice. She only knew being pushed to her limits, ensuring she was at her best.

Salome knew how to slow her heart and quiet her breath. She learned how to move without making a sound and to stay so still that it seemed impossible she was anything more than the shadow of a statue.

And yet, the day before, Salome lost control.

"Will this really help?" She rubbed her arms, trying to smooth the goosebumps rising on them because of the uncertainty buzzing under her skin.

With a sigh, Godiva nodded. "When you find your lungs fighting against you and your magic pouring out too quickly, I hope you will remember this lesson."

For nearly an hour, the witches went over the breathing techniques each of them preferred. Sometimes, it worked to close their eyes and count ten steady breaths, starting over if one wasn't smooth. Or perhaps they'd imagine filling up five goblets with five steady breaths. It was about the focus, the stability, the succession of each breath after another.

Sylvia soon found them hidden in their pocket of the library. If she found it strange to see them seated in a pentagonal formation, she said nothing of it even as she and Salome made their way into the corridors.

"I suppose you heard what happened," Salome said.

Sylvia shrugged. "Everyone has."

Nobles didn't bother with discreet gossiping. Perhaps they were still deciding amongst themselves how to feel about the recent events. They were free feel what they felt until the king gave his command. He said nothing so far.

"Let us take a different route then," Salome decided.

That earned her a suspicious look. "Are you looking to cause trouble?"

Salome smiled and took her away from Rene, linking their arms and heading to the meeting rooms. The l'Issalya brothers intercepted them along the way. They trailed behind since the witch circus wasn't there to keep an eye on Salome and she kept her distance from her own guards. She hoped the brothers kept each other on their best behavior, at least until she accomplished what she intended.

Maybe if she hadn't shown Ellasya that she had shadow magic, someone would have interfered before she interrupted the king and his councilors. No one stopped her when she banged on the doors of each room, pushing them open until she found the one in which the king was hidden.

As she stormed inside, Vincent stood. His eyes were lit with amusement. "Is there something wrong?"

"We have important matters to discuss."

"Right this moment?"

She nodded. "This meeting is over. You may continue it later."

It was the duchess, Irene, who stood up and offered her spot to Vincent's right. Salome grinned at her and murmured thanks as she took her seat. Irene patted her cousin on the shoulder, then set about ushering the others out of the room.

"Am I expected to leave as well?" Sylvia asked from the door.

For a second, Salome considered it. "As you wish."

"Farewell for now then." She swept away without another word, shadowed by her guard. As always, she appeared to have no interest to remain in the king's presence, no matter how much he'd cared for her in the years since her father's execution.

Vincent sat down, watching Salome like he half-expected her to attack.

"They are at your command," she reminded him, gesturing to Fabian and Oscar.

"And I am at yours."

He motioned for them to leave. She leaned her arms on the table and smiled, sweet as a girl with good intentions. He leaned back, folding his arms behind his head, and waited. They stared at each other for a long moment.

"You are not avoiding me, are you?" Salome asked.

"That was never my plan," he said, but paused. She didn't like the look in his eye. "Our situation has changed, however. Spies will surely send word to Pavalla of what happened."

He didn't yet know that the Alliance would be saying something as well.

"And you suspect them of the assassination attempt?"

"It is a possibility."

She inhaled and prepared for betrayal. Vincent waited until she was ready to speak.

"One of my men did not return with me from the city. I now have doubts of trusting my own guards and companions."

With those words, she gave up her place with the Alliance for good. She put suspicion on them, purposely. He wouldn't know who exactly they were. To be cautious of them was enough.

And his choices might reveal his loyalty to her, as Rosalia.

"Where would you prefer to be?" he asked. "With me?"

His mischievous smile made her throw back her head and laugh. Surely, he didn't mean it, but that didn't matter. It could be charm, or a sign he truly cared.

"No, the witch circus seeks to protect me. They also intend to be my instructors and ensure that I do not cause any trouble with my magic." She shifted in her chair, still uneasy. Things changed. She was more than a girl, than a liar and a thief. More than the king's betrothed. More than human.

He nodded thoughtfully.

"Will you make time for me?"

"I will do my best," he said.

Though she wanted to believe him, she didn't. Still, Salome smiled. "Do not allow me a moment to miss you, Your Majesty."

He took her hand and kissed her palm. "No need to worry about a thing."

She didn't believe this either but nodded.

"I shall have your belongings brought to the witches' rooms."

"Thank you, Vincent." Before she left the room, she turned back to him. "I understand why you did not warn me. I feel no anger toward you. I'm simply afraid that we will grow distant when it should be the opposite."

Without giving him a second to answer, she slid out into the hallway. The advisors, apparently, refused to venture far and lingered in the corridor. Whatever they discussed was too important to wait until later, even if the king dismissed them. Salome smiled sweetly as they parted to allow her through.

"Go, rejoin the king."

They obeyed, to her delight. A spark of power that danced at her fingertips. Power was never something she craved, but it did feel good. Riches would be better, yet that remained out of reach. She was escaping from her rooms with the Alliance, only to be guarded by witches.

All she could do was hope she made the right choice.

Chapter Twenty-One

By nightfall, everything perceived to be her belongings was brought to the witches' rooms. They were secluded on the far end of the castle, away from distrusting nobles, with access to a tower that enabled them to see all the way to the city.

Their rooms had a tapestry with a map of the world, stitched only with black threads, outlining land and water. None of the nations were named, nor were there any defined borders. Some of these places she'd seen herself, traveled by ship and walked the streets. Yvette had her sitting in taverns and at ports, listening to conversations and picking up languages along the way.

It was cozy here, a home. There were quilts made from fabrics that could have belonged to old cloaks, as well as plush pillows made of silk, satin, or velvet. Every soft surface was stacked with them, some ruffled or tasseled and all sorts of excessive.

"The pillows are all Della," Maris explained. "She likes to be comfortable."

"And they are the epitome of comfort," Della said.

It was a little nomadic and a lot of fun—and something only accomplished with money. Maybe they were richer than she realized, a result of their work around the world. Blood bindings and financial rewards must enable the possibility of a lavish life.

Or it was time stretched so far that made it easy to grow wealth. When one lived longer than the average mortal, what were the limits?

Maybe working with them wasn't so terrible or terrifying. Maybe it was another path to the life she wanted: comfortably rich. Wealth meant being able to do anything and go anywhere and be whoever she wanted to be. Wealth meant she was free and no longer bound to debts or worrying about affording the necessities.

A new life—it felt like a dream.

Smiling, Salome plopped herself onto a pile of cushions and cocooned herself in a blanket. Then, Salome looked up at the ceiling. It was painted gold, a little gaudy but suited to the castle.

"You look like you belong here," Godiva said from where she sat at the dining table with Thema. There were candles all over the surface in various stages of melting. It smelled like sugar and vanilla, reminiscent of a bakery in the early hours of the morning, preparing for the day.

Salome raised an eyebrow. "A new member of the witch circus?"

"That requires much training," Godiva said. "Years of practice."

"I'm a quick learner." She'd picked up new languages within a handful of months. She learned mannerisms and accents to be over a dozen different people. To be part of the Alliance, it was essential to be quick and useful. Useless things were discarded.

"Magic can be easy because it's half instinct, but what we do with our performances? There's more than you realize."

"Some skills require more time," Thema added. "Muscles don't appear overnight."

She had some, but not enough. Not like the bulky soldiers in the training room, or anyone who lifts themselves up with only rope wrapped around their wrists. Salome could scale buildings. She didn't have the strength to support her weight on a single vine like Della did, especially not for a long time. And though she knew she was brave, dancing around fire was much too dangerous for anyone without control over flames like Maris.

"Did he have everything brought here?" Maris asked.

"I believe so," Salome answered. Chests full of dresses and jewels were stacked in the corner. The Alliance didn't need these things. With her, at least they were useful.

"Well, then the king would like you to have a few more belongings," Maris said.

As the words left her mouth, there was a knock on the door. Salome got up to answer it. There was a messenger waiting, a box wrapped in silk ribbons in their hands. They stood staring straight ahead as if they were afraid of looking any of the witches in the eye, including Salome.

People distrusted the witches already. How would they feel about one who controlled the dark and had a criminal past?

"A gift from His Majesty," the servant announced and offered the box to her.

Smiling, Salome accepted it. "Send him my thanks."

"Yes, my lady." The servant bowed their head, then turned and hurried away.

Once the door was closed, Salome turned back to the witches. Vincent already had jewelry brought to her on multiple occasions: diamond necklaces, bracelets with topaz beads, rings that looked like flowers molded out of gold.

Each gift was an apology for being late, or not being there at all.

There was no apology, no indication of when she'd see him next.

She got him to do what she wanted, separating her from people who would use her and abuse her. With his help, she now stayed with the witches to be protected and trained.

He said it was fine and he wasn't afraid, but where was he?

Salome set the box on the couch, then sat beside it. Her fingers itched to pull at the ribbons, the greedy side of her that eager to hoard expensive treasures. Before she came here, she would sell them off herself to add to her repayment to the Alliance.

Once she plucked the ribbons apart. the lid of the box came off easily. Another necklace sat inside. At first, it seemed like a simple gold band that would hold tight to her throat and clasp at the back, but there were details upon closer inspection.

"What is it?" Della peered over the back of the couch.

"Don't state the obvious," Maris called before Salome could answer.

"A gold necklace with engravings that make it look like a tiara under the right light." Salome never saw anything like it.

Her contacts were all through Elias, but she could have new buyers. Who would resist something like this? One of a kind, gorgeous, elegant—something fit for a queen. The trouble would be navigating a market that was, for the most part, controlled by the Alliance.

"You know you don't need that life any more, right?" Maris asked. She came to Della and wrapped her arms around the smaller witch in an easy embrace. "No lying, no stealing—"

"I'm still pretending to be someone else," Salome said.

"It isn't necessary with us."

Salome shook her head. "What if someone heard these things? You can't simply listen to my thoughts to discover all you need to know?"

If it worked like that, why all the questions? All the urging? Unless they needed Salome to open to them willingly in order to understand her. She didn't know where to start. There was too much to unravel from the knot that was this life.

The four witches collectively sighed.

"Consider your priorities," Godiva said. "Our most immediate concern is your control over your magic. We will deal with the Alliance should they take action."

"And the king?" What would he do when he discovered she wasn't Rosalia?

The witches exchanged some looks. Godiva spoke up. "We must ensure he sees reason when the truth comes out. Your role in the balance wins over his laws."

But he was bound to his duty to uphold the kingdom's laws. No exceptions.

Maris added, "He'll have the full truth one day. He needn't know everything now."

"If you can only offer one thing today, let it be your name," Thema said softly.

Slowly, Salome turned to meet Maris's gaze. The fire witch nodded.

My name is Salome Visaya.

Only Maris could hear it, and she smiled in approval. "Focus on the good you can do and trust that we can accomplish our task, so long as you are with us, Salome."

How strange it was for her name to be uttered by someone outside of the Alliance. It felt like she was stepping out of one world and into another.

At the very bottom of the box, Salome discovered a note. It was tucked away like a secret, like he almost did not expect her to empty out all the contents to find this little message.

This is only the beginning, Vincent wrote in his elegant scrawl.

It felt like a promise, something she could truly have for herself.

Except that wasn't true and there were more important matters than her infatuation. He had a kingdom to rule. Though she temporarily evaded the Alliance, Salome had a new world of magic to explore, a light witch to find, and demons to eliminate.

Focus, the witches said. And she would try.

This thing between them had an inevitable end, and it was nothing compared to what they both had to do for this world.

Chapter Twenty-Two

It was the first of a parade of gifts. Little things, mostly jewelry. Rings, bracelets, necklaces, sun-like earrings, and star-shaped hairpins. None of them had the personal touch of the deck of cards that Vincent had given her a month and a half ago.

Which was mostly untouched until the witches decided that it might benefit Salome to practice using them. They hoped her magic could reveal what was to come.

The stack sat in front of them in a neat pile.

Most times, her touch did nothing. Images didn't shift. Visions didn't appear. She saw nothing but the cards as they were made, nothing strange or unusual. It took hours of groaning over failed attempts before Thema designated herself as Salome's instructor.

"It's exciting," Thema said.

Salome frowned. "You can control inanimate objects. It looks like the same ability."

"No, it's different. Watch and see. We'll draw out *your* magic and then you shall be impressed." Thema beamed. Her teeth were bright as the moon against the night sky. "We're going to go over different types of readings."

"How many?"

"Ones that require a minimal touch of magic, and some that demand very much."

Thema showed her different arrangements of the cards. A simple reading of three cards, with varying answers depending on the question posed by the person being read. Some arrangements were pyramids, or an elaborate web-like formation. A single card was even an option for the simplest of readings, should there be limited time.

"Some can read cards without your gift," Thema said. "Though the interpretations are different. They must memorize every card and what it might mean on its own and in combination with other cards."

How lucky Salome was, Thema said, to hear the cards as storyteller, to see the images shift at her touch, to simply hear and see. That was her gift: simplification of a story.

Attention, intention, and expectation.

Those three things determined how her magic presented itself. The more she paid attention to the everything around her, the better she could recognize the specifics of what needed to be done. With an understanding of what she could and would do, she made her intentions clear. All she needed to do was focus on them. Then, she needed to know what she wanted to happen and how. Her expectations would ultimately affect the outcome.

All of it left very little room to allow one's mind to wander. The loss of focus could lead to magic going terribly wrong. Not just flowers blooming in the wrong shade of color, or fire failing to build to more than a flame. It could be water turning to poison, or the air becoming toxic. It could be light so bright it made the skin blister and burn, or darkness that latched permanently onto the eyes.

Salome tried a single card reading and received the King of Hearts. There was nothing at first, no change to witness.

"Imagine what you saw before," Thema suggested.

Eyes closed, Salome tried to remember. She never had the gift of visualizing the world in her mind, but that moment of awe was hard to forget. The first thing that came to her was the look on Vincent's face, his shock and uncertainty, a flicker of pain. Then she remembered his eyes, how they softened upon meeting hers.

When she'd first held the card and it changed, her hands were steady. This time, they shook. There was no strange sensation and she heard nothing unusual, but it felt as though there was a breath at her ear whispering *look*.

She opened her eyes.

The card displayed Vincent, partially turned away from her.

A change, but nothing significant. Salome dropped the card with the rest and sighed.

"Magic is attention, intention, and expectation. It's what you make it," Godiva said.

There were those three words again. Salome rolled her eyes. "I'm not sure what I'm supposed to expect."

Only a few days had passed, but her head already felt like it might burst with all things she'd learned. This was only the beginning. She dropped her chin onto her hands and stared at the cards, pressing her palm to the image, and willing it to return to normal.

"Your mind is blank. Ask a question," Maris commanded.

"Like what?" Salome asked.

The fire witch shrugged.

There was a scream of annoyance in Salome's throat. When she swallowed, it felt like a heavy rock sliding hesitantly down her throat. They were supposed to be helping her, but perhaps she was waiting for a direct command when the solution demanded creativity. She could explore ways to make it work. To summon magic and bend it to her will.

"Be patient," Godiva said.

What is your true image?

Salome didn't speak the words aloud, but she glanced briefly at Maris, who nodded. Yes, she'd heard. Now she had to focus. Her eyes returned to the card, and she mouthed the question again, still not making a sound, speaking to the card.

It flickered, blurring like it was in movement, until she narrowed her eyes and concentrated on visualizing the original illustration.

Soon enough, it came into focus, but slowly.

Too fucking slowly.

This wouldn't work. It needed to be faster.

She couldn't focus when she could hear the countdown in her head, the clock reminding her of how much time she had until the con was meant to end.

A month and a half had already passed. She was more than halfway through the time she expected to be here with the Alliance. Would the end of this charade have a wedding or an execution? It felt like the latter no matter how much the witches assured her that it wouldn't happen.

The Alliance would decide what to do with Salome long before then.

Keep her or kill her—she wasn't eager to find out.

Thema sighed and shook her head, seeming unable to understand how hours upon hours of lessons might be frustrating. Learning, to the water witch, was the most exciting thing in the world. It was fun to sit around and read and absorb information. It was, apparently, exciting.

Not to Salome. She itched for movement.

She wanted to see what her next gift might be. It hadn't arrived yet. Surely, Vincent wasn't *that* busy with whatever his advisors tossed his way.

"Do you need to find him?" Maris asked. "Staring at the door won't summon him here."

Annoyed over losing the secrecy of her thoughts, Salome shot her a glare. Maris, however, had already redirected her attention to setting the firepit ablaze to warm the rooms.

"One of us might go with you as a precaution," Godiva said.

"I'm not a danger to myself or others."

"Maybe, maybe not," Thema whispered ominously, peering over the book she now held.

Salome crossed her arms. These last couple of weeks, Fabian and Oscar were there whenever the witches weren't, standing guard like loyal servants to the crown even though she wasn't yet the queen and never would be.

It didn't matter that the entire kingdom now believed she had magic. To them, she was still Rosalia d'Ilumias, the innocent daughter of a baron. They might have seen her and Vincent in the training rooms, but they didn't know about the skills she'd picked up with the Alliance.

Salome smiled as she opened the door. "Don't worry about me. My guards are perfectly capable of keeping me safe."

Fabian offered an arm to her. "Where are we headed?"

"To the king's rooms. I am certain he will be overjoyed to see me." She only hoped he was there. Having to hunt for him through the castle again would drive her to madness.

"Don't be long," Godiva said.

With that, Salome took Fabian's arm and Oscar closed the door. It was a quiet walk, the halls cast in a low light from the cloudy day. Sunset loomed close and servants were beginning to light the sconces to flood every room and corridor with candlelight to keep demons at bay.

"Have there been any attacks lately?"

Though Fabian seemed uncertain, Oscar had no qualms about answering.

"In the kitchens, last night, there was an appearance. No one was seriously harmed, though. The staff are learning to keep them away."

Salome said, "The witches said nothing about it."

"As they are currently focused on you, my lady, they made sure our court physicians were capable of attending to any injuries caused by the demons," Oscar explained. Though he sounded confident and sure, he kept a hand on the pommel of his sword.

Was it a habit or a remaining sliver of fear?

Those scars on his body couldn't have all come from battle. Some looked less like cuts and more like bits where his skin melted, then struggled to heal smoothly.

She asked no further questions. Wherever the demons vanished to, they weren't bothering her now. All she could see were shifting shadows and eyes peering at her from the dark.

Not her imagination, not like she once thought.

At Vincent's door, the brothers stepped aside, and Salome took the honor of knocking.

"One moment," Vincent called from the other side. A bit distant, like he was far away. There was a bit of rustling and heavy footsteps before the door opened. He looked somewhat frazzled at first, his brow furrowed in confusion. As he took in the sight of her, however, he brightened.

"Did you grow impatient?" Vincent asked, grinning.

Salome slipped past him, and the door closed behind her. Then, they were alone. The urge to grab him by the collar of his shirt sifted through her briefly. From the look in his eyes—dark and slightly dazed like he was in the grips of a daydream—he debated the same thing.

"Perhaps," she said, and sat in an armchair.

He sat on the armrest beside her, quiet and contemplative, but unable to keep his hands away. He touched her hair as if admiring silk ribbons, then trailed his fingertips along the side of her face. So feather-soft it gave her goosebumps and chills. Her reaction made him smile.

The curve of his lips reminded her of how it felt when he'd kissed her, the way he'd laughed against her mouth or captured her moans with his tongue. Salome crossed her legs in hopes of stifling the feeling that began blooming between them.

"Were you planning on coming to see me?" she asked.

"Of course."

"Then you took too long."

Another man might have been offended. Vincent laughed. "There were some matters that required more time than expected. I promise I had not forgotten you."

In approval, Salome grinned.

"However, we ought to discuss a matter concerning your staff," he began. The serious expression he now wore worried her. The pause didn't help either. He was thinking about his choice of words, how he wanted to say things. "Your handmaid has been loitering around."

That wasn't surprising. Annoying, but that was all. They wouldn't stay forever and, eventually, they would confront her. She'd tried to avoid the Alliance as much as she could, but they were still here.

There was unfinished business. Loose ends to tie up.

The Alliance cleaned up after themselves, even if they left chaos in their wake.

"Remaining with the witches may be in my best interest and I wouldn't want my former staff to suffer because of that," she said.

There was some truth to it. This was her staff, after all, or Rosalia's. It was her duty to determine how to proceed. If he thought it necessary, he'd intervene. He had that authority.

"Perhaps they could assist the castle staff," she suggested.

"If that is your wish."

Salome nodded. "Now that's out of the way, tell me that you have more gifts."

He shook his head and chuckled, bringing her hand to his lips and laying a kiss on it. Though he'd done this so many times and pressed his lips in far less innocent places, Salome couldn't help but smile. He was sweet. But this damned king made a fool of her. She wanted him too much. Craved him.

Desired him. Heat washed over her like wild ocean waves during a wicked storm.

It was so ridiculous, she was almost tempted to yank her hand away.

"I do have something for you," he admitted, releasing her hand then escaping to another room. His bedroom, she thought, catching a glimpse of navy-blue curtains hanging on a canopy bed as well as some clothes on the floor. Only his, thankfully, considering the colors and fabrics matched his usual attire.

A couple minutes later, he re-emerged with a small basket draped in a fuzzy, cream-colored blanket that seemed to move.

"What is it?"

Vincent approached slowly. "Let me show you."

And then he lifted the blanket. A tiny ball of black fur was inside, curled into a crescent. As she cooed, the little thing lifted its head. Enormous, golden-yellow eyes blinked sleepily up at her, and her heart was stolen.

He brought her a kitten.

"Does he have a name?" Salome asked, her voice soft with reverence. In awe.

Vincent set the basket on the ground. "That is yours to decide."

The kitten mewed and clumsily clambered out of the basket like it didn't yet know how its limbs worked. Then, seeming to give up on trying to walk gracefully, it rolled onto its belly and swayed back and forth. It froze suddenly, like it remembered there was an audience, and looked at Salome. When she crouched and stretched her hands toward it, the kitten hurried over and nudged her palms with its little head. Her heart must have grown three sizes in that moment, and she couldn't help but coo with delight.

It was so sweet, so small. A fragile little fluff that head-butted her again and again until she scratched behind its ears.

"A boy, I think," Vincent said. "Only a few months old."

So kind, so cruel. Forcing her heart to make space for more. She didn't know she could love a thing so much without even knowing it. She picked up the kitten and held it to her chest. He licked at her fingertips and purred.

Oh, the kitten purred so furiously, it seemed he certainly loved Salome too.

Lucky, that's what she was. This was good fortune.

"Fortune," she said. "That will be his name."

Vincent smiled and nodded with approval. "He's yours."

Salome placed her new kitten back in the basket and stood. She stared at Vincent for a moment, then launched herself at him. He laughed as she gripped the sides of his face and pressed their lips together. Again and again, she kissed him and kissed him.

And a little part of her dreamed that this could be real.

Chapter Twenty-Three

Wherever Salome went, eyes followed.

The nobles seemed unsure of her now, nodding and murmuring greetings as they crossed paths. Many of them would glance back and then there would be whispering.

"Could it be possible that now everyone is more wary of me than they are of you?"

"That could be a good thing," Sylvia said, her face expressionless. "When they seek friendship, they want something from you. You cannot trust that anyone is genuine."

"You are highly optimistic."

Sylvia turned her attention to the shadows on the ground. That day, they sat at the edge of the fountain located in the courtyard. Movement surrounded them, messengers from the castle and the city coming and going with various bits of news and entertainment. There were very few nobles around, though, all of them hiding inside. Some of them could be seen peering through gilded windows, watching the two young women with unconcealed curiosity and judgment.

All Salome wanted was some fresh air and time to plan her next nighttime trip. It felt like ages since she was able to creep around. She didn't even need to steal anything.

Still, an idea crossed Salome's mind that perhaps if she had enough gold, she might be able to satisfy the Alliance enough to get them to leave her alone.

Wishful thinking, really. Her magic was certainly worth more.

From the corner of her eye, she spotted Elias and Euria watching her from afar. Rosalia's once protectors were sent on patrol with the royal guards and soldiers, almost always away from wherever Salome intended to be that day. Amalia, too, had a new assignment as one of Irene's staff. Vincent took Salome's suggestion seriously and ensured they were occupied.

Now the truth was out, there was no need to hide. She could sit here in the courtyard, utterly exposed to attention, and practice what the witches thought might help her.

"Am I supposed to see more than a little rabbit?" Sylvia asked.

Shadow puppets. How exciting. Such a mundane task that Salome imagined the witches were teasing her about how little progress they think she made with her magic over the last several days. Yet, when Sylvia asked that question, Salome lost her focus, and the image of the rabbit lost its shape and turned to a dark smudge on the ground.

She frowned and wiggled her fingers.

The smudge shuddered a little bit, like a leaf rattled by a breeze. It began to shift, then became more defined until it very clearly became a horse. With a wave of her hand, the horse began to gallop over the shadows formed by her and Sylvia's skirts, as if the curved lines were hills to run across.

Grinning, Salome asked, "What else?"

"Give the nobles a bit of a scare. They could use one."

Poor girl, so bitter and resentful.

As Salome's hand flattened against her thigh, the image of the horse dissolving instantly. Then an idea struck her, and she lifted both hands, cupping them together as if trying to catch rain.

Smoke-like shadows drew toward her. They swirled together and twisted around like a serpent flicking its body around in anguish and agony. Then began to take shape. Salome narrowed her eyes and silently pleaded with the shadows to obey her.

It wasn't as easy as she thought. She could feel Sylvia's eyes on her, but the other girl didn't say a word. Sylvia always held back or said something vague, unusual, or bleak. She was here, at least, and felt more like a friend than anyone else in this black marble cage.

"Attention, intention, and expectation," Salome whispered aloud.

"Is that how they teach you magic?"

"It sounds silly coming from me, doesn't it?"

"Quite," Sylvia said.

"Well, it should work. Allow me to focus."

That hadn't been a challenge when it came to physical activities. She was excellent at picking up tricks from the Alliance, copying movements shown to her for quick, quiet pickpocketing of all sorts of things. She mimicked the combat training positions and moves like she was a mirror. Magic, however, was different. It felt like making something out of nothing. It felt like trying to grab a handful of smoke.

Salome returned her attention to the puff of shadows above her hand and set to craft an image of her new kitten.

Slowly, the shadows started to solidify. As if it wasn't smoke after all, but fur.

Maybe, if magic was a conversation, she only needed the shadows to listen.

She always heard the shadows, and sometimes she responded. Whispering in the dark, her voice and theirs. It used to feel like a little girl's imagination playing tricks on her. Not anymore.

She begged them to play along. To create.

And the shadows decided to accept the game.

A miniature of her kitten formed in her hands. A silhouette, rather than a solid figure, light as snow. When the shadow-Fortune looked up at her from where it curled in her palm like the real one did on its cushioned bed, it blinked hollow eyes, instead of golden yellow.

"How cute," Sylvia said.

The shadow cat suddenly disappeared, extinguished like a flame. A bead of sweat rolled down the side of Salome's face.

"It was a safe choice." Salome crossed her arms. "No one wants to see demons."

But as she looked at Sylvia, she realized the other girl's face was locked in an expression of horror as she looked at something behind Salome. Sudden fear rushed through Salome like a flash flood. She almost didn't want to turn around, but her curiosity won over, as always.

A tall figure swayed like silk in the wind. Its limbs were bent unnaturally though, and its hands had fingers too long and too pointed and dagger-like.

The shadow creature opened its mouth in a wide, mocking smile split its blurred visage in half. It had teeth like needles, long and pointed and pitch black like the rest of it.

Around her, there were screams.

"Demons!"

The courtyard erupted into chaos. People inside the castle rushed to the windows, drawn by the commotion. Salome's heart beat furiously in her chest, so powerful that it felt like it would explode out of her. But as she looked upon the creature, she realized it couldn't be the demons. It was day, the sky clear blue without a single cloud to disrupt the expanse of color.

This wasn't a demon.

This was her own magic.

She knew from the tightness of her muscles, the weight on her back, and the feeling of strings at her hands extending to the willowy figure. It felt like it did when she'd held the false cat, like she was still exerting power.

If her fingertips twitched, the figure trembled.

"Somebody get the witches!" someone cried out.

Fabian and Oscar drew their swords. Salome stretched out an arm, wordlessly commanding them not to move.

"Did you do this?" Sylvia whispered.

It was either horror or amazement in her voice.

The shadows cackled with cruel delight, and Salome wondered if they were a manifestation of her true soul. Blackened like rot, naturally wicked. She flexed her hands, stretching her fingers to far it felt like rope was pulled and pulled and pulled until it was so taut that it finally snapped.

The creature exploded in a thin cloud of dark smoke that dropped to the cobblestones, settling like a harmless fog, before dissipating completely.

Salome felt a heavy gaze on her like she carried an unconscious body on her shoulders. Glancing around, she eventually found Irene and Amalia standing in the main doorway. The former had one hand pressed against the archway, the other held over her heart. Amalia, however, had her hands clasped daintily in front of her.

When their eyes met, Amalia smirked.

It sent a chill down Salome's spine. The witches might see potential in Salome, but the Alliance already owned her, and she'd only become more valuable to them.

That look told her that they would not let her go.

This reprieve wouldn't last forever.

Dread settled in her stomach like an anchor in the sea, and she stood, ready to confront Amalia. A hand then came over hers. Salome nearly yanked her hand away before she realized who it was. The ward didn't offer a smile that might be considered comforting. Her expression was blank, and her touch was barely there, more like a feather on her skin than fingertips.

"They are afraid of you."

Sylvia referred to the nobles, the ones gathering around the courtyard in clusters with royal guards and their entourages forming a protective shell. They whispered to each other, not bothering to conceal the beginnings of gossip about the future queen.

Rosalia d'Ilumias, powerful but dangerous. Betrothed to the king and perhaps the downfall of the kingdom. It was too easy to imagine the terrible things the nobles might say.

"There's no need to be," Salome argued.

"Let them be frightened. Now you know they will not seek to get in your way."

People feared the Alliance and the power they could exert. It hadn't extended to Salome. This wariness was different. It meant eyes on her rather than averted gazes.

Everyone was truly watching her now.

There would be no running.

Chapter Twenty-Four

It wasn't long before Irene sent a messenger to request a private audience with Lady Rosalia. Her job as an advisor to the king enabled her access to all sorts of information and privileges. She always knew what was happening in the castle. But she was also there.

No matter how much Salome tried to remember Irene's expression, her mind returned to Amalia. That threatening smirk, the looming danger.

The walk to the meeting room was a long one.

Nobles stopped walking when they noticed her, moving to the side to watch as she continued ahead, trailed by Oscar and Fabian. All conversations ceased in her presence. Perhaps they were scared that her shadows could mimic the demons, if she wasn't the one to summon them herself. That was dangerous.

That could have gotten her banished—or executed.

She wasn't worried, though. She knew what she was guilty of, and it wasn't demonic.

If she needed a reminder, she found it when Amalia tried to approach her. With a shake of her head, guards ushered the red-haired woman aside.

"Keep her away," Salome told Fabian the other day. "I don't trust her."

The brothers obeyed her command without question.

She needed her magic to be stronger, a weapon and shield more than a trick or illusion. She had to make use of it and she had to learn to do it quickly. Every second of the day, she practiced. It strained and exhausted her, but there was no time. The only option was to be relentless.

If they came for her, she had to be ready to defend herself and fight.

"I can promise no one is bringing out pitchforks," Irene said without looking up when Salome entered the room. "On the battlefield, maybe, but not to our door."

Papers were scattered across the mahogany table, parchment rolls covered in drawings and scrawls. Irene leaned over them with her brow furrowed in concentration. It appeared very business-oriented, like the duchess was examining the state of the nobles' affairs.

"Wasn't that a concern already?" Salome asked. "After the situation in the city."

Irene sighed. "That was also a problem. This time, however, I refer to the nobles."

"Ah," Salome said with a single, solemn nod. As she smoothed her hands over her satin skirt, she considered her next words and sat down. "They thought they understood me. Now they must reevaluate."

Unlike Vincent, the duchess didn't take the seat at the head of the oval table. Instead, she seated herself somewhere in the middle.

Curious, Salome peered at the documents, the criminal in her gathering intel.

"There's a dispute between two families about the contents of a will," Irene said quietly and scratched some cryptic notes on the edge of a roll of parchment. Like a secret language meant to record her thoughts.

"I thought you wished to speak with me," Salome said, leaning back in her chair.

Though she hoped she looked nonchalant, she was going over her options —keep Irene on her side, ensure the king observed the Alliance, figure out how to reveal the truth without being beheaded.

"Oh, truly, I do." Irene lifted her head to reveal a desolate expression. "Vincent often takes care of these matters, you see, but he is not around."

"I have seen very little of him as well. He has sought my forgiveness through gifts." Far too many. Eventually, she would decide what to do with them. Selling them was her best option, but that would draw unwanted attention to her activities.

Right then, Salome even wore one of the bracelets Vincent gifted her during his absence. All those meetings and trainings, yet he made time to prove he thought of her. She toyed with the bracelet, then lifted her wrist to show Irene the little bauble that showed up at her door that very morning.

Irene squinted at it. "That is not an heirloom. He must have commissioned it."

If it had been someone else, Salome would have cackled. But this was Vincent and the thought of him trying to decide what he wanted for her, only her, and planning with jewelers made her blush. She couldn't resist smiling as she held up the bracelet to the light. It was simple: a thick, rope-like chain with three knots and diamonds lodged between them.

Irene resumed her work, crossing out scrawls on scraps of parchment and underlining a few things on the official documents. Somehow, she'd come to a decision and discovered important facts made permanent by ink and an illegible signature.

And then she moved onto the next pile.

There was no fun or adventure in re-reading documents and making notes. Besides, Salome's handwriting was terrible if she wasn't mimicking someone else's. For some reason, her own writing ended up looking slightly chaotic, as if she couldn't decide what to be.

"These are royal duties for you to look forward to, my future queen," Irene almost sang. "I know it all looks tedious, or perhaps intimidating if you are one to loathe sitting still in contemplation, but it can be rather… restorative, I might say. A meditation of a kind. Some days, I find it calming."

"Now that, I find hard to believe."

That made Irene laugh. "You discover interesting details about the court, if anything. Think of it like gossiping, except here, you must read between the lines to find the secrets."

She pointed at a paragraph in a new document. Salome followed where the duchess indicated, reading about a knight's living situation with recently awarded new lands. He sectioned some of it for his servants and commissioned a new building to house them.

"All this work is to please his lover."

"You discovered that simply by reading this?" Salome wondered, almost awestruck by the duchess's attention to detail. Her tongue felt stiff with the formal way she spoke as Rosalia. With Irene, however, she felt the need to talk and talk if only to keep up with her.

"Well, I cheated a little. I know the man. He's a romantic," Irene said with a grin.

They gossiped a little more about others, laughing between revelations, and stopped only when thinking they heard someone. Fabian and Oscar remained stationed outside, hopefully unable to eavesdrop.

"It's important to know about every person in this castle. Take dear Sylvia, for example—we used to be neighbors. Her family's estate was beside mine, near the Pavallan border. Though we aren't friends anymore and she'd lost her status, it's essential to know anything you can."

Salome nodded, but Irene wasn't finished.

The sunlight seeping through wide-open windows gave Irene a glow, and yet her voice darkened. "You ought to be careful around her. Girls like *that* are more volatile than you might imagine. She cannot be trusted."

Salome wondered if the same could be said about Irene. "Could I trust *you*?"

The duchess had a plethora of knowledge about the kingdom and its people. She could easily grab for power, and maybe that made her enjoy all the work Vincent hadn't been able to do.

Irene raised an eyebrow. "You don't think I'm genuine?"

"I have been warned to assume no one is."

The duchess laughed. "Well, I cannot argue with that."

It seemed an hour or two passed before Irene finished her work. She cleared her throat and set all the parchment aside. "Now, for the reason I called you here—"

"Are you allowed to summon me once I ascend as queen?"

Irene laughed. "No, unless you allow me that privilege. Though, let's be clear, I did not summon you; I *requested* your audience. You honored me with your presence." She leaned back in her chair, folding her hands in her lap.

Salome squirmed as if she was in an interrogation.

"How are you feeling?" Irene's voice was slower and sweeter. Usually, she was like a lightning strike, sharp and quick and impossible to pin down. "It cannot be easy after all that's happened."

"No, it is not."

"One of your guards claimed that he went off to follow your attacker. We have since kept an eye on him, as well as the rest of your staff. I also heard that you asked Vincent to keep them away."

"I do have suspicions," Salome admitted quietly, jaw clenched.

"It is not that we do not trust you. Vincent has made it clear time and time again that he has full faith in you," the duchess rushed to say, hands up in surrender. "Our concerns lie with your staff and the likelihood that they have betrayed you. It is not uncommon, especially when rising in power. After all, that is why Vincent keeps me close. Any distant relative could seek the throne should he abdicate or... worse."

"Becoming royalty is a hazard to one's well-being," Salome intoned. It was something she'd rehearsed with the Alliance if anything went wrong. That could even be a failed assassination attempt that she had to explain away.

"Exactly," Irene agreed. "And that is unfortunate. You are rising to power and there are many who are unsure of what to think of you. The other nobles... well, they are not all forgiving. You frightened them."

"With the shadows?"

"And the servant girl who died."

"That was an accident," Salome insisted.

"And the demon you conjured?"

Salome dropped her face into her hands and groaned. Even she was terrified by the thing her shadows became. "It was more of a puppet that looked like a demon."

"And yet it seemed out of your control," Irene said softly.

"No one would have been harmed."

No matter how much she trained to become Rosalia, no one would be able to prepare her for this situation. Even if the Alliance suspected she had magic, it seemed unlikely that they imagined it to be like this.

But maybe Salome needed to become something terrifying, if only to keep herself same from them. The more she thought about people fearing her, the more she wondered if it wasn't so terrible after all. People might leave her alone if they thought her too powerful to fight and they had no one with magic to rivals hers on their side She didn't want to be dependent and rely on anyone's protection. The stronger she was, the less she'd need to.

Irene's amusement now resembled pity.

"We will protect you and ensure the people believe in you as queen," Irene began, placing a hand on Salome's shoulder. It was warm and very light.

Hesitant, maybe. "We must ensure the witch circus remains with you, teaching you control."

In the many days following the incident in the city, that was exactly what happened. She learned much about the history of witches and their attempts to conquer the world, only to cause chaos and summon natural disasters. She knew about her shadow magic, and the counterpart in light magic, and how these types could be the most dangerous because of how the world needed balance in those two things. Not elements, but essentials.

"I am doing the best I can with everything I have learned thus far."

Irene nodded. "We understand and we are with you."

How often had Salome felt alone? Like there was no one to defend her or protect her, other than herself? Now, not only did she have the witch circus, she had a king and his top advisor. She had his friends and his family and him.

She only wished all this was for her. Not Rosalia.

Salome crossed her arms on the table and laid her head on them like a pillow. "You would make a better queen than I."

She was in this masquerade for almost two months already. She was still searching for her escape and desperate for it. At times, it felt like all she'd accomplished was transferring her dependency on the Alliance to the witches.

But she couldn't allow someone else to have such control over her life. It was hers, after all, and she would never again be anyone's puppet. The Alliance would be out of her life soon enough. The witches could teach her and train her, but they could not decide how she lived.

Irene shook her head. "That is not a burden I wish to bear. Let my cousin hold his crown and keep it far from me."

Throughout Salome's training with the Alliance, the thing they always taught her was to look for the route to winning. Staying here, still pretending to be Rosalia... that wouldn't let her win. But her greedy side wondered how she could keep all the things she loved here: the jewels, the witches, the magic, the romance.

If he wasn't a king, would they have stood a chance?

Would he have chosen her over duty?

She looked down at the bracelet on her wrist and was tempted to rip it off to toss it away.

Chapter Twenty-Five

A city cloaked in darkness. Fire that burned black and smelled like sage. Air so thick, it felt like inhaling water. The sound of screaming.

Shrieking.

Someone pleaded for their life.

Salome jolted up in bed, sweat beads dripping down her cheek like tears. Her chest rose and fell in heavy movements, her heart pounding and her lungs seizing with panic. It was a dream, a nightmare. Here, in bed, she was safe and the images she witnessed weren't real.

She couldn't see herself in those dark visions and yet it felt like she was the source of chaos despite never wishing for such power or mischief.

The bedroom door opened slowly. Della peered inside. "Are you alright?"

"I need a moment." Salome's voice sounded feeble and sad.

"Can I sit with you?"

Salome sat up straighter, pulling her knees to her chest, then patted a vacant spot on the bed beside her.

Della climbed onto the mattress and kneeled in front of Salome. Maybe this was a mistake. The wide-eyed stare was a little too much for this evening.

"Eventually, you will have to tell us more about you."

Nodding, Salome said, "A little bit at a time."

"Is it a lot?"

She didn't know how to answer that. "Maybe."

"How about how you became Rosalia?" Della suggested.

It was a gruesome story with details even Salome didn't know. She didn't want to know because it never mattered to her. All she needed to know was that the real girl was gone and wouldn't get in the way of the Alliance's plan.

Lady d'Ilumias was dead along with her son before the Alliance got involved. The baron was at sea in the beginning. Now he was likely lost beneath the waves. He hadn't come home nor had interfered with their scheming. Certainly, he would have learned of his daughter's betrothal to the king.

"They killed her, and I took her place," Salome said simply.

A minute passed.

Della didn't blink. "Is it that simple?"

Of course not. "Yes."

"Are they going to kill you too?"

Salome paused before answering. "I don't think so."

"We wouldn't let them."

As if someone brought out the sun after days of darkness, Della smiled brightly and opened her arms. At Salome's hesitance, she wiggled her fingers and nodded encouragingly.

Salome crawled over and accepted the embrace. The earth witch was easily enveloped by Salome's arms. Della even nuzzled in close and sighed happily.

It was like a protective shield around a child, but Salome wasn't the savior. Nor was Della. It felt like a surrender and Salome found that she didn't mind it so much. There was still much to accept. This was a step in one direction and nothing more. It was only that thinking that calmed her.

"It isn't so bad to ask for help," Della whispered.

"I'd rather not."

"Think about it."

Salome didn't agree nor disagree. They sat in silence, holding onto each other, listening to how they breathed. Deep inhales and exhales, slow and steady, until it felt like the tight coil of her body loosened.

"If you cannot sleep, perhaps it is time for some work," someone said from the door.

Reluctantly, Della pulled away and they both looked to see who interrupted the moment. The other three witches stood there, half-smiles on their faces and sleep clinging to their eyes.

Soon, they were all dressed and wandering the castle grounds. In the dead of night, there was a slight chill that ruffled the foliage in the garden and the flowers in pots stationed at doorways like inanimate guards.

Salome dressed in her thief's clothes, as suggested by the witches. Perhaps they understood her preferences for attire to blend with the dark. It felt more like herself.

"Where are we going?" Salome whispered.

Maris stretched out a hand to the empty corridor and extinguished half of the candles. Shadows cast immediately over sections of the floor, creating an obstacle course of light and darkness.

"Tonight, we're going to call upon the demons," Godiva said.

Salome reached for her daggers, but she hadn't brought them. No blades would be used tonight, she was told. She could only use magic.

"While they remain in our world, we must be ready for an attack from any direction. You need better control over your magic, and we need to make that happen now," the wind witch continued.

"We don't have much time," Thema added.

They stood in the shadows for a stretch of time that felt like ages. Her skin itched like there were bare branches scraping at it during a walk in the forest. Cold sweat dripped down her back, born from a nervousness she'd never admit to feeling.

Days went by without a word of the demons. They were still around, somewhere.

Salome shuffled her feet across the tiled floors, looking up and down as if she might spot them lurking in a corner. There was nothing but darkness. The shadows swirled around their ankles like affectionate serpents. Hissing and calling her name, they almost seemed malevolent. At least now she knew they were harmless to her.

"Control them," Thema whispered. "Make them still."

Salome stretched out her hand, extending her fingers as far as they'd go. She half-expected her bones to crack from the effort. At first, nothing happened. Staring straight down at the shadows at her feet, she silently pleaded with them to listen. They hummed a song that made her think of starlight, but that wasn't what she wanted.

"Don't ask. *Command*," Godiva urged.

She squeezed her eyes shut and curled her hand into a fist.

This time, she didn't ask or plea or beg. She didn't hope or wonder or wish.

She told them, without speaking a word, to be silent. She told them to listen and obey.

All the shadows went motionless and quiet, lifeless again as they should have been.

Thema took Salome's hand and squeezed it. She was proud. This was progress.

Perhaps she could hold her own when it was time to fight. Another battle was bound to arise. Her readiness was essential. She would not be in the field and ask to be protected. She would be there to fight, compelled to be there by some unseen urging. Something telling her that she had to go.

Like there was something waiting for her.

"Are we just going to stand here and wait?" Salome asked, keeping her voice low.

The shadows were twitching now, becoming as restless as she was, though she wished to hide how she felt. Magic made things more visible. Even her fist loosened.

Maris shrugged. "Do you want to go further?"

The witches weren't afraid, so they split into two groups. Salome remained with Della and Godiva, while Thema and Maris went another way. This exercise was meant for Salome to practice her magic.

If being around certain people helped her improve, then they would focus on that in her lessons until she grew accustomed to having a bit of an audience.

"Should we try the dungeons?" Della asked.

Godiva shook her head. "Let us try the courtyard."

And so they ushered Salome along, pushing her toward open skies and fresh air. She was in awe once she stepped outside, tilting her head back immediately. It was a bright night with stars dotted across the darkness and a half-moon shining in silver. So beautiful, she smiled.

Her father had tried to paint pictures with the stars, crafting shapes by connecting the lights and weaving tales about Tala, the goddess of stars. A daughter of a god, one of three goddesses who ruled the sky. Salome never knew if he made up all the stories or if they were real myths from Villasayas.

"You won't find the demons there," Godiva said.

"Look ahead," Della added.

Salome crossed her arms and looked across the cobblestones in search of movement. There wasn't any, not even the sway of shadows. The trees were still, too.

Unusually so.

"Something is out there," Salome whispered.

Della nodded. "I feel it too."

What could her earth magic do here and now? At least with the shadows, Salome could create anything that came to mind. Godiva could blow down a house with one strong breath if she wished it. But against the shadows? She only saw how Maris fought them.

"If they appear, is it up to me?" Salome asked. Her mouth felt dry, and her throat itched. She longed to claw at her chest to remove the invisible weight on it.

The witches didn't immediately answer.

Her body shook, and she didn't understand why. Fear was something she overcame countless times. Fear was natural when the Alliance plucked you from the street and raised you among criminals. She pressed her hands against her middle in hopes that it might stop the nausea rolling through her.

Slowly, Salome began her retreat. She backed up toward the doorway, ready to race through it to douse herself in candlelight. Her bed was calling her, even with the nightmares that might greet her again.

"Calm yourself," Godiva said.

"I will, but—give me a moment."

That was all she needed. With their permission, she bolted with no direction in her mind. All she needed was to run, to feel her heart pound and lungs seize with labored breaths, but in a better way. Active, not afraid.

When she finally slowed to a stop, Salome didn't know exactly where she was. It must be somewhere of little importance, somewhere she never needed to traverse in the night.

"*You.*" A whisper behind her, a masculine voice she instantly recognized.

Salome whirled around, tucking her mask over her face before she faced the king.

"What are you doing here?" Vincent was so serious, all business with a hand hovering over his sword.

"I have done nothing wrong." She held up her empty hands in surrender. The only weapon she had on her was tucked into her sleeve, a needle-like blade. "No crimes shall be committed by me on this night."

"Then what are you doing here?"

"Simply seeking fresh air."

There was something about seeing him in the night, dressed like this, that brought butterflies into her stomach. It felt like restless wings fluttering inside it of her, eager to escape. She lowered her arms and walked toward him.

By the time she was a mere breath away from him, he began pulling his sword from the scabbard. Salome placed her hand on his, pushing it down. This wasn't the time for a fight. He exhaled slowly. Despite the bit of light illuminating the corridor, she couldn't see him clearly and that was good. That meant he couldn't quite see her either.

If he did, he might recognize her. Though she wore a mask over the lower half of her face, she hadn't hidden away her eyes. And now they were locked with his. Near-black meeting a smoky quartz brown.

"We're not fighting."

"Then what do you want?" he asked.

She answered truthfully, "I don't know."

It had been a while since they'd been this close. Her body remembered every intimate moment, heat rushing through her in response. She looked at his eyes, his lips, his hands.

They stood there without saying a word. He allowed her to remain near. She couldn't help herself, reaching for him once she found a bit of courage. She placed her fingertips on the side of his face, tracing his cheekbones and jawline.

Touching his mouth was taboo. Though her fingers twitched, desperate to know how they felt, she couldn't get her to hand to stray close enough. Her arm fell limply to her side. They wouldn't stay like this forever. These moments were born in the dark and stayed there. The dark where the shadows woke up from their short-lived slumber, called by her pounding heart and her blooming anxiety.

She took a step back.

"Please, let me be. All I wanted was a walk."

For a second, she didn't think he'd agree. That sense of justice and righteousness in him might have forced him to deny the request. After all, despite not committing a crime this time, she did it many times while she was a guest here.

"Just this once," he said.

There was another moment of quiet that unsettled her.

"And? There must be more," she said.

Vincent shook his head.

"Tell me."

He clenched his jaw. "Go. That was what you wanted. I shall not follow."

"No, I'm curious now. Do you feel the same that I do?" Salome took a step closer. Her heart thundered.

He answered with silence and a gaze that traveled the length of her body. It was a slow, appreciative journey. As he looked upon her face, she lowered her eyes, only to notice his hand rising as if he might touch her.

Salome leaned toward him.

If he looked long enough, he'd see every familiar thing about her. That he knew who she was and that he'd touched this body before. Intimately, hungrily. She licked her eyes and savored the memory.

"There is something," he said.

His arm dropped and he flexed his hand.

Without warning, Salome surged forward and somehow Vincent was prepared. Her hands gripped his shoulders while his latched onto the sides of her head. They pulled each other close, stumbling toward the wall. Their lips crashed together so intensely, Salome instantly lost her breath, but she didn't care. Her mouth moved over his, enjoying the feel of it. Her tongue darted out to catch a taste and his lips parted.

When she met his tongue, she almost groaned. Kissing him was paradise. It was all she wanted to do from now on. She kissed him like it was the only time she'd ever get to, fierce and passionate and almost ready to cry. She never wanted it to end, but it would. It had to.

If they continued, he'd remember. He'd feel everything he'd already felt on her body. Her mouth, her hands, the curves that he had gripped nights before. Heat continued to bloom, and she needed to extinguish it before she was too alight.

As she pulled away, she commanded him, "Do not follow me."

He couldn't even if he wanted to. That hand she'd pressed to the wall was trapped there, his own knife from his belt stabbed through the sleeve of his fine shirt and lodged into the wall. He could escape, but he didn't seem the type to tear apart his clothes unless out of desperation. How wasteful of a tailor's work, especially considering the quality made for a king.

Laughter swirled in his eyes instead of anger. A lazy smile graced his lips, and she placed her own on them one last time with her gauzy mask in between. A second later, she raced away to be swallowed by the shadows.

She was running faster than she did when she and Vincent encountered the demons. Unaware of direction or destination, she kept going. Legs pumping, feet flying off the ground.

All she thought was to go, go, go—and forget that unforgettable kiss.

Salome thought she was free, nearly back to her rooms. And then she collided with Amalia. The sight of her was alarming, not only because Salome didn't expect to see her, but because they were a mirror image of one another. Both wore their dark leathers, masks over their faces, holding themselves in a defensive stance.

"What a coincidence," Amalia said.

"I don't want trouble."

"You cannot avoid us forever," she began. "Or forget why we're all here."

For money. For greed.

All the gifts she'd received over the last several days came to mind. If she stayed with the Alliance, remaining in her rooms with them, each of them would have a replica by now while the real one was off to the black market. Instead, Salome hoarded them for herself,

"They're coming. They will not give up until they get to you, dead or alive."

It was a promise.

Chapter Twenty-Six

On the day that marked one month until the royal wedding, Salome woke up to banging on her doors and raucous laughter. Her guards were out there, failing to interfere. She even heard Fabian's faint chuckling.

When Salome opened the doors, she found Irene waiting impatiently there with Eulalia, wearing matching linen gowns of green and gold. A peace offering in the form of a plate of ensaymada, soft and sweet bread topped with sugar and cheese, in one hand. Four other girls stood behind them, dressed in plain dresses of silver and gray, hair plaited neatly with their heads bowed in demure respect.

"What are you doing here?" Salome asked, crossing her arms. She narrowed her eyes at Fabian. He averted his gaze, cheeks reddening.

Irene grinned. "Tonight is the masquerade."

Salome winced. She'd forgotten.

A feast was scheduled, with dancing to follow and a great number of people both highborn and lowborn in their best clothing. Hundreds upon hundreds of barrels of wine and sweet mead. She and Vincent were the only ones to be unmasked, dressed in gold for prosperity and happiness. Everyone else would conceal their faces. Since she arrived in Ellasya, the kingdom's best seamstresses made multiple visits, measuring her, and inquiring about her preferences. Usually in the early hours, only for a few minutes at a time, especially since Amalia always quickly shooed them away.

Vincent was responsible for all the poking and prodding she'd endured. Vincent, who remained absent and distracted, though he continued to send gifts. One evening, he even sent a set of pauldrons to her rooms. Silver and rose-gold, delicately engraved pieces of armor, and a perfect fit on her shoulders. She couldn't find them this morning, though, when she was taking stock of her belongings. Thieves were tricky, as she knew from her own crimes, and it was essential to keep track of where things were.

For tonight, Vincent sent a delicate, golden circlet. Perfect for a queen.

Her guests forced her to sit, poking and prodding at her. From sunrise to sunset, her skin was pinched, her hair pulled into elaborate designs.

Irene and Eulalia simply sat back and laughed. Their process was shorter and simpler. It took no time at all to ready them in their matching aquamarine gowns.

All day, she sat in front of the mirror, transforming into someone regal and mysterious. Her eyes were outlined in kohl, more obsidian than smoky quartz. Her hair hung to her waist, loosely curled. Gentle hands placed the dainty circlet from the king on her head, white gemstones cut like the moon and stars in the front, surrounded by golden vines and flowers.

The seamstress brought in Salome's gown, and she stepped into it. It hugged her body but flared out at the hips. Long cape sleeves hung off her shoulders in glittering gold fabric that trailed across the floor.

Salome twirled for his guests.

"Queen Rosalia d'Ilumias!" Irene applauded.

Laughing, Salome waved them off dismissively. Excitement bubbled inside her, filling her with frothiness. She didn't notice the twitching of her own fingers at first, not until she saw movement from the corner of her eyes.

The excess emotion made the shadows stir. The excitement she felt roused them from their calm and now they wanted to react. Her guests hadn't noticed. They were too occupied giggling to each other over something that Salome couldn't her. There was choral humming occupying her attention, twisting around her giddiness and contorting her thrill.

She closed her eyes and focused on her breaths.

Slowly, she inhaled, then exhaled. Once, twice, and thrice more, until the fluttering in her stomach slowed. As she looked around, the room had returned to normal. The sound of quiet conversations came clearer.

Breathing, apparently, did work wonders on magic.

As the sun descended and the moon rose, Salome finally stepped out of her rooms.

Though she no longer had Amalia at her side, she could hear the other woman's voice in her head, reminding her to behave. To dazzle the king and the crowd, but never forget who she truly was—*nothing and no one.*

The Alliance had lost their leash on her, but they remained, like ink stained on her skin.

She spotted Amalia lurking nearby, a secretive smirk on her pale lips. She saw the castle fill with new guests and imagined half of them to be members of the Alliance.

Waiting for the right moment to act.

Fear hung onto her like fog before a rainstorm. She'd reminded Fabian and Oscar to ensure her staff were kept away from her, but there was only so much they could do. Maybe the Alliance wanted her on edge to ruin it all herself.

There would be a party, but she wouldn't fully enjoy it with this dread.

The castle was transformed. All candles were lit with flames swaying like dancers. All the marble polished, gleaming like crystals. Banners hung from the ceilings, gold, and silver and white, the metallic threads shining and shimmering in the torch light. The chandeliers had tassels with tiny bells attached to some of the threads, jingling faintly.

In the throne room, dozens of people crowded inside, all dressed in their most decadent attire with matching masks. Generous swaths of bold fabric adorned each guest, some in romantic reds and orange sunsets and jewel tones. Some matched with their partners. Some were single and wore more muted colors.

"Rosalia!" the king called out and stood.

The crowd parted for him. Silence claimed the room, conversations dying and music fading. She found Amalia in the crowd, still dressed plainly but still present. There was a goblet in her head and a pin in her hair that must have been a knife.

She did nothing but raise her drink in a quiet toast.

Salome would not do the same. She turned away, as if she could truly ignore what was bound to come at any moment.

The shadows began to lowly hum a song that only she could hear, ominous yet eager.

Vincent walked toward her. As everyone watched their reunion, Salome focused on him.

Irene and Eulalia bowed their heads to the king. When he stopped, they disappeared into the crowd, the former dragging along the latter, who protested quietly.

Vincent had tied his hair back neatly, his facial hair trimmed and cut with clean, defined lines. His clothing was golden, almost like armor, with a leather breastplate detailed in bronze and gold. His coat was the color of dark honey with chocolate-colored brocade, matched with trousers and boots bearing tiny golden embellishments.

"My lady Rosalia," he said, bowing low. No fear or hesitation in his eyes when he rose.

She bowed her head. When he looked at her, so near, it was a little easier to ignore the shadows. The weight upon her chest was removed. She felt like the taut rope wrapped around her middle that drew her to him was slackened.

She felt safe, strangely enough, like if she could trust anyone, it was him.

There was something about him that was warm and welcoming, something that pleaded with her to relax and give in. It was utterly new and strange and as she was a curious woman, she was inclined to explore that. Without the Alliance's command, it felt like she could do that now.

When he held out a hand, she accepted it. A shock raced through her, travelling the length of her arm until she felt herself blushing. Like a woman in love for the first time, except this wasn't love. This was a charade.

"Thank you for all the beautiful gifts," she said.

"I wanted you to know that I missed you."

"Then why did you not visit more?"

He ran a hand along his jaw. "I wanted to, I truly did."

"Perhaps you are too distracted," Salome suggested. "And this is poor timing."

His gaze turned sharp. "There is never a good time, but this has been delayed too long. A union should have been secured the moment I became king and I've failed in my duty, but no longer."

There was no consoling in those words. None of that gentle, insistent demanding to find her pleasure like the one night she shared. She wanted that man, the one who felt lust and pursued it, not this one who decided to switch out passion for the mere concept of duty.

"Those are not the words of a romantic," Salome said.

"I am trying to protect you—"

"Are you? From what? I'm more inclined to think that you have been avoiding me."

He brought her to the center of the room, holding her in a position of a dance. She allowed him. Let him think he had control while she made sure he knew she had more questions. She had the urge to move closer though. Being so close reminded her of their thrilling midnight encounters. Of daggers and stolen kisses, tension, and teasing.

No one else ever offered such excitement.

He pulled her close. The music played louder. As he leaned in, he inhaled the scent of her perfume. She felt his breath on her ear and shivered. It seemed impossible the Alliance could ruin this.

"I always want to protect you." He tightened his grip around her waist.

"Do you think that I am incapable of protecting myself?" The shadows at his feet stirred, awakened by seeds of fury. None seemed to notice. Only she could hear the low hissing. She fought for calm, to regain control, breathing slow.

As she steadied, so did the shadows.

"Then let me be your shield, as you are your own sword."

Her tongue twisted with unkind words that would ruin whatever they had together. Pretty words could easily prove untrue.

He sensed her hesitation when she did not smile. "After the wedding, you shall be in all the meetings. You will know every plan, every success and failure. You will not only fight beside me, but we will also lead this kingdom as a team."

"Is that so?" No clever words came to her now.

"We shall need to prepare you for that role, but it will take time."

Salome never desired a crown or a throne. She didn't want to lead. The idea of being trained into queen was too much. There was no room in her mind to think of it. Already, she was being taught magic. Soon, she'd be part of the fight.

It was too much. She wanted to make it simple. To be selfish. To seek pleasure and nothing else.

She wanted him, not just riches or freedom. She wished she could keep him. It was terrible and greedy and undeserved, but it was what she desired—without the crown and a kingdom to rule.

"Dance with me," Vincent whispered. A plea, not a command.

How could she refuse? With a nod, she allowed him to take the lead, to manipulate her body with the music. Slowly, it made sense. Stepping together, spinning, leaning in and out. Hands touching, bodies close. The shadows fell silent as the music entranced her.

Once the song ended, Vincent stilled, breathing heavily as he held her. Her own breath was ragged. The bodies around them blurred.

All they saw and all that mattered was each other.

"Don't leave me yet," she commanded.

He obliged. A smile replaced the dark, lingering concern on his face as the musicians began another song, smooth and romantic. A traditional Ilaryan dance, like a competition, where two partners fought for the lead. Palm to palm, pushing and pressing, spinning around one another, trying to take the steps first without falling out of rhythm. She laughed breathlessly at the end, winning by managing to capture his hand between hers.

He looked at her like seeing the stars for the first time, before he kissed her fingertips. She felt another shock, right where his lips touched her, though silk gloves covered her skin. The witches insisted on it, unless she wanted to make use of her clairvoyance. If she could read cards, they'd warned, she'd likely read palms as well. Perhaps she'd already started to.

"Another one," he begged.

This time, it was her turn to accept and oblige. Intrigue rippled through her as he gestured toward the musicians. They nodded and picked up their instruments, playing a tune reminiscent of another place.

Of a song she vaguely remembered, hummed by her mother.

Of Villasayas.

"For your mother," Vincent said.

Her heart stumbled. Her breath caught. This bit of truth tied her to the baron's daughter. Her own mother lingered in memory.

Together, they entered the dance. Movements re-enacted a flirtation between a couple, a hide-and-seek rhythm of weaving steps. Other guests joined the dance in pairs. While Salome had some knowledge of several cultures, including arts like their dances, the Villasayan dances were always her favorites. They felt like home.

By the end of the song, her heart was light and fluttering.

In front of everyone and in the center of the room, he placed a delicate, feather-light kiss in each of her hands. Her face warmed, the affection and intimacy almost unbearable, as she remembered his lips elsewhere on her body.

But, in the silence between songs, he became solemn.

"I hope you will forgive me for my absence," he said.

"The witches made sure I was not alone."

Salome didn't know if she could call them friends yet. The history and bonds between them seemed impossible to breach. At times, she felt like an outsider peering through a window into their lives, wondering when she could come inside.

They separated at last, breaking the chain-link of their fingers.

"Forgive me, I must leave you for now. I have guests to greet," he said. "Enjoy the night. I hope to see you once festivities have ended for the day."

They held each other's gaze, the stability of it flickering once when she glanced at his lips. Vincent pressed a kiss to the corner of her mouth. It felt like shooting stars flew across her skin and her face felt too warm.

And then he was gone, disappearing into the crowd.

Salome was left to wander, avoiding the gazes of masked guests. Her hands twitched at her sides, beckoning a shadow to dart around her ankles like a serpent beneath her skirts. Abel glowered across the room, but the king's men stood in his way. Elias and Gerard were likely nearby as well, but the room was packed, and she couldn't spot them.

The crowd suddenly parted. But not for her.

Four women walked in. A hush settled over the room as they beheld the witches. They wouldn't be performers tonight. No theatrics or acrobatics. They came straight to Salome, footsteps accompanied by the clink of chained jewels around their ankles. With them, she was safe, and reminded that she was stronger now. She could handle herself, but their presence ensured she didn't have to face anything alone.

"Why a circus? Why perform?" Salome asked once crowded within them. She'd held onto this question for too long, too distracted by all the other things she longed to know and the topics they found most important to discuss.

Thema answered, "A combination of reasons, really. To inspire fear and awe. To practice our magic freely. To revel in the beauty of what we can do and remind the world of it."

"We travel the world, performing for the kingdoms that hire us," Godiva continued, and smiled. "No loyalty to anyone but each other. If you can do good in the world *and* do what we love to do, why hold back?"

Thema beamed. "That is why we are who we are and do what we do."

They were better people than Salome, with kinder hearts and an inclination to generosity. In comparison, Salome felt weak and vulnerable and too young to understand the world.

People kept glancing in their direction, whispering. Each witch was dressed like her element with matching masks. Women made of flora, flame, wind, and water. They soon teased the crowd with little displays of their magic: a flame on a tongue; floating liquid to lips; wisps of air lifting hair to expose bare shoulders; flower petals raining over couples.

Including Salome and Vincent when they reunited, looking like a pair of suns in a sea of chaotic color, bold and unburdened by the mystery of a mask. He touched the circlet on her head, the necklace around her throat. Sweetly-scented yellow petals fluttered around them.

The shadows curled around her ankles, refusing to remain dormant when there were dark figures spinning across the floor beneath dancers' feet. Salome fought to find some solidity in the fingertips brushing her skin, brief touches that made her smile and soften. Enough to subdue the unease stirring the shadows.

Guests praised her, congratulated her. They must have decided to shower her with joy rather than fear her and her magic. It didn't feel genuine, though. Polite, maybe, and she couldn't decide if that was better or worse than their suspicion.

For a few fleeting seconds, she missed the Alliance for all their roughness and abrasiveness. That was all she knew these last several years, and what she accepted as all she deserved. She even searched for them again in the crowds, finding Abel and Gerard guarding the exits, while Amalia and Euria were close to a cluster of servants. Her former staff didn't wear any masks, a sign that they were working rather than participating in the celebration.

When she met Amalia's eye, the red-haired woman smirked. Euria kept her remaining eye turned away though, as if she didn't want to witness what might happen.

Salome glanced around the hall, searching for some sign of danger, calculating the distance to each exit. Tense, she shifted her legs to rub against the blade strapped to her thigh and touched her wrist to check for the thin knives tucked in her sleeves. If a fight was coming, she was ready for it.

Would the Alliance risk it though?

The shadows stirred, roused by the flash of unhappiness and brewing chaos inside her.

A touch of sunlight settled on her bare shoulders and the shadows retreated.

A soothing touch, like a soft kiss on the grow. The light witch was here—playing, not fighting. Like it was a game to keep Salome guessing. An image came to mind—a flash of white-gold, a figure in a shimmering silver dress slipping between tendrils of light.

But who and where?

There were too many people, all masked. All faces concealed.

Her frown caught Vincent's attention, and she twisted around, looking for the witches to inform them of what she felt. What she thought she saw. Maybe they felt the magic too.

"Is something wrong?" he asked, rubbing his thumb across the back of her hand.

Salome shook her head.

"Have you noticed tonight's response to you?" he began. "Everyone can see how you shine, and they are not afraid."

Though the guests kept their distance, he was right. They glanced with interest, offering soft smiles, and looking at her like she meant something. Like she made them hope. All she had to do was lose control of her emotions and unleash her dark magic, then they'd turn on her.

It had already happened. It could certainly happen again.

The witches were always near. Protecting her, watching her, guarding her even as they enjoyed themselves—dancing, their heads thrown back in laughter, their fingers locked, their gowns lifting as they spun together. They tipped back crystal goblets of sweet wine. Della stole kisses from Maris's lips and left some on her wrists and hands. Thema and Godiva never left each other's side, hands interlocked.

The sights inspired longing, melancholic bells chiming in her chest. She swelled with the desire to be with them and like them, unafraid and never alone.

Hours quickly passed, a blur of music and magic. At times, she caught glimpses of Irene, dancing with various masked men, including Fabian. Eulalia flirted with a guard who barely glanced at her, which only amused her more. Oscar, distinguishable by the scars on his neck and jaw, conversed intimately with a man in the corner of the room. Duke d'Aryllia, his attire matching his wife and sister, but he focused on the soldier, leaning close.

Through the night, Salome danced until dizziness left her leaning against Vincent. She drank and dined. She laughed and leaned in for kisses, blushing as though she never kissed so eagerly before. As if she never kissed him before. The thief found more passion in him than his betrothed, but it didn't matter.

The way his eyes followed her, the daze in them, showed her that he wanted both the girl she pretended to be and the one in the night that he couldn't trust.

But the enchantment soon shattered.

The main doors of the throne room flew open. The musicians stopped abruptly. Dancers slowed their steps. Eyes turned toward the intruder—a young boy covered in dust and grime from travel. He was breathless and frantic, eyes searching. He ran through the crowd until he fell to the king's feet.

Vincent knelt, listening as the boy's shoulders heaved with labored breaths, gasping out his news. When Vincent stood, his mouth was set in a grim line, eyes darkened. He looked at Salome before glancing around the room.

"King Sebastian of Pavalla was attacked last night and claims we sent the shadows to his door," the king announced.

Multiple guests gasped. Some clutched their chests, eyes filled with horror.

"In two weeks, his army will attack our southeast borders whether we meet them or not."

Stillness replaced the carefree, celebratory demeanor of the guests.

"And so, we will fight again."

While the monsters quieted in the castle, they still ravaged the world beyond. The witches' protection didn't extend to the kingdom's enemies, or anywhere far from the capital. Their power was limited.

Salome went to his side. Vincent slid a hand around hers and gripped it tight, like she was the strength he needed to speak.

"We will fight them until our last breath or theirs."

Chapter Twenty-Seven

LATE IN THE NIGHT, WHEN THE CELEBRATORY MOOD FADED INTO an ominous hush, someone banged loudly on the door.

Salome was in the rooms she shared with the witches, but alone while they surveyed the castle. It wasn't uncommon for Pavallan spies to try to infiltrate the walls following a call to battle. Guards were placed at the door, though, to keep watch over the king's betrothed. They should have known not to wake her. Everyone else ought to have been too fearful to disturb the witches.

With a dagger in her hand, she turned the doorknob, hoping it was only Vincent who come to uphold his earlier promise.

Before she could properly open the door, her guest slammed it open, and she stumbled back. A hand grasped her wrist.

When she saw their face, she stopped breathing. Bodies moved around them, filling up the space, trapping her. The shadows shuddered awake, unaware of what to do, waiting for her command. She was too stunned to make one.

"You were like a *daughter* to me," Gabriel said. "You ungrateful little fool."

The thing about liars was they knew how to use their eyes. Most people revealed the truth in them. Not Gabriel, who taught her that himself, the king of liars and thieves. So, when he spoke, she couldn't distinguish truth from falsehood. All she saw was her fear reflecting in his eyes.

"You were, but not anymore," he added. Without another word, he tilted his head.

Something came around her throat, a metal rope cutting into it. As she choked and the world faded, her only thought was that family would never hurt her like this.

SHE WOKE BEFORE THEY REALIZED IT AND WAS LISTENING intently, gathering every bit of information she heard and hoarding it like blackmail. The back-and-forth swaying told her they were in a cart, traveling away from the castle, she guessed. Taking her away from everything she was learning to love.

Heartache was poison. She felt it in her bloodstream, the way it burned through her.

"Is she really so valuable?" Amalia mumbled.

"I don't understand why you hate her," Euria said just as quietly. "When you have magic, you keep it, and you wield it."

Never true friends. Never family. Only ever using each other.

They discussed spies, and earnings, and servants in the castle. They talked about soldiers they'd bought, suites they'd ransacked. The details were hazy though. No specifics. To speak like this, they must have been certain Salome had no way to escape.

It sounded like Gabriel and Yvette were reaching for more power. Like they were tired of working in the dark and decided it was time the nobles were unburdened of their status.

In silence, she lay there, held steady between trunks that must have been some the Alliance had brought to Ellasya. The shadows didn't feel present. Somehow, Gabriel knew to keep her unconscious and prevent her from using magic against them.

Briefly, Salome wondered where the witches were, and then decided it didn't matter. They didn't need to be here. She could handle this. The cart came to a stop, and someone disembarked, causing the cart to sway. She opened an eye to peek at her surroundings and found Euria sitting inside with her, her good eye turned away.

As Salome sat up, she flexed her hands, and the shadows drew to attention. She called them to her and commanded them to be ready.

"Will you tell me what's going on or will you force me to use magic against you?" Her voice remained low, ensuring no one else would realize she was awake.

Euria looked at her in alarm. No screams, as they were taught. Her one eye darted from Salome's face to the shadows curling up to form figures of dark fog. As thoughts flickered through her mind, her throat bobbed, and then Euria nodded once.

"Where are we?" Salome asked.

"Just passed through the far gates of the city."

"And Gabriel? What is he planning?"

"A coup," Euria said. "They want to overthrow the king."

"Why?" Salome's brow furrowed. Weren't the Alliance all about puppetry? Holding the strings without being held accountable for what their dolls did?

Euria shook her head. "He hasn't told me. It's something about one of the former queen's brothers? Apparently, he'd struck a friendship with Gabriel and Yvette in their youth, but it all went wrong. No one knows how much the royal family knows about the Alliance."

There wasn't need to say more. It was too risky to continue operations. This also meant their purpose in the castle wasn't solely to increase their wealth, but to gather information on the royal family, to see what they knew.

To see if and how the Alliance could strip them of their crown.

"Don't kill me," Euria pleaded, her voice soft. "Aren't we friends?"

Salome almost laughed. None of them were. Their loyalty was to their own lives, to the power the Alliance held over them.

"What do they want with me?"

Before answering, Euria looked aside. Was someone approaching? Salome wiggled her fingers and the shadows slid toward the other woman.

"Taking you back to headquarters so they can keep an eye on you. You're an asset now, Sal, and they won't give you up," Euria said hurriedly, hands up in surrender. A sword lay beside her. There wasn't any sound of movement around them.

That wasn't their decision to make, and she had no intention of being their weapon.

Salome was about to speak when someone gathered a handful of her hair and yanked her back. Gritting her teeth, Salome looked to find Amalia, right before the red-haired woman dragged her out of the cart. Euria sprang to action, grabbing her sword.

Two to one.

With a glance, she caught sight of a riderless horse. Maybe that's why they stopped. The cart driver likely needed to relieve themselves. Amalia made quick work, slamming Salome to the ground and tying up her wrists with a string of smooth beads. Though she attempted twisting to see what they were, she figured it out when she felt the world go quiet, even the breeze lost its voice. She reached for the shadows, calling to them, and heard nothing.

The Alliance knew how to deal with magic.

Salome began thrashing, trying to free herself. Every kick she aimed, Amalia dodged, along with headbutts. No matter how hard Salome pulled against her new restraints, she couldn't get out. Curses flew from her mouth, and she wondered if the shadows were screaming for her, shrieking against the barrier that came between them. The quiet was startling—and enraging. She felt the darkness of the world like fabric over her eyes rather than something calling to her.

Was this how others felt? Afraid of the dark instead of curious about it?

"Fight me!" Salome snarled. "*Fight me* instead of chaining me!"

"Is it working?" Euria asked Amalia.

"Evidently."

They spoke like she was nothing, like she was no one. If she wasn't full of hatred before, she was now, and she didn't care that Euria had asked her not to kill her. Amalia stood and wiped her hands on her trousers, smirking down at where Salome kneeled on the ground.

She would break her thumbs to free herself, but first, she pulled herself to her feet. They had no idea what she could do, nor did she. Maybe they could find out together.

"I'd die before Gabriel could have me," Salome said. "I will *kill* you all."

The words slipped from her lips before she could think. Her voice had become hoarser, like her throat had been sore or something damaged her vocal cords. It was almost unrecognizable in its inhuman cruelty.

Amalia blinked in surprise, her hand tightening on a short dagger. It frightened her.

Good.

Salome was not the same person who'd arrived here with them. She was stronger in many ways, and she'd learned things from the witches. Though Amalia had tied Salome's wrists behind her back, she had no trouble using her enhanced flexibility to bring her arms to the front. Training with the witch circus included lessons on magic and physical skills. To perform with them, she had to prepare her body.

And witches were stronger than humans. Salome felt that change in her too, the slow growth of her muscle strength and endurance. There were many reasons why she needed to learn control.

Her eyes shot to the daggers in Amalia's hand.

"Don't be a fool," Amalia warned.

Still, Salome lunged.

Amalia dodged her, but Salome caught her sleeve. It knocked the red-haired woman off-balance, and she stumbled. That flash of unsteadiness enabled Salome to hook her foot around her opponent's ankle and push. Amalia nearly fell, but Euria caught her and shoved her back to Salome.

Back and forth, they attacked each other. Salome stayed on the offence, barely breathing between hits. Euria and Amalia circled her, launching attacks at the same time, but using more defense than Salome. If she hadn't trained with them all these years, maybe she would have fallen against them. If she hadn't trained with the witches all day for weeks now, Salome would already have surrendered.

She knew her strengths now, and she had more reason to keep fighting.

Her new skills didn't stop Euria from slamming Salome against the cart. They didn't prevent Amalia from cutting the inside of Salome's hand when she tried to steal the redhead's dagger. And yet she was faster, taking hits and landing ones herself within a single breath. She could hear the other two panting as Salome continued.

A kick to the thighs. An elbow in the chest. Her foot at their knees, her own knees in their stomachs. Euria launched a fist at Salome's mouth and slammed her knuckles against her lips. Blood dripped from them when she stepped back and gasped, but Salome lunged again.

When Amalia moved to strike, Salome grabbed her arm and twisted it behind the former's back. Amalia cried out as Salome pulled, fingers digging into her wrist until she dropped the dagger. Before anyone else could grab it, Salome kicked it into the air and caught it.

As soon as she had it, she sliced apart the beaded rope on her wrists.

She slashed it along Amalia's arm not a second later, and when the redhead reached to cover her wound, Salome grabbed the other dagger. The thing about Amalia was that she never did get over the habit of reaching where she was hurt. It was easy to kick her down once her blades were gone, and Salome focused on Euria.

The one-eyed young woman was fast and strong, but she was tiring. Salome was faster, still breathing evenly, and now she could hear the shadows again. As she dodged Euria's next blow, Salome cut the remaining rope from her arms.

Once freed, the shadows shrieked. Salome winced at the shrill sound, stunned momentarily, and Euria took advantage of it. She surged forward, following when Salome stumbled away. It didn't seem to occur to Euria that the restriction on her opponent's magic was gone. She didn't realize that the shadows were able to converge until they struck her.

A scream flew from her lips as the shadows sharpened to swords. They sliced through her tunic, pinning her to the ground. No fatal blow, but they wanted it. Salome could taste their bloodlust on her tongue—or was that her own feelings?

Red was the color of rage, and it filled her vision.

But the sound coming from Euria made her pause. This was her doing, this pain. Salome gasped suddenly, eyes widening. Someone grasped her wrist, and she twisted to see who it was. The same time she lifted the dagger, the shadows rose like soldiers flanking her. They were shapeless, floating fog, and when she went still, so did they. Like they were one and the same.

Gabriel pulled her to him.

The disappointment in his eyes was as startling as it was agonizing. Did he really believe in her? Did it really upset him that she wouldn't choose his side anymore? Something feral in her took over and Salome bared her teeth. She flexed her fingers, ready to strike.

Amalia was on her feet again, grabbing Euria's discarded sword and moving to strike.

"Stop!" Gabriel commanded. The redhead froze. "We're letting her go."

"But—"

"She won't kill us," he said, and smiled.

As if she loved him like a dutiful daughter. No, she was afraid. As much as she wanted to kill him, to kill them all—she couldn't do it tonight. Euria was proof of that, tearful and trapped against the dirt. The shadows pinning her down evaporated, but she lay there, bleeding.

"I won't give up on you, Salome. I won't let them keep you," Gabriel promised. "Now you know what I'd seen."

She could have killed him then. Used the shadows like weapons and wield them against these people who had once been family. People who'd she protected and who had protected her too. Who taught her strength and relentlessness.

It was Gabriel now who slung a string of beads around her throat. He tied it tight, making her choke, and knotted it in place.

"You have always been valuable and now you are *priceless*."

Not long ago, she would have swelled with pride and joy over such words. Now, she looked at him in horror. This inevitable magic was something he anticipated all this time, as she wondered. He confirmed it to her now.

He yanked her close and pressed a kiss to her forehead. At the same time, he tugged on the beads and made her gasp, before shoving her away. Salome stumbled.

With a nod, he said, "Go. You're free."

How long did she have? She looked up, instinct telling her to check the stars for the answer. The night sky was littered with their light, twinkling like candles in the distance, but of course, they said nothing.

"For now," Gabriel added. His smile was cruel. "I'll keep an eye on you."

It wouldn't be easy. She knew him well enough to know he'd punish her for not obeying, for not coming with him now and letting him offer her some freedom. Whatever time she had, she'd take it.

Salome turned and raced back to the castle.

Chapter Twenty-Eight

SILENCE REIGNED FOR SOME TIME ONCE SHE RETURNED TO THE witches' rooms.

The first thing they did was snap apart the string of beads at her throat. Thema whispered curses under her breath as she took them away. It didn't look foreign to them. If anything, it was familiar.

"We should talk about what happened," Godiva said. "All of it."

Salome chose not to inform Vincent that she was nearly abducted during the time. All she decided to do was send a messenger to tell him that she sent her staff back to the d'Ilumias estate, to explain their sudden absence. She was too much of a coward to use the moment to tell him the truth about who she was and what she was involved in.

The witches, however, demanded more.

"They let me go, but they'll be back. I don't know when. Gabriel was here, and that's unusual for him." Salome swallowed.

They waited for her to finish, like they could sense something less unsaid. She ducked her head and closed her eyes, letting rage and disgust wash over her. Without the beads, it felt like she was attuned to the shadows again. They rippled in response to her emotions.

"He called me *priceless*." Maybe that was the most terrifying part of the ordeal. Their inevitable return and not knowing why they would wait.

Did Gabriel expect her to choose the Alliance? Did he want to see her fall in the king's eyes before she sulked and returned home? He would do that. He would revel in her humiliation.

"We won't let them take you," Della promised. "But we'll keep watch. If it comes to a fight between us and the Alliance, we can handle it. Together."

Did that include Salome? Did they trust her abilities?

Did they know what Salome had sworn? She'd meant it with her whole heart.

I will kill you all.

She would never belong to the Alliance again, no matter what Gabriel thought. Their plans—she wanted no part of them. Vincent's crown could be theirs for all she cared, but that was all they could have of him. She'd kill them first.

This was the world she'd grown up in. How was she to leave it if she now seemed even more part of it with such thinking?

"Whatever you have done in the past is in the past. You are ours and we are yours," Della told her, a softer sweetness in how she spoke. "It is what you do now that matters."

"I didn't kill them," Salome said. But she wanted to. She would.

"We cannot spend our energy without certainty that it's necessary, nor do we take offensive action. We can only response, and if we must—"

"They will forget you ever existed," Maris finished.

That seemed impossible. The organization was so big, she couldn't know who was in it, and who they would have to defend against. What if they were outnumbered and overwhelmed? What if the Alliance had magic users?

Maris was looking at her yet said nothing about those thoughts. "We should discuss your magic."

Salome curled up the couch, her legs folded beneath her and her hands resting on her thighs. She stared at them, palms up, as if she could see the magic at her fingertips. Did they sense the bloodlust in her? Were they worried? She didn't want to look at them and find out.

"The kind of magic you bear is volatile. It is dark and dangerous," Godiva said.

"It's different than ours," Maris said.

"Do not go into the shadows when they beckon," Thema warned. "They will claim you and use you until you are nothing but a husk. They are magic born of witches who lost themselves to the shadows. Listen carefully and you'll hear the ones who came before you."

A shudder raced through Salome's body. A new terror hitting her now.

"Never let them take command," Godiva added.

"How? Am I supposed to always be calm? Never think or feel?" It went against who Salome was. Loud, emotional, and always thinking about who she was supposed to be, what she needed to do, where she wanted to go. And now, with the terrifying reality of what she did was stark as the moon against the night sky, it seemed impossible.

Godiva looked to her sister.

"Thema knows best. She struggles the most with the control," Maris said.

Strange, seeing her calmness now, the concentration in place. Perhaps there was something lurking beneath the skin. Perhaps, while Maris's anger was like stoking a fire, Thema's was a raging storm waiting to be released.

"It is still difficult," Thema agreed. "But it *does* get easier. It simply requires focus. You must know what you want to do and remember who you are. You must tell it what to do or else it will act on its own. Magic is greedy, eager to take and consume."

Godiva continued, her voice solemn, "Voices call, hands reach. Ones belonging to the ones who gave in, who lost their way. Magic is all around us, the shadows will always exist, but luckily, some people are able to learn how to control it."

A cautionary hope. She could control the shadows, but it wouldn't come easy.

There would be temptations.

They stayed in the room all day. There was no morning walk with Sylvia, no afternoons with Irene—nothing scheduled to lure her outside. Salome could talk about her childhood, how she grew up poor despite her parents' dream to find adventure across the ocean, how they left their islands behind for it, how she ran away in hopes of making their lives easier.

And then the Alliance, finding her trying to pick at Gabriel's pouch of coins, then taking her in. She picked up the different tongues by listening at the docks, eavesdropping on conversations between merchants. They liked that and offered her a place to stay in exchange for her talent.

From then on, she was theirs.

Whenever Salome started to become upset, Thema led her through breathing exercises. Eyes closed, mind quiet, lungs expanding and deflating. Long, drawn-out breaths until each one came out evenly.

As evening fell the shadows woke. Maris lit every inch of the rooms. Godiva summoned melodic wind, until the soothing sound overwhelmed the whispers. They ate dinner in silence, though Salome kept glancing to the doors. Vincent remained absent, still occupied in a meeting. She picked sullenly at the sansrival the kitchens prepared for her in hopes of impressing the future queen. The cream was thick and smooth, the layers of meringue light and airy, a little crunch added by crushed cashews. Nostalgia stabbed her as she recalled how her mother had wished to make it but was unable to afford the right ingredients.

Once they finished their food, Salome laid out the deck of cards as Thema directed. Face up, laid out on the floor.

"Do you remember what we told you?" Della asked, sitting across from her.

Attention, intention, and expectation.

"You cannot tell your own fortune, as far as we know. It hasn't been done." With a wave of Godiva's hands, the cards shuffled and flipped over, the faces concealed.

Salome scooped them into a pile and then fanned them toward the air witch. Godiva chose three and laid them on the floor, side by side, faces up.

Ace of Spades. Three of Hearts. Queen of Diamonds.

The Ace was the first to change, twisting into inky smoke before reappearing as an anatomical heart swirled in black, silver, and gold. The Three of Hearts shuddered, then stretched and twisted into interconnected knots. Different scents rose from them: saltwater, sweet roses, and firewood. The faceless Queen of Diamonds changed last, twitching until the skin darkened and features emerged, soon showing Thema.

And so, Salome read. "The Ace of Spades, a metallic heart—the ability to love intensely. The Three of Hearts, knots of attachment. And then there's the Queen of Diamonds—the person of most importance to you, your sister by blood."

Looking at Godiva, she saw pride and picked up the cards. The images returned to their original design as she slid them back into the deck.

"Have you experienced any palm reading yet? Visions that fill your mind when you touch someone's hand?" Thema asked. They had warned her before the masquerade.

She shook her head. Not really. A flash, once, of images that didn't last in her mind.

Maris clucked her tongue. "Clairvoyance is easily controlled. The darkness in you is our concern."

Salome frowned. Maris looked at her nails, seeking something interesting to inspect within them. She even raised a flame on the tip of her thumb and bounced it between her fingers like a party trick.

They instructed her to perform various tasks, from closing her eyes and performing breathing exercises, to imagining the shadows inside of her, imprisoned in her body. She had to think of it in a labyrinthine design, a process of navigation and technique to fully awaken her magic.

A couple hours later, Salome opened her eyes to find the witches staring at her, patient and unperturbed. Maris had an eyebrow raised while Della smiled sadly.

Salome closed her eyes again. She submerged in darkness but found no doors or paths. She hardly heard the whispers of the shadows. All her life she was a fast learner, picking up skills quickly, taking instruction in stride. Not this time. She felt nothing but the usual call of the magic, the shadows stirring, watching and waiting.

We're right here, they seemed to say. *Come on.*

Gritting her teeth, Salome tried to calm herself. Slow breaths, muscles relaxed, mind clear, allowing her instincts to lead. But they led her nowhere.

Salome opened her eyes again and crossed her arms. She knew how to get their attention, to speak with command rather than ask for their compliance. What to do with them when she wasn't in danger was a whole other challenge.

"We didn't say it would be easy or immediate," Maris said.

Della tried to be reassuring. "As time goes on, you'll learn more about what you can do. Your power will only grow, and we will be with you along the way to guide you."

"Then what can I do right now?"

Godiva smiled knowingly. "Guard your thoughts and feelings. Your magic will come naturally, instinctively."

"Read the books I gave you," Thema added.

Della laughed gleefully. "It will get better, I promise! You've only begun to awaken."

"But we'll go to battle—"

"We will be with you the whole way," Godiva promised.

Salome watched, waiting to see the air witch's eyes shift or her hands to twitch, for some sign that she didn't mean those words. There was none, only a patient gaze and a small smile. Acceptance and understanding, all in that one expression.

One day, though, she would find her parents. Salome looked at Maris. The fire witch nodded, hearing her thoughts and accepting them. And so, she could have power and freedom, magic in her grasp and a chance to go where she willed, to see her parents again. That kindness was something she never thought she'd have.

There were choices now and people who would stand beside her as she made them.

She had lost one family but now had a new one.

Chapter Twenty-Nine

"Stay focused," Godiva instructed, tapping Salome on the arm.

"I *am* focused," Salome said.

With a battle looming, they decided to work on her combat skills with magic. The witches, however, weren't worried about how she could handle daggers or swords. They wanted to see her use her magic as an offensive and defensive.

Killing was not an option and so they were intent on her control. It was too easy to lose her grip on her magic when her emotions ran high and, once the leash loosened, there was no certainty of the ensuing chaos.

All they wanted was to see her craft more figures and make them attack without killing. It seemed easy enough. Making them dance and using them for combat, however, were apparently very different.

Beads of sweat trailed down her forehead as she narrowed her eyes at the ball of shadows hovering above her hands. This was the least complicated part, but she'd done it so many times that day, her body felt ready to collapse into bed.

"What are you trying to imagine?" Thema asked.

"A cat, like Fortune." Salome jerked her head at the black kitten curled up on the cushion beside her while she sat cross-legged on the floor.

"Just one?" Godiva asked.

The mimicry of her pet solidified and pranced on her hand before climbing up her arm. She commanded it to sit on her shoulders, then to wrap its little body around her neck. It obeyed her instantly, and Salome beamed. However, the witches didn't look impressed, even when the shadow kitten yawned and revealed rows of shark-like teeth.

"Create an army," Maris suggested.

"*That* would be interesting." Della nodded in agreement.

The focus she put on creating copies had her grinding her teeth. The shadow cat crawled off her shoulders to sit on the floor in front of her. Black, smoky shapes moved toward it, floating like fog. Salome pressed her hands to the floor, imagining a large cluster crowding around her.

Two more appeared, sitting beside the first, and stared at Salome.

"A few kittens won't save you in battle," Thema said quietly.

Blowing hair out of her face, Salome tried again, dropping more of her weight onto her hands and closing her eyes in concentration.

"That's three more," Godiva observed.

Salome kept her eyes closed and breathed deeply.

"Five more."

Ten in total. Ten kittens sitting in silence as if they were statues. Though Salome was curious to see how they looked, she kept her eyes closed. Learning quickly was one of the things she was proud to say she could do. But there was no knife at her gut, a silent threat if she shifted her position wrong. There was no one calling her useless or weak or pathetic.

And yet she felt like that was happening now. Something tickled her cheek, then the back of her neck. The sensations made her shiver, and she felt her focus beginning to collapse.

"How many do you think you can make?" Godiva asked.

A couple hours later, there were over a hundred shadow-formed cats. They climbed all over the floors and the furniture, terrifying Fortune with their too-many teeth. Salome stood with her hands on her hips, surveying the rooms with pride.

Her body, however, ached as though she tried to climb a mountain. Like she scaled the side for hours upon hours with the sun mercilessly bearing down on her. Every breath she took felt heavier than normal, her energy sapped from all the effort.

Della urged her to sit, clearing away the shadow cats on the sofa. Once there were none in the way, Salome plopped down and exhaled loudly.

This was different. There was no stress forcing her to fight. It was calm, as it should have been, so she could learn to channel at any moment. They already knew she could conjure enough to survive if needed. It was the rest of the time that needed refining to ensure she had complete control.

"Magic takes a toll on the body," Godiva explained. "And all the emotions you feel—"

"Please forgive me for being able to feel," Salome interrupted.

"Magic is instinctive and reactive. When you are on the field, it will manifest your emotions in ways none of us may anticipate. The best we can do is try to provide your mind and body with methods for channeling how you feel," Godiva said, waving the cats away.

Salome stretched her fingers apart, then pulled them into tight fists. All the cats disappeared into a puff of black smoke that Godiva sent away with a light gust of wind. As the room cleared, Salome slumped against the sofa cushions.

All that use of magic took a toll, and she needed time to recover.

Salome closed her eyes and listened to the witches tell her about things that felt secret. They were the only witches of their kind in the world, the only ones attached to a single element with an additional, unrelated ability.

No matter where in the world they were, they would find each other.

But oftentimes, they endured cruel, gruesome treatment prior to coming together, becoming a group strengthened their magic and assured they would never be alone. They could rely on each other for energy, like mirrors reflecting sunlight around a room with only one window to brighten it.

Many years could pass before another witch came to be.

After all, the witch circus was much older than Salome, though they never disclosed their exact ages. Godiva and Thema were buried alive in the deserts of Miraunis, surviving only because of their magic allowing them to breathe under the sand and quench their thirst by drawing water from around them.

In Yoreal, on the continent across the Viridian Ocean, Della attempted suicide. When her family had a funeral for her, the dirt around her coffin leaked inside and healed her, bringing her back to life.

The small village in Tyrea where Maris was born tried to burn her, fleeing when she commanded the flames to burn down every house instead. Across time, witches were not regarded with kindness.

It was well over a century since the witch hunts across the Ocean though. So many had fled from the Westerland continent, the survivors describing families turning on one another out of fear.

"I felt it when you were born," Della said with a thoughtful frown. "Didn't know where you were, just that you arrived. While I can't control shadows, I saw them shifting around like hounds lifting their noses to follow a scent. It was only recently that I sensed we needed to be here in Ilarya."

"What about the light witch?"

"Someone else had been waiting for her. I felt it when she was born, too, but it felt like someone was mocking me, making her presence available to me, then taking away once I tried to focus on it," Della explained.

It was too strange to listen to her speak this way of such things. Like Maris, she was much older than she looked. Physically, she appeared youthful and sweet. It didn't match the wisdom and experience of her words, or the suggestion of her age. How old was she if she was mature enough to be able to sense when Salome was born nearly two decades ago? How old were these women and how long would they live?

How did they look so young? Would Salome be like them?

"Witches age differently," Maris explained. "Once we reach adulthood, our aging process slows significantly."

"So how old are you all?"

All four witches laughed, but none answered. They continued with lessons, sharing stories of their magic going wrong, of beautiful places they'd visited, and watching wars decimate entire peoples, unable to help where they were not invited. Interference was like cursing yourself. Tornadoes emerged where they never had before. The ground split open and swallowed palaces a witch had built with her magic. Tsunamis came from mere lakes and drowned villages where a witch governed. Lightning struck the homes of witches who tried to help a human rise to power.

The only time the witch circus became involved in politics of some sort was when they were asked. Blood magic was required to bind themselves to the rulers. Just as they'd done with Vincent's parents to assist them in their war against their eternal rival, Pavalla, where the shadow demons exacerbated their animosity toward one another.

There were other types of magic users, such as humans who used tools to create illusions or do readings of someone's fate. Some focused solely on incantations to perform magic. Others could use natural materials to craft magic-infused concoctions that could change an individual when ingested. Sometimes that meant transforming them into other creatures, or simply altering their physical appearance to some degree. Other times, that meant stopping the heart to fake death, or perhaps change an individual's natural scent to smell of fresh roses.

As she previously learned, some humans could read cards to discuss a person's fate or fortunes. Some could touch a palm and, like Salome, images would come to mind about what the individual would experience in the near future. It wouldn't be as vivid as Salome's visions but could be accurate depending on the person's inclination to magic.

And what decided an inclination to magic?

There was no certain answer. People searched for it across centuries. There were plenty of theories involving ancestral history or geographical impacts. Some theorists imagined it was related to personality. Skills could be learned and perfected, some said, and so anyone with dedication could learn magic.

"Our magic is natural and instinctive. We can strengthen it with amplifiers and practice maintaining focus, but much of what we can do is something that simply feels right," Thema said, then frowned. "Or stifle our magic, as the Alliance had done to you, though I cannot imagine how they discovered that."

It was a new topic for her to research, it seemed.

"Our performances require the development of skill, though, which is why you would not immediately join us for a show," Godiva explained.

The weakened state of Salome's body began fading. She now felt as though she downed some sugary drink that filled her muscles with short-lived energy. And so, the lessons resumed.

"Now, can you craft a weapon from the shadows?" Maris asked.

The idea made Salome grin with delight.

Chapter Thirty

THE NEXT FEW DAYS WERE A BLUR OF IRON AND STEEL.

Countless soldiers filled the castle and courtyard. Camps rose outside the walls, filling the fields between the castle and the city. Every soul in this kingdom knew the inevitable—another battle was coming, and all needed to be ready for it.

Those closest to the castle came the day after the celebration. Others soon followed. Those closest to the battleground would meet them there. Soon, all those soldiers would head to the southern border, prepared for death.

Two weeks until they fought again.

Less than four weeks until the wedding.

Time was running out.

Dinners were long and eventful. Halls and corridors filled with movement and sound and life. There was hardly a moment of peace and silence. Vincent scarcely had time to see Salome, passing her in fleeting moments, or sitting beside her at dinners with only glances to spare. Sometimes his hand would brush against her, fingertips trailing along her thighs or his knuckles against her breast. Teasing her, reminding her of when she had his touch, and making her want it again. There were no more gifts this time. He had even less opportunity to put those together.

It wasn't his fault. She still couldn't bear it with a smile.

Salome locked herself away one day, content in the peace of relinquishing the charade for a few moments. There were limits to her pretending. She would fight with him, but she'd never lead and take part in preparations. That was a queen's duty, a queen she'd never be.

She should leave before the wedding. The witches were bound here, but Salome wasn't. She'd have the chance to find her parents before returning to the witches for more lessons. Where that would be, though, Salome didn't know. It all depended on if she told Vincent the truth and she didn't know how to accomplish that.

Peace came to an end when Irene pounded on her doors, shouting from the other side. The sun had only just risen, but Salome was sitting on her bedroom floor with Fortune in her lap before a single ray could break through. The witches left long before sunrise, off to the city. Salome hadn't quite listened when they told her why while she'd been half-asleep.

"The king awaits his lady!" Irene sang, loud as the morning bells, likely waking the whole castle.

Upon opening the doors, Salome found Fabian and Oscar with her. This was one of the few times Salome had seen them recently, others replacing them the king and his advisors that they were now required to attend more meetings. Fabian offered an apologetic smile.

"I can't say no to her," he said.

Oscar snorted. "*Her*? Or just any pretty girl?"

His brother responded with a pained expression. Rolling her eyes, Salome ushered Irene inside, who blew them a kiss before shutting the door behind her.

"What does he want?" Salome tried not to wince at the lack of refinement in her question. She blamed it on the early hours.

Irene was endless life and energy, boundless and bright, as if she already forgotten about the terrible ordeal Salome endured with the Alliance. Before she learned that attachments only made life more challenging, Salome would have easily loved a girl like that.

Irene grinned widely. "He wants you in the training room."

"Did he send you to fetch me?"

"No, I intercepted him on his way here. Now he must wait." There was a devilish glint in her eye that made Salome laugh.

"Allow me a moment then," Salome said before rushing off. She threw on a loose white shirt, some tight-fitting trousers, and a comfortable pair of boots.

Within seconds of emerging, Irene took Salome by the hand to lead the way. An image burned in Salome's eyes—bare skin, bodies entangled. Fabian, armor on the floor, and Irene's pale hands on his brown shoulders. His hands gripping the soft flesh on her hips.

Instantly, Salome snatched her hand away. Already, she'd forgotten to be careful. Already, she'd stolen a secret. Before she came here, seeing such a thing would have made her laugh with delight. A secret! A little piece of blackmail! But now, she felt wrong.

And she didn't like that. This feeling might stop her from doing what she needed to do to survive, even at the expense of another.

What she done was explore magic she didn't yet know. She stretched a muscle that wasn't yet strengthened. It felt like she had a weakness rather than a skill.

Irene turned, frowning as she drew her hand to the chest, hurt in her eyes. Everyone knew what she could do with cards and shadows, but they didn't know she could steal their secrets from the palm of their hands.

"I need another moment."

Before Irene could speak, Salome rushed into her room, closing the door and leaning against it. Eyes closed, she willed the images away, but the scent of sweat and feminine perfume clung to her nose, remnants of what she saw.

A knock at her door jolted her. When she didn't answer, they knocked again. They knocked thrice more.

"Lady Rosalia?" Fabian called.

"Almost ready," she answered, rising, heart racing. Salome plucked the first pair of gloves she found, a soft tan linen, and hurriedly put them on. Finally, she opened the door.

Fabian and Oscar waited patiently. Oscar glanced at her gloves.

Along the way, they offered her advice for sparring. Stand wider, don't lean forward too much, guard your expressions, don't get arrogant. Fabian poked her. Oscar smirked when she jumped. At least they believed she didn't have the necessary skill to win a fight. It would be all the more delightful when she won.

They had her laughing by the time she entered the training room.

Inside, it reeked of sweat, blood, and steel—reminiscent of her training with the Alliance.

Vincent was already there, along with several soldiers in various stages of undress with wounds and scars visible on exposed skin. Irene stood among a group of women, wielding a bow and a quiver of arrows. As Salome entered, their gazes met, and Irene smiled.

Vincent broke off from a fight, straightening while his opponent froze. His sweat pulled his black shirt close to his chest and his hair hung loose around his face. As Salome approached him, he threw her the sword he was holding. Real steel this time, singing in the air as it flew.

She struggled to catch it and it clattered to the floor.

Behind her, Fabian laughed, then coughed, as Oscar elbowed him in the chest. Salome rolled her eyes, bending to pick up the fallen sword. All these good-humored people around her calmed the chaos in her mind, the dark, deadly thoughts that she struggled to send away.

"Are you ready?" Vincent called.

Another man offered his training sword, bowing graciously when Vincent accepted. The room stilled and silenced, all bodies stepping aside and awaiting the king's command.

"No magic," he warned her. "We fight fair."

"What if I don't fight fair?" she purred, lifting her sword into dueling position. She bit her lip at the voice she used. Too late to take it back. Too familiar to the thief in the night that stole the king's kiss.

Something flashed in his eyes. Too brief to decipher.

She tried to switch to a flirtatious smile, to remind him about their bout in bed and how she'd looked at him that night, rather than the teasing in corridors, the chasing and temptation.

"I suppose no one truly fights fair on the battlefield." He grinned.

He tapped his sword against hers. It vibrated lightly in her hands, singing to be swung and slashed. The sword's handle was slick from his sweating hands. He looked weary but delighted by the prospect of a contest, reminding her that he was a soldier before he became king.

"What are you waiting for?"

He laughed. Her heart thrummed at the sound of it. "Ladies first."

With that, she lunged.

She swung and stabbed and slashed. He dodged every attack, swaying and side-stepping. His sword met hers, their blades ringing at the impact. This steel could wound. No more games, no more teasing and taunting.

It became his turn to push, to swing his sword down on hers. The strength of the strike made her step backward, the soles of her boots slipping against the floor. He grinned. She narrowed her eyes and shoved.

Back and forth, they lunged and dodged. They swung and parried. Ducking, diving, dancing around each other. She laughed breathlessly, falling in love with the way the steel sang. He was steadier, stronger while she struggled, still clumsy with the long blade. He identified her weak points easily, toying with them, making her correct her movements.

His skill with swords was so great, it felt like magic. At one point, he pinned her to the floor with his sword at her neck. A mixture of amusement, disappointment, pride, and unease played across his face.

She surrendered, and they fought again. A few minutes later, she downed him. Her foot was on his arm and her sword at his heart.

His chest rose and fell with each breath. His eyes never released hers.

Be proud, she wanted to say. *Be in awe.*

Something unsaid hung between them. He wasn't smiling or laughing.

"Did you let me win?" she asked, stepping back, and removing the sword from his chest.

The joy in her win fell fast. Maybe it was that she already felt weak. Maybe the witches leaving her behind today made her feel vulnerable and alone. Maybe all that had happened and all the dark things in her mind put her on a dangerous edge.

Vincent shook his head as he pushed off the floor. Once standing, he towered over her. Arm limp, sword at his side. Reluctance made him tense, the ridges of muscle on his stomach prominent through his shirt and the knuckles over his sword paling.

"Fight me *properly*. What are you afraid of?"

Vincent's jaw tightened as he glanced away. But not before she noticed the flicker of doubt in his eyes.

"*Tell me.*"

"I am not certain it is wise for you to—"

"To what? Fight?"

He turned his back to her.

"Are you doubting me?" she asked.

She shouldn't have been so angry with him for going against what they'd agreed upon. She was still lying to him. It wasn't fair to expect him to speak truth but every day with him was laced with her deceit. And yet she was hurting, heart aching, wondering why she wasn't good enough no matter who she pretended to be.

"My lady, it's different out there. It's not a game." Still, he wouldn't look at her, like he couldn't face her when he revealed such uncertainty about her ability to stand her ground.

That isn't fair. The rage began to rise. The shuddering strength of her power left her trembling where she stood, panting as she glared at him. The shadows rose around her, extending like columns of black smoke as the room began to darken.

No matter who she was with, she was doubted. Of all the things that could upset her, it had to be this. Though defiance surged through her, rage overwhelmed it. Time made her grow stronger. Her years with the Alliance turned her into a weapon. Now she had new advantages. She was deadlier, not weaker, and she wished all would understand.

The sword in her hand dropped to her feet.

Someone exclaimed in horror. Vincent whirled around and called Rosalia's name, the sound muffled like her head was underwater. Her hands shook beyond her control. A halo of pale hair entered the room, a brightness between the dark. Around her, the shadows hummed, louder and louder.

Her muscles loosened, control slipping away as her hands numbed and the world blurred. Panic spread like venom through her veins. She could feel their hunger carving into her like an empty stomach.

We'll take care of everything, they promised.

She imagined her fingers, hands, and wrists turning black like they had been plunged into soot. Her knees buckled.

Fabian and Oscar grabbed her arms, holding her up and keeping her away from the king.

But she wouldn't hurt him. She couldn't. Salt stung her eyes. A hint of copper touched her tongue as she ground her teeth and closed her eyes, trying to focus, to find the calm and quiet place she required.

Your power will only grow with time, the witches had said.

Is this what they meant? What they feared?

"Rosalia," Vincent whispered softly. "Look at me, love, just look at me."

His hands were on her cheeks, thumbs on her lips. The name didn't belong to her, but his affection did. This sweetness was hers to claim.

His eyes searched for hers, but hers could not settle.

The brothers held on, keeping her from folding into him.

A ray of light, bursting from the windows, settled on her skin. It embraced her, wrapping around her like a lover. It kissed her skin with the sweetness of sugar and honey.

The light witch was here. That strangely brought her comfort. Salome searched for her in the crowd. More people filtered in, clustered by the doorway, drawn by the commotion. Unfamiliar faces peered at her, curious and concerned.

Irene watched in silence with her hands curled into fists. Concentration filled her eyes, an unwillingness to look away. As Salome met her gaze, Irene flexed her fingers and lowered her gaze.

The door slammed shut, like someone wanted to prevent others from bearing witness.

Look what our queen can do, she imagined them saying. *How dangerous she is.*

As Salome closed her eyes, she tried to breathe. It took a few moments, a few struggling inhales and shaking exhales, until each breath came steady.

Slowly, agonizingly slowly, the shadows hissed and began to retreat.

They loosened their hold, whispering like traitors begging for forgiveness before the axe or noose. She felt the magic sigh with defeat, the weight on her chest lifting away, the tingle in her fingertips fading. The chorus of voices crashed and collided with one another, becoming incoherent.

She did not need more demons, especially ones who wanted to control her. But perhaps they were an extension of her own existence: greedy for power, willing to take advantage of weakness, flighty and frightened and ambivalent. They took everything she thought she knew and twisted it all. She was familiar with chaos, but this was a worsened version, and they weren't even on the battlefield.

There was no doubt that she could survive that fight. Her only wonder now was what sort of wreckage she could create despite how he did not think her capable.

Vincent's fingers trailed from her cheeks, down her neck and arms. When he reached for her waist, she pulled back, unwilling to look him in the eyes. "I'm sorry, Rosalia. Forgive me for being afraid."

He sighed, leaning his head toward her like preparing to share a secret. He brought his hand to his chest, pulling out a locket. He didn't open it, only clenched it in a fist.

"This damned war is nothing but loss. For all of us, including myself—my mother, my father, my sisters and my brother…" he trailed off. Here he was, so willing to be vulnerable.

As soft murmurs filled the air like the buzz of many insect wings, her gaze flickered around at the many faces filling the room. Fighters, servants, nobles.

Vincent sighed, full of frustration. "What if I lost you as well?"

"You won't," she swore. "So long you believe in me, in us, and our strength." But she would have to protect herself too.

Again, he pulled her closer and she leaned into the embrace. To complete the con, she told herself, to keep him close until she could run. But this was a war she was willing to fight. A king she was willing to fight for. She hesitated to try to understand her desperation to be there on the battlefield with him, other than changing fate foretold in the cards. He was too good to die.

She came here for the kingdom's wealth, not its well-being.

But she stayed for her king, for newfound magic, for sisters, and freedom from her cage.

He placed a hand around her face, fingertips stroking her cheeks softly. Gentle and caring and the kind of person she should fight to be with. With his other hand, he passed the fallen sword. She gripped it like a lifeline, hoping he saw her strength before any similarities between her roles as Rosalia and Salome the thief. Let him see her capabilities before anything else.

Let him see that she wanted to stand by him, regardless of who she was.

"My warrior queen," he whispered with a smile.

She tightened her grasp around the sword. Fingers pressing into the handle as though she could meld it to her hand. She had to be stronger, less afraid. She had to prove she could fight for herself, that she herself should be feared, rather than someone deserving of worry.

A little part of her wanted to prove that she would be a great match for him as she was, not who she pretended to be.

Chapter Thirty-One

WHEN SHE WALKED THE CORRIDORS, EVERYONE AVOIDED HER eyes. Salome couldn't tell if it was because of her magic or because she walked among the witch circus as one of them.

Salome kept her head high as she walked from the library to a set of stairs leading into a tower. Her hands shook, but she hid them within the folds of her wide skirt. After hours of staring, of the witches trying to calm her breathing and Vincent going off for an audience with citizens, she needed a change of pace.

"Are you certain no one will be there?" Salome asked the witches.

Maris looked up, trying to peer up into the tower. The staircase wound around and around, twisting around a center that offered rails to grasp as one ascended. "I hear nothing."

"Only birds," Thema added.

This tower was where all the messenger birds were housed. All news from across the kingdom and around the world would be found here, a small roll of parchment clutched in talons.

"Make sure it smells lovely," Della whispered to Godiva. "Or else Maris will become a grouch."

The fire witch gently shoved the smallest one, and they laughed at a private joke. The other two merely rolled their eyes as if they could not bear another moment of the sickeningly sweet romance. Thema hurried around them, climbing up the stairs with more impatience than usual.

Apparently, she didn't like heights. Thema's knuckles paled as she gripped the railing with both hands, using it to propel herself higher. Laughter followed her as the rest of the witches climbed up the staircase. Then, when the water witch reached the top, there were gagging sounds at the stench.

Grinning and shaking her head, Godiva rushed to reach the door to freshen the air, as Della requested. It was a quiet, secluded space and an interesting change of the scenery.

The only sounds with the gentle cooing from the messenger pigeons. They ruffled their wings every now and then, sending snow-white feathers flying around. Salome swatted them away as she moved to the window.

The view from it was incredible: a stretch of green grass between the castle and the city, grooms taking the horses on a little walk around the field, the glass windows in the city catching sunlight and twinkling in the distance like stars during the day. The sky was blue with thin white clouds coasting lazily. A gentle breeze caressed her skin as she closed her eyes and leaned out slightly.

"That's terrifying," Thema mumbled. "You have lost your wits. I shall stay safely tucked away in the corner." Lucky for her, Della was kind enough to craft a stone chair so she could sit and relax. The latter, however, seemed unlikely as she lowered her head into her hands. Her breathing steadied to a meditative state.

The fear and discomfort that must have filled Thema's mind manifested in the sky. The thin clouds became thick, gathering tight together, and the sky darkened. Perhaps unintentionally, she summoned a storm. Before long, it began raining.

"So, what can we discuss today?" Salome always did like the rain. There was something wonderful about it, the way it sounded and the way it smelled.

"Multitasking," Godiva said. "A weapon and your magic at the same time."

As if on cue, Della placed her hands against one of the walls. Stone scraped off as though she'd taken a shovel and carved out a chunk. The loose piece soon transformed into a staff and Della tossed the new weapon to Salome. Unlike in the training room. Salome caught it smoothly.

Della laughed and applauded, and Salome bowed. She placed herself in a fighting stance, waiting as Della crafted another staff and threw it to Maris.

Without looking, Maris caught it in the air, then bent her knees and leaned forward.

Grinning, Maris asked, "Do you think you can win against me?"

Salome surged forward and attacked without thinking. Their weapons clashed briefly. Maris pushed Salome back, following as she stumbled away. Again and again, she swung the staff in her hands, relentless. All Salome could do was defend herself.

"Call upon the shadows!" Godiva reminded her.

Salome had to remove one hand from the staff, the weight of it more evident when held by a single arm. With one hand freed, she opened her palm, and waved her fingers in a beckoning motion. It took a moment, but then the shadows at her feet lifted from the ground and swirled around her hand.

It took her a few moments to figure out what to do with it. All the offensive moves Maris made kept her distracted. Magic required focus and most of hers was set on their fight. Sweat dripped down her face and back as she struggled to keep up with Maris. She had endurance that would make any highly trained soldier deeply envious.

Salome needed to be like that. She needed to be better.

"Years of practice," Maris said in response to Salome's thoughts.

"Use your magic," Godiva said again.

Salome huffed angrily and brought up her free hand just as Maris swung at her again. This time, instead of meeting the oncoming staff with her own, Salome brought up a tiny shield. It was solid enough to catch the stone weapon, sturdy despite being made of shadows, but barely large enough to block her torso.

Della clapped.

They tried again and, the next round, Salome brought the shield up quicker. Then they made her switch from holding the staff with both hands, to immediately bringing up a shield. Once she grew accustomed to that, they dropped their weapons and took a break.

Maris leaned against the window beside Della. Meanwhile, Salome propped herself by the door and exhaled. The wind witch brought the breeze over to help cool down her sweat-drenched body.

Wiping a hand over her brow, Salome looked over at Thema and grinned. "Are you—"

Maris suddenly interrupted. "Get away from the door!"

At that same moment, the door swung open and revealed an individual dressed in ratty traveling clothes. They had a bag slung over their shoulder with parchment spilling from the opening and ink on fingers grasping the strap.

They lunged for Salome, yanking her close. The shadows rustled and rose to action. They looked like ropes made of smoke ending in spearheads. Everything slowed. Salome stared straight into the messenger's eyes.

No, not a messenger.

"Sleep well, Salome," the assassin said and smiled.

The shadows stabbed into their body, tunneling through their torso, but it was too late. The assassin did what they came to do: they snuck a needle under Salome's skin. It pierced the soft flesh at the base of her throat.

Blood began to pour from the assassin's body, and they fell to their knees, dead almost instantly. Their body slumped over, blood pooling around them and slowly dripping, oozing down the stairs.

Only the Alliance would do this. Gabriel said they'd come for her. Was this what they meant? Surely, he'd know he couldn't kill her, and he didn't seem interested in that.

This was a message, then. A reminder that they were still there, waiting, testing her.

Punishing her.

She'd killed with her magic again. She imagined Gabriel gleeful about it, pleased that her instincts were deadly, and how useful that would be for him.

All it did was fill her with disgust.

The poison was already spreading in her body, racing through her blood to destroy her. She could feel it working to kill her as quickly as possible, her vision blurring and muscles going weak. Salome yanked out the thin needle out of her neck, then her legs gave way and she crumbled to the floor. Another day, without this attack, she would have been horrified by getting so close to the filth scattered across the stone tiles.

She gasped for air as her throat swelled, clawing at it. Her eyes bulged in panic, and she scratched at her skin as if opening herself up might free herself from the poison now killing her.

If time had slowed earlier, it moved too quickly now.

Della screamed in horror. Whatever was happening, the agony must have accompanied a gruesome effect on her body.

Before Salome could throw herself out the window to spare herself the devastation caused by the poison now deep in her system, Godiva and Maris grabbed her arms. They pinned her to the ground despite her thrashing. There was a scream trapped in her swollen throat, a violent storm made entirely of her own voice with the rage befitting a wicked typhoon capable of decimating the largest of cities.

Blood covered her hands. It was on her face, on her neck, everywhere she'd tried to scratch and claw. In her writhing agony, she'd made a mess of herself. The blood stuck to her skin and clothes, set on reminding her of her body's destruction.

Thema suddenly appeared over her, hands outstretched.

"Stay calm," Thema said. "Stay *still*."

All Salome wanted to do was to jump from the tower and die. What would have terrified her if it suddenly came to mind was now the only thing she wanted. Maybe the poison infected not only the body, but the mind too. It would kill her, surely. Death was better than this torture.

Gabriel was punishing her. He wanted her in pain.

Maybe he knew the witches would take care of her before she died. He wouldn't kill her and lose such an asset.

He must have wanted her to suffer and be afraid.

It felt like something was cutting her skin into segments, then slowly pulling it away from her body. It felt like someone had doused her in oil and lit it with fire. Her insides burned and burned. She wanted to scream and cry but all she could do was make muffled sounds and fight against the hands holding her to the floor.

Thema worked her magic, hands pressed to Salome's throat. Her skin cooled like she was dropped into a bathtub filled with ice. She gasped at the sensations slamming her body like a tidal wave. Thema murmured inaudibly to herself, removing one hand from Salome's body to lift it above them. Liquid rose like a waterfall in reverse, moving upward and out of her bloodstream. It climbed into Thema's palm, pooling within it.

And then the pain was gone.

Thema released Salome and leaned back. There was sweat on her forehead and a sleepiness in her eyes. The weight on Salome's arms and legs disappeared and, instantly, sat up. All the witches moved back, allowing her space to breath.

Salome said through clenched teeth. "They want to frighten me if they can't kill me."

"I don't understand," Della said. Her voice sounded so young, belonging to a child instead of a woman who'd been alive for several decades. Though Salome expected to find a glimmer of fear, there wasn't any. Instead, Della looked devastated and furious. Like she herself was ready to destroy the world to punish the people who commanded this.

Salome got to her feet, albeit shakily. Her clothes were a wreck, ripped apart and covered in her blood.

The assassin lay lifeless on the floor. She stared it for a long moment in silence. It seemed none of the witch circus knew what to say to her. What could they even say? How could they comfort her? It was tragic that a third attempt was made on her life, but the message was clear: the Alliance wouldn't give up until she was dead.

They would ensure she knew how they felt about her betrayal.

Slowly, wordlessly, Salome began to go down the staircase. There was movement behind her, footsteps of someone coming close, but they kept some distance from her.

"Let her go," Godiva said quietly. "She won't hurt anyone."

"Not anyone innocent," Maris corrected.

Salome whirled around on them. Her hands balled into fists, like she was ready to fight. They didn't understand that the Alliance would force this violence out of her however they could. Even if they weren't present, they still played with her strings, and she didn't know how to get rid of them.

She wanted to kill them.

To kill anyone who did their bidding.

"Go, then. Run. Wreak havoc. Come back to us when you're finished and try not to destroy the castle during your tantrum," Maris said, her amber eyes flashing with annoyance.

They didn't like her ambivalence, but neither did she. They didn't like her violence, but it was up to her to learn how to handle it. Somehow.

Turning around, Salome continued her descent down the staircase, seething with frustration and hopelessness and self-hatred. With every step, the space around her grew darker as she called the shadows to her hands. Her fury and bloodlust beckoned.

Perhaps she could only be free if she eliminated the Alliance.

Chapter Thirty-Two

SHADOWS SWIRLED AROUND HER, BLACK SPIRALS ACTING LIKE A protective shield. She had snuffed out all the lights and doused the hallways in darkness.

Her blood burned with rage.

How dare they?

Salome couldn't stop the vicious thoughts that swarmed her mind like angry wasps emerging from a damaged hive. The world around her was swathed in darkness now, the shadows drawn out to fill every inch around her.

Before she arrived at this castle and donned the name Rosalia d'Ilumias, the blood spilled in eons was rarely at her hand. This time, it was. Multiple times. What innocence she had was long since abandoned the moment her magic properly awoke.

And now it was alive, twisting around her like a black tornado. Her nostrils filled with the scent of wood smoke and rosemary.

Maybe this was what she had to become if she wanted to survive. It wouldn't have been the first time she transformed into someone more violent and self-serving. That was what she needed to do in order to make it through all those years with the Alliance.

She loathed it. She despised how there was no more softness or gentleness, and how she needed to pursue this if only to have hope.

Any noble who crossed her path scurried away, clutching their valuables to their chests as if she might steal those away. They weren't the ones she wanted. She had no need for gold and jewels now. Perhaps, from here on, she never would need that again.

There was enough danger in her life. Maybe she couldn't end the war herself, but she could help the witches in their mission. And she could eliminate the threat of the Alliance, knowing that Gabriel wanted her back.

Instead of being powerless, she could do what she had control over.

She had magic. She would use it.

"I will not be punished," she said quietly. "I will not be killed."

All she could see was her rage and her hurt and her fear. It was darker than a starless night where the moon was cloaked in thick clouds. Her fear was a disease she couldn't cure, tearing through her with more violence than the poison that was injected into her neck.

I will not be killed.

Somehow, she found herself in the kitchens.

As always, Salome had to do what needed to be done to move forward with her life.

The staff scattered as she lifted her head, except for one. They couldn't move, not while they were pinned to the pantry door with chains made of shadows locked around their wrists and ankles. Still, they tried to free themselves, pulling at their restraints.

She didn't know their face, but she knew the arrow-shaped mark behind their ear.

The one that said they belonged to the Alliance.

"Let's send a message," Salome said as she approached them.

It didn't occur to her how anyone might react to seeing her like this. Or why she might be targeting this individual. Excuses and explanations came to mind. She thought of the assassin in the training room and the similar mark on their body. A mark Salome also bore, though none had noticed so far. If it was up to her, no one would ever see it, and she could keep all her secrets.

"Someone else is listening and watching. I do not know where or how or who they are, but I know they are lurking," Salome whispered. She kept her voice sweet and girlish, just as Yvette often did when she was enraged.

The spy recognized that. It was evident in the way their eyes widened and the increasing panic that led them to tug faster. The shadows wouldn't loosen their hold though, and Salome had no intentions of letting them go.

"No matter what they do or who they send, I will not go to them."

They should be afraid of her. They should learn that she wouldn't be so easily commanded by them anymore and she never wanted to go back to them. She wanted to be free and maybe that made her terrible. Salome was selfish enough to fight for that.

But not happily, not with pride.

There didn't seem to be other options. The Alliance would only respond to severe action.

Before the spy could scream, the shadows around their ankles came undone. Before they could kick out their legs or try anything to free themselves, those shadows delved between their parted lips and dived down their throat.

The sight made Salome gag, tears springing to her eyes, but she couldn't look away.

I have to do this, she told herself. *It's the only way.*

Theonlywaytheonlywaytheonlyway...

The spy choked and gagged, eyes bulging, face turning purple. They looked at Salome at blood vessels burst, as their throat seemed to expand like a balloon, overfilled and ready to burst.

They twitched and thrashed, fingers stretching to reach for their mouth.

Desperate to breathe, desperate to remove what was entering them.

Until something snapped. The spy's head twisted unnaturally, and their body slumped.

It was not a pretty way to die.

The shadows slithered away. It was only once they dissipated like morning fog drifting away that she felt in control of her body again. The heavy weight that felt like a mask over her face and pulled her limbs like marionette strings vanished, too. All the strength that kept her standing upright was gone.

It was the only way.

Salome fell to her knees. It brought her close to the body now slumped on the floor. Black marks covered their face and throat like someone smeared paint over their skin where the shadows touched them. Smoke slid out of their mouth like drool. Their eyes remained open, frozen in fear.

This was her doing.

Knowing that, she turned away and emptied the contents of her stomach on the stone floor. Sobs shook her body. She wept and gagged and trembled. Her body felt heavy and worn-down, exhausted from such violent effort.

She didn't know how long she sat there. The witches arrived at some point. They sat with her, cleaning up the scene as best as they could and keeping servants out of the kitchens.

Using magic so much that day left her feeling drained. Her arms dangled uselessly. She felt like she had no ability to move. Not even her eyes strayed from where they focused, despite how she could not seem to see anything. She wanted to sleep.

"This is why we need control," Godiva whispered. "Fear and anger tend to cause a strong reaction. Our elements go into a protective state that can turn violent."

Godiva continued speaking in a hushed voice, combing her fingers delicately through Salome's now-tangled hair. The rest of the words didn't register to her, though she was certain they didn't matter. One of the witches was missing but without being able to focus her vision, she couldn't tell who was absent. Only Godiva's presence was certain. The rest was a blur.

"The king is here," someone said.

It was said so low, Salome almost didn't hear it. She turned around, her unfocused gaze searching for him. The scent of him hit her first: citrus and leather. And then his voice.

"Rosalia, love," he said. His voice was warm and gentle, and she didn't think she deserved his sweetness. "Let me take care of you."

She softened. There was something calming about him.

Whatever it was, it helped. She wanted to keep that. to hold on even if she had no entitlement to the waves of peace washing over her at the sound of his voice and the faint fragrance of him.

But the stubborn part of her determined to keep her independence reared its ugly head. On instinct, she leaned away, but he held out his hand, waiting. Eventually, she would give in. How he knew that, she didn't know, but something told her he'd understand. That he would take care of her. She imagined him brushing back her hair, kissing her brow, cleaning away dirt and grime, and waiting until her storm settled.

Salome was certain he sensed it too. Something that told him to be here, with her, because he knew her in her many dimensions, even if he didn't yet realize how much he knew.

He saw her in the night but didn't know her. He saw her in the day and thought he did.

Maybe he was suspicious. Maybe he wasn't.

But the reality was that his soul must recognize her soul, just as hers recognized his. There was something connecting them, some invisible thread woven around their hearts. It hurt to think about it, to imagine it might exist.

How sad that of all the places she could go for peace, of all the people who could offer her comfort, it was only King Vincent of Ilarya who could soften her heart and make her feel safe.

If she could only have that now, she had to seize the moment. Salome took his hand and Vincent tugged her to him. She slumped in his embrace.

Here, held in his arms, she sobbed.

She cried over the love she was certain she felt for him and for the violence she caused. She cried over her weakness and lack of control. She cried out of loneliness and despair, knowing she had a home and destroyed it because it was an awful one. She cried because she was pulled into a new family and she felt like she didn't belong, not yet and maybe not ever.

She cried, and he held her tightly. He spoke so quietly, it was like sharing a secret.

"You're with me. You're safe. I'm here," he said.

Desperate to keep him close, she clutched his arms and buried her face against his chest.

"I will kill them all," she vowed. These were the words of a girl forced to do terrible things to stay alive. Who would keep doing such things so long as she needed. But she didn't want to listen to herself. She wanted to hear his heart and match it with hers.

"Who?" he asked.

Salome shook her head. There were so many secrets between them, so many lies.

"I may know who they are," Vincent said.

At that, she lifted her head.

"My parents knew of an organization of thieves and murderers. They were dangerous people who tried to enter our home and take control of the kingdom. I have tried to dismantle them and rid us of them, but with the war, it is not an easy task, nor one with which I can provide my full attention," he told her, his eyes downcast as he held her close. "It would not be difficult to imagine they would come after you if it suited their agenda."

The Alliance was right to be concerned about his knowledge of them.

But what had he done? What did he intend to do?

If he knew of her association with them, she was bound to hang for her lies and deceit, for the crimes she committed against him. If he urged the right person to speak, he'd learn of all she'd done over the years—the people she hurt, the things she stole, the laws she broke.

She'd have to kill them before he could find out or prove to him that she was different. That she was someone he could trust, and that she was someone to keep close, not someone to sentence to death.

"I will kill them all," she said. "Whoever they are, whatever they want, I'll kill them."

She was nothing and no one, but she could change that.

They would fight in the war against Pavalla. She would fight at his side and prove herself an ally. With the witches, she'd work to get rid of the demons, to find the light witch and stop her from wreaking more havoc in this damaged world. For him, for herself, so he would be safe, and she would be free.

His heartbeat was steady, solid, and he was warmer than sunlight. Quietly, he stroked her hair and kissed the top of her head. The tenderness forced the tears in her eyes to fall, rolling down her cheeks.

They sat there in silence, knowing she truly meant those words.

Something told her that, of all people, he would allow her to hunt them down and destroy them. He didn't even know all that they'd done to her. But she thought he might understand. She imagined him letting her go out into the night in her dark leathers, both standing under the moonlight, staring at each other. Both determined to do what seemed the right thing to do.

He held her hand in his, palm to palm. She saw what would happen if they both survived the battle. The future wasn't certain, but if they lived, this would come true. She would make sure it did.

Chapter Thirty-Three

IF SALOME COULD BE ANYWHERE IN THE WORLD, SHE DIDN'T KNOW if she'd choose to be here. Ilarya was a cage of its own kind.

Where would I run?

She had her hand on the glass covering a framed map on the wall, illustrated with bits of folklore and fantasy. It had only a portion of the known world, a detailed map with Ilarya in the center. The Viridian Ocean and Villasayas to the west. Veirelle to the north, Laisia to the east, and Pavalla and Miraunis to the south.

That didn't include the other continent on the other side of the Viridian, or the ones far south filled with snow and untouched territory.

She'd at least visited the Westerlands before, only to discover that she felt even more like an outsider there. Everyone was so pale and looked at her with the clear belief that she didn't belong there.

Her finger drifted to the Villasayas islands. Images filled her mind of white sand beaches and turquoise waters, dormant volcanoes and looming mountains in the distance, palm trees swaying and forests promising branches of fruit and flowers.

A loud knock startled Salome and she withdrew her hand from the map.

The doors opened, and Vincent entered. "Are you ready?"

A grand dinner was being held, a formal farewell to all those heading off to battle in a couple of days.

He smiled as he held out a hand covered in paint. Black and bronze and gold, making her suspect that he had been painting her, making her vain heart sing.

She looked down at her own hands, the black silk gloves covering them, then took his. No shock, no jolt, no burst of the senses. The witches recited words that echoed faintly in the back of her mind. She was the one that men should fear. What she could do was dangerous.

Salome could never truly fear the night, not when she was part of it.

In the Great Hall, Vincent led her to a table overlooking the large space. He kissed the inside of her wrists instead of her hands, finding her pulse and pressing his lips there. Warmth traveled up her arm and when she met his eyes, there was mischief and lust.

She was calmer when he was close. Soothed like ice on overheated skin. Once they were seated, he kept a hand on her thigh, stroking absently as his attention was diverted to others in the room.

The other day, after they left the kitchens, Vincent had led her to his rooms and helped her undress. When her skin was exposed, he kissed her bare shoulders, and ran his calloused hands down her arms, over her waist and hips. He'd murmured comforting words to her before helping her bathe with a warm damp washcloth. Every touch was gentle and caring and a promise.

He was with her. Everything would be okay.

Maybe, if she could stay at his side, she could believe that.

His uncle, General Bruno, sat beside him this evening. There was even more silver in his hair now, more weariness in his eyes. Like this, right before another battle, General Bruno earned an image of a war-hardened man, his hope dim, and his body tired.

At least he wasn't afraid of her. Or maybe he and the other nobles now saw her as a new weapon, something to help them win all the battles with little bloodshed on the Ilaryan side.

"When we return, we can celebrate our victory and your union to my nephew." Bruno's smile was tinged with sadness but his eyes soft with tenderness.

Even Irene was quieter than usual, seated alongside her husband.

"If you were wondering," Irene began, her voice low in a whisper. "Everyone knows what happened. No one shall ask of it, but they know."

Salome glanced around. "And?"

"A powerful queen could be our downfall or our victory. You control the shadows and see the future in the cards, and our hands." Irene gestured to Salome's gloved hands.

An observant woman already thinking of the steps ahead. She had no smile, only a knowing look in her eyes as if to say there was no secret that could be kept from her.

"Are *you* afraid of me?"

"Not at all." Irene shrugged. "But I am curious. Did you see something about me?" No patience nor malevolence was present in her words or tone. The only indication of her displeasure was the slight purse of her lips.

Salome sighed. "I didn't intend to."

"Think nothing of it. You are still my *friend*, I hope."

"Of course," Salome said.

Better friends than enemies. She'd accept that as long as she could.

"This magic is merely...very new and strange."

"Did it frighten you?"

Salome shook her head.

There was no guarantee that what she saw was an absolute or a fragmented possibility. Was it a precursor to death? Or simple insight into what was to come? She could ask the witches, but they weren't too nearby. Though present for tonight's dinner, they dined among the guests instead of the advisors, staying distant from the politics.

"Let us trust each other," Salome said.

Finally, Irene smiled. "I'd like to."

The night went on. Irene continued to tease and ask questions until finally divulging that she would also ride into battle. A reassurance, perhaps, that someone Salome knew and could trust with her life would fight beside her.

Their conversation paused when others came to speak with Irene. A fight for her favor and her influence over the crown. Others glanced at Salome with uncertainty.

Vincent laced their fingers, palms pressed together on the table, leaning in every so often to inform her on what he learned from others, from idle gossip to political matters. He revealed the Pavallan army was drawing close, spotted by scouts near the border. Some villagers were evacuating their homes while others prepared to fight.

Messengers came and went. Soldiers entered to grab food and say some goodbyes.

A sense of dread dawning over the people as the battle loomed, though. Liveliness extinguished as bellies filled and wine bottles emptied. The excitement of each nightly event faded faster and faster as the likelihood of death drew closer.

Half of the guests left when a man with a grim expression walked into the hall.

He bowed deeply. "Your Majesty." His eyes flashed to Salome, so brief that she might not have noticed if she wasn't staring intently at him. "They're here."

For a second, fear seized Salome. She nearly expected an army to barge in—or maybe even the Alliance, come to try to kill her. Instead, four men entered the hall with a shrouded body on a stretcher.

She didn't realize her hands were shaking until Vincent held them, pressing a kiss to her knuckles. His eyes held a sadness seen right before delivering bad news.

"Forgive me. If I had known they would arrive tonight, I would have warned you."

Slowly, she pulled her hand away. "Who—?"

"It's poor timing," he continued.

"Vincent, please."

After a moment, he lowered his voice and said, "Your father was found."

An image of her true father flashed in her eyes—warm, brown eyes and thick black hair, eyes crinkled with laughter despite the weariness hanging over his malnourished body. But that wasn't who Vincent meant.

It was Baron d'Ilumias.

"Unfortunately... he's been dead for several weeks."

Time slowed. Every gaze shot to her.

The remaining guests whispered a quiet chorus of similar sentiment. *Poor girl.* Pity filled their eyes. All Salome could do was try to breathe evenly, to prevent the shadows from waking and wreaking havoc.

Nothing in her wanted to know what happened. She had no interest in how disfigured the body had become. Death was ugly. She'd seen too much lately. Now this was coming up like a submerged recovered treasure and all that was lost now rising to the surface.

This was another message from the Alliance, a reminder of how she'd gotten where she was and all the casualties that made the charade possible. Waves of nausea rolled through her. If they forced her to look, she wouldn't have to feign sickness.

Portraits of the baron hung in the halls of the d'Ilumias estate, but the baron's presence could never be felt. His home was empty and cold as a result of his lost family and his long absences. She did not see him then; she didn't want to see him now. She didn't want to think about what she was doing with his daughter's name.

Missing for months. Dead for several weeks. The Alliance slaughtered him and his daughter. They left a man to rot where he died until they had a use for him.

The message was clear: The Alliance did not forget the pieces of their games.

For a moment, Salome stared at the body, horrified.

And then she stood and bolted.

Fear and relief hit her the second she stepped outside of the room, but she didn't stop. Her heart slammed against her ribcage, trying to break free. Her lungs burned; her hands shook. She was going to be sick.

At the base of a tower staircase far from the hall, she slowed, finding sanctuary there. Salome propped herself onto the steps and pressed her back to the stone walls. She glared at the pale marble statue standing guard at the bottom. A veiled woman, the hint of a smile hidden in the carved folds of fabric. Beautiful and blissful in enviable oblivion.

Vincent called for her, slightly breathless.

The corridor was empty except for them. No guards, no servants, no wandering nobles. Moonlight and starlight spilled from the open archways overlooking the gardens. He sat next to her in silence. After a few moments, she leaned into him, and he cradled her head in his lap.

"Don't tell me how he died," Salome muttered, closing her eyes. She wanted to be relieved. He was dead. He couldn't condemn her. But his corpse was a reminder of what the Alliance could do. They could have hidden his body but allowed the king's men to find him.

It was no accidental discovery. It was purposeful.

All that was hidden would be revealed.

"There is nothing wrong with grieving for your father," he whispered.

"I never thought there was." She didn't cry. Perhaps she should have.

A daughter should have mourned her father, but the baron was not hers to miss.

Fear was made of talons gripping her heart and lungs. She felt like her body was brittle and time was sand slipping out of her hands. The Alliance would not stop, and they would not forget and she may never be free of them.

Quietly, Vincent swept back the strands of hair that had fallen into her face.

"We could die at any moment. This could all be over."

"We might die before we're married," he said.

She choked back a laugh or a sob. She couldn't tell which.

"Is that what weighs on your mind these days?"

Vincent was calm, his eyes unfocused in the shadows. A few candles along the walls lit the corridor. She found comfort in that, in his certainty of safety, though she knew if she let go and listened, she would hear the shadows.

"A significant concern," Vincent admitted as he leaned forward, his elbows on his knees. His hair hung around his face, dark curls grazing his cheeks. "Life is short. If I could spend every second with you, I would."

Salome glanced away and caught sight of the hem of a white gown, red and gold embroidery along the edges. Maris. The flames grew, flickering, assuring that she was nearby. A friend and a guardian, even if she didn't deserve it.

"I cannot grieve for a man I hardly knew," she whispered, more to herself than to him. "And I cannot bear the pity."

Rosalia lost her father. Salome lost her security. But she couldn't leave him, not yet.

"Are you afraid, love?" His voice was soft.

She imagined all he could see was a grieving girl, struck silent and solemn by a corpse. He understood loss, a terrible thing to find common ground on.

"You ask that often." A hoarse laugh escaped her throat.

He swept his thumbs across the backs of her hands, warmth pushing through her silk gloves. The goodness of him made her grateful, caring when she careened into chaos, anchoring her before she could fight or flee.

When he looked up, he wore a crooked smile. "Not an ounce of fear then?"

"None at all," she lied. But she heard the demons pushing against the shield around the shadows, fighting against candlelight.

"Another reason why I need you."

Salome shook her head. "That is not true at all."

"It is. Unlike you, I am terrified," Vincent said, touching his forehead to hers for a second. "I require every ounce of your courage and, selfishly, I need you to stay alive."

Salome sighed. He was watching her carefully, waiting to see what she had to say. Listening attentively, like every word she said mattered. No one else ever looked at her like that.

"If it is safer here—"

"I'll find my way to the battlefield with or without your permission. You cannot command me to stay."

"Rosalia—"

The way he spoke made something within her crack.

"My father is dead, my family gone. You and the witches are all I have now." The steadiness of her voice vanished the second she succumbed to his arms. In some way, he truly was hers. The shadows sought her, the witches claimed her, but she wanted *him*.

He was the calm force she craved. He was gentleness and goodness and grace.

If she fought alongside him, if she could protect him and make sure he only remembered her as someone who was trying to do good, maybe she would deserve him. Maybe she could fool herself into believing that.

If she had to say goodbye, she would do it herself. Not now, not yet, but soon.

At least, before then, she can ensure he'd think fondly of her when she was gone.

"I refuse to lose you," he swore.

"You do not even have me yet," she said with a sad smile.

Perhaps he never would.

Chapter Thirty-Four

The night before they left for battle, Salome sat in Vincent's room.

Fear made him fragile. Dark circles slept under his eyes and a mosaic of dried paint splatters coated his hands. This little moment together felt like a final gift.

When she'd walked in, he kissed her immediately. His beard scratched against her cheeks, the ends of it rough from a recent trim. Desperation entwined in his every movement, hands gliding over her arms, up her neck. His fingers wove into her hair and pulled her close, as if terrified that she might slip away.

She clutched him with the same desperation. Time would run out soon enough. She wouldn't waste any opportunity to touch him, to be with him. It required no acting to sink into his embrace and meet his passion with her own.

He did not speak of fear or war, just kissed her and held her and hoped. Delirious with his desperation, demanding and delighting in what she offered.

"Please," she whispered, and that was all he needed.

With the door locked, they made quick work of each other's clothes, stripping it away until they were both bare. Vincent growled lowly with appreciation, kissing her from her throat and down her middle before stopping before her legs.

He kissed her there too. Kissed and licked and sucked until her legs were so weak, she had to plead for a spot to lay so she could enjoy his attentions. They ended up on his bed, tossing aside sketchbooks and canvases and paint supplies to have enough room together.

They made love. Tenderly at first, then harder and more desperate, before becoming softer with each other and savoring every movement they made together. Salome burned under his touch, delighting in how he knew how to please her.

And then, once they decided that they'd had their fill, he pleaded, "Let me paint you. Let me never forget how lovely you are."

Despite her initial reluctance, she couldn't refuse him. The painting would one day vanish with her. The memory of this moment would be her gift to him.

His eyes darted between her and the canvas. A content smile sat upon his lips. Tonight, he was all disorder—his gray shirt wrinkled, his dark trousers splattered with paint, his eyes slightly dazed. He sat upon a stool as he worked, its true color hidden beneath layers of paint.

Salome lounged in a plain brown armchair, dressed in a now-wrinkled pale-yellow chiffon gown. Her black hair was loose, hanging around her shoulders with moonstone and obsidian beads woven into braids by Sylvia earlier that morning. Her eyes were lined with kohl, dark and bold against her tawny brown skin. Her cheeks were overly warm from blushing at the lustful way Vincent kept looking at her, her lips swollen and red from kissing. Her body was soft and relaxed, sated after he well he'd tended to her.

War was tomorrow. Tonight was for them.

"Tell me everything I don't know," she begged as he adjusted her limbs. Light hands lifted bits of her hair, fingertips grazing her cheek. As if he was afraid to touch too much and reignite his desire, distracting him from his task.

"Where would I start?"

"Anywhere."

Vincent paused. As he leaned back, he cleared his throat. "I always wanted to be a painter. My father would take me into the forest and encourage me to explore. At the end of the day, he would remind me who I was: a prince, a boy who would have to be selfless, who couldn't spend his time trying to paint the trees."

He bore the burden of royal blood before the crown was ever bestowed on him. But within forests, it was easy to forget the rest of the world when one saw nothing but trees and earth and sky. When Salome was little, they were her second home as well, where she climbed and ran like a wild creature before she'd left her village behind to lighten her parents' burden.

Before long, Vincent became engrossed in his work again. The canvas was his target, the paintbrush his arrow. His eyebrows drew together, eyes narrowed, jaw tightened with determination.

She imagined a little boy with black hair and big, brown eyes gazing at the world with wonder. Shielded in the shade, blissful and innocent as he painted what he saw. The crushing sadness of the brush taken away, the trees fading into the distance as he returned home.

"Did it break your heart?"

He shrugged. "He was always kind."

"Ah, he taught you kindness?"

"And my mother taught me to be a hero." He smiled fondly.

Despite her urge to lean forward, Salome remained still, the perfect muse, but couldn't stay quiet. "Why do *you* have to be a hero?"

Heroes lost too much. Heroes sacrificed. And heroes died.

"Someone has to be," he said.

She giggled at the feather-light fingers on her neck when he adjusted her. Almost guilty for making his task more difficult, she forced herself into a perfect statue for a bit longer. "But why you?"

"Because I have the power to do something."

Her face scrunched up as though she bit into bitter fruit. When he glanced up, he chuckled. Salome couldn't see the humor though, only an ivory skull, the skin melting away, a hero's death foretold in the cards.

A servant girl later brought them food and drink. The sight of the paint-splattered king, sitting on a stool while Salome lounged in front of him like a goddess, had no effect on her. She was in and out without a word. An intruder in their moment when he was a simple artist and she, his muse.

This evening, Salome's hands were bare and vulnerable, though she kept her fingertips far from his palms. His eyes lit up when he had to adjust her position, delighted by their nearness.

There was nothing to fear—no demons to disturb them, shadows weak as the candlelight filled the room with warmth and brightness.

Finally, Vincent sat beside her. Closing his eyes, he breathed deeply, slowly, like sleep was creeping on him. Freed from playing muse, she rose to inspect his private rooms.

Scattered books, disorganized on the bookshelf in the corner of the room. Three windows covered by heavy curtains in dark grays and metallic shades. Upholstered couches and chairs with paint bottles cradled between the cushions. Not much space for visitors.

Her eyes caught on a portrait of her sent by the Alliance, hanging beside paintings of his family. One of his parents in their white-and-gold wedding clothes hung in the center. The other of Vincent and his siblings, the four d'Allorias children.

"My family," he said.

And she was among them. There was so much she could say, but she couldn't speak.

"My sisters and my brother. We couldn't wait to ride into battle with our mother once we came of age. When my sister Viviana went, she brought back such magnificent stories."

She turned around.

Vincent took a deep breath that shook his entire body.

"I was second after Viviana, meant to look after the younger ones while she went off with our mother and father. Our parents were taken first, weakened by the price of witch magic to save us. My sister returned to the fight and left me to protect the younger ones—but I failed."

Kneeling, she rested her head against his legs. Her hands searched for his. When she found them, she placed a kiss on his knuckles. Her fondness for him was stifling, strangling her heart. His voice wavered and it made her ache.

With another shuddering breath, he continued, "They beheaded Viviana on the battlefield. My younger sister, Lorea, rode out in the night to reach another truce once the battle had ended. Only two riders returned, both traumatized after witnessing demons take her.

"The youngest, my brother Laurent." His face twisted into a scowl. "He was so reckless. He demanded to come to battle with me. Angered by what we lost, he charged in alone, and did not stand a chance when he was surrounded on the field." As he spoke, his hands curled into fists. Frustration and fury bore down on him, an ache resounding in his voice.

Salome couldn't fully understand it. Leaving her parents meant she had very few memories of them, and the Alliance could be called her adoptive family, but she never truly felt loved or at home with them. Now, she had the witches, but her relationship with them was new. For now, she could only imagine his loss and pain.

"War is a wretched thing," she said.

Vincent nodded. He blinked repeatedly and widened his eyes at the ceiling, trying to fight his fatigue. Salome grinned. He was insatiable, unsatisfied with the short time they had together. How could she feel nothing for this man? It was never possible. He was too easy to fall in love with.

"Tell me more tomorrow. You should rest," she decided, standing.

He rose with her, knocking his knees against her legs and reaching for her hands. Palm to palm, he laced their fingers. "Stay with me."

Visions swarmed in her mind: a crowned helmet falling, crushed by the enemy's feet, a storm of arrows raining upon an army, dark shapes in the sky, figures in white-gold light.

She tried to resist the dizziness as the images danced before her eyes.

"One more thing," he insisted, anchoring her to reality. A shy smile graced his lips as he led her to a smaller room, gently pulling her by the fingers and granting her some relief from fate.

Paintings upon paintings filled the room, stacked atop one another. Some of the royal family, of green and golden gardens, of the view of Ellasya from the tallest tower, and so much more. Piles of paintings that should have been displayed for all the kingdom to see, not stored in secret and covered in dust.

He directed her attention to the corner of the room, to what he tucked away there.

A suit of armor like the one in her visions. She turned, almost nauseated by the mere sight of it so soon. Beside it, there was a smaller suit, a mixture of dark metal and leather with flowers and celestial objects in yellow and rose gold, including a helmet with a matching crown.

Propped up beside it was a sword, covered by a black sheath bearing golden patterns of moons, suns, stars, and the brightest yellow blossoms. A matching shield stood nearby. Together, they made up a queen's armor. Bearing the star and the suns of d'Allorias and the moon of d'Ilumias.

Despite all his doubt, all his fears, Vincent still saw the warrior she might be. It did not matter that guilt would gnaw at her, that the d'Ilumias symbols did not belong to her.

If she could have nothing else, she wanted this.

"It's for you," he whispered. Vincent stood behind her, her back to his chest. His heart pounded despite his calm. As he leaned in, his lips moved against her hair, stretching into a smile.

She could have wept. She didn't deserve this man and his gentle, good heart.

"When the sun rises, our journey begins. At nightfall of the seventh night, we will meet the Pavallans at the Woods of Palvary." He paused. "We fight together. They will not see our fear."

Salome looked him in the eye. "There is nothing to fear."

Except the demons, unleashed on the world when the moon and stars were smothered by the clouds and the night was at its darkest.

"Will you stay?" he asked.

As king, he could command it, but there was no need. "Tonight, I'll stay."

He led her to the bedroom again and lay with her on the mattress. When he kissed her, he moved slowly, running his nose across her skin and sighing. Salome closed her eyes when they weren't face to face, focusing on every sensation as he kissed and touched her with his mouth and hands. It was when she was on top of him, riding him, that she interlaced their fingers and held his gaze.

"I'm yours," she said.

For now. For tonight.

This was all she could have.

Chapter Thirty-Five

Hours later, they rode their horses side-by-side through Ilarya. Vincent led at the very front of the formation, adorned in his regal armor. She lifted her head high, riding on the king's right. A place of power beside him.

Together, they would survive anything.

Survival was all that mattered. No bloodlust, only determination aided by her young magic. The shadows were silent, awaiting her command. She focused her mind on holding their leash until the perfect moment to let them go.

General Bruno rode on Vincent's left, banner in hand, the star and the suns on near-black blue. The witches rode on Salome's other side, donned in dark leathers with engraved details of their elements and their faces concealed by skull-shaped, black lacquer helmets. Not entertainers, but warriors wielding their own weapons—Della held an axe, Thema a crossbow, Maris a mace, and Godiva bore a pair of swords strapped to her back.

The l'Issalya brothers rode in the row behind, Irene and Duke d'Aryllia with them. Together, they rode through daylight and darkness at full speed, making camp when necessary. Hundreds upon hundreds of people were ready to fight against Pavalla, to face death and look it straight in the eye. All for their kingdom and their king.

Along the way, they passed several villages. People waved flowers and threw them on their path. Those who could join their horde said goodbyes to loved ones. Some wept. Others howled for victory.

Salome tried to feel nothing for them. Most had no real armor or weapons. Villagers came with what they could, from shining swords to dulled axes and farm tools. Whatever they had, they raised them to the king, pledging themselves and their lives for the sake of protecting their homes.

Fools, she thought. But she was a fool too. She was here with them, after all.

The day of the battle, Vincent spent the morning speaking with Bruno and talking with the soldiers and commoners. Each person mattered to him; each life should be remembered.

He met with Salome right before the battle was to begin, helping her onto her horse though she hadn't needed it. Together, they ventured to a field where the Woods of Palvary separated the kingdoms.

The heat died down as night drew near, made bearable by Thema and Godiva cooling the air and Della's enchantments on the armor to make them light but sturdy. More breathable in hopes of helping them survive longer.

It wasn't the weather painting Salome's brow in sweat, but the battle looming ahead.

"Are you afraid?" Vincent asked.

Salome clutched her helmet in her lap. There were no soldiers in sight. No flags waving in the setting sun, no hint of human life within the trees. One might think this place was deserted and forgotten.

"No," she answered. "Not of the folklore about the Woods, at least." Though she grinned, she knew now that the stories were never just stories.

Wind ruffled the forest's leaves, whistling then howling. The trees seemed to touch the sky, a dark wall of green and brown, shadows spaced between them, concealing the stories embedded in the Woods of Palvary.

Thema removed her helmet for a better look.

The Woods of Palvary were a place of death, the nearby villages claimed. Decades ago, countless battles between the kingdoms happened here. The battles moved to other parts of the border, stretched along the vast fields. Superstition kept them away from this place, afraid of supposed curses.

Until tonight.

People stopped fighting here out of fear. A story of survivors who came back, eyes clouded, bodies broken, mumbling incoherently. They weren't as their loved ones remembered them and died shortly after their return. Some blamed the war. Some suspected there was more.

Centuries ago, there were no trees, only open fields. The trees, they said, were born from the bones of the fallen. The bloodshed nurtured seeds and roots. Magic made them rise. After every battle, the Woods thickened with new trees. A seemingly cursed place now, where battles weren't meant to be fought. But blood still spilled.

If Euria were here, Salome would have asked if this was the place to hear the witch's heartbeat. Was this her grave? Was this the birthplace of Ilaryan folklore?

"This is the place," Della whispered.

Godiva nodded slowly.

When a deer burst from the trees, the horses huffed, stomping their feet on the dying grass. Thema lifted a hand, blowing wind back to the trees. The deer darted back into the safety of bark and branches. Salome wondered if it was true, that seeing a wild animal marked one for death.

Nearby, a soldier who nocked an arrow lowered his bow.

"We shouldn't be here. Why did they want to fight here?" Della said. "I can feel magic in the trees—a curse, a warning." She pulled off her helmet, glancing over at the other witches before her gaze wandered back to the Woods.

"Are the tales true then?" Salome asked.

"Some were created to protect the innocent animals who seek refuge in the forest. Some things are not meant to be known to humans," Maris said, eyes narrowed.

Yes, some of the tales were true. This place was laced with magic.

"Are we cursed?"

"Only if you kill the animals, I think." Della dismounted and kneeled on the ground. The grass ruffled as Della placed her hand on the earth, forming a path in the grass that raced to the trees. Her hair was bright in the fading light, a bold yellow against her armor as loose strands waved in the breeze.

"They're here, waiting." Her voice was low and uneasy.

Salome squinted ahead. "How do you know?"

"A heavy weight trampling across the earth. Human and horse. Fewer numbers than ours." Della's smile faded as she mounted her horse again. She shook her head, trying to make sense of it.

The horses continued their protest, pulling on reins and stomping.

Whatever it was, the shadows felt it, freeing themselves from wherever they'd hidden. As they awakened, they called to Salome by the dying light.

"The wind—" Thema began, voice hoarse. "They were waiting but not for us. There is a reason they have fewer soldiers." Her eyes widened and suddenly, she shoved her helmet back on and lifted her hands. The reins fell, but the horse kept steady. Her arms bent as though the wind pushed back.

And then a deafening roar came from the sky.

The air filled with the scent of smoke and charred remains. No wonder Pavalla was ready for battle. They surely assumed with this help, they would win, and the war would end. War had raged too long and now magic had a bigger role than before.

Everything was changing. This wasn't a rivalry between kingdoms anymore.

This was a show of power.

"Those should not exist here," Godiva said.

A shower of flame burst from the mouth of a dragon the size of a castle. Thema countered, sending streams of water to extinguish them.

Midnight-blue scales gleamed against the darkening sky. Eyes glowed green as emeralds as though gems sat within the dragon's eye-sockets. It roared and flapped the wide expanse of its wings. This was the wind Thema had fought.

These were creatures of legend, not seen in over a century.

"You didn't train me for this," Salome said.

Maris shot her a glare. "None of us expected this. We will have to focus on the beasts. You keep your attention on the ground."

"It will tire her out too soon," Thema said.

And then soldiers burst from the trees with four smaller dragons above them.

Behind Salome, people screamed.

Thema kept repeating the name *Zsiona*. A far-south continent, almost mythical, surrounded by waters no ship could sail through. Thema said it like a curse, like saying it would send them back where they were meant to be.

The dragons dipped low. Ilaryan soldiers shouted and ducked.

But Maris fought back. The flames on her fingertips danced in her eyes until she shot them forward. They were arrows of their own, lengthening as they reached for their targets. It wouldn't hit the dragons, but Maris didn't seem to care.

Vincent called for Rosalia to stay close, as if he thought she might charge into battle all on her own. For his sake, she turned to him, unsheathing her sword in one smooth motion.

"I won't die today," she promised.

"I won't let you."

She laughed and slammed her helmet onto her head "You're my king, but you don't control me."

No one did anymore.

The last of the sun dipped below the horizon. The shadows came alive, surging to Salome. She hunched over the saddle, a burst of agony in her chest like they tried to yank out her heart. Before she understood what the shadows intended, humanlike figures formed from the pieces of dark around them.

"Be careful," Maris warned. "Don't lose control."

Salome couldn't speak. She couldn't say that she didn't command this. It felt more like she called to them and then they used her as a conduit.

The leash slipped from her hands, and everything happened at once. All she could do was gasp and clutch her chest like the air was torn from her lungs. The figures charged faster than any human. Faceless figures running across the field to meet her foes. There was no death for them, only disintegration, and they could rise again.

Della sent boulders barreling toward their opponents. Vines sprouted from the ground, wrapping around the legs of the Pavallan horses and dragging them down. Their riders soared, then crashed to the earth, held prisoner by vines.

Godiva charged ahead, positioning herself between Salome and the battle. "Remember our warning: do not use your magic to kill. There are far too many lives involved here tonight and all that death will corrupt you."

"I *know*."

"If you must kill, use anything but your magic."

"Be careful," Thema cautioned.

"You've already experienced the bloodthirsty kind of instinct. Resist it," Godiva said.

Frustrated, Salome opened her mouth to question the command, but Maris interrupted. "Our power is not endless. Do not use it to kill. Not tonight." There was a warning in her voice, but she had no chance to say any more as they turned forward and charged ahead, straight into the other army, weapons raised.

Someone shouted in terror. Salome looked up in time to see arrows raining on them.

Vincent's voice overwhelmed all other sounds, shouting orders and commands, but nothing telling her to run and hide. This was different from the Alliance's in-and-out routine, grabbing what they wanted and getting away. She had to fight, to prove she could, to show she was strong enough to be in battle. Vincent worried for her, the Alliance thought her weak without magic, the witches feared what she might do.

She had a few things to accomplish tonight.

Fight to the death. Prove them wrong. *Survive.*

Grinning, Salome lifted a single hand, palm up to the night sky. Urged by instinct to stop the arrows, as she'd done before. A shield of shadows formed above the Ilaryans within the archers' range. The arrowheads bounced from the shadows and fell uselessly to the ground.

The dragons swooped down, rising when she raised the shield. Wind from their wings pushed back, dispersing it like smoke.

When she tried to reform the shadow figures, she found it difficult to breathe, like a hand was around her throat. When she looked for the other witches, Godiva shook her head. The shadows were weaker now. She could barely hear them, as though they settled to catch their breath though they had no lungs and no need for air.

The other army approached.

Salome readied her sword and shield despite the heaviness of her limbs.

Maris called out, "You've done too much too soon, little one. Wait until the weakening has left. Then fight again."

"You'll live," Della assured her. "You aren't used to using your magic so much and at such distances. The more experienced you become, the easier it will be. For now, the weakening will come sooner than it does for us."

No magic. No shadows to guard her. She was not a witch in this battle, not anymore.

Soon, they were mid-field, racing through the ranks. No colors to tell each fighter apart, only certainty in direction. The sound of steel rang through the air, swords meeting swords, swords meeting shields, and dragons screeching in the air.

In the distance, lithe figures of light waited between the trees.

Chapter Thirty-Six

SALOME SCREAMED AS SHE TUMBLED, AND DIRT FILLED HER OPEN mouth. Swords swung down at her. She rolled, narrowly avoiding the enemy blades, until she managed to lift her sword and shield at her assailant.

Her blade burrowed into flesh. Not to kill, just enough to bring them down.

"Are you trying to spare them?" General Bruno growled. "Get up!"

She rose, swiping at the blood splashed onto her cheek. When she stumbled, he pushed a hand onto her shoulder to steady her.

"I'm fine," Salome said, shoving him away.

Concern flashed in his eyes before he was forced to fight again.

No time to talk. The battle raged on. Now Salome was on her feet, fighting face to face. She sought Vincent in the cacophony, searching for his armor. Too many bodies, too much blood flying between them, preventing her from finding him in the fray.

"The queen!" someone roared. "To the queen!"

At first, Salome looked around before realizing they meant her. They came at her from all sides. Weapons slammed down on her. Sparks flew as metal clashed with metal, sword to shield. The flashes of light caught on her queenly armor, drawing more attention her way. Someone grabbed at her, arms wrapped around her middle.

She threw her head back, her helmet colliding with a bare skull. She kicked out her legs, shoving away someone trying to trap her. Her boots found a throat, and the impact sent them to the ground. Her assailant was then suddenly ripped away.

Fabian and Oscar flanked her, protecting her like a barricade.

On her feet again, breathing heavily, she bowed her head to them.

The brothers stayed close. The battle went on.

Her armor stayed strong, even blow after blow. It dented, it rang, but remained unbroken. Her sword sang when she swung it. She screamed at the effort of her tired arms but gritted her teeth. Someone always came over to help her. Sometimes it was a common soldier, grime on their faces as they nodded then rushed away. Sometimes it was one of the witches, reminding her that they were close.

In those moments, when she stepped back, she appraised the battleground.

Between the trees, figures of light stood like guards stationed at the gates of a proud city. Anyone who dared come close met streaks of light shaped like swords, slashing easily through human bodies.

The light witch was there.

But every time Salome stepped toward the trees, someone blocked her path.

Above, the dragons soared and swooped, grasping Ilaryans in talons and squeezing. Tighter and tighter until human form was unrecognizable, until they were blood and bone and unrecognizable pieces. Bodies littered the ground, seeping into the earth. Daylight would later reveal earth stained red, bones like uplifted roots. Heads torn from bodies, cracked skulls, broken spines. Even the horses were feasts for the beasts.

Witch-fire and dragon-fire filled the once-empty field. An unseen shield surrounded the trees, though, preventing the flames from spreading and slaughtering the life within. Only small streams of blood trickled toward the trees, siphoned by magic.

The ground shifted and turned, trapping limbs and locking enemy bodies to the earth. A wall of fire as tall as the trees prevented retreat into the Woods. Wind roared louder than a hurricane, blowing people down.

It encouraged the Ilaryans to fight harder.

There was a count at one point, a pair of Ilaryans competing against each other. With their swords, they slashed, stabbed, and lunged as though their feet were winged and they had magic instead of willpower and bloodlust.

She laughed at their rivalry until one had his head separated from his shoulders. The survivor screamed in agony, like he'd been gravely wounded. His friend's head rolled to her feet, hidden in the helmet, but she could imagine his eyes. Brown and wide open, his laughter frozen on his face.

Salome yanked off her helmet and vomited until she was empty.

Though there was a hint of bloodlust running through her, she couldn't stomach death's stench of rot and ruin. The shadows reveled in horrors that made her retch, delighted by the gore. When her weakening waned, they dragged limbs into crevices opened by the earth witch, imprisoning their opponents. There were shadow hands with endless arms, reaching upward with clawed hands around fragile mortal necks.

Trying to stop them felt like forcing her own fingers backward, pushing until the shadows brought human soldiers to unconsciousness rather than death. Soldiers collapsed, alive but barely.

Her disgust mingled with the delight of the shadows.

In the distance, someone called out in fear for Rosalia.

Salome twisted around, searching for Vincent. When their gazes met, he smiled with relief, but a Pavallan blocked him when he took a step toward her. Her fingers twitched and the darkness around her pulsed, ready for more. She fought for control, to hold them back.

Inhale. Exhale. Inhale. Exhale.

Please, they begged. *Let us fly.*

Somehow, she knew what they meant—her familiar, well-loved daggers. They weren't with her now, but the shadows could take their form.

No killing, not with her magic.

So, she suffered with her sword, slick and painted red with human blood.

Salome only called on the shadows when a figure charged too quickly. A Pavallan woman this time, raising an axe in the air. The shadows felt Salome's panic when she was unable to lift her sword in time and answered her call.

Black smoke and tar turned to blades in the air and flew at her attacker, cutting through the woman easily. Shock formed in her features even as she fell.

Salome dropped to the ground, panting. Maris was at her side in an instant, roughly pulling her by the arm. She left a red handprint where she touched, remnants of the fire witch's killing. Salome grimaced, wondering what evidence of violence lingered on her own body.

"Enough!" Maris snarled. "Don't allow the shadows to inflict such violence."

A ring of fire surrounded them. A wall between the witches and the rest of the battle.

"You'll be dead if you keep doing this," Godiva shouted. Her helmet was gone, lost in the madness. Streaks of blood coated her cheeks. Every time someone came within three feet of her, Godiva raised her hands and sent them back with air, a force of wind and will. The strength of it sent the Pavallans on their backs, unconscious. "When you feel weakened, it is your body telling you what it struggles to bear."

Magic wasn't weightless, it seemed. Magic was a muscle that could be overexerted.

"What am I supposed to do?"

Della and Thema joined, and the four shielded Salome. Without looking, Della lifted a hand. The Pavallan soldier behind her fell, their ankles encased in stone. Godiva swept a hand sideways, sending gusts outward. All within five feet of them blew backward. Those closest received the worst damage—necks snapped, dead before they hit the ground.

"Stay in control. Try not to kill with your magic," Della whispered. "Win by wounding."

"What about *your* magic?" Salome gestured to the death around them.

"We've had ours for decades. You don't yet know all there is to know about what *you* can do. Shadow magic is different; it's inherently deadly." Thema looked pained to say it, like it was a secret she'd been keeping. "The voices you hear in the shadows are the ones who came before you, who were claimed by the magic itself. You are at risk of that, especially when your magic is so young and untamed."

It wasn't fair. They treated her like a child. *Little one.* Fondness laced with inferiority.

Their elements never betrayed them, surviving the demands of combat. Resentment raced through her, red-hot beneath her skin. Her fingers twitched. Too weak to do real damage, all she did was make the shadows expand and contract.

"Little one," Della said. "We will take care of you."

She didn't want caretakers. But fear of falling apart made her nod. Salome tried to be soothed knowing the witches were not the Alliance. They would guide her and stay with her. And one day, she could be as strong as them. Maybe stronger, maybe that was what they feared.

A loud screech came from the five dragons circling high in the sky. The beasts tossed a body between them like a toy, unidentifiable as human or horse, with flesh falling off the bones and blood dripping.

Godiva fumed. "These beasts should be exiled on Zsiona. How did Pavalla get them? How did they bind them?"

"Too late to wonder," Thema said, shaking her head.

"What do we do then?" Salome asked.

"For now, there is nothing we can do except attempt to slow them," Godiva said.

Maris scoffed. "This is a feeding ground."

Her fire was useless, a mere caress across their bodies. Only their human opponents felt the heat, wailing in agony as their bodies charred.

Della glanced their way and vines emerged from the ground, wrapping around the Pavallan soldiers' bodies—blinding, gagging, and binding them where they lay. The only sign of her displeasure was the downward twitch of her lips.

Godiva gestured above. "Dragons do not mix with demons. Notice they haven't landed."

The beasts remained aloft in the sky and avoided Salome's shadow figures. Perhaps they understood the wrongness of the demons, or the things that looked like the ones plaguing the world, and the fact that they did not belong here.

Moonlight and stars blinked away, becoming concealed by clouds rolling in.

The dragons retreated, fading into the dark as the lights winked out. At the same time, dozens of demons rose from the earth. It was difficult to notice dark shapes in a darker night, but what she saw was wicked. The demons had bodies of tar and oil, and yet they tore through human bodies like feather-filled pillows.

Both armies shouted in alarm as their comrades fell. They retreated to the light, seeking flame before demons sought them. The demons were not like the dragons; they did not have a side, claiming whatever they found.

"I can't even set the field on fire to send them away," Maris snarled.

"That would kill everyone," Della said.

"Yes, *I know.*"

The shadows under Salome's control hissed. Ready to rise, but too weak to move. It was her fault, her lack of training preventing them from action. They required her energy, and she was too drained.

Maris sent flames around them and into the sky. A streak of white-gold light also burst from the center of the battle. It sent the demons away but didn't destroy them. Meanwhile, figures of pale light coiled limbs around shadowed bodies, drowning them in brightness, squeezing until they dissolved into thick smoke.

The demons stayed away while the field was ablaze, only rising when the flames faded. They kept their distance from bright figures, shrieking at the sight of them before sinking into the earth.

"She's here," Salome breathed.

Della touched her arm. "We don't know whose side she's on."

"But we can find her!"

Godiva shook her head, grabbing Salome as she began to push out the barrier the witches made around her. Something in her was desperate to simply see her. But Godiva gripped her wrist. "The fighting is not over."

Fire kept the demons down. Demons kept the dragons away.

Humans fought each other regardless of the monsters above and around them.

"End this!" General Bruno shouted nearby. "Surrender!"

Enemy soldiers surrounded him. One laughed. But the fight raged on. A blur of metal and blood, nearly impossible to see in the dark. Even the witches re-entered the fray, raising weapons again when enemies were too close to keep away with magic.

Salome did not know where to look, only where to swing her sword. Her arms burned with the effort, exhausted from hours of fighting. Too long, too much. Della ran over, noticing her slowing steps. With a secret smile of hope and urgency in her eyes, she shoved two daggers into Salome's hands.

"Fight, little one. We need you to live." Della's hands covered Salome's, forcing her fingers to grip the handles before she darted away.

The blades were unfamiliar but beautiful and balanced. She sent them flying, blades burrowing into the neck of a Pavallan man about to kill an

Ilaryan. He looked at her as blood spilled over his lips and he crumbled to the ground.

His opponent turned. She didn't immediately recognize him—his hair had fallen into his eyes, strands stuck to skin covered in blood and mud. He looked confused, glancing between the fallen man with the daggers in his neck and his betrothed.

"Today is not the day we die," Salome reminded the king.

"No, it is not." But something wavered on Vincent's face, in his voice.

Recognition, maybe. But he had no time to think, and she hardly had a chance to react. They were too absorbed in the sight of each other to notice who was behind Vincent. The figure approached quickly, seizing the moment of vulnerability with a derisive laugh. He adorned obsidian armor, a crowned helmet, and a torn cape thick and darkened with blood.

And he held his sword to Vincent's neck.

Salome lunged forward, but the crowned man pressed the blade tighter against the exposed skin. Vincent locked eyes with her and shook his head slightly, trying not to cut himself on the steel at his throat.

Someone shouted Vincent's name. Another shouted for Rosalia.

She looked around, eyes wide and heart-pounding.

"Hello, Vincent."

"Prince Ricard." Vincent's hands twitched on his sword.

Oscar tried to charge forward, but three Pavallans held him back. "Let go of him!"

Fury contorted his features over his nearness to his king, yet too slow to stop this from happening.

"Enough!" the crowned man commanded. "Tell your soldiers to lay down their weapons."

"Yours first," Vincent said.

The violence around them slowed as the commands spread through the battleground. Those closest began lowering their weapons.

The crowned man smiled. His skin was darker than Vincent's, more russet brown, and half of his handsome face scarred. His hair was pitch-black and long, hanging between his shoulder blades, stringy with drying blood.

The fighting died around them, a ripple effect as both Ilaryans and Pavallans looked to their leaders. Irene burst through, followed close behind by Fabian, his face bloodied and bruised. Her bow was broken, her quiver empty, but she held a short dagger. Rage and devastation radiated from them once they absorbed the scene.

She felt a hand on her shoulder. Bruno was there, steadying her, offering comfort. But Vincent's death wasn't the fate she had seen, not at all what the cards suggested, not like this. She gritted her teeth. When she inched forward, Bruno held onto her armor, holding her back.

"Are you going to surrender?" the Pavallan prince asked.

"Here I thought we were friends," her king said, charming but mocking. "A friend would know that I would not allow things to end like this."

A sneer distorted the prince's face. "Get on your knees."

The witches surrounded the two of them. No Pavallan soldiers were near enough to stop them, though there was never a chance they could.

"Are you threatening me?"

"I would not dare." Vincent inclined his head toward Maris, her hands gloved in fire. "But she might."

"This will hurt, I promise," Maris said with a smirk.

The Pavallan prince lowered his sword. A short-lived hesitance. The sword rose again, the edge against Vincent's throat. A sliver of skin split. The prince's face hardened, harsh angles highlighted by Maris's fire.

"It does not need to be this way, Your Highness," Vincent said.

"The conflicts in your kingdom have spilled into mine. The magic is worsening, Vincent. My *father* nearly died. Any possibility of peace is ruined."

Vincent turned slightly, only to be pushed to face forward. The prince's sword dug into his neck, drawing blood onto the blade. "And my life is the punishment?"

Salome took a step forward. Vincent glared at her. She stilled.

"My death seals yours, Your Highness," Vincent continued. "If I die, you die. What glory comes from that?"

Maris lit a ring of fire around them. Salome stepped away, lifting a hand to shield her face. Bruno held onto her, keeping close. Vincent's gaze still upon her but warmer now. He smiled, unafraid.

"No one wins the battle if we both die," Vincent said.

"Nor if you all burn," Maris added.

The prince glared at her, then glanced around at their audience. Flames danced in the eyes of those present, a reminder of his fate and theirs. It was his choice.

Prince Ricard sheathed his sword and turned away. "Count your dead and I'll count mine," he decided, facing the remains of his army. Slowly, the prince turned, surrendering but walking off like a victor.

"We saw your beasts, Your Highness," Vincent said.

Prince Ricard paused. "Then you should be afraid. Your army might have witches, but mine has wings."

"End this war, Ricard, before it's too late."

The prince laughed—a cold and unfeeling thing. "There is no end to what our families started."

It was dawn when they finished counting the bodies, identifying as many as they could to bring news to loved ones at home. Some Pavallans remained, gathering remnants of the dead—jewelry and bones, heirlooms tucked into pouches. Bodies covered the field, the stench of death like a rotten veil.

The sun rose, painting the horizon a hazy gold.

As the remaining Pavallans began their trek home, Salome saw her shining in the dawn. Skin pale as the moon, white-gold hair, the sickly color of her cheeks replaced with rosiness, a sinister smile on her mouth as she rode away with her guard.

Sylvia, with sunlight bursting from her hands and blood dripping from her lips.

And she retreated with the Pavallans.

Chapter Thirty-Seven

During the ride home, it was a silent trudge through the summer rain.

In the capital city, the people called for celebration. They cheered for their kingdom, their king, their future queen. Returning warriors embraced weeping loved ones and music filled the streets.

But Salome felt the blood on her hands, heard the cracking of bones, sensed judgement against her for her sins. She felt like she ventured too close to death, a bleak feeling burrowing deeper into her with every step home.

And she thought of Sylvia—bitter and blithe enough to unleash terror on the world.

Once within the castle, Salome raced to her rooms. Servants hurried around, preparing what they could for the celebration that would last the whole evening. They stayed out of her way as she barreled through the corridors, trying to get away, desperate to escape and hide. Her guards broke free from the returning army to follow her.

"Lady Rosalia—" Oscar called as she turned a corner into an empty corridor.

She whirled around, shaking her head. "I *can't* be there and celebrate tonight."

All she could hear in her head was that this war would never end. It would only worsen.

"War is a terrible thing, my lady. Enjoy the moments free of it." Oscar took a step back.

She must have looked like some wild creature, wide-eyed and snarling. Her hair was a gnarled mess of knots. Her hands curled, shadows twisting at her feet like smoke. There was too much dirt and blood on her even now, a proper scrubbing still necessary. Though she quickly bathed and changed her clothing on the way home, Salome reeked of war. A permanent stench in her nostrils now.

She was a terrible thing, too. With a stinging in her eyes, Salome escaped, thinking of the deaths wrung by her magic. Each step was brisk and stiff with clenched fists and weary muscles.

Her guards kept their distance, unwilling to leave her be. Once she passed through the doors to hers and the witches' rooms, they would be unable to follow her.

"Little one—" Maris's voice was so loud it ricocheted off the walls.

Salome turned, a hand already on the door handle. "Is it too much to ask to be alone for a while?"

Whatever she felt, she didn't want them trying to decipher it yet. She didn't want them to offer sympathy. Not for the first time, she resented that she rarely had a moment to herself.

The fire witch frowned. "No, but you must calm yourself."

Della emerged from behind Maris. Her ivory skin was smudged beneath her eyes, tainted by sleeplessness. If she opened her hands, the fingers digging deep into her palms, Salome imagined wilted flowers and blackened petals. But nothing fell as her dainty hand grazed Maris's waist.

Maris shivered as though Thema's ice broke through her natural blazing heat. She grew a hint of a smile that was like smoky, lingering remnants of an extinguished flame.

"Don't let the darkness consume you," Della pleaded. "Or else you'll become a monster of your own making." From her lips, it almost sounded beautiful—shadows, lusting for Salome's body and power, as if they needed a vessel and Salome was the perfect size.

"I can't make any promises," Salome said. Della's world was a lush garden, full of life, and she'd opened the gates. She reeked of sweet vulnerability. But Salome snapped back into reality and turned cold. "Now leave me alone."

When they did not turn, she looked at the l'Issalya brothers, now stationed on either side of her doors like dutiful statues.

"You're relieved of your duties tonight."

Oscar glared at her. "You cannot command that."

"Let me grieve for the innocence I've lost over the last few weeks, Oscar. Leave me alone." Salome sighed. "*Please.*"

She wasn't the queen. They could choose to ignore her commands.

"Just this once—for you," Fabian decided, gripping his brother's arm.

Oscar gave a resigned nod. "Stay in your rooms and rest. Do not leave them."

Salome yanked the door open, then slammed it shut. In her rooms, the dozens of candles had been lit by servants expecting her return. She imagined smothering the brightness with shadow, letting the smoky tendrils envelope the light and choke it.

Dark temptation, a satisfying stillness in the front borders of her mind. Now aware of the consequences, she was stifled with fear. She remembered the tar-covered hands, the darkness on her eyes, the choking grip.

A quiet mew drew her eyes to a ball of soft, black fur. Fortune lay curled on a pillow-bed on the floor, tail swishing, and golden eyes expectant. Her bedroom was his kingdom, and apparently, she was trespassing. He blinked his eyes at her, so unusually large they looked as though they belonged on a caricature rather than a cat. Crouching, she petted him. Fortune pressed his head into her hand, urging her on with his purring.

"Don't miss me if I don't come back," she said.

Half an hour later, she was masked and strapped with daggers over skin-tight leather.

Slowly, she pushed the door open, wincing when it creaked. Weary eyes won over her guards, now snoozing at their stations. Drooping heads and useless hands, legs miraculously supporting their dead weight. Still there, as the king likely commanded, but not paying attention, as she requested.

Music roared through the castle, haunting and aching and joyful and winsome all at once.

She made it to the gardens before she heard someone behind her.

The king stood there, dressed in dark silks. "No parties for criminals?"

No drunkenness on him, nor drowsiness. Maybe he had new ghosts. What images tore through his mind? Were they as bloody as the field? Was he waiting to see what horrors his people would endure after a battle by the Woods?

"Probably not your kind of party." Salome gripped the dagger she'd withdrawn upon hearing his footsteps.

Parties in the Alliance often had thick crowds of criminals, boisterous laughter, and shameless boasting. Some of them had a wickedness that sickened her. A tendency to violence against the innocent and vulnerable. She, at least, preferred to prey on the rich and privileged, the ones who could handle a bit of loss. It twisted her stomach to target those who were kind-hearted and generous, who would suffer greatly if even a little of what they owned was snatched away.

Still, while she went along with the Alliance's feasts and delights, laughing with them and bragging about her own crimes, she liked to think that there was a border between good and bad that she danced around. A gray area between worlds.

He eyed her with a look she could not explain. Something thoughtful, something vague. Instinct told her to run. Curiosity made her stay. Confidence told her that she could handle it, whatever it was that made him look at her this way. She held the dagger downward, her thumb tapping impatiently against the pommel.

"I saw you on the battlefield," Vincent said slowly. "There is no need to pretend."

Salome jerked back in alarm and tipped her dagger toward him.

For some reason, he smiled. "Rosalia—"

She almost laughed. Maybe she should be relieved.

He didn't know the whole truth. This thing between them could end here. From the corner of her eye, she spied the witches lingering by the dying hedge maze.

Moonlight shined off amber eyes. Maris stepped forward as Salome's decision flashed through her mind. She would confess and everything would change. Since Vincent was strong and capable, he didn't need her. She could go and disappear, and he'd be better off.

It ached to think that.

"Little one—"

Vincent jolted at the sound of Maris's voice, only just noticing her presence. The witch didn't glance his way once.

"Are you sure?" she asked Salome.

Perhaps it wasn't the good time. It was doubtful that moment would ever come. The truth would come out and if anyone revealed it, being the one to decide that was her preference.

Salome focused on the king. "You don't know me; you never have. Rosalia is not my name. You're a fool for failing to account for your noble families, for thinking I was her."

He looked at her, confusion wrinkling his brow.

"She's dead, Your Majesty, and I took her place."

The witches strode forward. The king stopped smiling.

Armor clanged as guards approached. Not just any guards, but the l'Issalya brothers.

"What are you saying?" Vincent demanded, striding forward. When he reached for her masks, she didn't stop him. He ripped them away, hands shaking like he was afraid of what he'd find.

She felt bare and vulnerable. Clay-like, cracking as he exposed her face.

His eyes recognized the details, yet he remained confused. If he wanted to see some physical signs of her deceit, he found nothing. He never knew Rosalia, only associated her name with Salome's image.

A tentative hand with calloused fingers grazed the soft curve of her cheek. She twisted away, leaning back like his touch disgusted her. His reaction was exactly what she intended: hand yanked back, eyes darkening, jaw tight, the tenderness carved away.

That hurt him.

An apology perched on the tip of her tongue. She struggled to swallow it and remember that all she'd done was for the sake of survival.

"Then who are you?" His voice sharpened to steel. It turned dangerous.

"My name is Salome Visaya. I've lied to you. I won't any longer." She wanted to hold steady, to speak with pride for her accomplishments. For months, she'd fooled a king and all his court. She'd stolen every charming moment and snuck into his heart and his bed.

But, for the first time, she felt guilty for it, now that she wasn't so desperate to use his riches to earn her way out. No more hands itching for gold, only a gaze searching for remnants of affection. She couldn't find it, not with the armor he'd now built around himself.

Vincent's gaze went sharp, then dull.

His eyes became cold, like he felt nothing.

If the pain in her chest had come from a blade rather than the look on his face, it would have been fatal.

As Vincent lifted an arm to grab her, air rushed between them. With the strength of hurricane winds, the air witch sent Vincent stumbling back.

"You will not harm her," Godiva warned. "Our agreement ends the moment you do."

There were other witnesses, though. Fabian and Oscar continued to approach, hurrying to their king. Vincent focused only on Salome. Like she was not just a thief and a liar, but his enemy. Seeing that made her stomach twist.

"This has to happen," Salome said, glancing briefly at the witches. "Don't interfere."

Godiva narrowed her eyes but nodded.

Vincent growled. Gripping his sword, he gestured to her. "How? How was this possible?"

"I have a resemblance to her, along with shared inheritance. I had help to become her, to convince you of who I was."

"Who?"

"The Alliance," she said.

Recognition filled his eyes. Maybe he remembered their conversations about them, about how his parents wanted to weed them out and destroy them. Resentment turned to hate, his lips curled, teeth bared in disgust. The sight of it stung so painfully it nearly brought tears to her eyes, but she couldn't look away. She wanted to see everything, every spark of pain she ignited.

"I've been with them for years. They were the ones who sent all those assassins. I betrayed them by joining the witch circus and trying to leave them, but they'll come back for me." She took a deep breath that rattled her lungs. "Now—now I can't stay any longer."

"You aren't going anywhere," Vincent decided.

For the first time he looked away, only to jerk his head toward her.

She didn't understand until the l'Issalya brothers grabbed her arms and forced her to her knees. Her dagger fell from her hands. Pain coursed through her legs as they met the gravel. Salome didn't resist, though the impact made her grit her teeth and freed her tears. They fell like blood from a fresh wound.

Using magic, she could fight them back. The shadows wouldn't act now though, not while she wasn't afraid or facing death, nor had an interest in commanding them.

With an enraged scream, Della surged forward, but Maris held her back.

A flicker of Vincent's affection for Rosalia had him silent, staring at Salome. His concern came and went as quick as a flash of lightning. Eyes widening, mouth parting slightly—until he turned away. At his side, his hand clenched into a fist. She saw the trembling fingers though.

Vincent whirled on the witches. "Have you known all this time?"

Though Salome expected Godiva to speak, it was her sister instead.

"Apologies, Your Majesty, but one of our own comes first," Thema said.

Salome nodded.

"Informing you would only harm her," the witch added.

Vincent spat at Thema's feet. Spoken with the same derisiveness heard in the village, he grumbled, "Witches."

Salome winced like she'd taken a blow.

At that, Maris released Della, ready to charge with fire blooming in her hands. Della grabbed her as Thema snuffed out the fires by taking Maris's hands.

"Don't interfere," she said, then to Vincent, voice cracking, "I'm sorry."

For once, she meant it. How strange it was. She couldn't remember the last time she'd uttered an apology so earnestly. If only he understood how much that meant, how much she felt for him. It was foolish of her to feel anything at all, let alone love. She did love him though. She couldn't lie to herself about that.

She loved him and lied to him and gave him nothing but agony now.

"Take her," Vincent commanded.

The l'Issalya brothers said nothing, yanking her up.

When Salome glanced back, Vincent held a hand to his chest as if wounded there. Vincent remained half turned away, head down and shoulders shuddering, as if sobs were wretched from him. As if he was in agony.

Whatever the wound, she felt it too.

She'd stabbed first. Of course he'd strike in return.

As the l'Issalya brothers dragged her through the castle, she remained expressionless while her body hung limp. She did not struggle, even as the entire Ilaryan court saw her dragged like a doll down to the dungeons.

They passed dozens of cells, most full of groaning prisoners slumped like life was leeched from them. They threw Salome into the furthest one. She fell onto her knees and stayed there.

"You would have been a brilliant queen," Fabian said.

"I never wanted to be one."

Once in solitude, Salome allowed herself to feel the horrible things she'd attempted to hide away, to fully fall apart. Still kneeling, her head fell into her hands as the tears came freely. A sob wracked her chest, as painful as a boot to the ribs. She tried to choke it down, but only made it worse. The cries and wailing of the other prisoners drowned her out.

Chapter Thirty-Eight

SHE WAS LEFT IN THE SILENCE OF THE DARKNESS, THE windowless, comfortless madness to which she was condemned until the king determined the date of her execution. Off with her head, put an end to the mess she made.

It was almost a comfort to have a quick death.

The dungeons were too dim to keep darkness away. Being there was another whisper of encouragement for the demons to come out and play. Only three sconces lit the dungeons, spaced far apart with short, dying candles. No scent to mask the stench of prisoners forced to relieve themselves in their cells and no one willing to clean it up.

Was this the punishment for the prisoners? Forcing them to breathe in ruined, rancid air? Letting the darkest things feed on their souls until perhaps they had nothing left? This was what happened when one disappointed the king. He let them rot, suffer, and face the night. This was a new side to the king and his kingdom.

Glory above, gory below.

The monsters were here. Banished from the world above, they lived in the dungeons below. Her stomach turned, and her muscles tightened as if she could fight before they feasted on her.

In the surrounding cells, a prisoner groaned. Nails tore at cell doors. When a demon rose—a mimic or a malform or a combination of both—the moaning ceased. In the cell next to hers, she caught a glimpse of a little girl with a dislocated jaw, eyes sewn shut, and hands like a hawk's feet. The cell door rattled unnervingly as the little girl unleashed a vulgar laugh in response to the prisoner's whimpering.

Then, nothing.

Then, sounds of slurping.

She retched in the corner.

In the following days, Salome kept her eyes squeezed shut and a shadow-shield around her body. She listened to the shadows' disjointed speech, finding their voices easier to bear than the tortured prisoners. The shadow demons took their time, eating their share little by little. Here, they could be patient. Here, they could take their fill and come back for more.

Eventually, Vincent came to visit her. Grim and dreary, like a storm cloud hung over him and the sun never shined anymore.

Salome was surrounded with black smoke when he walked in, all shadow and sorrow, too tired to assert control. He was a beacon of light with the torch he carried, filling her cell with a golden glow. She heard him lock it into place on the wall.

Vincent coughed to grab her attention.

As she exhaled, the smoky darkness around her dissipated. "Go away."

"You're miserable," he answered.

The sound of his miserable voice piqued her interest.

Did he know what happened down here, that banishing the demons from the world above sent them snarling below? Did he know that his prisoners were feasts for monsters?

"I'm biding my time." She tried not to sound bitter. She failed.

From the corner of her eye, she could see the calloused palm of his hand pressed against the cell bars. When she turned fully, still avoiding his eyes, she noticed how languidly he leaned against the door. One hand against it, one arm above his head, comfortable to stare at her like she was his personal performer.

"This cell does not suit me, I'm afraid."

"Would you like a throne instead?"

She lolled her head around, a dull gaze falling on him.

He smirked, just slightly.

A thought struck her like lightning, as vivid as a bolt against the night sky. Salome launched at him, boldly pressing her hand against exposed palm. Instantly, her eyes rolled back as images roared to life behind them. Too intense in sight and sound and stench.

Three arrows buried in the palm she touched. Three arrows tearing through the other. All six trapping him against a blazing tree. Blood pooled around him. Dead or dying, broken all the same.

Vincent yanked his hand away.

"You're going off to battle again," she stated in a daze and a hoarse voice. The images terrified her more than she would ever admit. Guilt came with such a confession. If she had never told the truth, she could have been there, protecting him.

He struggled, eyes shifting and teeth grinding. "I can fight without you."

"This time, you'll *die*," she hissed. "What I saw—"

"You cannot frighten me like this."

She slammed her fists against the metal bars. "You *will* die! I don't want that. Despite all that I have done, I don't want you to die. Don't go."

"How can I believe anything you say?"

He leaned away, dismissing her.

Salome screamed wordlessly in frustration, grabbing the bars and rattling them.

Come on out, the shadows crooned. *Let us out and we'll lead the way.*

An image appeared in her mind, a door of smoke and shadow, promising freedom if she opened it. Salome closed her eyes, willing the images away. When she opened them, Vincent was watching her without tenderness or longing. What she saw was a broken man, looking as though he lost everything in his heart and now all that remained was a shell of who he used to be.

For a moment, they stared at each other. A contest to see who broke first.

"Vincent, you can't go—"

"Did you ever love me?"

She regarded him, the bleak look on his face.

"No," she said, for his sake. She turned her face away.

Maybe it was love. She didn't know. All she could do was hold onto the fact that there were too many lies for it to be entirely true, but it was close. It was something more than what she'd felt before.

Vincent whirled around, refusing to look at her like the mere sight of her was revolting. His hand moved to the sword at his hip.

"When I return, you'll be executed."

And then he was gone, taking the light and her pride, and leaving her to fume.

This wasn't her fate. Salome could not see it, but it did not feel true. But she closed her eyes and listened to the murmuring symphony from the darkest corners, cancelling out the cackling and crying, the shrill sound of prisoners in their desolation.

Once, Salome had seen Vincent as a kindly king, a gentle soul, as he likely intended. They were two masks meeting their match. The man who condemned her was someone different, a facet of him that he'd hidden until now. Cold eyes, closed-off heart, capable of condemning her to this place.

"I'm sorry," she said again, even if he couldn't hear it.

And she meant it.

And again, she wept and wished she wasn't who she was.

She was nothing and no one, far from a queen. She was a con artist, and this was bound to be her destiny after all she'd done. This was the path she'd chosen, one that led her straight to the royal executioner.

Chapter Thirty-Nine

MOMENTS AFTER GRUMBLING GUARDS REMOVED A SHROUDED body, she had another visitor.

Pale arms with long, puckered scars slid through the bars of the cell door. Signs of damage done to themselves, of fatal injuries that somehow had long-since healed. History written in two wordless lines. Within the hands, there was a sunflower at peak bloom. Bright yellow petals around a large brown center.

A peace offering, a sign of friendship.

Salome sat in a corner, her legs pulled up to her chest and her arms around them. She lifted her head from where it rested on her knees.

"Hello, little one," Della cooed. "You've made quite a mess of things."

Maris appeared beside her with a torch in her hand. Their eyes examined the damage done to Salome's by a few nights in the dungeons. Della wrinkled her nose. Maris looked slightly disturbed.

Slowly, Salome got to her feet and approached the cell door.

"They've brought me enough food and drink to keep me alive, but I haven't seen the sun in days, or any inch of the outside world." Salome's hands shook as she accepted the sunflower.

"The sun, moon, and stars are magic of their own," Godiva said.

Thema trailed her, barely a step behind.

"Are you all here to preach and tell me that everything will be alright?" Salome crossed her arms. "I could get out on my own, if I wanted to."

"Instead, you've chosen to punish yourself like this," Maris retorted.

Punishment, yes. That was what she deserved. Rosalia hadn't deserved to be killed by the Alliance so Salome could take her place. The king was good-hearted and romantic, too easy of a mark. And then all those people claimed by the violence of her magic.

She was a woman with an inclination to the night, to the darkness of the world. What could she offer except death and destruction? It was better to hide in here where the only glimpses she got of the outside were visions, even if she didn't know what was real.

The night after Vincent's visit, Salome thought she saw Sylvia. Ward of the king, witch of the light, bane of Salome's existence. She'd crouched in front of Salome while she was half-asleep, eyes swollen from hours of crying.

Sylvia murmured gently, but Salome didn't understand. All she knew was the hand stroking her hair affectionately, the warmth of the touch that felt like a bright summer's day on the beach, and the smell of daisies.

But when her vision focused, no one was there.

The first nights were the worst. Someone decided to snuff out the candles and locked the doors. She imagined that same person ensuring the hallways were flooded with light, ensuring demons remained down here with the prisoners.

One rose from a puddle of shadows and crawled right up to her on eight spindly legs like a spider. It opened a mouth to reveal a tunnel with rows upon rows of small, razor-sharp teeth and a breath that smelled of rotting flesh. A tongue slithered out and dragged across her face. She nearly vomited before she couldn't bear it any longer and brought up a shield of shadows. The demon slammed spear-ended legs against the surface in hopes of shattering it and gaining access to her.

She couldn't sleep after that, dozing briefly, only to be woken by a new demon as hideous and hungry as the first. Shields required focus and all those hours awake carved dark circles around her eyes.

Salome wondered if she should ask them what took so long to visit.

Though Salome didn't voice her questions, Maris decided to answer. "There were some matters to sort out before we could see you. Then the king believed we would release you and refused us entry. We thought it best to wait."

A more important matter came to Salome's mind. "I saw *her* on the battlefield. Did you?"

"We did," Thema said quietly.

"So, Sylvia is the light witch."

Della nodded solemnly and leaned against Maris.

"Yes, that girl revealed some awful things." Maris looked pained. "After the surrender, she came to me and opened her mind, allowing me to see the things she'd hidden from us all while she watched you. Like us, she knew you were coming to Ellasya and it was all too easy to get close to you."

Salome closed her eyes. Though she couldn't say it aloud, she admired that cleverness. They'd used each other.

"And what did you see?" Salome asked.

Della squeezed Maris's hand.

"She's been working with Pavalla since she was a little girl. The l'Essalia estate is near the border, enabling easy communication. When their schemes were discovered, her own father took the fall. I didn't see the witch mentoring her and shielding her from us, but this witch taught the girl to drink dragon blood to amplify her magic, failing to inform her that doing so takes a toll on the body." If Maris looked menacing before, she looked worse now with a dark, murderous look like in her eyes. Salome half-expected her to breathe fire.

Della murmured something to calm her.

It was never just about demons. It was anger and power and purpose.

Failed plans fueling Sylvia's hidden motives.

Godiva paced in front of Salome's cell door, wringing hands covered in rings of black tourmaline, hematite, and obsidian. Her necklace of rough-cut citrine swung with each step.

"This is much worse than what we anticipated," Thema said. "We must call upon every bit of our power."

Godiva nodded. "We have our own amplifiers. You must have some as well."

Salome leaned forward. They only mentioned them before.

Grinning, Maris gestured to the array of jewelry they donned. Jewelry adorned minimally, now worn in near excess. Rings upon rings, bracelets stacked on arms, necklaces and headpieces and earrings. Amplifiers to strengthen their magic.

Della wore a pyrite headpiece with rose quartz and apatite gemstones woven into her honey-golden hair. A pink tourmaline band wrapped around her arm with drooping chains of small obsidian and aquamarine beads.

Maris wore layers of gold chains with selenite and agate and half a dozen rings, both silver and gold with an array of colorful stones. Godiva and Thema were adorned with matching red and black gemstones on rings, bracelets, and necklaces, though Thema wore significantly more.

"If we wore them all the time, it would seem suspicious," Thema said. "Some people know what it means to wear so many stones."

"You ought to see what I put inside our armor." Della sighed dreamily.

Godiva added, "Some of us are more powerful. Some have better control. Some, like myself, cannot do as much as other witches of our element. It is an eternal balancing act."

Della reached into the pockets of her charcoal gown to pull out a necklace with smoky quartz pendulum and another with amethyst and fluorite braided with gold and silver chains. Salome donned them eagerly.

"I don't understand why you stay here when you could leave and do more with your life," Della wondered. "And with us."

Godiva continued, "But if you bind yourself to us, you cannot use your magic for murder or ambition."

It was a chance at a different life, with no more pretending, as she always wanted. Of course there were strings. Dreams didn't come so easily.

"Fine," Salome conceded. "But we must go after Vincent before he gets himself killed."

They nodded. As if she had any power in this deal. The witches, at least, seemed to genuinely care about her as more than a pawn.

"There is more," Della and Godiva said together. "Your word is not enough for the binding. This kind of deal requires magic with consequences."

Like a king and queen losing their lives so magic might save their people.

Magic had to be balanced, a give and take. This was a contract of a kind.

"Of course," Salome drawled. "But, as I said, I don't need your help to escape."

Maris grumbled quietly to herself. "Why are you even here then? To be dramatic?"

Ignoring her, Della said, "It's not the escape. It's everything that comes afterward."

"Because Sylvia is my counterpart, you need me to get to her."

Silence met her.

"I'm your only hope," Salome said.

"Our best option, perhaps, but not the only one," Godiva answered cautiously. With some reluctance, Godiva opened her hands, revealing over a dozen small, glass crystals. "We only need a few drops of your blood for the binding spell."

Blood magic.

The shadows hissed at the crystals.

Maris offered a small knife, slipping it from her sleeve. "Come, little one, we don't mean to harm you. With this, you become included in every agreement we make. The magic in the world will acknowledge you as part of us, not a single entity."

"This is for your protection and ours," Della said.

And everyone else. The unsaid words hung between them.

Despite her discomfort, Salome offered her hand through the bars. Maris made a cut across Salome's palm then pushed it onto the crystals. The red spread faster than she anticipated, spilling over them. Then the witches began to chant. More hands, pale and dark, cold, and hot, wrapped around each other.

All four closed their eyes as they spoke in synchrony, words incomprehensible. It was hypnotic, like silk spun from their voices. Tingling sensations sprouted in her hands and feet and spread through her limbs, like many-legged insects crawling beneath her skin.

Then, as her body began to surrender, she felt the gentle tug and then harsher wrenching of the shadows from her, from everywhere. They roared with rage, becoming black fumes encircling her. Bloodcurdling agony filled her ears, shrieking her name. Her magic was terrifying—too strong, overwhelming.

But then the shadows were gone, forcefully shoved back into her like returning a ripped-out heart to her body. Caged. Contained.

Only the groans of the broken prisoners could be heard.

The hands lifted away.

Her cell door creaked open. All four witches moved away so Salome could exit. How easily she could have done this, slipping shadows between the lock to open it, or even one of her hairpins. On her own, she had nowhere else to go, no plan to escape or funds to sustain her. With them, everything was different.

It was quieter and easier to breathe as the shadows began seeming docile and partially dormant. Like she had a better grip on their leash now.

"You don't have to steal anymore," Godiva said.

Salome pouted. "There were some things I wanted for myself though."

Maris laughed low, rolling her eyes. "Predictable. I kept the armor aside for you."

"And I have Fortune! He's been very pampered and well-fed," Della promised.

Then Salome searched for her daggers in the pocket of shadow made from her silhouette, as Thema once showed her. No longer hiding who she was, she could use them as she wished. With a grin, Salome unsheathed a pair of them and spun them between her fingers.

Godiva looked unimpressed with the little performance.

"Are we going to war?" Della whispered, grinning widely with giddiness. "Are we going to save the king?"

Salome nodded. "I won't let him die."

Chapter Forty

THE WITCHES WERE NOT WELCOME AFTER THE KING LEARNED OF Salome's deceit, their complicity in keeping her secrets, and how easily they chose her over their agreement with Ilarya. An agreement that killed his parents.

He dismissed them and bid them leave at the earliest opportunity.

And yet they returned to battle for that man.

The blood binding was still in place.

They were only hours behind the king and his soldiers, yet horrific destruction greeted them on the field. Half of both armies already cut down. Blood and filth were everywhere.

It was a massacre, and Pavalla was winning.

Soldiers moved in sharp synchrony, bringing down Ilaryans with easy blows. Metal through metal and leather then flesh and bone. Beyond them, the Woods of Palvary seemed denser, darker. Woods infested with wicked things, demons with clawed hands and long teeth glinting like silver blades between the shadows of the trees.

The cursed magic here was stronger than before, strengthened by all the bloodshed. As if the countless deaths had seeped into the earth like a sacrifice to gods. Salome felt it when she inhaled, like a cold, winter breeze sinking into her lungs, rooting itself there with talons and teeth. It appealed her own dark magic, like it was an old friend.

It terrified her more than all the bodies across the bloodied, muddied earth.

"Look to the skies," Godiva urged, gesturing upward.

The sun was slowly descending, shielded by racing clouds and rescinding its light. Between the clouds, dragons wove and roared. Each flap of their wings seemed to make the clouds shudder, like even they were terrified.

Thema was all wide-eyes and amazement as she spun around, staring up above. "Feeding them regularly makes them loyal, but this is different. This is *amazing*. No one has written of anything like this."

Della shook her head. "No good comes from their presence."

"We did not come here to ogle dragons," Godiva said.

"Enough." Maris nodded to Salome. "Let's find your king."

"And what of you?" Salome asked the sisters.

"We search for Sylvia," said Godiva. "The light witch is young; she can be swayed onto a safer path..." she trailed off, as though her hope was a dwindling flame. She set her jaw and looked ahead, searching for Sylvia already.

With that, Della shoved Salome forward. For the first few steps, she stumbled, until finding herself into the center of the chaos. No killing by magic, only steel and shield.

Maris and Della remained close to Salome as Godiva and Thema went off in search of the light witch. Having them flank her was strange, and different from the first battle. This time, she felt like she was one of them, a sister in this family. She had the urge to smile, but it felt wrong to find a speck of joy amid the monstrosity of battle.

Then, any time a Pavallan drew close, the shadows reacted. Her assailant's shadow would rise from beneath their feet, lifting to form a shield between them and Salome. Preventing the shadows from doing worse felt like chaining her limbs.

They yearned to do more.

A hand burst through, claws scraping at armor. Salome pulled back, like trying to leash a thrashing, snarling animal.

They were hungry, demanding a taste of death.

"*Focus*," Maris whispered beside her. "Keep your mind focused."

All she knew was that she needed to save him. As her blade met bodies and blood splattered her armor, she continued searching for him. Everything was a chaotic blur, movement around her like a violent breeze.

He was supposed to remember her. To do that, he needed to live.

She couldn't move on knowing he was gone. That the world had lost brightness.

The second she found him, the world sharpened. It was like she saw clearly for the first time, instead of feeling like she was peering out a foggy window.

The king's blade was locked with another's, and his knees buckled. The fear of loss urged her forward, faster, eager to reach him. She left Maris and Della behind. The battle enveloped them.

A Pavallan soldier barreled into Salome with only a shield in her hands. She pounded it against Salome's sword over and over, each impact making Salome's legs tremble.

The shadows screamed in outrage. They pulled at invisible restraints, wishing fervently to lunge free and slice her apart with black blades.

Wordless shrieking filled her head with gory images of the harm they wished to inflict.

Though the woman was strong, Salome refused to lose. She let out a cry and dropped her shield, grabbing onto her opponent's with her now-free hand and yanking with all the strength she could muster. The woman's eyes widened. In that split-second hesitation, Salome slammed the shield into the woman's neck. It slid in easier than she'd imagined, sinking into flesh like a knife through butter. Too soft of a body and too sharp an edge.

One of them had to die.

It wouldn't be Salome.

Only the stunned expression remained on her opponent's face as she fell, taking Salome with her. All the while, she kept gripping the shield, trapped where it had sliced into.

She looked away and released the shield. Without her weight put into it, it slid out of the woman's neck and dropped to the ground. Then Salome turned, yanking off her helmet, and emptied her stomach on the grass.

As she lifted her head, an arrow whizzed by and shallowly cut her left cheek.

She straightened and turned, eyes wide to see Irene standing a few feet away with another arrow nocked and ready. But slowly, Irene lowered her bow and approached Salome. Mud and blood marred her hair and skin.

Salome picked up her fallen sword as she got to her feet. "Was that supposed to kill me?"

"Despite all the love I have for Ilarya, I don't think I could kill a friend." Irene sighed, returning her arrow to its quiver than wiping her forehead with the back of her hand. The act smeared more grime across her skin.

Salome bowed her head. "Thank you, duchess."

"Next time, I'll kill you. You're supposed to be imprisoned," Irene said, but smiled.

Then, fast as a flash of lightning, Irene shot an arrow at a Pavallan that came up from behind Salome. The soldier collapsed, the arrow lodged in his exposed forehead and poking out the back of his skull. He fell backward, down onto the destroyed earth.

"Go and give my cousin a nice surprise," Irene suggested.

For a moment, Salome mourned the friendship forfeited with the truth. But then she raced away and found Vincent again, he was fighting someone else, no hint of fear or holding back. He stood firm. Graceful, a soldier more than a king. He didn't need her, not now.

But when he did, she would make sure he wouldn't fall.

She didn't come to fight for Ilarya, only for him.

To make sure they could both move on.

There were several bodies in her path, but she pushed and shoved and slashed until she stood in front of him. He removed his helmet and grimaced. She swallowed the hurt and stood straight, unbowed, and unafraid, despite her aching heart. Sweat stuck his hair to his forehead and when he wiped at his face, the touch left a trail of grime behind. And yet she saw his beauty. As the first day she saw him, he was too handsome to be real and it struck her like a blow to face, almost knocking her off balance.

He raised his sword. "Whose side are you on?"

"My own. And yours." *Always.*

His features softened. The aching in her heart intensified in that moment, briefly allowing hope that she could have a place in his heart too. It was so, so foolish and she shouldn't hope, but she did.

The moment shattered as someone charged in, another Pavallan woman with a battle-cry, charging at Vincent. She had an accomplice too. Salome dodged the blows meant for her, until she was suddenly met by pain.

A Pavallan man in a helmet and full armor smacked her hard in the face with his circular shield. Salome reeled. Blood dripped from her nose and into her mouth. Another hit came, another face full of blood. She spat it out, then charged.

Viciousness escaped its containment, flinging to the forefront of her consciousness. With a snarl, Salome slammed her sword at his neck, chopping again and again until head separated from body and the helmet rolled far away.

She didn't know this side of herself, and wondered if it was her, or an extension of her dark magic.

Gleeful laughter rang in her mind despite the sounds of clashing metal and screams around her.

As blood splashed against her face, someone whirled her around. She bared her teeth like an animal but softened once she realized who held her back.

"You will still be executed if you survive this," Vincent warned, and let go. "You cannot go unpunished."

His voice had a darkness that she should not have liked, but she did, especially the honesty in it. He was furious; it made her fonder. He was honorable, loyal to his laws, ruling over his heart with his mind. That way, he was safe from those who could hurt him as she had.

It had to hurt. Though it seemed cruel to hope he suffered from her actions, at least it allowed her to imagine that she had a little bit of a hold on his heart. A gentle thing now forced to steel itself after her attack against it.

She shook her head and smiled. "You'll have to catch me first."

And then she dashed away, giddy after finding him. Like this continued strength renewed her energy despite the calamity around them. Corpses covered the ground, forming obstacles to her escape. It reeked, too, with the air rancid from fecal matter and human decay.

But when she glanced over her shoulder, Vincent wasn't following.

Of course, he wouldn't, no matter how much she wished he would. He had a battle to win before playing her games. She searched for him, desperate to see him alive and fighting fiercely. The kingdom could fall for all she cared, but he couldn't.

Hope filled her that his need for justice would keep him alive.

She scanned the crowd and found a girl of white-gold approaching, shimmering like sunlight on the sea. Sylvia, dressed in lightweight armor colored bronze and gold, and her pale-yellow hair in an unraveling braid. She held no shield or weapon, somehow serene amidst chaos, smiling within a cloud of screaming agony.

Wild eyes, gray like a terrible storm, with dark circles beneath them struck Salome as beautiful and terrifying.

A glittering, golden wall separated the two of them from everyone else.

"If it isn't the Queen of Hearts," Sylvia cooed. "I promise I haven't come to kill you. I need you alive for what I have planned." There was no softness in the way she spoke, no tenderness in words that should hold meaning. This wasn't the girl Salome had known.

"Lucky me."

"And I'm sure you won't kill me any time soon." She smiled, white teeth gleaming. "After all, your powers have just awoken, haven't they? The beginning is the most brutal part."

The taunt was bruising and made her feel inferior. It infuriated her.

"You could have done so much good."

"Like *you*? How high and mighty, like your beloved king. We're the same. Two criminals who betrayed the d'Allorias family, though differently than I did. We were made for each other, bound to each other, and we will *always* need each other."

Salome shook her head. "I don't need you at all."

"For a seer, you fail to see what will come to be."

"What do you see that I don't?"

Within a second, Sylvia snatched her hand, pressing palm to palm and digging her fingers into the back of Salome's hand. "I can see all that you've done, all you have seen and felt before. That's my gift."

Could she smile further? Could her lips widen, and her teeth sharpen, more monster than maiden?

Before Salome could speak, Sylvia turned to a ray bursting through the clouds. Bliss bloomed on her face before she leaned deep into it and vanished, the golden wall gone with her. Sylvia stepped through that sliver like it was a door. Salome's fingers itched, longing to try it with the shadows.

Night crept closer now in Sylvia's absence. Her light had illuminated the battle.

Without her, there was only burgeoning dark.

From the rubble of limbs and blood, a Pavallan soldier stood separate with an arrow ready, staring at Salome before firing. Another Pavallan took a shot, then another and another. Within seconds, half a dozen arrows soared toward her.

As if they knew who she was to the king before she revealed the truth.

She didn't think. Blinded by emotion more than the sweat and blood dripping into her eyes, she lashed out. She searched for threads of her magic, struggling for a moment. Once found, Salome pried them free.

In the back of her mind, she thought she heard a whisper. A plea. *Don't.*

She didn't know if it was Maris or something else, but it didn't matter. It was too late. In her panic, she released the leash she held onto the dark magic at her fingertips. She unlocked a cage of feral beasts. All she needed to do was give them freedom to survive the onslaught headed her way.

She was desperate. She had to, so she did.

The shadows cackled with glee as they rose, multiplying in shapes that matched her shadow from the setting sun. They charged forward together, swiping the arrows from the air and racing toward the assailants.

With amplifiers and her new binding to the witches, she was stronger. She could do dangerous things like this.

The Pavallans froze, staring in horror at the monsters.

The shadows began to slash and tear apart the flesh in their path, seeking only to spill Pavallan blood. The voice in the back of her mind screamed at her to pay attention, to wake up from the darkness enveloping her.

Yes, she was stronger.

But embracing that came with her own suffering.

The consequences came quickly. Her skin warmed and crackled. Large blisters began forming on her skin, every inch ablaze, in agony.

It raged and burned and ravaged her. It was as sharp as a whip and as hot as a fire.

It hurt *everywhere*. Removing her skin from her body would have been less painful.

She screamed, spitting blood from her mouth.

She clawed at her skin, trying to take the pain away, and screamed and screamed.

Somehow, Maris made her way to her, uttering things Salome couldn't understand. Maris clutched a handful of beads of garnet and black tourmaline. Healing her, Salome realized, and the blistering across her body.

"The binding could kill if you try to break it," Maris explained.

So, she was stronger, but only if she behaved. She understood, despite the agony.

Forcing her eyes open, Salome searched for the king. Vincent was on the ground, reaching for his sword with blood dripping into his eyes and arrows shot through his hands. Three through each palm, like she envisioned. There was no tree behind him, the only thing that hadn't come true, but the Woods were in the distance.

Above him, the Pavallan prince had his ornate sword poised to kill.

Ready to end the king's life, to destroy Ilarya with one strike.

Maris's eyes widened. "Don't—"

But what choice did she have? If she had the opportunity to do something good, to keep the soft-hearted king she loved alive, she would make any sacrifice. Maris would have done the same for Della, for all the love they shared.

Newly born bloodlust flared again. The blood magic binding urged her against what she wished to do.

Salome screamed and reached toward the two royals.

Prince Ricard's own shadow rebelled against him, now a gateway from the shadow world to this one. Hands burst free, grasping his legs, then reaching higher and higher until the talons curled around Ricard's neck. And then they squeezed, strangling him until his body could no longer stand, his eyes closed, and his heart stopped.

She felt his heart slowing, his lungs giving in, as though her own hands gripped him.

The pain returned, a ravaging agony of fire and sun against her skin. It was inside too, a constricting pain within her throat, airway blocked. The blaze of a thousand suns all at once.

Maris' voice was an echo in an empty cave. More muttering, more spells. Her voice was all around her, the urging and pleading to heal faster. The incoherent words muddled together, words in a language that Salome never learned. All Salome wanted was to close her eyes, to sleep for a little while and recover after that.

"Salome!" Vincent's voice was thick with fear.

Like he wasn't ready to lose her.

Like he hadn't already sworn she would die at the executioner's axe.

She willed her eyes to stay open despite the pain. She wasn't going to die, it wasn't possible. But he wouldn't look at her like this ever again. She wanted this memory, this knowledge he'd keep her alive if he could.

Maris would heal her, slowly but surely. Maris wouldn't let her die. She trusted the fire witch, all the witches. Maybe one day they would give up on her, but not yet.

"You reckless fool," he muttered as he held her head up. The arrows had been pushed through his hands. He bled profusely. She could feel it in her hair.

Heal him instead, she wanted to say. *Heal him first.*

"You cannot die. Not like this." Would he still have her executed? He pushed hair out of her face and spread blood across her forehead and cheeks. "Are you afraid?"

All she could do was nod. Inside of her, fire raged and ruined.

She didn't want to cry, but she did until pain won, and shadows kissed her eyes closed.

Chapter Forty-One

TIME SLOWED AND SHE NO LONGER REMEMBERED WHAT DAY IT was. Salome felt like she was adrift somewhere in a dark, windowless room. Her only movement was her chest rising and falling with slow breaths.

Her eyes wouldn't open, not even to locate the bit of warmth dancing over her skin like a bonfire was nearby. She wanted to pull it closer. Maybe her fingertips twitched, and someone recognized her wish. A thin sheet drew over her body and she wanted to sigh with satisfaction but couldn't. Wherever she was, she felt adrift and disconnected from the real world.

What she could see was terrible. Figures slinking through a forest with branches like bony arms and the holes in the bark like piercing silver eyes. She felt like a ghost, only able to observe. The figures wove between the trees, walking sticks in hand as they navigated the uneven ground. Roots rose from the dirt, dusted in fallen leaves that crumbled under their feet.

It was impossible to make out who these people were, concealed by hoods and shapeless cloaks, or if they were even human.

Her palms itched as if someone swept their fingertips across them.

"There isn't much time," someone whispered, their voice was soft and feminine. "But you must see this. The past comes for the future. You and I will make that happen."

The voice sounded different, injected with a confidence she wasn't accustomed to hearing. Sylvia was here, her voice like a lover's breath against Salome's ear. The things she now saw became even stranger when matched to the words.

Now she wondered if she was catching a glimpse of the past, as Sylvia could.

If Salome stole identities as a con artist, then Sylvia stole secrets. Salome would steal them back. If Sylvia was so insistent that their lives were entangled, Salome would use that connection to its advantage. This place—maybe it was the space in the world where light and dark were twisted together, and she could speak to Sylvia without interference.

This was solely for them.

"Find me, or I will find you," Sylvia said.

And then her presence was gone, taking the scene with it.

Salome blinked, but all she saw was darkness.

Was she in the shadows? A realm where her magic resided, where the creatures lived when she did not bring them out into the open. She still couldn't move, couldn't navigate this space, or determine how much time passed.

The powerless terrified her.

"She's healing," she heard Maris say. Her voice was distant and warped, as though Salome was underwater. It didn't feel like drowning though. It simply felt like her body was heavy and rebellious against her will to move.

"How long?"

"As long as she needs," Maris said, the only voice she recognized.

Her concept of the world remained as vague as a shadow in the night. Every detail indiscernible, every sensation like a ghost. She still couldn't feel her body, but she was alive. She couldn't imagine herself giving up yet.

Another image came to her of demons writhing. She remained within this dark space, wondering if this was where she went in the aftermath of the terrors inflicted by her magic. But demons were here, snarling and frothing at the mouth. She braced for the impact of their twisted bodies against hers. It never came. The demons stopped a breath before her.

The beast had the head of a lion but a tunnel-like mouth ringed with teeth dripping with venom. It sizzled when it spilled over the demon's lips and emanated a rank odor.

This all felt like a terrible, inescapable nightmare.

No relief of morning light, and demons all around her.

Behind the lion-headed one, there were others, some standing on two legs with two spindly arms dangling at its sides. Its hands drooped to the ground, knuckles scrapping against the ground, sounding like a steel blade being sharpened with a whetstone. There were countless more in other shapes and sizes. No features on their faces except for a gaping mouth with a tongue long as a snake, red like garnets and shining with saliva that looked as sticky as tree sap.

They moved around her, circling like sharks around their prey, awaiting the moment they could get a mouthful of her.

Other demons appeared and disappeared. Some looked like skeletal wraiths swathed in ruined cloth. They swung about her like hanging corpses, yet never managed to get closer than a hair's length away. She couldn't stop them or push them away.

The shadows shielded her, though. The moment she acknowledged their presence, hushed crooning replaced the growls and groans of the demons. But she still felt trapped, no light in this prison.

Once, this would have terrified her. This time, she closed her eyes and let herself exist.

In the distance, someone called to her. She didn't recognize the voice at first. Hearing him plucked her heart like the strings of a lute, playing a song she almost hated because of the way it made her ache.

"Come back," Vincent whispered. "Do not leave me like this."

She wanted to open her eyes and yet she also wanted to sleep. Quiet, waiting, letting herself grow accustomed to the dark as her home, her sanctuary. Those words, though—she couldn't allow herself to believe anything would change once she woke.

So she embraced the visions that came to her.

She was one of five now. She had to recognize her duty to the world to use her magic for a grander purpose. Whenever she woke, she would have something to contribute to the witches' task. She would be able to point them in a direction to get to Sylvia and whoever she was involved with. Growing up with the Alliance, she always had a mission. This would be her new one. This was her new life. She would inspect every inch of it for what it might mean.

A seaside city with agonized screaming in the distance on a moonless night. The ruins of a fortress covered in ash and blood. A girl with pale hair and storm-gray eyes with sunlight on her skin and a secret smile on her small, pink mouth. A witch with deep brown skin and pitch-black hair, with eyes of an unnatural red and gold. A forest with trees that rose taller than any towers, a canopy of black and white flowers against dark green leaves and silvery branches.

Salome's path was set before her now.

Chapter Forty-Two

SALOME FOUND HERSELF IN A LARGE CELL ON A THICK BLANKET with cushions around her and one large velvet pillow under her head. She tried to sit up, but a hand pressed down on her shoulder and urged her to remain where she lay.

Sitting around her was the witch circus, donned in masks yet again.

"You don't have the strength to be conscious very long," Maris said.

Della was who pushed Salome down, though. Both had dark circles around their eyes, dramatic against their pale skin. Godiva and Thema sat on the other side of her, the latter with a pile of books that Salome recognized as the stack from her bedside table.

"How long has it been?" Salome asked.

Godiva and Maris exchanged a look. That hesitance sent a flash of panic through her. Did they know where she was? The state of her mind? Those strange visions? Were they real? Was any of it real? Was it magic?

"Using your magic that way..." Thema began. "Well, it can have a heavy effect on the body, especially for a young witch like yourself."

"Your stamina will come with time," Godiva said gently.

"Unless you kill yourself by trying to break the binding," Maris added.

Salome looked around. It seemed someone had tried to clean up the space, scrubbing at all the grime that had built-up over the years. There was also more light than she remembered from the last time.

It might have been a different cell, a larger one, since the four witches fit inside.

With a groan, she swatted Della away and sat up. She crawled backward until her spine met a stone wall, then sagged against it. Once she went still, Della carefully nudged a pillow behind her lower back. They were all watching her, worry plain on their faces.

"Are you just waiting to yell at me when I'm better?"

"You were gravely wounded," Godiva said.

"I'm fine. Say what you have to say."

"Not yet," Thema decided.

Godiva raised an eyebrow at her. Thema briefly met her eye but said nothing. Her calm demeanor was almost amusing, as if she wasn't surprised that Salome would have done the foolish, dangerous thing she'd done. The Alliance certainly would have expected her to break any rules they made if she wasn't under supervision.

It was Maris who eventually broke the awkward silence.

"Your former employers tried to come for you again," she said.

"This time, however, it seemed they wanted to send a message," Godiva added.

"A simple one: *no loose ends.*"

Salome shrugged. She wasn't afraid of them or what they might do, especially now that she was a new woman, a shadow witch, and she wouldn't let them govern her life anymore. Feeling the four witches watching her expression carefully, Salome gave them a smile.

"Let them come," she said.

"That was our reply." Della giggled. "Come for us; see what happens when you make an enemy out of witches."

But the Alliance wasn't the immediate threat. They could try to kill her all or drag her back into their chaos and she would defy them each time. Her involvement with them, however, was something to face. A silly, lovesick part of her that wanted to say sorry.

To Vincent.

No matter how he felt about her now.

As if the Maris understood, she said, "You won't die."

Salome nodded. "I know. Does he believe I will let the executioner take me?"

"Perhaps. No one knows how you will escape though."

With a yawn, Salome thought about shadows and doorways and how she would be able to say goodbye. Things were different. She'd deliberately saved his life on the battlefield, preventing the Pavallan prince from killing him almost exactly as she had envisioned.

She saved him. Would he change his mind? Did it change anything?

Her heart hoped that he would see her and know he couldn't condemn her. That a part of him felt for her as she did for him.

And when she left him, she'd be free.

She could see her parents amid her training with the witches and trying to stop Sylvia.

"Rest now," Godiva said. "We'll discuss more another time."

Once Salome returned to sleep, she found herself in the dark place again. This time, however, there weren't any demons confronting her. There were no visions. Her heart was steady, and her breath came easy. When she lost the feeling of her body again, she welcomed the weightlessness. She allowed herself to heal and cleared her mind of the king and the light witch and the fearsome things she imagined would soon come their way.

Chapter Forty-Three

WHEN SALOME WOKE UP, MARIS WAS LOOMING OVER HER.

Sweat lined her forehead and circles under her eyes darker. Long chains of various gemstones hung from her neck and a few rings covered her fingers. Maris's hand on Salome's forehead trembled slightly, but her eyes remained closed in focus.

"Will you finally tell me what happened after I tried to save him?" Salome asked.

"Promise to be quiet and I will," Maris said.

Salome agreed. As Maris healed her, removing the blisters and redness, she told her about how Della had grown a tree on the field to shade them, to protect them from stray assailants before they'd returned to Ellasya. Thema had provided buckets of water to soothe the irritated skin on Salome's body as she dreamt of ice and snow, relief from the thousands of suns wreaking havoc on her skin. She had dark visions of what was to come, what the war would bring, and what the witch circus would eventually face. Apparently, over a week had passed.

Salome wanted to know how they avoid all the possible complications. Other witches, more demons, a forest that feasted on blood, and ruins promising a story that hadn't been told in centuries.

She couldn't do anything if she was executed though. Her treason demanded her head, and his advisors would pressure him into following the laws set by his ancestors.

"So, despite saving him, I am still going to die," Salome said.

"Your reward is a private execution. No commoners."

"Oh, how kind."

Maris rolled her eyes. "The Pavallan king is deeply grieved by losing his first-born son and has surrendered. His second son, Rupert, is now heir. And another son, a bastard who had been living within the Ellasya castle walls, has returned home."

Salome raised an eyebrow.

"You know him. A young man named Rene, who presented his true father with the light witch."

Of course Sylvia wasn't alone. A con was a con and it could rarely be carried out by a single individual. The grand charade was even more complex than Salome's. Sylvia had another kingdom as sanctuary and savior from her crimes against Ilarya.

Salome grimaced. "My deceit seems small in comparison. So, what happens next?"

"Well, we can't stay any longer," Maris answered. Her forehead creased with concentration as she brought the bronze back into Salome's skin. "The king does not trust us, nor does his court. We are no longer welcome, and *you* need to be at your strongest if we are to escape this unscathed."

Escape. Of course. There was no other option.

It needed to be theatrical though. When Salome was involved, that was bound to be the case. She wanted her grand goodbye. Let them remember she was no ordinary girl, but not a danger—especially not to Vincent, her king.

A question came to mind and before Maris could hear it and answer, Salome asked it.

"What happens to the magic if I die? Is the balance lost?"

Before Maris could form a response, Salome grabbed hold of Maris's hand. Palm to palm, as Sylvia had done.

Salome's eyes rolled back. Images blossomed in the darkness. A bonfire in the middle of the night, sparks flying into the air, and dead bodies animated by shadows wrapped around their limbs. Skulls and skeletons rose from the soil. They were different from the visions she had while she'd been unconscious—more detailed, more dire.

When she pulled away, she grimaced.

Maris raised an eyebrow. "You're learning quickly. Already figured out how to get specific visions. And lucky me, getting to see them too."

It felt natural, seeking insights into the future. To look ahead and try to read the details in the flash of an image she received. The books probably said such an ability would only grow with time. And then what would she be capable of?

The infamous witch of the shadows, the reader of one's fate and fortune. It was a title for the storybooks, for legends. She hadn't decided yet if that was terrifying or enthralling. Fame had never been something she craved. For a con artist, it was a curse. It was easier to go forgotten.

"All that time unconscious allowed me to learn some things," Salome said.

"Meditation does that. Did you learn anything else?" Maris asked.

"We can't go far from Ilarya despite all the terrible things."

Maris snorted. "Yes, we are planning to stay somewhat close."

"You have a plan?"

"There's a caravan currently waiting in the courtyard, nothing ornate, but cozy," Maris said, getting up and opening the cell door. "You'll be taken away as soon as I let the guards know that you're presentable. They allowed you some time to recover, but no longer. The king's advisors demand to see you punished."

If the king's soft spot for her and the life debt he might owe her couldn't stop the axe from falling, then Irene's friendship couldn't save her either. Salome looked down at herself. The smoothness of her skin returned, the blemishes gone, but she was stuck in the most hideous dress, plain light brown and as coarse as burlap.

Barely a few minutes after Maris left, Fabian and Oscar emerged at the door. Without a word, they towed her out, tying her hands together behind her back with rough rope. Fabian avoided her eyes. Oscar, however, looked her straight in the eye before shoving her forward. Salome stumbled along the way, until the younger brother allowed her to use him to steady herself.

Quietly, they hauled Salome onto the platform in a secluded section of the courtyards, a makeshift structure of rickety wood. The only sounds were a gentle breeze and the rustling of feet and fabric as people sought a better view. Less than a couple dozen people in total—servants and nobles, all awaiting her death.

This was hardly private.

Vincent was there, gold crown upon his head. No leathers, only silk and linen in navy and marigold. Someone had neatly brushed his hair and trimmed his beard. His handsomeness stunned her for a second. How refined and important he looked in contrast to her. He held his hands behind his back and watched her carefully.

A somber smile formed on her lips. "Do you really hate me?"

"No," he answered, but she imagined that it was just for her sake. Yet in his hands, he held the deck of cards he painted just for her.

"You never loved me though."

"I could have. I was starting to," he whispered, low enough so that only she could hear. Nothing changed on his face, not a flicker of new emotion in his eyes.

It almost hurt to see how little he felt or was willing to show.

"There was never a chance." No bitterness, only the honesty he deserved, but not all of it.

"Perhaps I was afraid." His voice was tranquil and tender. At this point, she preferred the storm and steel. He should have been angry. He looked wounded instead.

Her gaze slid to the executioner and the block where she'd be beheaded. "And now you have other things to fear."

They were quiet for a second.

Then, lowly, Vincent said, "If you escape this somehow, I will come after you."

"How would I escape?" she asked sweetly.

He reached out, but she jerked away. In response, he pulled his hand close to his chest, gripped into a fist.

"You will see me again, Vincent." Salome faced forward.

Oscar shoved her toward the block. He urged her down onto her knees, but no further. She took it as what respect he had left for her.

"Salome Visaya," the king began. Her name rang like a curse on his lips. "You are charged with the crime of impersonating a highborn lady, conspiring against the king, and stealing from the royal family and the people of Ilarya."

Salome kept her eyes down and smiled. It didn't matter that he said those words. Already, he knew she would survive, though he didn't know what to expect. Neither did she, not really.

"The punishment for these crimes is execution."

There was no need for a trial when she pleaded guilty in front of the king and several witnesses. The king's word alone was enough to condemn her. Everyone now knew she wasn't Rosalia d'Ilumias, that she was a nobody before the witch circus claimed her and her magic came to light.

The spectators gazed at her—some mournful, others impassive.

Irene d'Ellsaria wore a black dress for mourning. Her husband stood beside her, dressed in dark gray, and her sister-in-law, Eulalia, in black. General Bruno stood nearby, hands behind his back, expressionless.

If her hands weren't tied behind her back, she'd blow them all a kiss.

Her smile soon faded as she saw a pair of too familiar faces.

Euria and Elias were somehow among them, a reminder that the Alliance was watching, waiting to see if their pawn would see another day.

Her mouth twisted into a cruel smile. Salome needn't reveal their identities. The king would find them on his own if they didn't come for him. The Alliance could try to take her back, and they would fail.

She was free now.

And one day, everyone in the Alliance would pay for what they'd put her through.

Today was to remind the world of what she was.

Her head was on the block, the early morning sun rising, slicing through the dawn.

The executioner poised over her, raising his axe above his head, prepared for blade to meet her neck and kiss her bones. His shadow created a pocket of darkness around her—beckoning her, humming, and cooing and singing her name. Long-clawed fingers black as coal curled, lulling, and seducing her with soft voices.

Someone saw the shadows reach for her and shouted.

But they were too slow. Salome leaned in and surrendered, falling through the shadows. Her body tumbled into it, tucked into a ball like dropping into water and hoping to submerge in the depths.

The last thing she saw from the corner of her eye was Vincent, reaching out as though he might catch her before she got away.

He didn't.

She wondered if he hoped to.

Chapter Forty-Four

THE SHADOWS SWALLOWED HER, ENVELOPING HER IN A DARKNESS like the one she'd spent days in, then set her free. Light burst through the pitch-black expanse that seemed endless.

Her escape.

Salome gasped for air as she appeared on the other side of the portal created by the shadows, a doorway only she could walk through. Death was only certain if she hadn't tried. The axe was falling. If that blade hadn't killed her, the shadows could have. Instead, they brought her to a brown and black caravan with ivory silk curtains inside the windows. It was so large, it could have been a small cottage.

The witches stood around it, waiting. There were no bags or chests with them. Whatever belongings they had were now inside their vehicle.

At the sound of Salome's gasp, they looked her way.

Godiva surged forward, catching Salome as she stumbled out of the caravan's shadow. Maris came behind Salome, fire burning away the rope still tightly knotted around her wrists, as Salome blinked and blinked until her eyes adjusted to the sunlight.

The witches seemed amused by how she appeared. Her skin was slightly burnt like she'd stayed in the sun too long. Consequences for her actions, hinting at the wrongness of them for going against supposed justice, but not as severe as what she'd already experienced.

No one was harmed. Nothing cruel or greedy or selfish was committed.

Not that Salome was ever eager to uphold law and order.

She straightened, smoothed out the hideous dress like it was the most stunning satin, and grinned. Part of her was tempted to bow and request applause for her successful feat. Perhaps her stamina was nothing compared to theirs, but they couldn't deny she was meant to wield magic.

Thema clasped her hands together. Her eyes lit up with delight. "I was hoping you'd figure that out! Did you read that in the books I gave you?"

"I did," Salome replied, heart racing and face flushed from the thrill. She managed some time to study, after all, and Sylvia showed it was possible with the light. They spent so much time learning, and she figured the books might help speed up the process. Absently, she rubbed her wrists where the rope once was. The skin there tingled slightly.

"We didn't think you'd make it." Thema added, smiling apologetically.

"Don't lie," Maris chided. "Della was fully convinced she would."

Della laughed gleefully as she leaned forward and braided agate beads into Salome's hair. Her hands made quick work of it, barely pulling on the locks. "You knew it wasn't your time to die. So did I."

"I heard you had a plan and assumed I was part of it," Salome said. "But first, a goodbye."

Certainly, no one would ever forget her. A thrill shot through her as she imagined Vincent fixated on that moment. His advisors wouldn't be pleased. Eventually, they would send out people to find her. If another battle was called, then she wouldn't be a priority.

She hoped Vincent would come after her himself. One day, maybe.

After all, he hadn't said a proper goodbye, and she'd made a fool of him.

"He underestimated you," Thema said.

Godiva, meanwhile, gestured for them to pile into the caravan. Mouth pressed tight, eyes darting from castle to caravan, insistent hands making shooing motions. Thema stepped toward it first, pressing a hand on the side. The caravan shuddered, then vanished, even when she removed her hand. Turning back to them, Thema grinned.

"Manipulate within." Maris gestured to herself, then to Thema. "Manipulate without."

One could affect the mind of a person and the other could affect the world around them.

Thema tugged open the door and waved them inside. The other three allowed Salome to enter first. It was as big as it appeared on the outside. Inside, there were some benches made from chests covered with thin cushions, plus a couple of small beds covered with quilts and pillows. Candles were lit along the edges of the four windows. It reminded her of their rooms in the castle. They must have recreated the aesthetic from the one here to make it feel like home.

It was wonderful.

If they were to have a nomadic life, this was a good way to live that way.

A familiar little fluff was here to join them on their journey: Fortune, curled up on a violet velvet cushion. He looked up, waking suddenly from his slumber, and slowly blinked his large, golden eyes.

Warmth like sunlight filled her, along with an ache. She finally had her freedom and the chance to be herself, but the memory of Vincent's grieving eyes haunted her.

She imagined the kingdom referring to her as the almost-queen, the deceiver of their king. She wondered what that would mean for him, if their hope would crumble. Only this soft-hearted king could make her worry about the consequences of the con.

"He'll soon begin the chase," Salome said with a sigh. "He'll try to play the hero."

One day, it would get him killed—but she would try her best to keep that from happening. He could chase her, and she would let him, and he could try to be a hero and she'd try to stop him, but that was all it would ever be.

The two horses in the front huffed and stomped their feet, as if they were too eager to leave.

Once they were settled inside, the horses set into motion. Godiva's work, as evidenced by the gentle waves she made with her hands toward the front of the caravan, like she urged the horses forward. The carriage jostled slightly before steadying.

Salome sat beside Godiva, hands in her lap, leaning against a pile of plush cushions. The air witch reached out and placed her hand atop of Salome's, but she looked out the window, at what they left behind.

"With us, you can be who you truly are. You have nothing to hide and no worries to keep you awake. We'll be with you always," Thema said.

Godiva smiled, almost timidly. "We can do incredible things, all of us. It's easier to be together. Witches have fallen apart on their own."

"Together, even if the Alliance will come for me? For us?" Salome asked.

Godiva laughed. "Let them try."

"What are they to us? We could destroy them with ease if we wanted," Maris said. Her voice was so serious, and she kept her gaze averted, avoiding eye contact. Della reached into her lap and linked their fingers in silence.

"You are ours now. You have our love and loyalty. *Forever*," Della swore.

The other three nodded in agreement.

Salome smiled, reveling in the feeling of the possibility of being free. Briefly, Salome glanced at the shrinking figure of a decadent black castle. The gold on its embellishments glinted in the sunrise, winking like it shared a secret. The towers stood sharp against the blue sky, the walls smooth and elegant, and the roofs like the pointed end of a blade.

This could be the last time she ever saw this stunning place.

Looking back at the witches, Salome asked, "Where are we going?"

"To the Laisian border in the east," Della said, excitement evident in her voice, though her attention was on making a crown of pink and white flowers atop of her head. She stuck her tongue out as she did her work. "A kingdom said to be ruled by a royal family of faeries. Not quite true, but we'll be safe there."

"And there will be some people with knowledge that could be useful to us for what may be ahead," Godiva said.

"Oh, don't make it sound so dreadful! Laisia is *lovely*," Della said and laughed.

Salome grinned, closing her eyes. She'd heard some of the tales spun around the world. It was impossible to know what was true unless one was welcome there. The witches, it seemed, were one of the few who were.

"We will have to come back one day," Godiva said. "But we cannot stay."

As the castle faded from view, they settled into silence.

"He'll come for us," Salome said again.

There were so many details that felt embedded in her memory—the dark of his eyes, the glow of his smile, the feel of his lips on hers. She felt caged by what she felt and what she had with him. It felt like she would never forget.

Her mind and heart had decided he would stay with her, especially if she could never truly have him.

He was lost. She left him. That was how it was supposed to be.

"Won't catch us though," Della declared, disrupting Salome's thoughts.

The caravan rolled forward, pulled by horses assisted by magic that lightened the weight of their little home. It moved smoothly, as if there were no cobblestones under its wheels.

Outside, royal guards on horseback scrambled across the roads, searching for them. Vincent wasn't among them though.

Now they had more important matters to discuss. Thema was already looking over a map and making notes in a small book using a thin quill. Godiva spoke to her quietly, gesturing to a few areas on the map that her sister marked with ink. Meanwhile, Maris and Della made themselves comfortable on the cushions, their eyes drifting closed.

Salome looked at her reflection in the window and saw someone new. She had her name now, and a new title to go with it: the shadow witch of the witch circus. There was something else though, something that struck her as dark and terrifying in her own image. Not a trick of the eyes, but a reflection of her identity. She marveled at herself, entranced with her eyes and how the white in them had darkened to obsidian.

Thank you for reading! Did you enjoy? Please add your review because nothing helps an author more and encourages readers to take a chance on a book than a review.

And don't miss more in *The Witch Circus* series coming soon. Until then read HELLFIRE AND HONEY by City Owl Author, A.N. Payton. Turn the page for a sneak peek!

You can also sign up for the City Owl Press newsletter to receive notice of all book releases!

Sneak Peek of Hellfire and Honey

The battle hammer cut through the air in front of me. I spun away and an unpleasant breeze brushed my face in its wake. I waited for the sharp whip of fear, but exhaustion left only static in my head and an ache in my hands.

My opponent's muscles bulged as he lifted his hammer. I moved again, and the weapon plunged into the dirt. Perhaps he didn't recognize me in the darkness, or surely his strikes would be more accurate.

The vampire swung the hammer as though it were weightless. He was fast —too fast. Sweat soaked through my dress and cooled my skin. My lungs cried, but there was no time to catch my breath.

I dodged another swing. He was rested, fresh. I was not. He swung. I moved. Again. Again.

A swatch of silver moonlight escaped its cloudy prison. A beam of light illuminated our battleground, revealing the flicker of recognition in his eyes.

"Princess Salvatore." His growl of my name carried a distinct promise. New motivation bled the vampire's eyes from black to silver. He wanted to feel the life leave my body and carry news of my defeat to his king.

Armed with fresh resolve, his strikes quickened. Inhuman speed blurred his hammer and I narrowly avoided the attacks. The metallic edge of blood pooled in the back of my throat. He didn't give me an opening to slice with my sword and exhaustion threatened to drag me down. A few more swings and my head would be crushed against his hammer like meat on a butcher's block. The war would be over – my people defeated.

The last of my magic churned in my chest. I hoped I wouldn't need it for this fight, but the raining of cold iron around my head argued otherwise. I poured power onto the battlefield and my magic hunted for its prey.

The sneaking tendrils found the vampire. They wound around his legs, licking his skin and savoring the taste. The magic was savage, hungry, but I forced it to slow. If I worked the power too fast, he would feel it and flee. Too slow and his strikes would finally find me.

He swung the iron block and I sidestepped too late. His hammer crashed onto my sword. The force jarred my arms, and a cascade of glass splinters flowed down my shoulders. The hit emptied my lungs and locked me in place.

Leisurely, and with a faint smile, the vampire lifted the hammer again and aimed at my head.

The pattern of battle narrowed the world to a pinprick, this moment, the trajectory of the weapon toward my undefended face.

His hammer arched overhead, death in his eyes.

I pulled on my magic and pain stabbed me as power rushed from the depths of my soul. The twisted strands locked around the vampire's legs, arms, neck, and head. With a final heave that tugged the last wisps of power from my body, I hardened the magic coils to chain and drove them into the ground. The vampire's face twisted and he fought me, but his ability to block magic was weak. I dug the chains deeper and deeper into the dirt. His arms froze above his head and his knees locked. He shook with the struggle against my power and the weight of the hammer he couldn't drop.

"You have not won." The words came out flat as he struggled to shape his lips. "Our King will soon wear your blood."

"That sounds uncomfortable," I said.

My sword hung heavy in my aching hands, but the bite of victory was sharp. I heaved my weapon from the ground and stepped close. The vampire tried to burn me with his gaze, but my magic held him immobile. The sword slipped through his stomach and under his ribs. I found his heart and for a moment, we stared at each other with an unfortunate understanding. He had tried to kill me, but I killed him instead.

I cut through his heart and the silver bled from his eyes. My magic slipped away and the body fell to the ground.

With a ragged breath, I lifted the sword and sliced off his head. Some vampires could heal heart wounds.

The rush of battle faded. I staggered to my feet, one hand clenching my stomach, and spat bile and blood into the grass. My magic was almost gone, exhausted from a full night of fighting. It had already started to recharge, but would take hours to reach maximum strength.

"Took you long enough."

I jumped.

The old man stepped from a tree's shadow, cast by the moon overhead. His sword rested on one shoulder and his armor sported dents and divots, hits taken from hammers, swords, and axes. Zavier's body, though aged, remained toned and athletic. He smiled, but I knew he was not amused.

"I'm sorry," I said. "Did you expect my fifth kill to look as effortless as my first?"

"For a moment I thought he had bested you," Zavier said. So had I, but admitting that would make Zavier march me straight back to the castle. "Five tonight? You must be exhausted."

"I don't feel great." Knots nestled in my shoulders and aches in my fingers suggested a fracture or two. The sharp taste of vomit lingered in my throat.

"Did you heal?"

"Is that a joke?" Zavier knew my magic didn't possess healing capabilities.

"Maybe."

"I didn't think you knew what those were."

"Always such wonderful compliments from my Princess."

"I live to serve. What's the battle report?"

Zavier's smile slipped away.

"Our scout team engaged a force of two hundred vampires. Reinforcements from our kingdom arrived within twenty minutes. We lost thirty-five soldiers and estimate the enemy lost about the same."

His words formed a noose around my heart. Thirty-five soldiers gone in the blink of an eye. Sons and daughters, mothers and fathers, who would not return home. Thirty-five funeral pyres I would watch from my castle windows and could only cry when no one was looking. Not that the Kingdom of Ededen cared if I mourned their losses. I barely held any of their favor, and only in part to my parents' disappearance.

The vampires had lost a similar number. Tonight's battle was unexpected, but we did well.

Thirty-five dead.

Zavier snapped me from my brooding. "I went to your room to notify you of the battle. Imagine my surprise when you weren't there."

I grimaced.

"Imagine your guards' surprise when you weren't there. Imagine the chaos that ensued as half of your staff searched the castle until we found the stableboy, who informed your Royal Guard and First Seneschal that you had left with the scouts hours ago."

"That's a lot to imagine."

"Sal, I need an explanation."

I sighed. I couldn't explain the failure I'd felt since my parents had disappeared, or the deep-rooted fear that they may have found the cursed Fields of Death and damned us all. Every decision I made carried my kingdom closer to the inevitable. I couldn't explain the restlessness, the call of the battlefield, how much my magic wanted to fight. I certainly couldn't explain the moments of hesitation wondering if my death was the right answer.

"I don't have one, Zavier. I needed out. The scouts hadn't seen anything all day and it should have been safe to go with them. I didn't expect to find two hundred soldiers on movement to their camp."

"We are at war. What made you think any scout mission would be safe?"

"Relatively safe."

"Sal."

I wanted to shrug off his criticism, but duty and responsibility reeled me back. I wrestled away from youthful urges of defiance. Zavier served as my First Seneschal, my closest advisor and second-in-command. He deserved an apology, as much as I could muster.

"I'm sorry, Zavier. I'm sorry that I disappeared and worried you."

He tipped his head. "Thank you, Princess."

Zavier held out his hand and I placed my sword hilt onto his palm. He fished a cloth from under his armor and ran it over the blade.

"You need a healer." He continued his systematic brushes across the metal. The motions betrayed a quiver though. His knuckles paled as he gripped the rag too tight. His lips pressed into a thin line.

There was more, something he wasn't telling me.

"Say it."

He remained silent.

"Zavier, what happened?"

My First Seneschal didn't look up from the sword.

"Three thousand more soldiers were reported joining the camp," he said.

"Our scouts didn't see them?"

"Not in time to gather our forces. The spies said they came from a back valley pass."

Thirty-five soldiers had given their lives in a well-fought battle. For nothing.

"These two hundred were a diversion. They kept us busy over here and snuck through a different way," I said.

"Yes."

"And we fell for it." I clenched my aching, broken fingers into a fist. The pain fed the coiling snake of anger inside me. Stupid, stupid. My father would have seen this coming. The serpent of rage stretched higher, ready to strike. Where could he be that was more important than here, with our people? "They waved a red flag at us, and we ran straight into it, like an angry bull."

"Yes, Princess. We did."

I clenched my teeth.

"There's more," Zavier said.

Of course there is.

"King Kadence was seen marching with his men into camp."

Great. The elusive King Kadence Hendrick of Vari Kolum hadn't been spotted since his parents died almost two decades ago, leaving their eight-year-old king of the vampires. His presence was an announcement of the vampires' assured victory.

The ground looked comfortable, inviting, and I wanted to sink into it and fall asleep. I didn't want to hear what Zavier would say next. I catalogued my injuries to prolong the inevitable. My fingers throbbed in a numb way that meant I had ignored the pain for too long. My arms were heavy, my back sore.

"Princess, I'm afraid our options are limited," Zavier said. "Do you remember what we talked about weeks ago? When it was obvious the vampires were establishing a siege camp instead of the usual raids and battles?"

We had talked about a lot of things. Strategy, movement, statistics, personnel, and supply numbers. Everything had changed since then.

But I knew what he meant. I remembered the conversation as clearly as I had felt my blade plunge through the vampire's heart.

"Yes."

"I think it's time to utilize that strategy."

"How do you know?"

He handed me my sword, hilt first.
"First we find a medic, then I'll show you," he said.

Don't stop now. Keep reading with your copy of HELLFIRE AND HONEY available now.

Don't miss more of *The Witch Circus* series coming soon, and find more from Kay Costales at www.kaycostales.wordpress.com

Until then, discover HELLFIRE AND HONEY, by City Owl Author, A.N. Payton.

Princess Sal's magic bought her people peace and security, but she'll never be safe with the vampire king in her castle.

Centuries of war come to a bitter end when Princess Sal's parents steal half the witch army and disappear. Sal is forced to surrender to the vampire king, Kadence, and bind her magic as part of their agreement. She will give anything to protect her people – anything except her heart.

When Kadence conquers the witch kingdom, he doesn't expect their princess to be as delicious as wild honey. He can't decide if he'd rather kiss or kill Sal, and his desire for her battles against his hatred of witches. Despite their attraction, Kadence can't forget their war-torn history. He must decide if he can overcome his past to make way for a new future – one that might include Sal.

But when scouts locate Sal's parents and discover they're marching a demon army toward the kingdom, Sal and Kadence must unite their people for a final battle. If they don't, bloodthirsty demons will consume everyone they vowed to protect. Can they work together to save their people, or will hellfire destroy them all?

Please sign up for the City Owl Press newsletter for chances to win special subscriber-only contests and giveaways as well as receiving information on upcoming releases and special excerpts.

All reviews are **welcome** and **appreciated**. Please consider leaving one on your favorite social media and book buying sites.

Escape Your World. Get Lost in Ours! City Owl Press at www.cityowlpress.com.

Acknowledgments

First, thank you to my mother for letting me dream and telling me stories. Thank you to my sister, Kyra, for being there despite all our battles.

Thank you to Angelica and Andrea for being my best friends for so many years. To Vanessa and Victoria for befriending me during dark times and a little bit of trauma. To Emily for your love and encouragement for so much of my life. To the barkads/PACU group for being family and community throughout my life.

To the Toronto Writer Crew, thank you for the years of cheering for each other and celebrating how far we've come along! Special thanks to June Hur for your kindness and sisterhood, to Roselle Lim for your persistent support and generosity, to Liselle, Louisa, Faridah, Rachel B., and the many others who have made such a difference. To the Filipino authors and bloggers, thanks for making me feel relevant, and to all the authors who shared their insight, I'd be clueless without your help.

Also, big thanks to Taylor Shaw who read the absolute disaster of my first draft and taught me some essentials, and to my early CPs, Rachel G. and Marina for your feedback and enthusiasm. And thanks to my elementary school teacher, Mrs. Bell, who recognized my writing as something important before I properly pursued it.

Of course, thank you to my agent, Lesley Sabga, and my first agent, K.M. Enright for believing in this book and fighting for it—and of course, the Seymour Agency team, for all your enthusiasm over the years. Thanks to my editor, Tee, and the team at City Owl Press for taking this book into the world!

And thank you to my cat, Kingslee. I'll miss you forever. You were my good Fortune.

About the Author

KAY COSTALES is a Toronto-based, queer Filipina author and poet represented by Lesley Sabga of the Seymour Agency. As a child of immigrants, it is important to her to always provide queer Filipino diaspora representation in her stories. She graduated from the University of Toronto with an Honours Bachelor of Science in Psychology and Criminology but doesn't use her degree for anything. You can usually find her constantly daydreaming about dark but magical things, with a little bit of whimsy and romance.

www.kaycostales.wordpress.com

 twitter.com/kaycostales
 instagram.com/bykaycostales
 tiktok.com/@kaycostales

About the Publisher

City Owl Press is a cutting edge indie publishing company, bringing the world of romance and speculative fiction to discerning readers.

Escape Your World. Get Lost in Ours!

www.cityowlpress.com

facebook.com/CityOwlPress
twitter.com/cityowlpress
instagram.com/cityowlbooks
pinterest.com/cityowlpress
tiktok.com/@cityowlpress

Made in the USA
Middletown, DE
08 October 2023